CHROMED: UPGRADE

A CYBERPUNK ADVENTURE EPIC

RICHARD PARRY

coming to you with a profitable endeavor. You make money, we make money."

"Fine." Eckers poured himself Scotch. "What's the other thing?"

"We're going to fix your roof," said Julian. "In fact, we want to invest in your business. We want you to be one of our strategic partners."

Eckers coughed, spitting liquid on the bar. "What the fuck did you say?"

"Bernie — do you mind if I call you Bernie?"

"Yes. No. I mean, sure. Call me what you like." Eckers wiped his chin.

Julian took the bottle from Eckers. He poured Scotch into Ecker's glass, the liquid sloshing. "Bernie, we want to enter into a business contract with you."

The shorter man squinted at Julian. "What's the catch?"

"There will be paperwork, of course."

"No, the real catch."

"Ah," said Julian. "This entertainment won't be Reed branded. There's ... commercial sensitivity at this early stage."

"Why?"

"Because it's new." Julian adjusted his shirt — *too tight, I haven't walked around outside in a while* — before putting the bottle down. "There is some risk."

"It could blow up in my face," said Eckers.

"It could," agreed Julian. "Without risk, there is little chance of reward."

"Right. What's your risk?" Eckers had fresher sweat stains at his armpits, nervousness already at eleven.

"The risk for us is that you're unreliable scum." Julian spread his hands. "You will probably try to sell us out. You may steal our product." Eckers swallowed but stayed silent. "We could lose a whole line over this. It's a risk we're willing to take, to ... expedite the product to market."

"It is?"

"Yes. Because if our risk is realized, we will fucking execute you."

Eckers laughed, stopping when Julian didn't join in. "You always negotiate like this?"

"This isn't much of a negotiation," said Julian. "I've made you an offer. It's a generous offer. A partnership from a major syndicate in your shitty, gasping, desperate business. All in exchange for marketing a new entertainment, a product people will line up down the block to buy. If you don't want the deal, we'll take it somewhere else."

"No, I want the deal."

Julian smiled like a wolf. *Of course you do.*

○

Julian stood outside *The Hole*, a name more apt than Eckers knew. Or maybe the fat man did. He drew on his cigarette, blowing smoke in a stream. "Your problem is you let greed get in the way of your good sense."

Your other problem is you're talking to yourself. Julian pushed off from the wall, walking back to his car. He managed to stifle the trembling in his leg by clamping a hand on his thigh, driving augmented fingers into weak flesh.

○

Why not treat yourself to *Chromed: Rogue?*

[https://www.books2read.com/ChromedRogue]

CONTENTS

Off Grid	1
Chapter 1	8
Chapter 2	15
Chapter 3	21
Chapter 4	36
Chapter 5	45
Chapter 6	52
Chapter 7	64
Chapter 8	67
Chapter 9	83
Chapter 10	90
Chapter 11	93
Chapter 12	114
Chapter 13	121
Chapter 14	139
Chapter 15	146
Chapter 16	149
Chapter 17	155
Chapter 18	160
Chapter 19	166
Chapter 20	171
Chapter 21	182
Chapter 22	190
Chapter 23	198
Chapter 24	207
Chapter 25	216
Chapter 26	223
Chapter 27	231
Chapter 28	240
Chapter 29	255
Chapter 30	265

Chapter 31   268
Chapter 32   275
Chapter 33   283
Chapter 34   286
Chapter 35   291
Chapter 36   297
About the Author   303
Also by Richard Parry   305
Glossary   309
Acknowledgments   315
EXCERPT: CHROMED: ROGUE   316
Company People   317
CHAPTER ONE   325
CHAPTER TWO   329

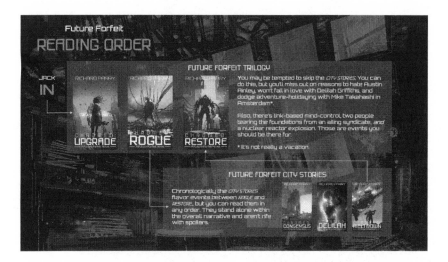

Want updates from Richard Parry? Sign-up and get a welcome bundle at
https://www.mondegreen.co/get-on-the-list/.
Find out more about Richard Parry at mondegreen.co
Published by Mondegreen, New Zealand.

Forever and always — for my Rae.

OFF GRID_

Never go off the grid. That was the rule. It kept Mason alive. If you had to, make sure you had a weapon and backup. Apsel's reach stopped where link coverage ebbed away to a gritty residue.

Mason had a weapon, but backup was a long ride away. *You're fifty percent there. Stop complaining. Get inside.*

Seconds was the kind of bar nobody would go twice. An old chipped door, the auto sensor broken, the sliders sticky with beer or blood. Mason shouldered it aside. The interior felt warm. Humidity stuck like a bad odor to the air. In its better days, it would have hosted over a hundred, the pump and beat of music making their own statement.

Today, fewer than a dozen people were nursing drinks, telling themselves the usual lies. He eyed a woman by the bar, working what magic she had left on a john, her use-by date well passed. The john looked no better, a long, stringy guy with fewer teeth than he'd been born with.

Neither were worth credits or paperwork.

He wasn't here for hookers or their clients. Mason was here for the promise of a lead. Most people would call it a rumor, but he'd spent enough time off-grid to know where truth lay among the grime.

Mason's optics scanned the bar, picking out the mods. *Seconds* wasn't the kind of place you went into blind. His first pass gave him nothing to cry about. Bionics done on the cheap, a knife where a laser would be best, out of fashion chrome making the wrong kind of statement. Nothing here was mil-spec.

Green neon flickered behind the bar, as tired and listless as the patrons. The bartender watched him, one chromed arm working a dirty rag over a dirtier surface. His eyes were underlined with a smatter of *hanzi*, the logograms giving off a soft phosphor blue bioluminescence. A couple of teenage *ganguro* girls were making out in a dark corner, the pastel of their eyeliner garish with the green from the bar. Mason's audio brought him the whisper of their bright clothes as they rubbed against each other.

Carter said this was the place. Someone had come in here, dropped credits into the old terminal on the back wall, and made a play to buy company assets. Mason brushed rain from his jacket, then made his way to the bar. His tailored clothes said *cash* and *syndicate*. No one got in his way.

Not yet.

Mason's overlay highlighted the bartender. No ID. No link. His optics showed a ghost who worked *down here* because *up there* was impossible. An illegal, like all the rest.

"Hey." Mason put a grainy photograph on the bar. A side shot of a man, orange mirror sunglasses on, greasy hair over a face gone soft and ugly. Carter had uplifted it from the terminal. "Know this guy? He's a buyer."

The bartender didn't look at the photo, his gaze touching the bottles stacked up in front of the flickering neon. The dirty rag paused. "I never heard of that mix. Been making drinks a long time now."

Mason tapped his finger on the photo. "It's a popular drink. Exactly the thing you'd get in this part of town."

The bartender shrugged. "Drink like that, might be expensive."

The rag resumed motion, his chromed arm picking up the green light and pushing it around the bar top after the rag.

Mason saw the *hanzi* under the bartender's left eye flicker, the glow stuttering. He pressed greasy notes down on the bar next to the photo. "I understand. Maintenance. Got to keep the kitchen in working order."

"Exactly." The rag stopped moving again. Mason caught a reflection in the chromed arm as a man walked in from the street. A sharp gust of night air followed him in, the faintest hint of sewage mixing with the acrid scent of rain. The bartender nodded to the newcomer. "It's killer out there." The photo and the money vanished, whisked away by the bartender as if they'd never been. He moved further down the bar, filling a cocktail shaker with dirty ice.

The newcomer sat next to Mason, a hint of Davidoff cologne washing off him. "Mind if I sit here?"

"It's a free country." Mason didn't turn, taking in the expensive suit cuffs out of the corner of his eye. Tailored sleeves went with the cuffs. Might be an exec out for some fun at the people's expense.

Might be syndicate trouble.

"That's the biggest lie I've heard this week." The man shook water from his coat, throwing the heavy jacket over a vacant barstool. "Hasn't been free since they invented the credit card."

"You don't seem to be suffering."

The man gave a quick laugh. "Business is good. What can I say?"

The bartender pushed a tumbler in front of Mason, the ice nestled in around a rich amber liquid. Algae in the drink sparked a bright pink, flecks of light flashing in amongst the amber and ice. "Your drink."

Mason nodded his thanks, taking a sip. The liquor was rougher than he'd expected. He coughed. "Christ." He saw a splash of white as he set it down. A scrap of paper was stuck to the bottom of the glass. *A note for my eyes only.* Money spoke a universal language.

The man next to him gestured to the bartender. "Whatever he's having."

"You really don't want to do that." Mason grimaced. "Last time I order the house specialty, that's for sure."

"I can handle it." The man counted notes on the bar. "These throwbacks need to get linked. I hate cash. It's too dirty."

"At least it's quiet." Mason took another swallow, then glanced at the stranger's tailored cuffs. He looked back down into his drink, reading the address written on the note. "It's probably as good a place to die as any."

A heartbeat of silence followed as pressure built in the air. Mason felt his lattice react, its prediction routines making his hands grab the bar's edge, heaving him over the top. A blast wave hit, tossing him against the wall. Mason's perception of time slowed as overtime flowed over him.

The fibers in his jacket stiffened to take the impact. Glass and liquor rained on Mason from the shattered bottles above the bar. His optics flickered as they adjusted contrast, first to the flash of light then the dancing shadows. A single neon filament above Mason stuttered out the last of its life in refracted green before the bar went dark.

"I'm glad you appreciate your situation." The man's voice came from the other side of the bar. "No offense. Like I said, business is good."

"None taken." Mason planted his feet against the bar, bracing himself in the narrow space. He pulled his Tenko-Senshin sidearm from under his jacket, the whine of the weapon soft in the darkness. The nose of the weapon tracked the man's footsteps as if it had a mind of its own. "Reed Interactive?"

"Good guess, but no. Metatech. Apsel?"

"Yeah." Mason listened for movement. *Careful. Metatech means mil-spec bionics. Keep him talking.* "What are they like?"

"Metatech?" The man paused. "They sure as shit provide better backup than Apsel Federate."

Mason's smile glinted in the darkness. "What makes you think I need backup?"

The man laughed as he made for the door. No hurry in it, like he did this kind of thing on a daily. "Buddy? You look fucked to me."

The door squealed a complaint as it opened, followed by a distinctive thud as Mason's opponent tossed in a grenade. *Get up, Mason. Move!*

Mason rolled over the bar. He hit the kitchen door as the grenade exploded, throwing him into a stove so grimy it looked like a movie prop. He fell hard, then pushed himself upright. His optics flickered in the darkness — *goddamn EMP* — then switched to thermal, the intense bright square of the Tenko-Senshin's energy pack outlined against the blue-black of the floor. Mason felt the cool calm of the hard link as his palm gripped it.

Only an amateur would rely on an EMP grenade against a syndicate asset. Top-shelf bionics barely noticed. *An amateur, or someone who really does have backup. You got what you came for. Time to go.*

"Mason?" The link flickered into life, Carter inside his head. Her deep, husky voice was tinged with a hint of concern.

"Now's not a good time, Carter." Mason went back to the kitchen door. A couple of tables burned, shedding sooty smoke. The heat from the flames scorched the center of his vision with white, so he switched back to visual light. "I'm busy."

"That's what I'm calling about." She paused. "Don't go out the front."

"You checking up on me?" Mason looked through the door's cracked window. The jumble of wreckage was unrecognizable. A mess of plastic and wood veneer nestled atop bodies. "I didn't know you cared."

"They used energy weapons. The signature is quite clear from sat telemetry."

"Plasma?"

"Looks like."

"Jesus. You get cancer from those things." Mason pushed the snout of the Tenko-Senshin ahead of him.

"No." Carter sounded annoyed. "You get *burning* from those

things. The fire would kill you, and you would hurt the entire time you were dying. You were lucky. And careless."

"Thanks."

"You're not going to be alive long enough to get cancer."

"Like I said, now's not a good time. You can list my failings later."

"Why not just go out the back?"

"Two reasons. First, they'll be expecting that." Mason stepped through the kitchen door, his feet crunching on broken glass.

"The second reason?"

"The bartender gave me an address. He's in here somewhere." Mason paused. "What, no snappy comeback?"

"It'll be expensive." Carter sounded doubtful.

"Put it on my tab. Did I miss a budget cuts memo?"

"I'll call a medivac." The link went dead.

Mason stepped over a body flung from the center of the plasma strike. He looked at it as he passed. *Not this one.* The radius of damage was from Mason's spot at the bar. His overlay plotted a line on Mason's optics, showing the point of origin.

A booth, no different from the rest. No sign of the *ganguro* girls who'd been there, the booth black and empty. A fluorescent light stuttered to life, then went dark as sprinklers kicked in. Muddy water trickled from the ceiling for a moment before dying out. Loose drips of dark water stuck to the ceiling nozzles.

Mason found the bartender sprawled backward against a broken table. His chrome arm was gone, the stump smooth and pale. *Cheap work. No anchoring.* Or maybe the guy didn't want to get that close to the metal. Mason scanned as he knelt. His HUD told the violent story of the bartender's injuries. Burns. Lacerations and bruising. "Hey."

The bartender coughed, the sound ragged and wet. "I tried to ... doesn't matter. Did you get the address?"

"I got it." Mason nodded to the door. "It'll keep a few minutes longer."

The bartender grabbed Mason's arm. "You don't understand. They're killing us."

"Killing you?"

"The rain. Your *buyer*. That's what's for sale. Don't you know?" He coughed again.

Mason stood. "Who was it?"

"What?"

"Who did you lose to the rain?"

The bartender looked at him, firelight playing across his features. The blue had faded from the *hanzi*, leaving gray marks like scars. "My brother."

Mason nodded. "Try not to move. A medivac's coming."

"I can't afford that." The man's eyes turned pleading. "Just leave me here. I'll be okay."

Mason looked at the Tenko-Senshin, the weapon's hum a gentle touch in his hand. He moved toward the door. Before he stepped into the street, he glanced back. "It's on the house."

"Which house?" The bartender slumped back. "Who'm I gonna owe for this?"

Mason didn't reply as he walked outside into the hissing rain, the door yawning behind him.

CHAPTER ONE_

"I don't know if I love you anymore." Sadie tightened a garter strap, grabbing a shirt from the pile on the floor. "That's all I've got."

"Seriously?" Aldo looked at her from the couch. "You're doing this to me now? We're on in five." They were in Sadie's dressing room. A huge mirror surrounded by ancient incandescent bulbs reflected their sins.

"I know, baby." She shrugged the shirt on. They hadn't taken the time to unbutton earlier. "But that's the way it's going to be." They were supposed to be readying for tonight's performance. But then the urge struck, and ... well, Aldo didn't get urges as often as he used to.

"Shit." The drummer rummaged around the pile on the floor, grabbing a pair of black leather pants. He felt in a pocket, pulling out a rumpled pack of cigarettes. He offered one, lighting it for her with an old-style Zippo, the skull motif etched on the side worn with time. "When will you know?"

"Know what?" Sadie worked on some black eyeliner. A rush job would have to do. She pursed her lips at her reflection in the mirror, then dragged on the cigarette.

"Jesus, Freeman! Whether you love me or not."

"I don't know." She put the cigarette down in favor of a comb, teasing her hair.

"You don't know? How can you not know?"

Sadie sighed, her shoulders sagging a little. She didn't turn away from the mirror. "It's not that easy."

"It's easy for me."

"No kidding. That was the fastest round we've ever had."

Aldo looked down at his crotch, then back up at her reflection. "Hey. You said you wanted it quick."

"I said I wanted to get it done before we had to go on. It's not the same thing." Sadie pointed to his pants with her free hand, still wrangling her hair with the other. "You should put those on."

"Why? What if I don't feel like playing tonight?" Aldo started putting a foot into the leather pants anyway.

"Are you five years old?" Sadie raised her eyebrow. "I guess I play without a drummer tonight."

"What?" Aldo stumbled as his other foot got caught in his pant leg. A year ago, he'd filled them out; now, not so much. *Too many of the wrong drugs.* "You don't have a band without a drummer."

A knock sounded on the door. "You're on." It was the stage manager Bernie, still carrying too much stress for his own good. "Don't do this muso shit tonight, Freeman! I got a hundred people out here who've paid—"

"Shut it, Bernie!" Sadie turned to face the door, a hairspray can raised in one hand. "I'll be on when I'm fucking on! Don't you have an ulcer to nurse?" She could imagine his wattled chin underneath bulging eyes in a sallow face, vein beating in his forehead. *Admit it, Sadie. You like pissing him off.*

"Musicians. You're all the same..." Bernie's voice drifted into an indeterminate mumble as he stormed off.

Aldo pushed an arm through a black sleeve, his movements sharp and angry. "You haven't answered."

Sadie gave a last flourish with the hair spray, pouting at her reflection. *Maybe too much grunge, Sadie.* "What? About the drummer? I don't need a drummer."

"Every band needs a drummer. But no. The other thing."

"I played two years without a band, let alone a drummer. What makes you think I need a band? Christ. Bernie's right, musicians are all the same." Sadie stood, grabbing her jacket from the back of a chair where she'd tossed it earlier. The leather was real, a parting gift from her father. It and the guitar were the only things he'd ever given her.

The guitar. Sadie looked at it, gleaming in the corner by the door. A shiver tapped its way up her spine. God, but she loved to play. Her hands itched to hold it.

"Jesus. You're breaking up the band?" Aldo's mouth hung open.

"What? No, unless you stay locked in your room tonight." Sadie pulled on her boots, the metal clasps jingling against her hands, then moved to the guitar. She almost reached for it but turned to Aldo instead. Her lips quirked, black lipstick against the pale white of her skin. "So. You playing tonight, lover?"

Aldo pulled the edges of his vest together, then ran a hand through his hair. Tall and lean. Dark hair. Dark eyes. *You always liked the tall dark and handsome, Sadie.* He dropped a lopsided grin at her, and she almost wanted to take it all back. "Yeah. I'll play for you, Freeman. Let's go."

She grinned back, then turned and picked up the guitar. "Okay. Let's rock this house." Sadie yanked the door open, letting her boots clank and stomp their own way to the stage. Time to *play*.

○

Her lips brushed the old mic. The air charged with the smell of liquor and sweat. It'd only take a spark to ignite it.

Ancient incandescent lights shone down on Sadie, bright and hot. Her fingers touched the strings, the sound almost gentle as notes leaked and flowed from the speakers. The crowd hushed, a giant's indrawn breath.

Like the feeling before a storm.

She felt the band behind her. Aldo with his electronic drum kit. The sound wouldn't be quite right, but it's what they had. Janice stood with her guitar, the digital board doing all the hard work.

Fakes. Impostors on her stage. That wasn't music. Sadie played at *The Hole* because of the people. They were off the grid, just like her. You'd be hard pressed to find a link in the room.

The mic in front of her smelled of excitement. It was time.

Sadie brought a hand down against the strings, the fingers of her other skipping against fingerboard. The crowd surged against the stage as the Seattle sound mixed with air made rich with their despairs and hopes.

The room grew heavy. People ground against each other, jerking and dancing with the music. She forgot about Aldo, about Bernie and his cut, and about how she would make rent. For a little while, the strings under her fingers were all that mattered, and she sang alongside her guitar until her voice grew hoarse.

Sadie stopped, the guitar's notes dying away. The crowd stumbled against the fallen beat. Sadie breathed, the microphone sharing her exertion with them. Her pulse pounded.

"Sorry." She smiled, lips to the microphone like a lover's ear. The room echoed with her voice. "I'm just tired." Sadie glanced to the side and saw Bernie in the wings, a scowl blooming on his face. Her smile turned to a grin, catching against her teeth.

"So." Sadie turned back to the crowd. *My people.* "Should I stop?"

NO. The roar washed over her. She closed her eyes in the face of it.

"Ah." Sadie's fingers touched the strings again, the sound walking around the stage. The crowd hushed for her. "I could use a drink."

Some hero in the crowd raised his bottle toward the stage. More followed, the press of bodies almost urgent. She held a hand up, stilling them. "Thanks. Just put it on the edge." The muscle along the stage let the hero deliver her drink. He had eager eyes and a face that wanted to be kind. "What's your name?"

"Mark," said the hero.

"Not Jax the Destroyer? Merlin the Merciless?"

"It's just Mark."

Sadie smiled again, fingers plucking strings, the sound of the guitar thanking him. "No shit, Mark. I guess not all heroes wear capes." She stepped forward, grabbing the bottle from the edge, the glass sweating against her hand. Sadie saluted Mark with the bottle before tipping it back. The beer was cool and clean, and she finished the bottle in a moment. She tossed the empty aside, a tinkle of glass reminding her bliss was fleeting. *But you can make it last a little longer.* "Thanks. Someone buy Mark a drink!"

The crowd cheered, shifting to the bar. Sadie glanced at Bernie. His scowl struggled to hold. People buying liquor always increased profits, especially in a place like this.

Sadie's fingers caressed the strings. She'd lied. Sadie never felt tired when she played.

Sadie shuffled the wad of dirty paper, counting notes. "Where's the rest?"

Bernie shrugged. "That's it. That's your cut."

"Bullshit." Sadie kicked off her boots to tumble into a wall. The mirror of her dressing room shimmied in complaint. "They were on fire, Bernie. They bought beer *and* a cover charge."

He shrugged again, his belly rising and falling with it. "What can I say. Cash is a rare thing. If you had a link you could check the books yourself." A smile crept on his face but found it foreign territory and left. "You think I'm trying to cheat you? C'mon, you're my star!"

Linked? Hell with that. "I think you'd cheat your mother if you thought you could get away with it. And I don't want shit in my head. Gets in the way of the music."

"The band doesn't think so." Bernie nodded to the door. "They're happy digital. You're the one with an ancient guitar."

"Ancient? It's a classic. It's the sound that pulls people in. Besides, you're confusing the issue." Sadie waved the wad of money, fighting red rage. "I can't even pay for parking with this."

"You don't have a car."

"It's because you pay shit. What if I just moved on?"

Bernie cocked his head. "I dunno, Sadie. Where you going to find someone who lets you play without a link? It's borderline illegal. I look the other way." He tried the smile again. "Because you're like a daughter to me."

"You make passes at all your daughters?" Her eyes drifted to his gut, then back to his face. "I think you let me play because I fill your bar every night. You bought a new car after I started here."

"It's a Toyota-Mitsu."

"It's a Lexus." Sadie pushed a chair in front of the mirror, straddling it backward. "Only reason you don't own a Mercedes is because it'd get stolen around here."

"Whatever." Bernie waved a dismissive hand. Sadie's blood got another degree closer to boiling point. "So, leave. Or stay. I don't care, but if you stay, make sure you're on time tomorrow." He pulled the door open, almost colliding with Aldo. "Christ! Aldo, talk some sense into your woman." Bernie shouldered past and out.

"She's not... Never mind." Aldo looked after Bernie, then glanced at Sadie. "You okay?"

"Just great." Sadie held up the money. "Here, take it. For you and Janice."

"You got your cut?" Aldo looked at the cash, not taking it, but also not looking like he wanted to know the answer. "Hell."

"Yeah, I took my cut." Sadie offered the money up again. "Go buy something nice. Like a beer."

"Beer's free. About the only thing that is in this place."

Sadie looked him up and down. "Just take it and go."

Aldo reached for her, his hand almost making it to Sadie's shoulder. It hovered beside her a moment. She wanted his hands on her like before it had gone bad. *It'll be okay. Go on.* Sadie held herself still, daring Aldo to touch her. To show her how he felt.

His hand dropped to the cash. "Right. See you." Aldo stepped out the door. Gone, like a missed taxi.

Sadie looked after him, then kicked the door closed. She brushed the tear from her eye, a streak of black left behind from her makeup.

That's why I don't love you anymore, Aldo Vast. It's because you're an asshole.

CHAPTER TWO_

Laia's eyes snapped open. She stared unblinking at the wooden ceiling as the sun's soft, warm fingers reached through the open window to touch her face.

The warmth of that touch woke her.

Laia reached, slow and lazy with sleep, cutting the sunbeam with her fingers. Ill-fitting wall planks let rain and cold in. This was the first time they'd let in sunlight.

So that's what it feels like.

Laia's hand pulled back to the collar at her neck. The hard metal left her skin chafed and raw. There might be sun, strange and wondrous, but the collar held her thoughts, a constant reminder she was a slave.

A scream cut the air. Laia scrambled from the pallet, scrambling to the open window. It looked out over a courtyard still damp from the rain. The old stones were turning from dark to light gray as the water dried. Morning mist began its walk to the sky.

Laia's eyes were drawn to another slave in the courtyard. The woman's eyes searched the sky, hand held against the burnished orange of their faded sun. Tears ran down her cheeks, her face wild with fear.

Abinal hadn't seen the sun in the fourteen years Laia had lived, the clouds and rain always constant.

No, sister. Don't fear the sun.

One of the house guards strode through a doorway opposite Laia, his haughty stride taking him to the slave in the courtyard. He didn't slow as he slammed his fist into her stomach, dropping her to the ground. "The Master has no time for your mewling. I will not warn you again."

The woman turned to him, hand still raised. "But ... how did I get here? Who are you? Where..?"

Her words were silenced by the house guard's sword, the blade glinting in the light as he held it high. He brought it down, red sluicing the dawn. The woman's head bounced against the old stones.

The rock drank blood as the house guard walked back inside.

Laia's fingers touched her collar again. Her sister slave's body lay cooling in the early morning. The collar reminded Laia she was special. Not a mindless slave like most, a Seeker, or worse.

I am Laia.

She looked at the terrible burning sky and felt hope.

The Master led Laia through the city, the stones under her bare feet rough. She couldn't remember the last time this way was dry. Rain usually pooled on the street, people's faces down.

Now they looked up as water evaporated under a sky turning yellow and angry.

Her skin felt warm, kissed by a star that hadn't the courage to show its face in forever. Laia almost smiled but caught herself in time.

It didn't matter. The Master turned to her, stopping so quickly Laia almost ran into him. He ran a gloved finger along her jaw. "You think there's room for hope." The Master's voice was deep and rich. A voice that could have belonged to a savior or a king.

There is no room for saviors or kings anymore. It is a world of devils. "No, Master."

"And you think this means you can lie to me." The *keffiyeh* hid everything but the Master's cruel eyes. He pulled his finger away. "Have you forgotten the pain so soon?"

Laia felt him touch her mind, the sensation slick and wet. Shuddering, she swallowed, mouth dry. "No, Master. I mean ... I haven't forgotten, Master."

"You're wondering why you can see the sky." He wasn't watching her anymore, turning to look at a Seeker pen by the road. It was a small one. Perhaps twenty or thirty men and women stood there. Laia caught sight of a small face. *Children, too.*

The Seekers were trying to get out, their normally white eyes clear. Clear, but confused, because they didn't know where they were or who they were with. But they suspected why they were there, and that gave them the strength of fear.

They pushed against the wooden poles of the cage, trying for freedom. Laia watched them, thinking of her next words. "I do wonder, Master."

"Hmm?" Her Master turned away from the cage, regarding her.

"I wonder why I can see the sky."

"It is because I sent the demon away," he said. "I sent it to the desert. I sent it to find your precious angel." The corners of the Master's eyes crinkled with a smile. There wasn't anything kind about it.

Laia bit her lip. *No.* "The angel—"

"The angel will be my slave, just as you are." The Master's eyes glinted. "You will remember your place, or—"

Poles on the cage splintered, and the Master spun as the first men and women broke free. The once-Seekers pulled wood aside for their fellows.

The Master glanced at Laia before striding toward the cage. He beckoned over his shoulder, and she felt the pull in her mind.

Her collar felt so heavy. *No.*

"Yes." The Master turned to look at her again. "Did you think I couldn't see your thoughts? Your plan to distract me so they could escape was foolish. That's why your city fell. You don't understand true power."

"Please—"

The Master spun away as the first of the escapees ran at him, a man with desperate eyes brandishing a broken pole as a weapon. The Master held his hand up, almost caressing the air, and the man stumbled to a halt. "I will show you true power, Laia. A reminder."

The man with the pole turned, running to the others. He hefted his weapon, slamming it into a woman's head. She crumpled. Another grabbed for the pole, trying to wrestle it free.

Now, said the Master's voice in her mind. *Now, reach out with your gift.*

She couldn't help herself. There was a channel made of pain in her mind, her thoughts guided down a single path of action, like a river to the sea. Laia tried to fight, the pain a searing heat. She fell to her knees, and—

The bodies were warm and wet. That man was just over thirty summers old, his body thin and weak as the work of a Seeker stripped him bare. The woman at his side was younger, her body remembering the harshness of last winter even if her mind didn't. She was tarnished, broken, and fragile. There, a child of just six, scars on his back.

Laia reached out, the first man screaming and clawing at his clothes. Wisps of smoke curled out from under the dirty rag he wore as a shirt. The woman at his side ran, stumbling to the ground as her skin flared, fingers of red fire reaching through black smoke to the sky.

Through it all, Laia's gift sang as she sagged to her knees, the collar's hold on her mind unlocked. The Seekers' bodies burned, their bodies curling as they charred on the dry streets.

"That, child, is power." The Master laughed. "Do not forget it. My demon isn't here to hold the Seekers in thrall, but you are. I have more than enough to make *you* do what I wish, and fear of you will hold them still as any demon."

Laia knelt, huddled over the old stones of the street. She'd thrown up but didn't remember it. Laia wiped her mouth, the collar clamping down on her mind once more. If she could just get free for a tiny scrap of time...

"No, girl. You will never be free. You are *mine*." The Master curled his hand into a fist. The pain ran through Laia, and she screamed, her back arching as she clawed the ground. People watched as the Master hurt her, powerless to help.

It went on, and on, and on...

Later, the Master's lesson still fresh, she sat with her brother Zacharies. He'd seen nineteen summers, unbent by the Master's iron will. It's why his room was little more than a closet. Tall and rangy, his hair was dirty and matted like hers. The old and dirty wood walls let the air whistle through along with a little light. There were no windows.

Right now, it was perfect. No one could see her shame and guilt.

Zacharies' eyes were glints of glass in the gloom. "Did he—"

"It is nothing, brother." Laia spoke quickly but lowered her face.

He stood as if to leave, rage hardening the line of his shoulders. "I will—"

"No!" Laia softened her voice. "No. Not today."

"If not today, then when?" Zacharies scratched under his collar. He leaned close, as if whispering would hide his thoughts. "The demon is gone. It holds no one in thrall anymore. His power is—"

"His power is stronger than ever," she said. "He made me..." Laia's voice wound down like an old clockwork mechanism.

When she had the courage to look up, Laia saw the understanding in her brother's eyes. "I'm sorry, sister."

"We should go."

"We should stay," he argued. "The angel—"

"The Master said the angel is dead."

"The *demon* is dead." Zacharies crossed his arms over his chest. "The angel has killed it."

"I do not think so," said Laia. "It is not what the prophecy says."

"To the hells with the prophecy," said Zacharies. "The control of the Seekers is gone. The rain has lifted. There is no water to carry the message. If that's not the work of your angel—"

"He is not *my* angel!" *Never say that. Angels can't be owned. Not like us.*

"Then whose angel is he? You're the only one who believes."

"No." Laia shook her head, collar nagging at her chin. "The Master believes."

"The Master torments you." Zacharies ran fingers through knotted hair. "He torments us all."

"Yes," she said. "But he also believes. He believes the demon still lives."

"Then where is it?"

"That is why we're going. To get the demon." Laia looked at Zacharies. *Please. Don't fight him. It's worse when you try.* "We have no choice, and..." She leaned closer. "If the angel is there, we will be free. Together."

Zacharies nodded, breathing out. He looked as if he was preparing to lift something heavy. "Okay."

"Okay." She spared him a crooked, sad smile. Laia's hand found his, and together they walked out to an Abinal baked warm and golden by an old sun.

CHAPTER THREE_

"I don't know why you don't go to the address, now you've got one." Carter sounded distant, the link hissing between them.

"You set the mission up, Carter. I'm just following through." Mason coughed, wiping rain from his face. "I'm curious."

He stood outside a crumbling building, too far from Seattle's high-rent district to attract buyers. *Hell, even low-rent districts would be an upgrade. This is a home for illegals with bad luck.* Rain lashed the front of the structure, giving old wood and concrete a glassy look. Five stories tall, and all of them ugly. He leaned against his Suzuki. The big bike felt warm from the run here. Mason left it on in case he changed his mind about going inside.

"Curiosity isn't a useful quality for you, Mason."

Mason smiled despite the weather. "Why's that?"

"Cats getting killed. You familiar with the expression?"

"Rings a bell," said Mason. "What I want to know is why a bartender at a shitty dive knew what you didn't."

"How's that?" Carter sounded more alert, a hard edge to her voice.

"He said the rain was for sale."

"He had a head injury."

"And here I am at the place where you said an Apsel energy signature was detected," said Mason. "An unauthorized reactor site."

"Following reactor signatures makes sense," insisted Carter. "Someone's trying to sell our shit. We're trying to find out who, and by we, I mean you. I sent you to the place where one of our reactors was used. Do you see how much sense it makes?"

"What doesn't make sense is why a bartender said the rain was for sale." Mason looked at the ruins around him. "The *rain*, Carter. Not a reactor." His optics' thermal showed no telltale heat blooms from bodies. Didn't mean people weren't cloaked, lying in wait.

The casual strays who made this place their home were nowhere around. On a night like this, that suggested they'd found death.

"You're probably right." Carter sounded as if she didn't believe her own words. "Getting to the buyer *is* a higher priority. The reactor site can wait. It's not going anywhere."

"I'm already here. This won't take a minute." Mason looked up at the falling heavens. "I've got to get out of the rain."

"You're within safe tolerance."

"That's easy for you to say. You're sitting pretty behind a desk." Mason ran a hand through his hair, examining the strands sticking to his palm. "You see this? Does this look like safe tolerance?"

"It looks like a day in the chair. Relax." Carter paused for a second. "Maybe two days."

"Maybe you should come out here and get wet."

"No thanks. Besides, you're going to die of cancer first, remember? And he's a *bartender*, Mason. At a place called *Seconds*, the most ironic bar name ever. He's not the FBI."

"People in my profession don't get to die of cancer." Mason looked at the building's dark and empty windows. A few stray shards of glass stuck to frames here and there, but the paint was long gone. The low building was an extravagance of an older world. Nobody put concrete into the ground unless they could get a hundred stories out of it.

Mason thought he saw a face at a window, but it shimmered and vanished. "Look, screw the bartender. You work your way, I work mine. He's one of my people."

"You don't have people." Carter snorted. "You've got an expense account."

"I think I'm getting symptoms."

"Like what?" Carter's voice turned serious.

"Check the feed. Was there a person in that window?"

Carter was quiet for a moment while she checked the mission recording. "No."

"Right." Mason coughed again. "Definitely symptoms." He brought up a tactical overlay in the top corner of his vision, setting it to play back the feed from his optics.

"Clever," said Carter. "Checking the digital against the real?"

"Something like that." Mason saw another face at a different window, an eyeless corpse with a wet gash for a mouth. The overlay showed a window, dark and empty. "The overlay gives me a headache."

"You could quit."

"No one quits. You know that." Mason walked away from the Suzuki, the bike powering down with a soft whine as the cowl locked into place. "You got a satellite view?"

"I'm working on it."

"You're working on it? What's that supposed to mean?"

"Christ, Mason. This isn't Fisher-Price in space. I'm getting a lot of interference. There are other interests at work here."

"Metatech?"

"Do you want the satellite, or do you want to know who's trying to jack it?"

"I want the satellite." Mason walked up chipped concrete steps to the building's double doors. An old wooden board lay against the steps, chipped paint advising *Vacancy - Apply Within!* He froze. "Wait. Someone's jacking one of our sats? That might be a priority."

"You do your job, I'll do mine."

"Jesus." Mason glanced up as if he could see a rogue satellite targeting him. "I don't want that thing pointed the wrong way."

"Have I ever let you down?"

Mason didn't reply. Carter had detailed stats on her mission performance, and it would be bad form to get into it with her now. Even if she'd dropped a catch, she'd make it look like he was the one supposed to catch it.

He pulled the tarnished knob. It tore from the rotted wet wood door. Mason tossed it aside. *It's a good thing they don't make 'em like they used to.*

Mason put his shoulder to the door, pushing it. The door squeaked, sticking for a moment, then groaned low as it opened into the gloom of the foyer. Something like a rat, but bigger, scuttled for cover. The overlay showed it too, which gave him pause. *What the hell was that? I do not want to meet the roaches here.*

He drew the Tenko-Senshin, clicking the weapon's light on. Clear and bright, the beam played across the room. An old reception desk watched him, boxes for hotel mail rotting behind it. A rusty bell still sat on the counter next to a heap of mouldering machinery that might have been a register.

"You're going to die, and they'll never find your body!" Carter's screech echoed in his ears.

"What the *fuck*, Carter?" Mason swallowed. "What the actual fuck!"

"I didn't say anything." Carter's voice sounded normal this time, laced with faint surprise.

"Yeah. Yeah, you did."

"Curious. It's progressing faster than I thought. With your augments—"

"You didn't just say I was going to die?"

"No." She paused. "I should have, though. Tactically speaking, you're not in a good place right now. It might have been the EMP."

Mason played the beam around the rest of the room. A curved stairway led up. An ancient man with a rotting face watched from the top steps. Mason closed his eyes, shaking his head. When he looked again, the stairway was empty. Mason breathed a little easier. "I tell you what."

"What?"

"Don't say anything to me until I talk to you."

"Nothing unsolicited?"

"Sure." Mason nodded. "'Unsolicited.'"

"What if I see something?" Carter sounded doubtful.

"Then you're just going to have to let me handle it. It's why Old Man Gairovald pays me the big dollars." Mason looked up the stairway.

High above him the roof was broken, faint fingers of moonlight touching the walls. Water was coming in from somewhere, the carpeted stairs sodden with it. "If I get out of this, I'll take you some-place nice."

Carter's reply was quiet, her voice uncertain. "Like where?"

"Nowhere like this place, that's for sure." Mason coughed again, something warm and wet hitting his hand as he covered his mouth. He wiped his palm against his pants without looking.

"Okay." Carter paused, then her voice hardened. "Try not to get yourself killed. I don't want to break in a new partner." The link went dead.

Mason put a foot on the first step, easing onto it. It creaked, the swollen wood giving easily under his weight. *Not that way, then.* What kind of asshole did business in a place like this anyway? A flash of lightning showed a ring of faces looking down at him. The overlay showed an empty stairway. He blinked a few times, rubbing his face with his free hand.

The Tenko-Senshin's beam bobbed across them, then they were gone. The hair on the back of his neck rose. "Definitely not the stairs. No problem." *And now, you're talking to yourself.*

He checked the foyer again. A door behind the reception desk offered promise. It stood slightly ajar, a sign saying *Staff Only* in what might once have been gold letters. Mason walked to it, his feet scraping and crunching on debris. He crouched next to the door, shining his light at the floor. Scuffs showed where the door had been opened. He touched the rough ridges of the floor before he stood, leaning against the frame.

Mason pushed the door slowly inward. Concrete stairs went down into the dark. He saw eyes blinking up at him, but the overlay called him a liar, the feed clear of hostiles. "Anyone down there?"

Silence. He waited, leaning against the frame. The giant rat thing made a mad scamper across the foyer's floor before disappearing again. Maybe the rat had the right idea.

Running away isn't what you get paid for.

A hysterical giggle tried to break free. Mason clamped down on it. He pointed the Tenko-Senshin's beam down the stairs. Peeling paper, the design faded, greeted him. A light switch, green with mold, was mounted at the top of the stairs. Mason clicked it a couple of times, the sound sharp against the background drumming of the rain.

He reached into his pocket for a drone, twisting the sphere and tossing it down the steps. It bounced, a scattering of red lasing out as it tumbled down into the dark. The drone mapped the room, because surprises were bad in a situation where enemy syndicates had stolen your corporate assets.

Mason waited as his overlay filled with the layout of the room below. He sealed the front of his jacket, shrugging as the helmet chattered out of his collar and lapped into place around his head.

"There's probably no one down there, Mason." Carter's voice was all business as the link came online.

"I thought I told you not to talk to me."

"Your heart rate's significantly elevated. I was concerned."

"You were what?" Mason put a foot on the stairs. *Time to go down.* "I think I misheard."

"Concerned."

"You got the satellite up?"

"Not yet."

"I'd be more concerned about that."

Carter sighed. "I can do more than one thing at once."

Something with a lipless mouth reached for him from the dark below. He blinked twice, feeling his heart kick against his ribcage. "It seems worse here."

"The satellite is worse here?"

"No." Mason coughed, feeling phlegm in his throat. "The ... stuff."

"Stuff? What are you, five years old?"

Mason leaned on the wall, his helmeted forehead resting against the peeling paper. He breathed in deep and slow, his hands shaking. He felt a little stab of anger at Carters' words, then he grinned as the anger pushed back the fear. "Thanks, Carter."

"What for?"

"Keeping it real."

"I don't know what you're talking about."

Mason continued down the stairs, the beam of light pushing back the darkness in the basement. Water trickled from a crack in the ceiling, the old concrete chipped in spidery lines. He played the beam along the cracks. "You getting this?"

"Yes." There was a pause, then Carter cleared her throat. "I don't think those cracks are that old."

Mason followed the cracks as they converged. He stepped past a support beam. It was charred and black along the side facing where the cracks converged.

He continued until he found a body. It was covered with a layer of carbon, black from head to foot. The corpse curled in a fetal position. Water had mixed with the ash, making a pool of dark ink around the body. Mason checked the feed. The body was there in digital too. *It's real. Someone burned to death here.*

"I think we're getting warmer."

Carter snorted. "Don't you think that's just a bit in bad taste?"

"What? Oh. Sorry." Mason tried for a smile out of habit. "Bad choice of words."

"Accurate, though. Find it, Mason. We can't afford to lose this one."

Seven men came at him out of the darkness, eyes milky from the grave. Their shambling gate brought them into the Tenko-Senshin's beam. Grasping hands reached for him.

They were on the feed. These weren't hallucinations. Dead men were coming for him.

Mason squeezed the Tenko-Senshin's trigger, the scream of the weapon deafening in the basement. The bright, angry blaze of the flechettes stabbed across the floor to the walking corpses. The heat from the weapon sparked and kicked at the air. One corpse ignited from the heat as the Tenko-Senshin pulled it to pieces.

Silence. Flames rose from the floor where a fallen leg lay, the smell of burned meat filling the air.

"Mason!" Carter's voice was loud in his ear. "What—"

"They were on the *feed*, Carter." Mason coughed again.

"That's impossible."

"You can see them, can't you?" He walked over to a burned patch on the ground where an arm lay, cut and torn from the Tenko-Senshin's barrage. He poked it with a gloved finger. "And you can see this."

"The dead don't walk. We know the hallucinations are just... They're an effect from the rain."

"This look like an effect?"

"No, but... Wait. What's that?" Mason's optics flickered once, twice, then a reticule highlighted a section of an arm. "That tattoo."

Mason leaned forward, poking the arm with the barrel of the Tenko-Senshin. The tattoo was typical Marine-style, the falcon, globe, and anchor blurred with age. A barcode was underneath, the six-digit service number faded to illegibility.

"Give me a second," she said. "I'll enhance that."

Mason's optics flickered again, highlighting the barcode and service number. A section popped into relief as image enhancing algorithms kicking in. Carter made a low noise. "Are you...? Jesus. You're *humming*."

"Yeah." She went back to humming. "I love my work. What can I say?"

"It's hardly the time, Carter."

"Oh. Right." She stopped humming as a chime sounded. "It doesn't matter, we're done. That arm belongs to... John Smith."

"John Smith." Mason raised an eyebrow. "His name's actually John Smith?"

"Yeah. From Nebraska."

"John Smith from Nebraska. What's his arm doing here? And when did he die?"

"That's the thing." She downloaded a military service record to Mason. Pages flipped over in the top right of his overlay. "Hah. According to the Marines, he's not dead."

Mason nudged the arm, then stood up. "Looks pretty dead to me."

"It's obvious, isn't it?"

"I'm a field agent. I didn't study sociopathy."

"Sociology. I'm a sociology major. Amongst other things."

"Whatever."

She sighed. "It's got nothing to do with sociology. It's logic. The reason why Specialist Smith doesn't have a deceased date on file is because you only just killed him."

Mason needed to get into the chair. He wasn't normally this stupid. "Specialist?"

"Career Retention Specialist. It's in the file."

"He was... Wait. He was in HR?" Mason looked at the darkness around him, then let the Tenko-Senshin's beam fill the spaces between the columns with light. *You're babbling. Get your shit together. Only little kids are afraid of the dark.*

"It's the Marines."

"I thought they shot people."

"They do. And they have an HR department to make sure they retain people who are good at shooting."

Mason let out a nervous laugh. "I guess that makes sense."

"I know you don't like HR, Mason, but this is a bigger issue, okay?"

"I don't follow."

Carter gave an exasperated sigh. "Talking to you is like talking to a child. You remember the atmospheric effect?"

"Sure. The rain."

"Right, the rain. We figured it made you see things."

"It does." Mason nudged the arm with his boot. "I saw a dead man walking."

"No, you didn't," said Carter. "You saw a live man walking, and then you made him a dead man. It becomes even more imperative we find the technology for the Federate. You need to get to that buyer and acquire the asset. To use your word, this is powerful 'stuff.'"

Mason chewed the inside of his lip, looking around at the bodies. Some were still burning. "They looked dead. They were attacking."

"Wait. I'll show you." Carter rewound the tactical overlay to the time Mason opened fire. "See?"

"Ah, Christ," said Mason. "I shot a bunch of vagrants, didn't I?"

"Yeah," said Carter. "But that's not the interesting bit."

Mason walked amongst the remains of the bodies. "What did Specialist Smith get kicked out of the Marines for?"

"Discharged."

"What?"

"They call it 'discharged,' Mason."

Mason sighed. "Okay. Discharged."

"He was attacked."

"It's the Marines. Gonna happen." Mason gestured around him. "He just got attacked again, after attacking me."

"You should read the file."

"Pretend I don't have time for that." Mason heard something scuttle in the darkness. He spun, pointing the Tenko-Senshin.

There was nothing there.

Carter flicked through the file, the discharge papers dropping into Mason's overlay. "He was trying to performance manage someone and got hit in the head with a chair. He couldn't walk properly after."

"So, I just killed an invalid? Way to make me feel better."

"The point is before," she sounded exasperated, "we thought the rain made you see things."

"It does."

"Right. But it also makes you see different things. Things that are actually there can appear different. That's assuming you believe you saw dead people attacking you."

"Have you been reading my Psych reports?"

"I get bored at night."

"Most people sleep."

"Most people aren't quite as high-functioning as I am." She sounded just a little too smug for Mason's liking. "So. Which is it? Did you just gun down a bunch of homeless guys in cold blood, or did the rain make you think a bunch of homeless guys were actually dead guys?"

"I need a drink."

"Later." Carter's tone turned businesslike. "You should finish your sweep."

Mason nodded. *Then get the hell out of here.* He walked toward the center of whatever happened here. The Tenko-Senshin's beam picked out bits of detritus on the ground. A lump of fallen concrete here, a mouldering box there. He passed another charred support column, this one cracked and broken in the middle, rebar showing through.

He played light over a smudge on the ground, nothing more than a smear of carbon. "I'm pretty sure that used to be a person. An illegal."

"It's not illegal, Mason—"

"You know what I mean. There are no implants."

"Or the fire was very hot." She paused. "I think you must be close now. Be careful."

Another support beam loomed from the darkness, blasted and twisted, concrete chunks missing. Beyond that, the floor sank into a smooth depression, the curve looking like the bottom half of a sphere. The concrete looked like it had been pushed down, the cracking suggesting something round and tremendously heavy had sat there. The ceiling was broken in a loose ring.

"There's no debris." Mason played the light up to the roof, noting where the top of the object must have punched through to the floor above. Water trickled in over the edge.

"I see what you mean. Where did the roof go?"

"I'm guessing this is the center of the blast. Whatever it was." Mason played his light around the area, picking up the remains of scorched cables. He followed them back to the remains of a reinforced case. The charred and twisted top was about waist height. An Apsel logo was still faintly visible on the leeward side. "What the hell?"

Carter paused for a couple heartbeats. "Is that the Federate's logo? Is our logo on that box?"

Mason grabbed the edges of the lid, pulling hard with augmented strength. With a creak and a flaking of carbon, the box opened. There wasn't much left inside, melted metals, burnt plastics, and glass.

"What is it?" Mason let his optics switch to thermal. The innards of the box were cold and lifeless. If it was Apsel tech, it had been burned out by whatever had happened here.

"I can tell you what it isn't. It isn't a reactor." She hummed again.

"Sure," said Mason. "Back to my question: what is it?"

"See if you can find a serial number."

"Come on. Look at it."

She sighed. "Fair enough. Wait a moment."

Mason started to lift fragments out of the box. His hand came up against a piece of metal, mostly intact. He rubbed his thumb against the carbon scoring on the side. "Check this out." He held the metal at arm's length, pointing the beam from the Tenko-Senshin at it. The light showed the Apsel logo, and the words *APSEL FEDERATE — ATOMIC ENERGY DIVISION.*

"That's ... *us.* You came here following a reactor signature, and you found a box of junk. Junk *we* made." Carter sounded almost confused.

"Maybe." Mason tossed the piece of metal back in the box.

"We can burn it." Carter paused briefly. "I've got the satellite online."

"About time. Can you kick off a strike?" Mason rubbed the back of his neck, feeling the tension there.

"It seems the best way. Let me send this up the line, see if they want to send a recovery team here."

"There's nothing to recover. We'd be better off nuking the site from orbit and finding out which circus division back at the ranch is screwing with us. If I got sent out here to recover a ... let's call it an *unauthorized* reactor, and we've got another team in play, someone in logistics is getting fired."

"See, it's that kind of commentary that keeps you in the field." Mason could hear the smile in Carter's voice. "Look, just let me clear it. At least it'll solve the problem around the paperwork."

"Paperwork?"

"The vagrants."

"Right." Mason started to pick his way back through the basement. "There's something I don't get."

"What's that?"

"The hallucinations? They're *real.*"

Her voice was wry. "They wouldn't be hallucinations anymore, would they?"

"That's not what I mean." Mason shuddered, thinking about the walking corpses. About a dead man from Nebraska named Smith. "I just blasted a dead man's corpse to pieces. Or I thought it was a dead man. The only thing left behind was an arm. You saw it on the feed."

"Yeah. I saw it."

"Here's the thing. What did Specialist Smith see in *me?* What made him and his buddies attack a syndicate man? That's not healthy behavior."

"What am I, the Oracle of Delphi? Come back in. We'll get you in the chair."

"I think it's getting worse. And I think it's worse *here*. At the center of whatever this is. Whatever was in this box."

"You've done your job. I'll put this in the report."

"Good." He sighed. "We don't want this getting out."

"What getting out?"

"I don't know. But you can be damn sure some reporter would have a field day if they found Apsel equipment at the center of..." He trailed off.

"I know." She laughed. "That's lucky."

"What's lucky?"

"I've got the satellite back, and would you look at that, I'm cleared for a strike. Get yourself clear."

Mason dragged himself back up the stairs into the foyer, walking through the crumbling entrance to the old hotel. He gave a last look around before walking back out into the rain.

The Suzuki fired up as he approached, cowl extending from the front. The lights on the dash blinked at the night as the rain fell harder. Mason climbed on, kicking the drive into gear.

"You ready?"

"Do it." Mason twisted the throttle on the big bike, pulling away from the hotel. He felt a pressure building in the air even over the rush of wind and rain.

Light, bright as a sun, stabbed down through the atmosphere. Clouds peeled apart, boiling and twisting as ionized air burned in a pillar of fire. The beam played across the hotel, fire raging up from the ruins as lightning flickered across the sky. Bits of concrete were flung into the night sky, leaving burning trails across the night. The orbital laser continued firing as Mason pulled further away. He watched in one of the Suzuki's mirrors as a dust cloud spread out from the sight of the strike, rain already pushing it back to earth.

It probably wouldn't even be on the news tomorrow.

Mason twisted the throttle a bit more, ignoring the warning flicker of red lights on the dash as the machine compensated for the shockwave. The front of the bike skipped, rearing from the ground as he put on more speed. "Carter?"

"Yes?"

He coughed. "I need to get in the chair."

"Yeah. Don't worry about the report. I said I'd take care of it. Good night, Mason."

"Good night, Carter."

CHAPTER FOUR_

The Apsel building touched the sky, the silvered glass exterior reflecting clouds blanketing Seattle. The ground, planed clear for a kilometer in every direction, was smooth concrete and neatly trimmed lawns brought into relief by clean white lights scattered across the premises. Flight traffic was steady in and out of the tower, air cars delivering their loads of early morning execs.

Mason opened a channel when he was five klicks out, still in the streets of the city. It would be bad to get a case of mistaken identity. "Mason Floyd. Specialist Services field operative, requesting clearance for entry."

"Copy your ident, Mr. Floyd. We've already got you on approach." The man on the other end of the link sounded bored.

"Just a courtesy call. You can never be too careful."

A pause, then a laugh came down the line. "You know, that's true. Especially after last week."

"What happened last week?"

"Someone wasn't ... what was the word you used? *Careful*. You're clear to use bay six." The bike's HUD, projected against the inside of its cowl, laid a map in green and red iridescent lines. He ignored it in favor of a mirror of the map that snapped into place on his overlay.

"I got it. Thanks." Mason kicked the bike up a gear, picking up speed. The reactor was barely working, the drive low and quiet. He opened a different channel. "Carter."

"Mason?"

"Ah, you're still up."

"I live for the job, Mason. You know that."

"You should get out some. Put on a dress and some pearls."

She snorted. "I'm not a pearls kind of girl, Mason. You know it's five-thirty in the morning?"

Mason grinned. His helmet's noise protection was good enough he didn't need to raise his voice. "No rest for the wicked. Beds aren't for people like us."

"Not the way you use them."

"Which brings me to—"

"No. No, it doesn't. I've woken up Sasha. She'll meet you at processing."

"She's going to be grumpy."

"Do you want your clean done grumpy or not at all?"

"I'll take grumpy." Mason approached the base of the main tower, bringing the bike into a wide concrete driveway lined by tall barriers. The Apsel falcon spread huge wings on the ground. Big enough to be seen from a distance, *Bay 6* was written in red letters above a wide metal door. A mix of other languages jockeyed for position underneath the label. They all said the same thing, more or less — *get lost, go away, this is not the door you're looking for.*

It'd be bad press if Apsel gunned down some throwback who couldn't read English.

Automated turrets looked down on him from behind razor wire, tracking his progress. "Those things creep me out. Each one is like its own little eye of Sauron."

"The eye of... Oh." Carter paused. "I didn't know you read. Fiction, I mean."

"Christ, I'm not some kind of barbarian. I read books."

"Books without pictures?"

"Go fuck yourself."

"Don't listen to what they say about you. I've always said there was more to you than—"

"Carter!"

"What? Get out there. Join a book club or something."

Mason pulled the bike to a halt in front of the door. Green light washed over him as lasers imaged him. *Just a last-minute check, right?* He remembered Smith-Benne. The agent came back with a small detonator on his car. They'd relied on perimeter radar back then. Mason was on the investigative crew.

They hadn't found all of Smith-Benne's body. *You can never be too careful.* "One more thing."

"What's up?"

"Thanks, Carter. I ... appreciate your help."

She paused. "Sure thing, Mason. Anytime." The link clicked out.

Mason tapped his fingers against the handlebars. With a clank, the doors opened, rotating yellow warning lights licking the walls. When the door was high enough he gave the throttle a small twist, entering the belly of the Apsel building. Even at this hour it was busy, techs moving around, servicing vehicles, loading munitions, and waving tablets at each other. He wove the bike through the people and machines.

He coasted to a halt, letting a total conversion stamp in front of him. It stopped with a hiss of hydraulics, torso swiveling to face him. He took in the spread wings of the Apsel falcon on its chest, the weapon launchers on its arms, and its face. It was huge, metal and armor stacked over four meters tall. "Harry. How you doing?"

"Pretty good, Mason." Harry pivoted, articulated feet clanking against the ground. "Just in for a service."

"Rough night?"

"It's the rain, man." Harry's voice echoed out through the room, and lights flickered up his chest plate. A red one pulsed insistently. "I don't know how you norms handle it."

"I thought you guys weren't hit by it."

"The visions? Yeah, got no problems with the visions. Sealed up nice and tight in here. No, this is plain ol' acid rain, Mason."

"I've got a raincoat." Mason shrugged, and his helmet lapped into his collar. "Still. I'm in for a checkup too. Maybe some sleep, if I can scrape up the time."

"Hah." Harry shrugged, big metal shoulders moving up and down with a whine. "If you'd do the conversion—"

"Not a chance." Mason nodded at Harry's mid-section. "I like eating too much."

"It's not that bad. You never have to wonder whether your diet's low-carb or not."

Mason snorted. "Sure, whatever. Take it easy, hey?"

"You got it. Have a better one." With a hiss Harry swiveled away, clanking across the bay. Mason nudged the bike into gear and let it purr toward a park.

He dismounted. "Open up. Service mode." A brief flash came from the instrumentation on the dash, then the bike eased down, the rimless hubs pulling in towards the chassis. Mason grinned to himself — no matter how many times he saw it, it reminded him of an animal stretching, his bike doing yoga's *downward dog*. The armored fairing flared wide, exposing the fusion drive, other mechanical components opening like a metal flower. Mason turned away and walked toward an elevator. A tech would be along shortly to look after it.

Something ghostly flitted at the edge of his vision but was gone when he looked. *God damn the rain.*

He'd best get himself to that med tech. The elevator doors opened silently in front of him. Mason stepped inside. "Medical."

"Medical, confirmed." The elevator spoke with a British accent.

A German company in America with a British butler? Now that's globalization.

○

The chair waited in the middle of the room. Cold white leather, like a dentist's without the happiness.

At least it's padded.

Also waiting in the room was Sasha Coburn, looking like she wanted to murder someone. She wasn't a morning person. Despite that, her uniform was crisp. This wasn't some hick Apsel outpost. This was the Federate Tower, and you dressed like it mattered, whatever time it was.

Consoles and medical equipment were in neat, ordered racks against the walls. Sasha sat in front of a console, the display bright with diagnostic information.

"Hey, doc." Mason took off his jacket, dropping it into a bin by the door. "Sorry to get you up so early."

Sasha looked over at him, giving him a quick glance up and down. He returned the favor. She had clinic-blue eyes, straight hair, and a mouth that liked to smile. Despite Carter yanking her from sleep, Sasha turned her bedside manner to eleven. A hint of that smile played on her lips. "You know it's never too early, Mason."

Mason grinned back at her. "Don't be like that. You're married."

She waved her ring at him. "A rock you can see from space and all that. What of it?"

Mason pulled his shirt off over his head, dropping it in the bin after the jacket. "You shouldn't tease a man."

She stood, walking to the chair. Sasha patted the seat, her ebony fingers contrasting with the white leather. Mason hadn't been able to work out if the black of her skin or the blue of her eyes were genetics or cosmetics. Not that it mattered, but he figured if it was cosmetics he should get the name of her clinic. It was top-shelf work. She raised an eyebrow. "C'mon. You know I don't get many kicks in this job. Do a girl a favor. Hop in the chair."

Mason sighed, mock-serious. His pants and underwear dropped in the bin. "This is harassment."

"I know. Get in the damn chair." Her eyes didn't leave him as he walked to the chair, settling in.

Mason coughed as his skin touched leather. "Jesus. Isn't there something in the hippo oath—"

"Hippocratic. You make it sound like I got my degree on safari."

"Sure. Isn't there something in your oath about doing no harm?"

"Yeah. It's not the top of the list, but it's in there. Why do you ask?"

"This chair. It's cold." Mason shivered.

"You big baby. I'll prep you a nice, warm cup of harden up when we're done." Sasha frowned, finger on her lips. "You want me to get you a blanket? Maybe a teddy bear?"

Mason bit back a reply. *She got up early so you wouldn't see dead men trying to kill you.* "We're good."

"It's just plasmapheresis."

"Remind me again why the bionics can't do this."

"Your nanotech needs something to fight." Sasha frowned. "We still haven't isolated what it is in the rain that makes you sick."

"You okay, doc?" Mason leaned forward. "You pull another all-nighter on this?"

Sasha clenched her fists. She shook her head. "It's just ... nothing's *working* anymore."

"Nothing?"

"Well, less than everything. I can't find anything in the plasma that looks like it shouldn't be there." Sasha walked back toward her workstation. "I'd say it's adapting."

"Adapting?" Mason shifted. "Why's this plasma...?"

"Plasmapheresis."

"Why's it still working?"

"I'm going to suck out your blood and spin it in a drum. Separate out the crap. If I had to guess, I'd say the hostile vector still needs to obey the laws of physics." She tapped her keyboard a few times. The environment shield lowered from the ceiling, settling around the chair. It was as wide as the grating on the floor. "I guess that's why they call them laws. Wait a sec, you might feel a pinch." An articulated arm descended from the ceiling, needles at the end of it. Mason watched as red light scanned his arm, then the needles slipped home.

He winced. "That's more than a pinch. You enjoy your job too much."

Sasha glanced at him. "Only with some patients. We draw straws to see who gets to work on you."

"I should be flattered... Wait, what? You draw straws?" Mason watched as the machine drew his blood, the red marching into the machinery in the ceiling. A hum sounded above. "I'm not a piece of machinery. Flesh and blood."

"Mostly." She gave him a long, slow look. "I'll be sure to raise your concerns with the ethics committee."

A returning line of red made its way from the ceiling down the other needle. It entered his veins. "Christ that's cold."

"It'll warm up soon. You're supposed to be a tough guy."

"Say, doc. These hallucinations."

Sasha turned away from her keyboard. "What about them?"

Mason thought back to the burning arm on the ground of the basement. *Hallucination my ass.* "I don't think—"

"Mason." Carter's voice rattled around in his head. "I wouldn't recommend it. Fastest way to get a trip to Psych."

"Sasha's okay."

"It's your brain." Carter clicked off.

Sasha raised an eyebrow. "You don't think what?"

"Never mind." Mason shifted in the chair. "How long's this going to take, anyway?"

He made his way up to his apartment and found her waiting for him.

He didn't feel tired, and if he had, Mason would have shoved it aside. *You can sleep when you're dead, Floyd.* A nasty taste lingered in his mouth, a relic of whatever cocktail Doc Coburn had given him before sending him off.

His apartment was how he'd left it. No one here except her. The shades were drawn, wan light struggling to make an impression on the lush black leather furniture and the woman who sat there. Mason pushed the door closed quietly behind him. "Hey."

She looked up. "Hey yourself."

"Get you anything? A drink?"

She stood, the sheer robe she wore falling open at the front. "I thought the whole idea of this was so you didn't have to worry about buying me dinner first." She smiled, raising her hand toward the TV, the art on the walls, and the view. "Quite a place you've got here."

"It's just where I crash. I got another place, out of the city." Mason walked to the liquor cabinet, pouring a splash of whisky into a glass. "I hope you don't mind. Had quite the day. I need a drink."

He heard her indrawn breath. "Jesus. Is that a Macallan?"

Mason glanced at her over his shoulder. "You know your whisky. Yeah. It's a fifty-seven-year-old."

Her bare feet brought her a few steps closer. "I... Hell. Can I try some?"

Mason pulled out a second glass. "Sure." The liquor splashed and gurgled as he poured. "Here." He didn't know her name. Didn't want to, either.

She took it from him, fingertips brushing his. She breathed in deep as she raised the glass to her lips, then took a sip. "God. That's really good."

Mason nodded, then reached into a drawer. He pulled out a pack of Treasurers, offering her one. "Smoke?"

"Christ. You smoke Treasurers too?" She took one, her nails a shiny red next to the silver filters. He lit it for her and she took a deep pull. "You sure know how to show a lady a good time."

"You should see me at a restaurant." Mason stepped to the stereo rack set into the wall, selecting a low beat. The antique Bang & Olufsen spread it out silky and smooth. Nothing made today sounded quite so pure. He put down his cigarette and whisky. "Do you dance?"

"Sure, baby." She put her own cigarette and whisky down, then moved over to him. She draped an arm over each of his shoulders. Her face was very close. "Whatever you want."

They rocked together in the center of the room. Mason touched her slowly, his hands running beneath her robe. "Do you mind if I ask you a question?"

She leaned against him. "Shoot."

"You seem like a nice girl—"

She snorted. "Right."

"And I'm wondering."

"Wondering? Like, how a nice girl like me ends up here?"

"Something like that." Mason touched her back, and she shivered against him. He leaned closer, kissing the nape of her neck.

She tipped her head back, making a low noise in her throat. "It's better than the alternatives." Her hand held to the back of his head as he nuzzled her. "Much, much better."

They danced for a few moments more as the light of dawn broke across the city, a sliver of heaven seen between the blankets of clouds. *Time waits for no man.* Mason took her hand and led her to the bedroom.

CHAPTER FIVE_

Bernie fidgeted in his creaking seat, his fingers tapping a rhythm as the rain drummed against the car's roof. That bitch Sadie made his ulcer worse, but *damn* she could sing. One of her tracks did laps inside his head. He liked the hard Seattle sound.

Come to think of it, he liked her hard body.

Bernie would get himself some of that. He always did. Bernie flipped open the old Buick's glove box, rummaging around until his hands found a memory sliver. It was ancient tech but needs must. Being under the radar was more important than driving his uplinked Lexus with an on-demand music system.

He slotted the sliver into the stereo, using a fat thumb to turn the volume up. Sadie's throaty voice eased out of the speakers, filled the cabin of the car, and drowned out the sound of the rain. Bernie leaned his head back, staring at the once-white roof. The cracked vinyl had a stain in the driver's side corner. He let his eyes wander along the pattern, thinking of the music, then thinking about what Sadie would look like naked.

A knock came at the window. Bernie jerked upright, knocking his bottle of Southern Comfort to the floor. "Jesus Christ!" Bernie reached into the footwell, rescuing the bottle, then spun the volume to low. He wound the window down with the ancient mechanical handle. *You're in charge. Prove it.* "You're late."

"You said six thirty." Haraway looked at him, eyes uncertain, her white Apsel coat showing a few spots where the umbrella she held didn't quite do the job. Her blond hair didn't have a strand out of place, framing a clinic-perfect face.

"So?"

"It's six thirty-one." She looked around, the deserted lot empty except for the rain.

"Like I said. You're late." Bernie jerked a thumb to the passenger side. "Get in, doc."

"I'm not a doctor." She walked around the car, shoes splashing through water. Haraway hauled the passenger door open, collapsing inside. Haraway puffed her umbrella a few times, shaking the water out. *Right on the floor of my vintage car.* "Nice music."

"Screw the music." Bernie eyed her. She was fine, no mistake. All the corporates were. They could afford it. "Why'd we have to meet?"

"I, uh." Haraway swallowed. "You know the rain?"

He snorted. "I know the rain. It's been pissing down for weeks. Bar staff don't turn up for work on time anymore."

She nodded, eyes distant. "I think..." She swallowed again. "I think we did that."

Bernie coughed out the swig of Southern Comfort he'd just taken. "What?"

"It's complicated."

"No shit." He offered her the bottle. *Get the bitches drunk, that was always a good start.* "A little southern hospitality?"

Haraway grabbed it from him and drank almost greedily. *If he could get her to go down on... Business first, Eckers. You know the rules. You always fuck it up when you forget the rules.* She came up for air, holding the bottle out. "You relocated my sister."

Bernie took the bottle back, letting his fingers brush against hers. She pulled back. His grin filled the small space of the car. *They always come around in the end. When they realize how much they need you.* "Remind me. Who's your sister?"

"Marlene Haraway. She told me about you." Haraway paused. "*All* about you."

"Ah." Bernie's grin stayed fixed on his face. "I remember. Younger sister, right?"

Haraway glanced at him, a look of revulsion on her perfect face. "That's right."

"Yeah. Real shame how she got in trouble with the syndicates." Bernie shifted in his seat, adjusting his crotch. "What's that got to do with it?"

"Nothing." Haraway's expression became guarded. "Everything. I know where the rain comes from."

"You said that." He waved his hand. "Spill, kid."

"We're trying to sell some tech." She craned around, trying to see through the rainy, fogged windows. Like she'd be able to see anything more than a couple meters away.

Always raining — it's always goddamn raining. "That's right." Bernie frowned. "Look, if it's about the test, that was—"

"It's not about the test." Haraway shook her head. "Okay. It's about the test. The test you did. Without me."

"The test site is where the rain comes from?"

"No." Haraway looked at her hands. "Maybe. It's complicated."

"Uncomplicate it."

She turned to him. "If you'd just *waited*, like I said, we'd have—"

"Couldn't wait," said Bernie. "Had a buyer."

Haraway blinked. "You've found a buyer?"

"*Had.* Gone on the wind. Someone blew up my meeting point."

Haraway scrabbled at the door. "I've got to go."

Bernie put a hand on her shoulder. "Doc, look, it's okay."

"It's not okay, Mr. Eckers." Haraway was tugging at the big old handle, the mechanism sticking. "There's only one reason why someone would... What did you say? 'Blow up your meeting point?'"

"Yeah."

Haraway looked him over. Saw his calm. She licked those delicious lips before speaking again. "You're not concerned."

"Nope."

"Why not?"

"Because I'm still sucking oxygen." Bernie leaned back. "*You're* still sucking oxygen. If they knew, we wouldn't be sucking oxygen."

Haraway tilted her head to the side before letting the handle go. "That makes sense." She paused. "We need to be careful."

"Yeah."

"No, Mr. Eckers. Really careful. This is big." Haraway smudged a window clear, looking out into the rain. "It'll change the world."

Bernie eyed her over the top of the bottle, then took a swig. "World might not need changing."

She turned back to him, her lips twisted. "*Everything* needs changing."

Bernie shrugged. He hadn't taken her for an idealist because she'd wanted money from the deal. Come to think about it, he didn't much care. He picked at his nose. "Sure. Needs changing. You still want to be rich?"

"No."

"What?" Bernie felt his heart skip.

Haraway smiled at him. She didn't look happy. Haraway looked *hungry*. "I want to be disgustingly rich. I want to have so much money that nothing can get in my way."

"Jesus, Doc, you had me scared for a second."

"No mistakes this time, Mr. Eckers," she said. "No blown-up meeting points. No reason for an Apsel satellite to perform an orbital strike. Nothing."

"No guarantees in this business, kid." Bernie scratched at his belly. "You know that."

She looked thoughtful, biting her lower lip between perfect teeth. "I know that."

"Why don't you come along this time?" Bernie leered. "Maybe after—"

"Are you insane?"

"I don't think so," said Bernie. "I sell shit. I make a percentage — a *good* percentage — on selling shit. I'm simple. Not crazy." *Just want to get mine. Everyone else is getting theirs.*

"I can't be there. If it goes wrong—"

"If it goes wrong, it's not going to matter if you're there or not," said Bernie. "They find me, they're going to find you."

"Are you threatening me?"

"Shit no." Bernie frowned. "You know how this works. It's just a set of facts. They'll stick my head in a jar and suck out whatever's inside. They'll find you."

She gave a slow nod. "They will."

"So, why don't you come along?" Bernie looked that fine body up and down again. "It'll give a buyer a little more... faith."

"Faith?"

"Don't hate the player," said Bernie. "Hate the game."

"You want me to give them faith?" She twisted to face him again, the Apsel coat pulling tight over her breasts. "The science is a little complicated—"

"Science?" He wasn't sure if he was keeping her talking for a good reason, or just to keep looking at her. She had a damn good clinic.

Haraway sighed, her chest moving under the coat. "The rain's not from here."

"What do you mean, not from here? Is it from Cleveland?"

She shook her head. "It's from much, much farther away. Trust me."

Bernie laughed, a small nasty sound. "Trust is in real short supply, kid. I tell you what would cut a deal, though."

"I'm listening."

"You."

"Me?"

"You. I tell you what. I'll bring some guys. Buyers with money.

You bring some product. And yourself. We'll see if we can make something work."

"Something?"

"What do you syndicate types call it? 'Contract transfer.'"

The car held them close, the only noise the rain on the roof. It seemed loud, urgent, as if it wanted to come in. "You want me to..."

"Look, doc. If you sell something big? They're going to have you executed."

"Yes."

"You don't care about that?"

"I care. Believe me. I'm attached to," she smiled, "'sucking oxygen.'"

Bitch is starting to thaw. Keep working it, Eckers. "You get a new contract, you get a new life. Protection."

She nodded slowly, coming to the same conclusion. "I'll need a space to set up."

"Just what are you selling?"

Haraway looked down at her hands. "I'll need to show you. And for that, I need to be there."

"So Apsel don't light us up from orbit?" Bernie tugged his shirt away from his paunch. "Or for insurance?"

"Insurance, mostly. I ... I think I can get it working right. So people don't die. So *we* don't die. Last time..." Haraway trailed off, looked at the rain again. "So much has already gone wrong."

"How big?"

"What?"

Bernie twisted to face her again. *This deal could be big. Could be the biggest you've run, Eckers. Play out the line. Don't break the hook.* "How big a space do you need?"

"Not very big."

"I've got a place. Off the grid."

"Do you have power?"

"I thought you Apsel guys were all about power."

"The demonstration has a certain fingerprint. If you'd listened to me before the test—"

"Bygones." Bernie waved his hand.

Haraway frowned. "It's best if it's near something Apsel already runs."

"Don't sweat the details. You'll get your Apsel reactor." Bernie put a hand on her arm. "But — well, doc. Don't jerk me around on this one." He let his hand linger.

She looked down at his hand, then pushed it away. "Don't worry, Mr. Eckers. It's a clean game of pool. And like I said, I'm not a doctor."

"Right, right." He nodded at the passenger door next to her. "Then get out. Be at *The Hole*. You know it?"

"No."

"Buy a map, then. Be at *The Hole*. Friday. Noon."

Worry crinkled her brow. "Can we do it sooner?"

"Do I look like an instant courier? No, it can't be done sooner. I need a new set of buyers after last time. And I need to get your precious reactor."

"I'm worried. They feel close." She rubbed her arms. "Friday it is." And with that, Haraway pushed the passenger door open, umbrella leading her way into the rain. Bernie watched her leave, his eyes on her ass.

He fired up the old Buick as she shut the door. The wheels crunched on loose stones and broken asphalt as he nosed it out onto the street. He grinned, the dim light from the dash lighting up his face. Bernie's hand touched the volume, Sadie's voice growing loud in the cabin. The car picked up speed, his belly bouncing against the seat belt.

They always came around in the end.

CHAPTER SIX_

The autolights shut off after dawn's glance through the windows. Louvers opened slow and silent to reveal the cloudscape clutching the tower. Mason hadn't slept yet. He stood looking out at the clouds beneath him, sipping whisky. Mason spared a glance toward the bedroom, catching a glimpse of black hair strewn across silk sheets.

"You ready to get to work?"

Mason coughed whisky. "Jesus, Carter. It's seven in the morning. I haven't been to sleep yet."

"It's closer to seven-thirty. You could have grabbed a couple of hours. What have you been doing with your time?" She sounded testy. "I've arranged breakfast."

"Breakfast?" Mason looked at his whisky. "I guess it is that time."

"You're not hungry?" Carter sighed. "You need to eat. Keep up your strength. It's going to be a busy day."

"You're a golden ray of sunshine, aren't you?" Mason tossed back the rest of the whisky. "I should get some sleep."

"You can sleep when you're dead. Harden up, buttercup."

"That's cold." Mason walked to the apartment's kitchen. "You should try field work."

"It's not my thing. I've a nice desk job here. I don't want to break a nail." She paused, her tone softening a little. "I don't need to die to show my loyalty to the company. And neither do you."

"You think?" Mason started to pull a few things from the refrigerator. "Cancel the breakfast order. I'll make it myself."

"We don't have time."

"Make time. I've got a guest."

"You've got a guest who charges by the hour."

"You're just cranky because I got you up at five-thirty."

"You didn't get me up." Carter sighed. "I didn't get any sleep last night either."

"Working late?" Mason put eggs and bacon down on the marble counter. He considered his choices. *You can do better.* Butter joined his breakfast pile. It was real, from grass-fed cattle. Harder to get than mil-spec ammunition. Mason had a guy who got it for him.

He put the butter down on the marble. His eyes wandered over the dark surface. Veins of white streaked the black. He wanted to touch it, feel its smoothness, its *realness.* Mason rested his fingertips against the cool stone for a moment, then raised his hand in front of his eyes. "I've still got the shakes."

"You were in the chair for an hour."

"It felt like longer."

She sighed. "This is one of the many reasons I don't do field work."

"You know what your problem is, Carter?" Mason fired up the stove. Expensive gas flames licked the skillet. He threw a good chunk of butter in the bottom of the pan. *Arterial plaque won't be what gets you, Mason Floyd.* "You never get out."

"I don't dance, Mason."

"Who said anything about dancing? But sure, dancing. You should try it."

"I don't want to try it." She paused for a second. "I don't think so, anyway."

"You don't think so?"

"Look, I've never really thought about it, okay?"

"Who's got their asshole dial all the way to eleven this morning? Okay." The butter had started to bubble, so Mason dropped bacon in the pan. "I just figured ... work bonding. I could take you out bowling. Or dancing." He watched the bacon for a little longer, then cracked some eggs into the pan, moving the butter around over the top of the eggs. Gentle heat was the secret to a perfect fried egg.

That, real butter, and real bacon. Everything was better with bacon. "You still there?"

"I'm here."

"I thought I'd lost you."

"Did you just ask me out dancing?"

Mason tucked a spatula under the edge of an egg, gently teasing it off the pan. *Flip without breaking. Don't want to look like an amateur.* "Not really. I asked you out bowling."

"I don't dance."

"So you said." Mason finished flipping the eggs. "We could play darts instead."

"It sounds like a date."

"It's a few drinks after work." Mason's eyes were drawn to the bedroom by the sounds of movement. "Christ!"

"What?"

"I've forgotten the toast." He rummaged in the pantry, pulling out a loaf of artisanal bread.

"I'd..." Carter trailed off, losing all her hard corners for a moment. "What?"

"I can't, Mason. I want to. But I can't." She sounded wistful. "I'd like to learn to dance."

"Hey, your loss." Mason cut the bread into thick slices, revealing seeds within the bread. They weren't fake soy texture.

"Your breakfast looks good."

Mason parsed that line through his head twice. "Are you ... *watching me make breakfast?*"

"It's my job."

"It's my apartment!"

"Sorry. I'll kill the video."

"It's also creepy as fuck." Mason looked at the bread. Un-toasted it'd have to be, or the bacon would burn. *I can't believe I almost screwed up bacon and eggs.* "I think this is the first time I've forgotten to toast bread for breakfast."

"It's been a long night. Cut yourself some slack."

"You're warming up."

"You've got a meeting with Gairovald at nine."

"And the temperature plummets again." Mason pressed a button on the Jura, watching it shuffle through its coffee ceremony. The smell of coffee hit as the espresso streamed into two cups. "Wait. Did you just say Gairovald?"

"Yes."

"As in, the boss?"

"That's right."

"Am I being fired?"

"Yes."

"Fuck!" Mason spun to face the windows, coffee forgotten. *Get your go bag. Take the stairs, not the elevator. Subway's a klick out, but you can make it.*

"Relax," said Carter, "I'm just messing with you. You're not being fired."

Mason felt the tension in his back unkink. "You're an asshole."

"Don't forget. Nine."

He held a hand up, middle finger extended. "This is for you."

"Cute."

"I thought you killed the video."

"I thought you weren't twelve. We can both be wrong, hey?"

"Seriously. Huge asshole." Mason thought for a moment. "Is someone else being fired?"

"Trust me," said Carter. "This one's right up your alley. Enjoy your breakfast. Don't forget to take some stims. They're in the medicine cabinet." The link clicked off, leaving him alone in his head.

Mason set up a breakfast tray. First, the pile of bacon and eggs on bread. Nestle the coffee in the middle. *Meeting old man Apsel at 9, huh?*

No problem. There was time for breakfast, and maybe a little something else.

Mason headed for the bedroom.

○

He was still rubbing his wrist where the stim hypo had bit his skin as Mason left the apartment. He'd left the woman in his bed, eyes wide over silk sheets, holding a white cup as she'd breathed the aroma.

Maybe she'd never had real coffee before.

Mason figured it was a bonus of sorts. She'd done good work.

He carried another coffee with him, a plastic lid over the Federate's logo on the white waxed cardboard. He passed other company employees in the corridor, people bustling on their way to work. White uniform clothing with the Apsel logo above the left breast.

These assholes need to not shop at the same store. Mason checked his own jacket and darker denim jeans, mylar and Kevlar invisible beneath the cotton. The utility of the clothing was more important than almost anything. Mason still wore the company's small falcon on the collar of his jacket. It was always best to show a little flair when meeting with the big man.

He waited at the elevator with a small huddle of people. They eyed him nervously; they all had different haircuts, some with face tattoos or glowing holos under the epidermis, others making their own statement with perfect, clean skin. Their eyes all held a variation on the same emotion: caution through to outright fear. They might not know him, but they knew what he was. A company man's company man.

Corporate acquisitions and recovery. Or a trusted killer, if the situation demanded it.

The elevator arrived with a soft chime. Mason stepped inside. "Anyone else?"

No takers. The doors closed, cutting them off from view. It might even have been justified; Specialist Services had a brand of its own. *Still.* "Fucking robots."

"Hmm?"

"Not you, Carter." Mason shifted the cup to his other hand.

"You're running late." Carter cleared her throat. "Again."

"Do you ever get tired of it?"

"Tired of what?"

"I don't know. Being treated like a leper."

"There hasn't been a case of leprosy in over fifty years."

"You know what I mean."

Carter paused before answering. "It's a bit different in ... my team."

"All doing the same work?"

"Something like that."

"You're lucky."

Mason could feel her smile through the link. He imagined it with some genuine warmth touched by about five percent sadness. "I don't know. You get to see more people than I do."

"It doesn't count if they're all assholes."

"Fair enough. Gairovald's been held up."

"So I'm not late."

"You're still late. He's *later.*"

"It's his dime." The elevator stopped, sliding open in front of him. Mason stepped out, people parting for him like a terrified Red Sea.

Mason walked down a long corridor, plush wool carpet — *real* — soft under his boots. He reached an open reception area. A white wooden coffee table rested between two leather couches. A black reception desk sat further in, the spread wings of the Federate's logo embedded slate in the wood. There wasn't anything subtle about it. *This is our house.*

He nodded to the woman behind the desk. "Nancy. How

you doing?"

"You're late, Floyd." Her face may as well have been the same stone as the Federate logo, but a smile twinkled in her eyes.

"I'm doing great! Thanks for asking. How are the kids?" Mason put the coffee on the desk in front of her. "I brought you a little something."

"You're an angel — but you're still late." Nancy reached for the cup, popping the top and inhaling. "I don't know how you still get real coffee."

Mason looked at the cup in her hands, thinking about where it came from. About what it cost to get it. *I'm no angel, sister. We both know that.* There was a convenient lie for these situations, and he tried it on with a smile. "I know a guy."

"You want to share the name of this guy?"

"Not really." He winked at her. "If you can go right to my supplier, well hell. I won't get favors ever again."

She tossed her hair, the smile reaching her mouth. "You can go in. He'll be along in a few."

"Thanks, Nancy." He stepped past the desk, then looked back at her. *Damn, but Gairovald has taste.* "See you later."

"Sure, Floyd."

Mason leaned back in a big leather chair as Gairovald Apsel walked in. He was an average height, average sized kind of guy. Despite that, life resonated from him like warmth from the sun.

Expensive suit. Perfect teeth. Hair salon-perfect. Gairovald wore the signature flower on his breast pocket — something pink today — as the man walked up to the big boardroom table.

The pair of guards who dogged his steps wore suits color matched to his. Their ebony skin was clean of blemishes or tattoos. Anonymous. Men who could be disavowed, if that's what was needed. They took up position either side of the door, their eyes locked on Mason.

We might be on the same side, but we're not on the same team, right?

"Mason."

"Sir." Mason stood, hands clasped behind his back. "It's a rare privilege to talk with you in person. What can I help you with today?"

"That's one of the things I like about you." Gairovald sat at the other end of the long table, gesturing with a hand. There was almost no trace of his German accent. "You're to the point. That, and you get results. Please, sit."

Mason let a small smile onto his face, sitting back down. *When the boss tells you to jump, you jump — sitting's easy.* "Thank you, sir. I'm just happy that I've been able to help with some of the company's ... opportunities in the past."

"Opportunities." Gairovald showed his perfect teeth. "You have a curious way of thinking. I read Carter's report on this morning's incident. You handled it well. However, it's not the end of it."

"Sir?"

"Are you aware of our research division?"

"It's one of our leading assets." Mason quickly scanned the numbers Carter served to his overlay. "Some thirty-four thousand employees and change. Mostly working on new initiatives. I don't have details. It's above my classification level."

"Something's run sour." Gairovald pursed his lips. "A rather unique piece of research has been stolen."

"Stolen." Mason tapped his fingers against the vast mahogany of the table. It was almost certainly real wood. "I see. This something is related to this morning's endeavor?"

Gairovald smiled with his mouth, not his eyes. "That's right."

"You asked us to find and recover the technology causing the hallucinogenic atmospheric effect." Mason coughed. *You need to get back in the chair. Get it done right this time.* "Not much was left at the site we found, but there was clear evidence our tech was involved."

"Our tech?"

"Atomic Energy." Mason frowned. "What I don't get—"

"Yes," said Gairovald. "Atomic Energy. Someone's been selling my property, Mason. Someone I employ, someone I've housed. Put food on their table, clothes on their back. They want to steal from me."

Mason nodded. "I'm guessing it's big."

"Why's that?" Gairovald straightened his cuffs, looking Mason in the eyes. "*Why* do you think it's big?"

"Because of them." Mason tipped his head to the guards on the door. "Because of you."

"You understand the situation."

Mason laughed. "I don't pretend to understand anything, sir." He leaned forward, putting a hand against the table. "I don't need to. It's not my job. But I promise you, if someone's stealing from the Federate — stealing from *you* — then I'll get to the bottom of it."

Gairovald looked at Mason in silence for a few moments. "I think I made the right choice. You're very dedicated." He held up a hand, forestalling Mason. "No, don't interrupt. Your file speaks for itself. It's time to up your classification level. There was a classified ... R&D project within Apsel."

"The rain?"

"The atmospheric effect, yes." Gairovald looked at a cufflink. Mason's optics zoomed in, showing an intricate gold affair inlaid with diamonds. "The atmospheric effect is a ... byproduct."

Mason thought that through. "A *byproduct?*"

"Yes. When you were sent to acquire the technology behind the atmospheric effect, we didn't know we already had it. The R&D project made no reference to this sort of outcome."

"That's a pretty big byproduct." Mason leaned back in his chair. "R&D didn't know about it?"

"It's not quite that simple." Gairovald held Mason's gaze. "It's one of my earlier projects. It's been mothballed for quite some time. It has significant future value to the Federate."

Holy shit. Gairovald hasn't done the heavy lifting on the science in thirty years. Mason nodded. "Okay, sir. So. New mission?"

"New mission," agreed Gairovald. "Different outcome."

"You want me to catch the thief."

"No." Gairovald stood, walking toward the door. He turned back to Mason. "No one steals from me. I want you to kill the thief."

Mason stared out the boardroom window for a long time after Gairovald left. He pressed his hand against the cool glass, the cloudscape stretched out below him gray and ugly. "Did you get that?"

"Of course." Carter sighed. "Why do you treat me like an idiot child?"

"For all I know, you could be an idiot child." Mason's lips twitched. "A savant, I mean."

"I get it."

"You know. Like a chess master."

"Mason? I got it."

"Speaking of getting things. Have we got a file?"

An icon flashed onto his overlay, information slipping over the uplink. "Of course," said Carter. "Some of this is from Gairovald's office."

"Some of it?"

"I don't spend my days surfing the Internet for porn, Mason. I do research."

"I don't know where you find the time." Mason flickered through the information. "Something's not right."

"Something in particular?"

"Sort of."

"That's not very particular, Mason. Do you know what 'particular' even means?"

Mason highlighted a section of information. "Here."

Carter was silent for a moment. "I see it."

The information Mason had highlighted was an image from the old hotel's basement, when—

Dead hands reached for him, the Tenko-Senshin screaming back at the darkness. His heart hammered in his chest, and he stumbled back as parts of people fell and burned in front of him.

—he'd found the epicenter. "This one. The image is from the box." Highlighted on the image was a charred piece of metal, the stenciled letters *APSEL FEDERATE — ATOMIC ENERGY DIVISION* still visible against the carbon scoring.

Carter was silent for no more than two heartbeats. "It doesn't have the R&D logo on it."

"You're pretty quick for an idiot child."

"This wasn't mothballed research at all. This was live tech, taken from Atomics."

"Maybe," said Mason. "It doesn't really matter though."

"It doesn't?" Carter sounded distracted. "I'm going to pull together a meeting between you and the department heads."

"A meeting, sure. The thing is, I don't care if the tech came from R&D, or from Never Land. Someone stole it. Mission's clear on that. Even if it's Peter fucking Pan, he's going down." Mason gritted his teeth at a memory that surfaced. Someone he'd trusted when he shouldn't have.

Carter cleared her throat. "I'm sorry."

"About what?"

"About ... your last handler."

"Yeah." Mason let a breath out, realized he'd been clenching his fists. "He made a bad call."

"You'd been working with him for two years. Did you have to kill him?"

"Yeah." Mason stood, walking toward the door. "Yeah, I did. He tried to steal from the company too."

She was silent a few moments. He let himself out. Mason tossed a nod to Nancy who caught it with a smile before heading for the elevators.

"I won't let you down, Mason."

"I know, Carter."

"You do?"

"Yeah." He clicked an elevator button, frowning at the old school tech. *Maybe Gairovald likes it retro.*

"You haven't even met me. How can you know?"

"I'm not sure." He stepped into the elevator. "Research level. Priority."

The elevator chimed, and a soft voice spoke. "Research level, priority confirmed."

"What?" said Carter.

"I was talking to the elevator."

"You didn't answer." Her voice was soft. "How do you know?"

Mason leaned against the glass of the elevator, his back to the clouds as the car dropped. "You haven't let me down yet."

She was silent as the elevator whispered down Apsel tower. Mason looked over the clouds. Lightning cracked briefly before the elevator sunk below them. Rain lashed the outside of the car. The city waited in the dark, far below. *The fucking rain.*

"I trust you too, Mason."

"Carter?" Mason watched the city approach as the car descended.

"Yes, Mason?"

"Don't get all mopey on me."

"I wouldn't dream of it." The link clicked off.

He smiled as the elevator car drew closer to the city. *Time to get serious.* He pulled his jacket close, then faced the elevator doors. Mason pulled a pack of Treasurers from his pocket, lighting one. The elevator chimed a warning at him, but he ignored it.

It was time to meet the department heads. Senior people. They made the technology that made Gairovald rich and powerful. They could make or break a career around here.

Mason's fists clenched and he looked at them, willing them to relax. *We'll see who's broken at the end of this.*

CHAPTER SEVEN_

The desert was oppressive. A hammer of sun, beating against an anvil of sand. Laia had never known such heat. The concept of a *desert* was as foreign as *freedom*. Words people said without understanding what they meant.

Cracked ground cobwebbed everywhere. Nothing grew here. Before the rain left, this might have been a mire. The smell reminded her of rotten things, now baked dry by Abinal's aging star.

Laia looked at Zacharies. He strained, sweat dripping from him to be lost on the dead ground.

The Master took no notice, the heavy whip in his hand moving slightly, as if it had a mind of its own. She watched the whip carefully, rubbing at the chafing under her collar, then wiped the sweat from her own face.

Zacharies held the divan above the desert floor, lifting and pushing it with his gift. The Master reclined atop it, sipping blue liquid from a chilled glass. Zacharies stumbled, and the divan trembled.

Blue liquid spilled over the Master's fingers. The whip rose cobra quick.

"Master." Laia spoke fast. She gave the air a gentle nudge with her own gift, making a soft breeze caress the slave master's dark robes. "We have arrived."

It wasn't a pure ruse. Those never worked. Truth was the best interruption.

A circular depression lay in the desert floor. Dirt became charred and cracked sand, melted in places to glass.

The Master looked at the indent, the whip holding a moment before lowering. "Good, slave." He stepped down from the divan, drink forgotten, glass weeping in the heat of the sun. Zacharies gasped with effort as he let the divan settle against the desert.

Laia stood with Zacharies as the Master walked the blasted desert floor. They said nothing to each other, but Laia worried for her brother. The trip had been long over the wasted ground. Despite the heat, he looked pale. She almost reached out to him, then remembered the collar at her throat. She sighed and looked away.

"Slave." The Master gestured at her. "Can you feel it?"

Laia felt out with her mind. Despite the collar, her gift hungered for this. She could feel *something*. A memory's memory. "It is..."

"What?" The whip twitched.

"It's hard to be sure. But I think it was here."

"Good." The whip fell back to the Master's side. "Where did it go?"

"I..." Laia faltered. The question was meaningless as *where do dreams go?* "It didn't go anywhere."

"Do you take me for an imbecile?"

"No, Master."

"Then don't treat me as one." The whip twitched again. "The demon is clearly not *here*." His voice was soft now. Laia dreaded the soft voice the most.

She pointed to the depression. "The demon was here, and then it wasn't. It's gone."

The Master considered her words before nodding. "Then we wait."

Laia felt Zacharies relax. There would be no holding the divan above the hot desert floor for the return journey. Not yet, anyway. She looked at the whip. If only there was some distraction out here.

Their Master was at his worst when he was bored.

CHAPTER EIGHT

The room's adaptive windows were tinted a dark gray for privacy. The lattice stretched under Mason's skin. It wanted grisly purpose. *Maybe later*. There would be plenty of time for violence come the meeting's resolution.

A black glass table sat between him and the room's three other occupants. The table's surface was full of images and icons. An information goldmine pulled from cam footage and Federate file storage. A few select pieces came from the public nets.

Carter hadn't said specifically, and Mason never asked.

Mason looked at the three of them. The fat black man, the woman in the lab coat, and a man so gaunt he looked like a cancer patient. *This is the best we can do?* The table was a barrier of sorts, a gold Apsel falcon etched into each corner, wings outstretched in victory. The barrier wasn't to keep them from him. It kept them from leaving. The evidence shown was an anchor, a thousand sins dragging them to earth.

Mason sighed, hands splayed on the surface. "It's going to be like that, is it?"

The fat black man looked like he wanted a piece, despite the sweat beading at his temples. *No doubt he feels I've dragged him from a very important meeting on corporate performance.* "Mr. Floyd. I'm not sure..." His volume wound right down as Mason glared at him. The fat black man's mouth hung open, flesh wattling around his neck, before giving a furtive glance at the one empty chair.

The empty chair said *this is why you fuckers are here.*

The woman spoke but looked like she didn't want to. "We responded to your request as quickly as we could." She was wedged between the fat black man and the gaunt asshole. They could have moved the chairs. Made things more comfortable.

It wasn't that kind of meeting.

Mason didn't care what their names were. She was the only one that looked like an actual doctor, white lab coat slung over some civilian threads. The gaunt man nodded in agreement, fiddling with his cufflinks. They looked expensive.

Mason gestured to the empty chair. "One of you is missing."

"Yes, but—"

Mason held up a silencing hand. *Let's get this back on track.* He held his hand out, palm up, at the gaunt man. "Military Applications?"

The man nodded. "That's right, Mr. Floyd—"

"Shut it." Mason pointed at the woman. "Medical?"

She nodded but didn't say anything. *Good.* He aimed a finger at the fat black man. "Let me get this straight. Porn?"

The fat black man swallowed. He'd already sweated through the armpits of his shirt, the dark red fabric stained black. "Entertainment. Synthetic Entertainment. It's not—"

"Right. Porn." Mason nodded to the empty chair. "Where is Haraway?"

The gaunt man figured it was his turn. "I was supposed to have a coffee with her this morning. She never showed."

"She heads up Atomic Energy."

The gaunt man nodded. "That's right. What—"

"I'm curious," Mason continued, running over the top of the guy like he was roadkill, "about what the head of Atomics might want with the head of Military."

His Adam's apple bobbing as he swallowed, the gaunt man paused, considering his words. *At least one of them's awake.* "She never said. Doctor Haraway—"

"She's not a doctor. Says right here." Information on the four heads of R&D shone under the cool glass of the table. Mason tapped the surface, Haraway's photo under his finger. Cut like a cute librarian, some top-shelf clinic work without a doubt. Mason gave the gaunt man a hard stare. "Is this position description inflation? If you're a doctor, you get a raise?"

"No. The thing is, she's brilliant."

"Are you fucking with me?" Mason looked the other man in the eye. "Are you trying to be *funny?*"

"I—"

"Do I look like I'm laughing?"

"What?"

"I asked if I look like I'm laughing." Mason leaned forward, his voice going soft. "Look me in the eye and tell me that I'm laughing. I *dare* you."

The gaunt man huddled back in his chair. "I don't understand—"

"No." Mason shook his head. "You don't understand. Shut it, fatty." Mason glared as the fat black man opened his mouth. The man's mouth closed with a snap and a wobble of flesh. "Of *course* she's brilliant."

The gaunt man swallowed. "What?"

"You said she was brilliant."

"She's—"

"Haraway is brilliant because this is Apsel Federate. She is brilliant because she is the head of the Atomic Energy division. Apsel Federate makes all its *money* from atomic energy. You," Mason leveled his finger at the gaunt man, "better come up with something a lot better than that."

The woman looked at her hands. Mason's overlay showed her

breath was shallow, heart rate elevated. Increased blood flow in her face. Stress markers from top to bottom. *About damn time they started to get worried.*

The gaunt man coughed. "Can I get some water?"

"Oh, I'm sorry. Didn't I offer you anything?" Mason's voice was still quiet.

"Uh. No."

"Then you can't have any water!" Mason's palm slammed down on the desk, making all three of them jump. "You people. You live your life down here in your labs. You have no idea what goes on out there."

The woman looked up, startled. Perspiration beaded her upper lip. "Out there?"

"You think this meeting's for your *performance review?*" Mason stood, looking out the window to the city below. He spoke, back still turned. "I thought you people were supposed to be *smart.*"

The fat black man stepped into the silence, like he'd been waiting for just this moment. "We ... what I mean is, Frank is right."

Mason turned. "Frank? Who the fuck is Frank?"

The gaunt man looked surprised. "I'm ... my name is Francesco."

"Good for you. You don't seem to understand what's going on here." Mason pulled out his Treasurers, tapping one from the pack. He lit it, the lighter's long tongue of flame reflecting in his eyes. Blowing out smoke, he leaned his hands against the table. "Any means necessary."

The woman gave a small gasp, barely audible, but Mason's audio caught it. She looked a deer in the headlights, ready to bolt. "We're ... being fired?"

"Do I look like I'm from HR?"

"But you said—"

"I'm not from HR. I'm not going to fire you." Mason took another drag on his cigarette, blowing the smoke toward the three of them. He leaned against the window. "Hell, if you've had a hand in this, you're just going to disappear."

Finally, they got it, the men a step behind the woman. She swallowed. "You ... can't." Her voice was very small. "I have a family."

"Yes. And Uncle Gairovald is very unhappy with you."

"I meant—"

"I know what you meant. Your husband. Your two kids. What are their names?"

"Sandy and—"

"Robert." Mason cut her off. He watched as her lips pressed together, leaving a bloodless line. "We keep detailed files."

"No."

"No?"

She started to stand. "Please—"

"If you leave this room, I'll assume you're one of Haraway's accomplices. I'll need to investigate your affairs." Mason took another drag on the cigarette. "Very closely."

She collapsed like someone cut her strings, looking at her hands again.

Mason looked back at the gaunt man. "Smarter than you?"

"What?"

"I said, is she smarter than you?"

Frank's eyes flicked toward the woman. "I don't—"

"Not her. Haraway."

"What?"

"You said she was smart. You were trying to be funny."

"I wasn't—"

"Is she smarter?" Mason turned away, taking another pull on the cigarette, giving the gaunt man a chance to collect his thoughts. Off balance was fine, but too far and he'd get nothing useful from them. When Mason looked back, he let his eyes find the fat black man before settling on the gaunt man. "Answer the question."

"Smarter than any of us."

"What was your meeting about?"

"Our meeting?"

"You said you were going to have a coffee with her today." Mason stubbed out the Treasurer against the table. Flakes of ash wilted to the ground. He pulled another one from the pack. The lighter flicked again. "What was the meeting about?"

"She said she wanted to talk about mutual interests. Getting our research teams to collaborate."

"Did she tell you she was planning to steal research from the company?" The silence lay over the three of them like death's shroud. "Do you know Apsel's policy on theft?"

The fat black man rallied. "Mr. Floyd, surely you don't think—"

"I don't know what to think, except that maybe you've stopped giving a shit."

"What?"

"Look at yourself." Mason waved a hand at the man's stomach. "You've let yourself go. The last time I saw someone that fat was in a bankruptcy case."

"My wife likes it."

"Your wife needs therapy. I wonder if Psych know about this." Mason's fingers tapped softly against the table. "Do they?"

The black man swallowed. "I—"

"I didn't think so. I'll book you in."

"I..." The fat black man's mouth opened and closed like a landed fish. No words came out.

"You understand, Apsel needs to know our people are the very best. Especially in the porn industry." Mason let his mouth twist in disgust. "It's no wonder she was able to steal it. None of you people look outside your own cubicle. I'm wondering if I should include this in my report."

"Your report?" The woman saw fit to look up from her hands. "What report?"

Mason flicked more ash to the carpet. It was plush, Apsel's logo in modest gray. "You must know how this is going to play out."

The fat black man leaned forward. "Play out?"

"Yeah." Mason dragged on the cigarette. "When I find out who was involved—"

"It was just Haraway," said the fat man, the words tumbling out of his mouth.

Mason raised an eyebrow. "When I find out who was involved, there will be a report. It'll highlight who was involved in the theft." He paused, feeling the silence grow. The three of them were trying not to look at each other. *The knives will come out soon.* "And..."

The fat black man leaned forward, his face desperate. "And?"

"And who was helpful." Mason nodded. "There's usually one or two who are willing to go above their job description. Work with us." A small smile tugged at his mouth. "Usually there's a bonus." He leaned back and watched them. He could almost hear the wheels churning in their heads.

It was the gaunt man who spoke first. "A bonus?"

Mason's smile broadened. *Gotcha.*

Mason stood in the corridor outside the meeting room, his cigarette burning out its life, ignored. He didn't want a cigarette. Mason wanted time. "What do you think?"

"I think none of them is going to get a good night's sleep for a month." Carter sounded bored. "I think you're wasting your time. I think you should cut down on your smoking."

"My smoking?" Mason looked at the Treasurer, the paper smoldering down toward the silver foil. He flicked ash to the carpet. "Why the hell would I do that?"

"You're going to get cancer."

"Again? That's a solvable problem." Mason watched the three R&D heads arguing with each other in the room. The fat black man was still sitting in his chair. The gaunt man was leaning against the table, gesturing with a hand. The woman stood alone by the window. "It's not a big deal."

She sighed. "Never mind."

"Why do you think that?"

"I said don't worry about it. Smoke all you like. Hell, even I'll order you some more. Treasurers, right?"

"No, I mean why do you think I'm wasting my time?"

Carter sighed again, theatrical enough for a stage performance. "You're like a child."

"Because I smoke?"

There was a moment's silence, then she said, "Children don't smoke."

"Some of them do. I did. When I was a kid." The Treasurer almost burned out. Mason dragged back the last of it before dropping the butt to the carpet, grinding it out with his shoe. "There are worse things."

"Gairovald's going to pitch a fit because you stubbed out a cigarette on the carpet."

"That?" Mason smiled, wondering if Carter watched him from the cams. *Of course she does. It's her job to keep tabs on you.* "It's all a part of the fiction."

"I think you're wasting your time because none of them know anything."

"You can't be sure of that."

"It seems likely. Haraway didn't turn up for work. If one of them was in on it, they'd have made a pretext to leave today before your meeting."

"Could be a double-blind."

"I've read their email."

"That's more like it." Mason pulled out another cigarette. "Must be tedious to read."

"You always smoke more when you're stressed." Carter paused. "Yeah, it's tedious. R&D, or some kid's birthday party, or a barbecue at the weekend."

"You understand the R&D stuff?"

"Mostly," said Carter. "It's not my area."

"Which one?"

"All of it. It's not like I spend my weekends reading up on nuclear energy."

"What do you spend your weekends doing?" Mason rolled his shoulders. "Almost time for round two."

"I'm not going out bowling, Mason, so stop asking."

"Jesus, Carter, who said anything about bowling?" He grinned. "It's like you're obsessed."

"Oh, for God's sake." Carter sounded like she wanted to slug him. "What's the plan?"

"I'm going in there with a bunch of coffees. I'll talk to them about how this has all been a terrible mistake."

"You're going to do what?"

"And then you're going to watch them. After they leave."

"I'm sorry?" said Carter. "I thought you said I was going to watch them. All three of them."

"That's right." Mason's grin grew broader. "Unless you had something else to do this weekend."

The link went dead. *That's coming along nicely.* Mason started to whistle as he headed off to the cafeteria. He'd never been to the one on this floor. The fat black man looked like a mochaccino kind of guy. The gaunt asshole probably had it black. And the woman?

Chai tea. Maybe with soy.

○

Haraway's office wasn't what he'd expected. Mason had pictured a lab with white walls, half-finished experiments on tables, and maybe some components scattered about, wires hanging loose. What he got after cutting the yellow tape crisscrossing the door was ... *different.*

The walls were dark, inlaid with wood veneer. Rainforest foliage flourished in planters around the room, big green leaves reaching for a sky they'd never see. When he walked in, the room warmed for him, light spilling from the ceiling like the sun. Underfoot was a carpet made with long twists of fibrous material. It reminded him of noodles.

Or grass. That was probably what Haraway was going for. The whole rainforest thing.

The middle of the room featured a small black stone table and a single lounge chair. Inset into the wall was a dispenser, standard fare for Apsel executives. He walked to it, punching in an order for Scotch. The machine spat out a chunky tumbler, a single hunk of ice landing a second later with a clatter. The dispenser measured an exact two fingers of amber liquid.

He took a sip, giving the office a tour. He started with the desk. It was glass and sat in the back corner of the room. His optics tagged the terminal on it, a small desk lamp, and the back of a photo frame. *Sentimental, Haraway?*

"What kind of woman are you?" Mason swirled liquor, letting its aroma join the rainforest scents. It was good Scotch.

"What?"

"Not you, Carter. I'm talking to myself."

"Do you need me to make a booking with Psych?"

Mason continued to walk the room, his feet silent on the carpet. "I don't get it."

"Delusions and confusion are common first markers for mental instability." Carter paused. "Are you sure you don't want me to call Psych?"

"What? No." Mason stopped in front of the small black table in the middle of the room. He leaned down to get a closer look, running his hand across it. It felt rough, almost unfinished. "Check out this table."

"What about it?"

"It's not smooth. The surface is trash." His optics clicked in to zoom.

"It's obsidian. Didn't you go to school?"

"I went to school. I was more into sports and watching cheerleaders. How can you tell it's obsidian?"

"Conchoidal fracture."

"Are you speaking English right now?"

Carter sighed. "You're going to be the one that breaks me, Mason."

"You weren't a cheerleader, were you?"

Carter cleared her throat. "We're not going bowling."

"Who said anything about bowling? Look, just drop the bowling thing." Mason tapped the surface of the table. "This thing is junk. The surface is uneven. You couldn't even put coffee on here without a high risk of a spill." He put his Scotch on it, the glass tipping slightly, the liquid off-level. "See?"

"Do you know what an atom is?"

It was Mason's turn to sigh. "Of course."

"I'm just checking. It's hard to know the edges of your education."

"Spit it out."

"Fine, fine. When molten rock cools—"

"Molten rock?" Mason retrieved his glass for another sip. It really was good Scotch. "I thought you were talking about atoms."

"When molten rock cools fast enough, the *atoms* inside it can't get themselves into a crystalline structure." Carter sighed again, like she was daring heights of theatrics. "When that happens, and you break the rock, you get a conchoidal fracture."

"You can see the atoms of this thing through my optics?"

"I can see it's black, looks like glass, and has conchoidal fracture lines. It's obsidian. She imported a giant hunk of volcanic glass for a coffee table."

"Why would she do that?"

"Maybe we can get her to Psych and find out. The point is, it's not a broken table. She got a table with rough edges on purpose."

Mason sat in the recliner beside the table, leaning back. He got a view of the ceiling, tips of the rainforest plants stretching fingers to the roof. "It's kind of peaceful."

"There's a sound system. Do you want me to turn it on?"

"That depends. What's she listen to?"

"One sec. Okay, here it is. It's rain."

"She could go outside and listen to the rain. It rains all the time in this city." Mason sat up. "Are you sure she hasn't been seen by Psych already?"

The gentle sound of rain's soft touch on leaves came from the room's speakers. A bird chirped in the distance. "How's that?" said Carter.

Mason stood. "It's not my thing."

"Want me to kill the audio?"

Mason walked toward the desk. *Last stop, Haraway. What were you working on?* "No. Leave it." *Damn, but it is peaceful.* He stepped around the desk, tugging the lamp's chain. A small pool of light spilled over the glass surface. There was an old-style notebook, real paper leaves and all. A pen sat beside it. Mason flipped the notebook open, looking at pages of equations, hand drawings, and meticulous notes. Mason left his hand on the notebook, the paper texture under his fingers comforting. He lifted his eyes to the photo.

A younger woman looked out at him, eyes sparkling. She was laughing at something just off frame. If Mason squinted just right, he could see Haraway in that photo, a little younger, and an entire lifetime away. Except this girl had green hair, and heavy black eyeliner.

Green hair wouldn't suit Haraway's corporate image.

"It's her sister." Carter cut across his thoughts. "She left the syndicate a few years ago."

Mason picked up the photo frame, flipping the latch at the back. The photo slipped into his hand. The writing on the back was full of loops and curls. A younger woman's hand, someone just finished with being a girl.

"Jenni — I'm free! See you soon." It was signed *Marlene.*

Mason tapped the photo against the desk. "What do you mean, 'left?' No one leaves the syndicate."

"She did."

"That's not helpful."

"Sorry, Mason." Carter cleared her throat. "One day she was here. Enrolled in some clever kids' program. Next day, she was gone."

"Missing?"

"As near as."

"What happened?"

"I don't know. The file is brief. She just left," said Carter. "Like I said."

Mason sighed. "She didn't *leave*."

"She didn't?"

"No." Mason turned on the terminal. "She ran away. Marlene Haraway, a promising young mind, ran away from Apsel. Now why do you suppose she did that?"

"How can you tell?"

"Because she sent this photo." Mason looked at the login prompt on the screen. "I hope you're better with computers than you are with people."

"Much better," said Carter. "Just pretend you're Jennifer Haraway. The computer thinks you are."

"Do I have to wear exec clothes?"

"I think all you have to do is be a little less of an asshole."

Mason winced as the screen in front of him flickered twice, the computer chiming. "Welcome back, Jenni," said the terminal, a cultured male voice coming from it.

"Who the hell uses a display these days?" said Mason.

"I don't understand, Jenni," said the machine.

"Pull up the last item worked on."

"I'm sorry, Jenni. As per your request, your files were deleted after the download."

"The download?" said Mason, leaning forward. "What download?

"You initiated a work plan download."

"What was on it?"

"You deleted those files."

Mason punched the terminal's off button. "Well, that was helpful."

"They wouldn't need you if it was easy. Security's already been in here."

"I know. I cut the tape on the way in." Mason swiveled in Haraway's office chair. His eyes moved back to the notebook. "Can you give me a scan?"

"Sure."

Mason picked up the book, opening it. He flicked the pages through in a smooth motion of ruffled paper. "Get it?"

"Got it," said Carter. "Okay, done. Digital copy of her notes is in your files." As Carter spoke, an icon danced into life in his optics, then slid off the side into the archive.

"Thanks, Carter." Mason turned the book over in his hands, then pulled open a few pages at random. The tech notes might as well have been hieroglyphs. He flipped to the end. A single word was scribbled on the last page. *Eckers.* He tucked Marlene's photo into the notebook. "I think I'll hold onto this."

"What for?"

Mason shrugged at the empty room. "I don't know, yet."

"At least you're not smoking."

Smiling, Mason walked to the door. "I need you to find some stuff for me, Carter."

"Sure."

"I want you to find for me anyone who was involved with Marlene."

"Sorry, I thought you said, 'Marlene,'" said Carter.

"That's right."

"Can I ask why?"

"You can."

"Why?"

"I don't know that either." Mason stepped through the door, then uplinked the command to seal Haraway's office. He watched the ceiling lights die, the room dipping into darkness, as the door slid shut in front of him. The plants might never see their fake sun again. "It's a hunch."

"A hunch?" Carter paused. "You want me to do a bunch of work on a hunch?"

Mason put his hand against Haraway's door. "Okay. It's more than a hunch. Haraway's sister... Wosshername."

"Marlene."

"Marlene, right. What would you do if your sister left the syndicate?"

"I don't know." There was doubt in Carter's voice. "I've never had a sister."

"I don't have a sister, but I figure if I did, I'd want to know where she is. I don't know if I'd leave all this," Mason gestured at the hallway, "but I'd want to know she was okay."

And maybe, just maybe, I'd want to walk away from it all. If I had a sister, and she yelled for help in the dark, cold world? Maybe that'd be enough.

Mason walked away from Haraway's office, tapping the notebook against his leg. "What does the word, 'Eckers,' mean to you?"

"Who knows. Password?"

"It's a pretty weak password."

"The weak ones are the best. When I was in training I used, 'password,' for seven weeks before anyone guessed it."

"No shit?"

"No shit, Mason." He could feel Carter's smile coming through the link. "Sometimes simple is best."

"Okay, let's say it's a password." Mason walked past a researcher, white lab coat and harried expression moving past too quick for a nod. "What's it mean?"

"I'm not sure I understand the question."

"You base passwords on stuff, right? Like your mother's maiden name, or a simple word. 'Eckers' is a pretty weird thing. It's a set of letters."

"Like a name," said Carter. "It could be a name."

"That feels right," said Mason. He paused in the corridor, getting his bearings. "Can you do a search?"

"Already running," she said. "There's a bunch of Eckers kicking around. Which one do you want?"

Mason held the notebook up in front of his eyes, then flipped to Marlene's photo. He looked at the girls' face, the smile, and then turned it over. *I'm free.* That's what she'd written. "I want one that's got a criminal record."

"Narrows it down a bit," said Carter. "You've got ten left. Why a record?"

"Anyone who's tied to a syndicate won't have a record. Not for this."

"Not for what?"

"Escape. She ran away from us. And her sister is trying to find her."

CHAPTER NINE_

The building was big and old, windows dark, some broken. A set of double doors at the front reminded Mason of a barn entrance, big enough to herd cattle through. A badly painted sign banged in the rain, weathered letters proclaiming *The Hole*.

"Now this shit is classy." Mason got off the big Suzuki, the drive powering down with a soft whine. "I thought the last part of town was trash, but this is taking it down a few more steps."

"It's a popular location. Before they lost the Space Needle, anyway," said Carter. "According to satellite surveillance, there was a significant gathering earlier this evening."

"Significant? Define significant. Ten guys? A hundred?"

"More like a few hundred. It's hard to be sure."

"Okay, that's significant." Mason's helmet snickered back into his collar, the rain falling on his skin. "Wait. It's hard to be sure?"

"Some members of the crowd didn't have a tag."

"Illegals, huh?"

"It's not illegal." Carter gave a growl of frustration. "It's strongly discouraged."

Mason snorted. "Yeah, sure. You and I went to different schools, Carter."

"You should get out of the rain, Mason."

"Yeah." Mason rubbed his cheek, feeling the rain already starting to burn his skin. "Okay. I'll go see who's home."

As he walked away from the bike, the machine's lights dimmed. Mason could hear the plink of cooling metal under the constant hush of the rain. His feet scuffed against a few stray pebbles, the street and sidewalk in disrepair. A Budweiser bottle lay in the gutter, the rain slowly burning the label from it. He pushed open the door. It swung open on surprisingly well-maintained hinges.

He'd expected a creak at least. It'd have gone well with the inside of the place, all blacks and reds. An actual stage stood against the back wall, lights and speakers cold and lifeless.

At least it had a full length, not-fuck-around bar. The rest of the room was just a big empty space.

Except for her.

A woman leaned against the bar like she owned it, a bottle of something amber in front of her like it was waiting for her to sin again.

She sat in a small pool of light, the dim room around her like a lake of gloom. One side of her head was undercut, long black hair cascading on the other. Black lipstick. Natural looks, not a hint of a clinic about her. She glanced at Mason as he stepped inside, then away as if everything about him was *boring*. "We're closed."

Mason smiled. "Bars never close."

"This one does. Fuck off." She took a pull from the bottle, swallowing big.

Mason shut the door, walking toward her. He nodded at the bottle. "May I?"

Her eyes moved to him again, giving him a proper once-over before looking back to the mirror behind the bar. "Sure."

He reached over the bar and snagged a glass, splashing liquor into it. He took a sip, coughing. "Fresh, isn't it?"

A small smile tugged at her mouth. She was pretty, if you wanted to dial up the grunge. Natural from the boots up. "That's one word for it. House specialty."

"I'd hate to taste what they do bad." Mason pulled out a pack of Treasurers, offering her one. She looked at the pack for a second, then took one with elegant fingers, painted black nails a contrast to the cigarette's silver filters.

He glimpsed calluses. Guitarist's hands, unless he missed his guess. The silver of the cigarette glinted next to her black lipstick as she leaned toward the offered light.

She gave a small sound of pleasure. "That's a good cigarette."

Mason lit one for himself. "Yeah." He breathed the smoke in, then sent the exhale cresting toward the ceiling. "What do you play?" Mason watched the smoke walk on lazy legs upward. "You look like a guitarist."

"Nothing you'd like." She watched him with more interest now. "Nothing straight and even."

"I don't think life's supposed to be straight and even," said Mason. "I think it's supposed to be crumpled."

"Sure," she said, but something had relaxed in her shoulders.

Still, tough crowd. "How about them Seahawks, yeah?"

She snorted. "Don't waste your time." She held the cigarette out from her, the glowing tip pointed up. "Are these ... *silver?* Did you just light me up a silver filter?"

Mason took another drag, the ember tip of the Treasurer flaring. "What do you mean, don't waste my time?"

She thought for a few moments, masking it with a pull from her cigarette. "Well, it's one of two things."

Mason nodded. "Sure. What two things?"

"More like one thing, with a bonus round."

He smiled despite himself. "Bonus round?"

"Sure. You came here, looking for someone."

Mason nodded. "That's a fair guess. It's four-thirty in the morning. Although I might have come in just to get out of the rain."

"I heard you drive up." She tapped ash directly onto the bar. "So you came to see someone."

"Okay." Mason sipped his drink. "I came to see someone. I figure you're here so you *won't* see someone."

"Very perceptive," she said. "And yet, here you are."

He smiled again. "But I'm not the person you don't want to see."

"It's not an exclusive club," she said. "I could not want to see you *and* someone else." But she smiled too.

"Sounds like you've got a list."

"I've got a list," she agreed. "Anyway. He's not here."

"The guy you don't want to see?"

"No. The guy *you* want to see." She frowned. "This is more confusing after a few drinks than I thought it'd be."

"How do you know it's not you?" Mason watched her.

She glanced at him again, then turned to the mirror. "It's not me. I'm the bonus round. And you're so not my type."

"I should be offended." Mason tapped his own Treasurer against the bar. "But I'm not. Name's Mason."

Those eyes watched him, the black lipstick pulling into an answering grin. "Good to meet you, Mason. He's not here."

"You said that before. Who's not here?"

"Bernie."

"Ah." Mason refilled his glass, then offered her the bottle.

She nodded, snagging it with her free hand, taking another long pull. "'Ah,' for sure."

"How do you know I'm here for Bernie?"

"Because he's an asshole."

"Fair enough." Mason thought that one through. "You work for him though, right?"

"Everyone's boss is an asshole."

"Mine's not."

"Yeah he is." She glanced at him. "Or you're the luckiest man in the world."

"Mason." Carter sounded bored. "She's an illegal, Mason."

"You're the world's giant cock-blocking overlord, aren't you?" Mason kept his comments to the link, nothing showing in the real.

"Just thought you should know. I get three heat signatures in the building, and only two of you are linked. She's not the other one."

"Why don't you take the rest of the night off?" Mason swirled the liquor in his glass before speaking in the real. "Jesus."

"What?" She looked at him, licking liquor from black lipstick. "You don't look the religious type."

"It's ... never mind." Mason stood. "Hey. You didn't tell me your—"

A door at the back of the room banged open, a man striding in. He was tall and thin, black hair streaming behind him. He stopped dead when he saw Mason. Mason's optics adjusted for the gloom, picking out the widening of the man's eyes. *Surprised, are you?*

"Who the hell are you?" The man started forward again, his long legs taking him to the bar. "We're closed, asshole."

Mason put his hand out. "Mason Floyd." He tried on a smile to match it. "I'm an acquisitions specialist."

The man ignored Mason's hand. "You can acquire yourself a way out of here. I said we're closed."

Mason's HUD was already working through a biometrics match, but neither of these two came up on the search. Neither of them was Bernie Eckers either. He put his hand back at his side. "Sure. Say, have you seen—"

"We haven't seen anyone. Fuck off, company man. Your kind aren't welcome around here." The newcomer grabbed the woman's arm. "Come on, babe. Let's go."

She looked at the hand on her arm, then at her cigarette, before looking at Mason. "It was good to meet you, Mason."

"Yeah." He nodded at her. "I didn't catch your name."

"No. You didn't." She grinned over her shoulder as the other man led her toward the back door.

"Hey." Mason wanted to follow her. "How do I get a hold of you? About your boss. If I need to talk to you again. You got a number?"

The man at her side threw Mason a look, all savage edges, but she smiled at him. "I've got a number."

"What is it?"

"If you can guess it, it's meant to be. I hope I see you around." And with a flick of hair she slipped through the door at the back.

That kind of hope goes both ways. "Well, Carter. He's not home."

"I could have told you that."

"You lack a sense of adventure. That's your problem."

"It might be. Your problem is going to be severe hallucinations in a few hours. Why don't you come in for another round in the chair?"

Mason's teeth glinted in the gloom. "You're such a romantic, Carter. I'll be in soon." He thought about the man who'd pulled the woman away. "I need a shower."

"You need more than a shower. She's not for you."

Mason ignored her. "And then I'll come back. Mr. Eckers and I need to have a conversation."

"Mr. Eckers. Hmm. I wonder." But Carter fell quiet.

Mason walked toward the street doors. "Carter?" The rain still fell in unabated judgment on the world outside.

"Yes, Mason."

"I need a meeting."

"Oh, Christ. *No.*"

"Really, Carter." Mason swung a leg over the bike, the HUD sparkling into life. A soft whine escaped from under the seat. "I think I need to talk to Metatech and Reed."

"You want to get your ass kicked again?"

Mason's helmet lapped into place around his face. "I was outnumbered. I did *not* get my ass kicked."

"You got beaten worse than a red-headed stepchild." Carter laughed. "No, it's fine. I'll set it up. I can never get enough of a good ass-kicking."

"Thanks," said Mason. He smiled inside his helmet. "I might bring a bigger gun this time."

"Bring whatever you like. But I'd call Harry if I were you."

"Harry?" Mason frowned, his foot knocking the kickstand back. He gave the throttle a twist, the fusion drive purring and growling under him. "That's a bit much for a *meeting*, don't you think?"

"It's your life, Mason. I'm just making suggestions."

"Well, suggest a meeting. Metatech. Reed. Somewhere neutral."

"Of course. I'll prep Sasha."

"Thanks, Carter." Mason was still thinking about black lipstick as the big Suzuki roared off down the street, front wheel skipping up to reach for the sky.

CHAPTER TEN_

Zacharies sat close to Laia, sharing his body heat. She was small, thin, the desert cold nipping at her. He looked at the Master, sitting warm by the fire that Laia had coaxed into life. She'd been exhausted afterward.

The Master hadn't shared his fire or his food. The night was hungry and cold. The desert waited in the darkness, patient. Zacharies sat with Laia at the edge of the depression in the ground. Zacharies held a piece of melted glass, the edges sharp and bright. He glanced at their master, then back to the glass.

"It'll never work," said Laia.

"What? Hush now. Sleep." Zacharies smoothed her hair, his sister's head against his shoulder.

"We both need sleep," she said. "You carried more than I did today."

He reached up to scratch under his collar. The metal left a rash, chafing his skin. He was almost used to the mark of being a slave. *Almost.* "I carried trash today."

She started up, looking into his face. "Not so loud! He'll hear you."

"So?"

Her finger pressed against his lips. "You know as well as I."

Zacharies tensed, then slumped. "I know. I wish—"

"I wish it too." Laia leaned back against him. She was shaking. They both wanted freedom. Or the Master dead. Both were the same thing. "It's so cold."

He hugged her closer. "The angel will come."

"I don't believe in angels." Laia turned toward the Master. "Not anymore."

"You must believe." Zacharies rubbed her shoulders for meager additional heat. "It's—"

"It's all we have." She'd been finishing his sentences for as long as he'd been finishing hers. "It's not enough."

"For what?"

"To dream of hope."

"It's not a dream." Zacharies held up the melted glass. "Where do angels come from?"

Laia pointed toward the stars, impassive and mighty above them. "From Heaven. From our dreams. It's the same." Zacharies nodded, resting his chin against her head. "Our dreams are worthless." There was something sick and tired in her voice. "They are the dreams of the lost. The fallen."

"Oh, sister," said Zacharies. "We aren't fallen. See, look here." He held the glass out to her.

She took it. "What am I looking at?"

"See the ground?"

"I see it." Her voice was quiet, small.

"See the stars?"

Her head tipped up. "I see them."

Zacharies fell silent for a moment. "Remember two cycles past when a rock fell from the sky?"

"Yes," she said. Another shiver ran through her. "When it fell, it burned the earth."

"That's right," said Zacharies. "It came from the stars. But it wasn't a person."

"What do you mean?" She turned the glass shard over in her hands.

"An angel wouldn't *fall*," said Zacharies. "An angel would land. An angel would bring the weight of the heavens—"

"—And step against the ground," Laia leaned away to look at him. "You think an angel landed here?"

"Yes, sister," said Zacharies. He glanced at their master again, and his voice turned mocking. "I think the angel has come. Like the rock, he is mighty, and the heat of his anger burned the sand to glass."

Laia ignored the sting of his tone and listened to his words. She leaned against him again. "I hope so, brother."

He stroked her hair again, saying nothing at all. But his eyes burned, watching their master next to his fire, as they shivered in the cold of the desert night.

CHAPTER ELEVEN

Mason pushed through the crowd. He felt like a salmon, forging upstream. He'd left his bike behind, too many people on the streets to ride. It had retracted the cowl, sinking into park mode, leaving him on foot.

He was used to crowds like this. Dense. Dirty. Hungry.

Neon signs flashed everywhere he looked. Mason felt surrounded by their stained color. The *hanzi* may as well have been in Sanskrit for all he could make out. Steam rose from manhole covers in the street. He passed a man with a trolley piled high with electronics, a faded Walmart logo in chipped plastic on the front.

A woman gyrated her hips, plastic raincoat open at the front. She was naked underneath. "*Nǐ hěn yīngjùn.* You want good time?"

Mason didn't look twice, walking into the anonymity of the crowd. There were always a lot of people out in Chinatown, but since the rain most people stayed inside. Plastic sheeting stretched across the sidewalk above him, a low-tech solve for weather that killed the poor. It was already mottled and rotting, the downpour beating against it. *This place always reminds me of Hong Kong.*

Sooner or later, someone would have to do something about the rain for good. *Not my problem.*

A man grabbed his arm. Mason ignored it, catching another man's hand reaching for his wallet. Mason gave a twist of the man's wrist, pulling out the Tenko-Senshin with his free hand. The muzzle pressed against the thief's head, the weapon keening. "If your buddy touches his pistol, you're a dead man."

The pedestrian traffic flowed around the three of them, willfully oblivious to what might be. Sometimes you got shot in Chinatown. Sometimes you bought chicken feet.

The man behind Mason spoke. "Let him go. Or I'll—"

Mason spun, the lattice twisting inside him, pulling the thief around as a shield. The man hissed with pain as Mason's grip tightened on his wrist. He could see the other man clearly now, acne spotting a face too young to carry anything more than a light fuzz. He wore a jacket patched and marked, chains lacing it, all under a head topped with *Harajuku* punk hair. "Or you'll what?" The Tenko-Senshin's whine was high-pitched, a red light flickering on the barrel.

The man Mason held groaned. The kid with the acne watched the barrel's light before looking down. "We don't want any trouble." He raised his hands. It was what Mason was waiting for. The lattice yanked, and he wrenched the man's wrist he was holding, pushing him into the kid with acne. The barrel of the Tenko-Senshin swung back out to the street, the whine getting louder.

A man who'd been crossing the street with murderous purpose stopped, looking at the barrel of the weapon. Mason's optics scanned him. *Same jacket. Same marks.* The goatee on this one's face was grown in. *Not a kid.*

Mason showed teeth. It wasn't a grin. "Back off."

"Hey, I was just—"

"You can do it from over there." The Tenko-Senshin vibrated, the whine above audible now, the lattice chattering along his arms as he held the weapon. "I got no issue peeling the skin from your face with this."

"Sure, sure." The eyes above the goatee flicked to the other two. "We were going anyway." He gestured at the other two. "Come."

The acne spotted kid looked at Mason, lips pulled into a sneer. "You're a dead man!" He slapped one of the marks on his jacket, chains jingling. "We're the South Sun Tigers, and no one—"

"If you're going to say no one kills one of the South Sun Tigers, friend, well. That's just the kind of thing that cries out for a demonstration, isn't it?" The crowd continued to flow around them. Despite his words, Mason spun the Tenko-Senshin back into his holster.

The kid cradling his wrist nudged the other one. They both looked at the man on the street. "Come on."

"Yeah." Acne Kid swallowed, his eyes bright. *Goddamn stims, makes people feel invincible.* "We'll be back, company man."

"If you think it'll help." Mason shrugged, turning back to the crowd. "I'm running late now, aren't I?"

"I told you to bring Harry." Carter sounded bored.

"What, so he could fire a plasma cannon into the crowd, or immolate some street punks with rockets?"

"You wouldn't be running late if you'd brought Harry," Carter said. "You'll come around in the end." Mason muttered under his breath as he pushed through the throng. "What was that?"

"Nothing." Mason looked around. "Where the hell is it?"

"Over there. See the yellow and red neon sign?"

"It's in *hanzi*, Carter."

"Yeah. So, that's the place."

"You sure?"

"I read Chinese," she said. "Clear as day. Says it's the *Golden Palace Restaurant*."

"Of course you do," said Mason. "You read Chinese, but you can't dance."

She sighed. "I didn't say I couldn't dance."

"Whatever." Mason pushed through the greasy plastic strip door at the base of the stairs, heading up. The carpet was old, stained, worn thin in places. It might have been red once. The inlay might have been gold. It was just brown now.

Something stuck to the bottom of his foot. Best not to ask what. Mason paused. "You sure this is the place?"

"I'm sure. You said neutral."

"I didn't say I wanted to get salmonella."

"You can't *get* salmonella," said Carter. "Besides, this place gets great reviews. Don't forget. You're running late."

Mason kept moving up the stairs. At the top was a long corridor running the length of the building. He walked down the dim hall, optics adjusting for the low light. A wooden door with a golden handle was waiting at the end. He listened, a hand on the knob. The noise of the street sank to a murmur. The door was clean, no hint of grime like the floor. He pushed it open.

The room was carpeted with a rich red pile, gold threads running through it. A large tiger's head in gold bared fangs from the floor just inside the door. He walked over it, looking at the partitions made of slatted wood, or something wood-like, that separated booths from each other. Wide tables set out with white china and black chopsticks. White double doors with round glass windows set at eye height led to a kitchen, which was at the back near where he'd entered.

Mason let his optics worry out the details, mapping the room, noting the blemishes. Around the walls weapons hung in racks, his HUD spitting up names and dropping their locations into the map it was building.

The restaurant was empty except for a table near the middle. Two men sat at the table. The HUD marked them, uplink IDs showing on the map in the corner of his vision. City records were downloaded, the floor plan in the archives overlaid against Mason's generated map.

Matched pretty close, give or take. As an afterthought, the HUD dropped uplink IDs from the kitchen area out the back, migrant workers doing whatever people did in kitchens. It's not something Mason cared enough about to find out.

"Eighteen Arms." Mason kept his comments to the link.

"What?" said Carter.

"All these swords. It's the Eighteen Arms of Wushu." He gave an over loud cough, so the two men would know he was there. *As if they didn't already.* "It's quite different on the inside. They've got some kind of medieval theme here."

"You don't say," said Carter. "That's not mentioned in the reviews."

"Let's do this." Mason walked toward the two men. One of them he knew. Even if he'd forgotten the face he'd remember the immaculate white cuffs. The cufflinks were made to look like small gears. He smiled, surprised to feel it genuine. "Hey. Metatech, right?"

The Metatech man stood, returning the smile and offering a hand. "That's right, Apsel. No hard feelings?"

Mason shook Metatech's hand, then turned to the other man. He noted sunglasses over an expensive suit. "Reed?"

"Right in one." They shook, then all three sat down. Mason couldn't help but notice that his back was to the door, Metatech and Reed with their backs to the window and the street outside.

Reed leaned forward. "What's this about?"

Mason held up a hand. "Can I ask a question first?"

The Reed man sat back, spreading his hands. "It's your dime."

"Sunglasses? Inside?"

Reed's face quirked, almost a smile. "It's a thing I'm testing. For the company."

Mason nodded. "Sure. Look, is there a waiter here? I want a drink."

On cue, a slim Asian man in white entered from the kitchen doors. Mason caught a smattering of *hanzi* in softly glowing green under the cuff of his white jacket. His optics marked the empty earring holes, like the restaurant didn't want their staff to show metal to the customers. The man's accent was thick. "Food? Drink?"

Metatech waved a hand. "Sure. *Píjiǔ?*"

The waiter looked at him. Reed snorted. "It's just *pí.*"

"You shouldn't rely on the link for easy translation, especially if you're using the wrong language," said Mason. "*Bīru o onegai shi.* Asahi, if you've got it."

"*Tsingtao?*" said the waiter. At Mason's nod he turned to the other two. "Anything else?"

"Whatever he's having," said Metatech. Reed nodded. After the waiter walked away, Metatech turned back to Mason. "*Bīru?*"

"He's Japanese. Not Chinese." Mason drummed his fingers on the table, then said, "Look, this meeting—"

"We're just having a couple beers," said Metatech. "It's not a meeting. There's no way the syndicates would sanction a *meeting*."

Reed leaned forward. "Just a couple of beers. On our own initiative."

The waiter came back with a tray, three green bottles frosty in Chinatown's mugginess. Glasses clinked against them. He started to put the beers in front of them. Mason waved the glass away, taking a pull right from the bottle. "*Garasu de kuru.*" *Comes in a glass.*

"You speak Japanese?" said Carter. "What the hell use is that around here?"

"*Watashi wa nihongo wo sukoshi dake hanashimasu,*" said Mason. "Look, I need to focus here." But the link was already gone.

"Problem, friend?" said Reed. He poured his beer into his glass.

"No, no problem," said Mason. "Just my handler checking in."

"I hear that," said Metatech. He and Mason clinked bottles.

"You guys know each other?" said Reed.

"Sort of," said Mason. "Professionally."

"Misunderstanding," said Metatech.

"A misunderstanding." Mason nodded. "Metatech here was trying to sell Apsel tech. Or buy it, I haven't worked it out yet."

"Buy it," said Metatech. "Didn't know it was Apsel." The other man frowned, straightening his cuffs. "Probably wouldn't have changed our course much if we had known, though. We might have brought a few more operatives." He smiled at Mason over his beer.

Reed nodded. "Misunderstandings. Wrong board memo at the wrong time, and we cop the shit, right? Happens all the time." It was hard to read his face behind those glasses. Mason liked to see a man's eyes when he was brokering a deal. "I had two of those last week."

"Ah," said Mason, taking another pull from his beer. "So, here's the problem."

"Problem?" said Metatech. "Something the Federate needs our help with?"

"Not really," said Mason. He put his beer down, turning the bottle so the label faced him. He started scratching it off with a fingernail. "More a ... friendly piece of advice."

Reed laughed. "You're trying to stop a sale."

Metatech started to laugh too but stopped when he saw the look on Mason's face. "Holy shit. It's something big."

A piece of the *Tsingtao* label came off, a bright red letter on a white background. Mason looked at it for a moment. "I had a meeting with the boss this morning."

"Right," said Reed. "So what?"

Metatech sat quietly for a moment. "*The* boss?"

"Yeah," said Mason. "Gairovald."

Reed spat out the swallow of beer he'd been taking, dabbing at his chin with a napkin. "I didn't even know he was in the country."

"He's not. Officially, I mean." Mason shrugged. "Just passing through."

"And he met with you?" Reed took another swig from his glass. "What division you work in?"

"Specialist Services," said Mason. "Acquisitions. Mostly."

"You really must be good enough to not need backup," said Metatech. "What's he like?"

"He's the boss." Mason considered the question. "Knows what he wants."

Metatech nodded like he knew. *Maybe he does — could play golf with the head of Metatech on a Sunday. No way to know.* "What did you lose?"

"No clue," said Mason. "We tracked the deal online, same as

you. Unspecified syndicate tech. We've worked out it's ours. Comes in a box about this high." He held a hand up to the height of their table.

Metatech leaned forward, his beer forgotten. "Recovery?"

"No," said Mason. "Remove and erase."

"Christ," said Reed.

"Why are you telling us?" said Metatech. "I mean, it's got to be golden. We'll all want a piece."

Mason nodded again. Another piece of the Tsingtao label peeled off. "It's a fair warning. If you want in, you have to go all in."

"All in?" Reed looked at him over his glasses, Mason getting a view of his eyes for the first time. *Worried.* "What do you mean?"

"Stock price might go up. Might go down too." Mason turned the bottle in his hands. "Or war. We won't stop until we ... resolve the loss."

Metatech snorted. "There hasn't been a war between the syndicates in—"

"What do you want out of this?" Reed topped up his glass from the bottle. "And why us?"

"Easy," said Mason. "I'm actually hoping you'll be smart enough to stay out of the way. Someone's trying to sell our shit, and they'll be trying to sell it to one of you."

"But why *us*?" Reed said. "Reed Interactive. Metatech. Apsel. What's the link?"

"Money, mostly." Mason looked at the Reed man, then turned the beer bottle against the table, the knurls on the bottom making a harsh sound. "They'll need a syndicate with the cash to pay for it. Look, we're the same guy, just different places. We all got our reasons for working where we do."

"Right," said Reed. Metatech nodded.

"And I know that when the rain came—"

"You think the secret to the rain is in this tech?" said Metatech.

Mason nodded at Reed. "Hallucinogenic effects released in the atmosphere? Only one syndicate specializes in synthesizing entertainment right into your brain. It's why I thought you might have been Reed, back at the bar."

"Figures," said Metatech. "I was after Reed as well."

"You assholes," said Reed. "It wasn't us."

"No, no," said Mason. "I'm pretty sure it was us now. Not our specialty, but it looks like it's our tech."

"How do you know?" asked Reed.

Mason remembered a broken building, shattered stone, and a blackened piece of metal with the Apsel logo alongside *ATOMIC ENERGY DIVISION*. The hallucinations were stronger there, somehow. He tapped a fingernail against the bottle. "Can't say. You know how it is."

Reed shrugged. "You don't want to sell it? This could be easy all around. Why try in markets that aren't your core business?"

"That's above my pay grade," said Mason. He grinned. "You can keep trying the other way, though." Reed's hand tapped the table. Mason nodded at him. "Something to say?"

"We tried to buy the rain."

"You what?"

"Wasn't on my watch. Didn't know it was the rain. While you two were getting acquainted, we'd already tried to get a demo of the tech. Someone wanted to set up a deal. Said they had something that would blow our mind. We sent a team to ... collect. Old building, outside of town."

Mason leaned back. "Building's not there anymore."

Reed nodded. "I figured. The deal was sour."

"It wasn't sour. Someone just didn't use the right protection." Mason took a last swig from the bottle. "You know who tried to sell it to you?"

The other man shook his head. "Sorry, Apsel. And you know—"

"You wouldn't tell me even if you did."

"That's it. You know how it is."

"So," said Metatech. He splayed his hands in front of him, looking at his nails. "What's the play?"

"No play," said Mason. "Nothing up my sleeve. I just want you to know. If someone tries to sell you a metal box with an Apsel logo on it? We're coming after that box."

"Fair enough," said Metatech. "What about—"

The door at the back of the restaurant banged open, street thugs spilling in like angry garbage. The lattice spun Mason around in his chair, optics doing a quick zoom. He picked out patches, chains, the *Harajuku* style overdone. He caught a familiar face covered with acne. His HUD already mapped out the five punks. Mason looked at where they were standing, noting the tiger on the floor.

"Ah, hell." His shoulders slumped. *These little cocksuckers are going to screw this negotiation up.* "South Sun Tigers. No shit."

"Mason," said Carter. "There's an enforcer class hybrid approaching."

The whine of servos accompanied the enforcer as it crouched low to shoulder through the entrance. Big metal hands pulled on the door frame as it shuffled into the room, marking and crushing the wood where they gripped. It stood up, looming an easy meter above the tallest of the South Sun Tigers. The metal and ceramic of its armor glinted in red. Chains had been welded to the armor in places, giving an approximation of the South Sun Tigers patch pattern. It flexed its shoulders, then slammed one metal hand into the palm of the other. A step took it forward, a hiss of hydraulics escaping as it locked into a fighter's crouch.

Metatech looked at Mason. "Friends of yours?"

Reed already had a gun drawn, an energy weapon pulled out from under his jacket. It was black and ugly, a short-nosed thing. "Christ, Apsel. We came in *good faith*." The energy weapon swung to Mason, then to the South Sun Tigers. Then back to Mason.

Mason's hands were up. "These guys aren't—"

"Hey, asshole." It was the kid with the acne, walking tall with a bunch of punks at his back. "I told you, *company man*, no one messes with the South Sun Tigers."

"That's not what you said," said Mason. The Reed man swung the weapon back toward the South Sun Tigers.

"What?" said the kid.

"That's not what you ... you know what, *fuck* this." The Tenko-Senshin was in his hand as if by magic. Mason didn't remember pulling it out. The lattice might have helped. He caught movement out of the corner of his eye as the Metatech man reached under his jacket, pulling out a weapon looking like a big staple gun.

"Going hot," said Carter. Her voice was flat. She'd put a box around one of the South Suns at the back, a thin man with a data jack in the side of his head. A cable, knotted and twisted, dropped down from the jack to a small portable rig. The man tapped furiously on the keyboard. "Prepare for interference."

Mason nodded. *It's time to dance.* He kicked off a targeting solution, the helmet lapping out of his jacket and around his head. His overlay marked the Tigers.

As an afterthought, he excluded the one with the rig, the overlay's box around the man flashing and dying out. Carter would be *pissed* if he stole her kill.

The Metatech man gave the staple gun a jerk, and the bulk of it fell into sections, linking together into a barrel. His other hand came out of his jacket, slapping a rectangle underneath.

"Link up. Kick into overtime," said Mason. The other two men nodded, their link requests already coming in. Their icons blinked on his overlay, then stabilized. Mason felt the familiar feeling of his lattice, warm under his skin. It felt like his heart slowed in his chest as his augments speed up his nervous system. The light in the room changed as his perception upshifted, the colors washing out. The South Sun Tigers seemed to pause, the one on the rig typing in slow motion.

"This isn't your play?" said Reed, his voice sounding stretched over the link.

"It's not his play," said Metatech, a flash of neural static following the words. "I've got the big one."

Reed clicked an affirmative. "I hope that cannon of yours can do the job."

Metatech's smiley came across the link, outlined in red. "It's something a bit special. From the boys in the lab."

"This is what I've got," said Mason, sharing his overlay with the other two. "Six targets. One of them's an enforcer class hybrid — all yours, Metatech. My handler's on the decker."

Reed marked the kid with the acne. "You look personally involved. I'll take him."

"Solid copy," said Mason. "Wait. You're leaving me with three?"

"Reed Interactive's into entertainment. We're not a bunch of ninjas."

"It's ninja," said Mason.

"What?"

"It's just ninja. The plural. There's no 's' at the end."

There was a burst of static from Reed's end. Then, "Ready?"

"Ready," said Metatech.

"Ready," said Mason. He felt the lattice reaching down through his arms, and he pulled the trigger on the Tenko-Senshin. The overtime played down his spine, and he thought he could almost see the individual flechettes leaving the weapon, silver flashes quickly surrounded by flames as they superheated the air, fire following them to their targets.

His optics cut out, the world going dark. The lattice coughed out of overtime with a jerk, his heart thudding and kicking back in his chest. He almost tripped, the wrench back to the real making him stumble. "Carter?"

Mason heard something thump *hard* to his left, feeling heat as the Metatech weapon fired. There were three snaps from his right as Reed's weapon joined in. He could hear their movements, quicker than thought.

"Carter!" Mason swung the Tenko-Senshin in front of him. "Carter, I'm blind." *The decker. Faster than Carter? Might just be a head start.*

Snow flicked across his vision, then cut back to black. *Think, Mason.* He was pretty sure there was a table behind him. He dropped to a crouch, duck-walking backward until his heel hit. He knocked his helmet against the table, then scrabbled for the edge and pulled it down, the clatter of plates and chopsticks almost lost in the noise of weapons fire. Mason hauled himself around the table. Flimsy, it would serve as visual cover only, but it was better than nothing. He felt the little Tenko-Senshin vibrating in his hand. After a moment, he clicked it off and put it back inside his jacket. His hands searched the floor, fingers feeling the hilts of weapons. He picked them up, feeling their weight.

A dollar says you've picked up swords, Mason.

His overlay kicked back in, tracing the room's outlines over blackness. A burst of snow rained, the overlay dropping off, before flaring back on.

"—On, but ... Understand?" said Carter.

"No, I do not fucking understand." Mason felt the table kick his back as small arms fire hammered it. Metal, sharp and hard, plinked off his helmet. "What the hell is going on?"

A scream cut across the room. Something arced and crackled on the far side of the room, and Mason's vision cleared. The overlay cut out, replaced by text scrolling up from the bottom right. He caught the words *system BIOS* and *reloading* as the text raced.

"You back with me?" said Carter.

"Yeah," said Mason. "Lattice is down. Overtime's not working."

"Their hacker was pretty good." Carter's voice carried something else. Maybe respect. "Not quite good enough. Your augments are rebooting. Give it time."

"I don't have time." Mason risked a look over the table. The thin man with the portable deck was on the ground, smoke wisping out of the side of his head, the hole where the jack was charred black. The remains of the cable to his rig had burned away.

Mason saw the Reed man was down, splayed back on the floor. Metatech wasn't anywhere to be seen, but neither was the enforcer.

The three Tigers he'd originally marked on his HUD were still standing. One had a red tattoo across her face. Another was a huge man, a set of chains passing through the skin of his face. The third was a man with a mohawk and the moves of a dancer.

"I see you've left me three." He considered the weapons he'd picked up. A pair of butterfly swords. *Right first time.* "I'm not sure, strictly speaking, that these are part of the Eighteen Arms of Wushu."

"They're not replicas. Stop whining," said Carter. "Just go cut a bitch, okay?"

Mason stood from behind the table. The three gang members paused, then the woman with the red tattoo smiled.

"There's still one left," said the woman with the red tattoo. "He's mine."

The huge man put a hand on her shoulder. "No. I want this one."

"We take him together." She shrugged his hand off, reaching under her jacket and pulling out a pair of submachine guns. "What's it going to be, company man?"

Mason looked at the guns, then into her eyes. "I think it's going to be like this. You're going to shoot your friend in the balls. Then I'm going to throw you out the window behind me." He moved from behind the table, his left foot sweeping out to clear debris. The lattice tugged at his calf, and his overlay flickered off for a second. Mason ignored it, breathing slow and even.

The man with the mohawk narrowed his eyes, looking at Mason's foot, but didn't say anything. He held back, fingers twitching at his side.

The woman laughed. It sounded genuine. "I'm sorry, but no."

Mason tucked the swords by his side, throwing himself into a tumble toward the big man. The woman's submachine guns chattered after him, tearing chunks from the floor. Mason's roll took him behind the big man, the woman still firing. A look of horror passed over her face as the big man stumbled, blood spraying from the bullet holes. *Nasty — explosive rounds.* Mason readied the swords, stepping over the big man's corpse. He swung twice, then stepped back.

Red Tattoo looked at the stumps where her hands had been. The submachine guns fell to the ground, hands still holding the grips. She backed away, leaving a trail of dark red on the ground, spatters raining from her wrists. Red Tattoo stumbled as her foot hit the table Mason had crouched behind.

Mason stepped forward, planting his foot into her stomach and pushing. She sprawled back, hitting the window, the glass cracking. Mason frowned, then did a spinning kick. He hit her high in the chest. The woman's body smashed through the window. A half a second later a thump came from the street below.

He turned back and looked at the big man's body. There were bullet holes up his leg and into his chest. *No groin shot.* "Close enough." Mason held the swords loose by his side, small drops of red falling from the blades.

A slow clapping sound made him turn. Mohawk had his hands held in front of him, fingerless gloves muffling and shaping the sound at the same time. The last Tiger said, "Impressive, company man."

"I wish you wouldn't call us that."

"It's what you are."

Mason shrugged. "It's no crime to have a job."

A feral smile lit Mohawk's face. "Come now. You take it a bit further than just a job."

"Maybe." Mason flicked blood off one of the swords, the drops spattering against the floor. "Still no crime. Now take you guys. Coming in here. Busting up the place—"

"We own the place."

"And attacking me and my associates. That sounds like a crime."

Mohawk put a little pout into his voice. "Aww. Did we hurt your delicate corporate negotiations?"

It was Mason's turn to smile. There wasn't anything happy about it. "You have no idea. Tell me, what's your malfunction?"

"My malfunction?"

"Yeah. You come in here, a bunch of big swinging dicks. Aside from," Mason tipped his head at the broken window, "your token female."

"She wasn't a token. She was my girlfriend."

"Unlucky," said Mason. "So you come in here, wanting to pick a fight with 'company men.' You can't win that fight."

"I don't know. It almost worked."

"Didn't even come close," said Mason. "Now it's just you and me."

"Sam is still out there."

"Sam?"

"The big guy."

"Ah," said Mason. "The enforcer."

"Yeah," said Mohawk. "I guess you'd call him that."

Mason took a step forward. Mohawk stepped back. Mason said, "Sam's a smoking ruin right now."

"He's a total conversion. Against a norm? Please."

Mason laughed, a little mirth in it this time. "That guy wasn't a norm. He was Metatech."

"Meta... Shit." Mohawk shrugged. "Okay, so Sam's probably dead. But we got one of yours." The man pointed toward the Reed man, lying still on the ground.

"He's not one of mine," said Mason. "We going to do this, or what?"

"Do what, company man?" But Mohawk moved, Mason following. The two men circled each other. Mohawk reached into his jacket, his hand coming out with what looked like the grip of a sword. There was no blade.

Mason looked down at the butterfly swords he held. "Don't you think that's a little unfair?"

Mohawk's lips were thin and nasty. "Sometimes it's got to be like that."

Mason's overlay fuzzed with static, then cleared. A blinking cursor on the bottom right spat out some text. The text said *ALL*

SYSTEMS ONLINE. Mason smiled. "Yeah. Sometimes it's got to be like that."

He tapped the lattice, overtime rising like a tide. The color washed from the light. Mason's tongue felt too slow and thick to speak. His optics marked the sword grip the other man held, highlighting the nano filament blade of the weapon as it slid out.

They ran at each other. Mohawk held his sword over his head, a classic *kendo* strike. Mason slipped to the side, the lattice gritty and unsynchronized as he stepped close. He struck, both blades entering Mohawk's back. Mason felt the other man shudder through the hilts of his swords.

The nano filament sword fell from his hands with a clatter.

Mason smoothed the lattice off, overtime dropping like a shroud. He tasted cinnamon and spat on the floor. He checked the other man. Dead, heart and spine severed.

Mason went to look at Mohawk's fallen sword. The handle stood from the floor, the blade fallen right through. He could hear a soft hum from the weapon. *Vibroblade, maybe.* He didn't touch it, thinking of the Tenko-Senshin in his holster. "Carter."

"Yes?"

"We're going to need a cleanup crew down here."

"They're already on their way."

"Cops?"

"Of course."

"Can you—"

"You talk to the cops," she said. "I'll talk to the chief of police."

"Thanks, Carter." Mason walked to the window, looking out. The steady stream of people on the sidewalk continued past and over the woman's body below. "I hate Chinatown."

The cop was a short fat man who smelled of bad coffee and too much work. His body armor didn't quite cover him, stomach pushing through between the chest and leg plates.

"So, *citizen*," said the cop. "You were just minding your own business."

"That's not what I said," said Mason. "I was trying to have a business meeting."

"Right. Minding your own business, like I said."

Mason looked down at the man. "You make it sound like it's ... what's that thing you guys do? That's it," he snapped his fingers, "like it's a crime. You do crime, don't you? Fight it, I mean."

"Look, pal—"

Mason held up a hand, stepping back from the smell that wafted from the cop. He watched the police drone as it hovered, taking evidence photos. Red and blue lights licked over the walls as it scanned, light lasing out in flashes of green to mark out things the tiny AI considered evidence. It stopped over the sword grip sticking from the floor.

The cop looked over his shoulder at the drone. "Got something to add to your statement? Maybe want to tell me about the sword?"

"No." Mason sighed. "It doesn't have to be this way."

"What?" The cop stepped forward, looking into Mason's face. Mason tried not to breathe. "What doesn't have to be this way?"

"Am I free to go?"

"Are you...? No, you're not free to go." The cop took a step back. "What's your rush?"

"Am I under arrest?"

"No."

"Then I'm free to go." Mason nodded to the man, starting toward the door. He stepped over the bodies on the floor. He paused by the Reed man.

The cop was a half-step behind. "Hey, buddy." He put a hand on Mason's arm.

Mason looked down at the hand. The cop followed his gaze, then pulled his hand back like he'd been stung. "Are you putting me under arrest?"

"I've still got questions. Wait a second."

"What is it?"

"I got a call coming in."

Mason nodded. "You'd best take that. It's your boss."

"My ... what?"

"Your boss." Mason shrugged. "I don't know about you, but I usually answer when the boss calls."

"Look, just... *Shit.*" The shorter man pointed at Mason. Mason's optics noted the armor of the cop's gloves were worn. *Police budgets don't stretch quite far enough, do they?* "Don't go anywhere." The cop got a distant look as he took the call. Cheap link, probably. No multitasking upgrade.

No overtime.

Mason crouched by Reed's body. "Carter?"

"Yes, Mason."

"I take it that the chief of police is calling?" He reached for the dead man's sunglasses.

"I hope so. I woke him up."

"How'd he take it?" The sunglasses came free. Mason looked them over. A nice pair, but nothing special. Nothing you'd be testing out for the company.

"Not well."

"Do I have anything to worry about?"

Carter barked a laugh. "You? You've got lots to worry about. There's a couple rival syndicates caught up in this now. One of them's got a dead agent. And you've managed to piss off a local gang."

"I meant, from the cops."

"Oh," said Carter. "Them. No."

"No?"

"No. The South Sun Tigers, though. Those guys..."

"I understand." Mason sighed. "Look, what do you think of this?"

He held the sunglasses in front of his optics so Carter could take a scan.

The overlay mapped the sunglasses, a manufacturer and model number appearing in the corner of his overlay. "They're sunglasses. Pretty expensive ones, but off the rack. Nothing custom."

"Right." Mason turned the dead man's face toward him. "Ah."

"Ah?"

Under the body was a spread of red, too shiny to be blood. "That's not blood."

"No," agreed Carter.

"This guy isn't dead."

"It's not a guy," said Carter. "Kick it to thermal for a second."

Mason's optics switched to the softer blues and brighter reds of thermal. He looked at the bodies around him, already cooling in death, then to Reed's body.

Stone cold blue, except for a rectangle of white heat at the body's core. "Is that a machine?"

"Yes," said Carter. "Reed Interactive sent a robot to meet you."

"It wasn't a robot," said Mason.

"You're sure?"

"Play back the video, Carter. It wasn't a robot."

There was a pause. "You're right. It wasn't a robot. Say."

"Yeah?"

"What's not a robot, but looks like one? If you were into synthetic entertainment, what's the next logical step?"

"Jesus, Carter. Is this a sexbot?"

"You always think in straight lines, Mason. Just bring it back with you."

"What about the cops?" Mason switched his optics back to visual light, glancing at the cop. The man's face was an unhealthy red.

Carter giggled. "I'll make another call."

"No, it's all good. Leave this one to me."

"It's always work, work, work with you, isn't it?" Carter dropped the link with a click.

Mason went to the cop, who looked like he was caught between running and standing still. "You done?"

The other man swallowed. "That was the chief of police."

"I know," said Mason. "Can I go now?"

"There's a small—"

"You're on the take from the South Sun Tigers."

The other man's eyes bulged. "Now just wait a goddamn minute—"

"No," said Mason. "No, I won't wait a minute. Here's what's going to happen. You'll deal with the Tigers."

"I—"

"You're on the take, but they're going to be upset with you for letting me walk. Way I see it, you need to get in front of it." Mason grabbed the Reed body by the jacket lapels. "Kinda sucks. Have a good night."

He walked from the restaurant, hauling the body with him. Mason made it to the big Suzuki. He linked to the bike, warming it up. He tossed Reed's body over the front near the handlebars, arms and legs dangling down either side.

The bike hummed, waiting. Mason reached into his jacket for the Treasurers, lighting one. He hoped Reed wouldn't come looking for their synthetic body before he had time to finish his cigarette.

CHAPTER TWELVE_

The *Hole* was comfortable, like a well-worn shoe. It was Bernie's place of business. Not just a bar, some throwaway commodity in a world that gave zero fucks about tenure or prestige. *The Hole* might die, but it was evergreen. Ready to be born again.

There were no customers at this hour, because *daylight* was when creatures of darkness scuttled for cover. Bernie hated his customers were illegals. Not because they flew under the radar, because that made disposal easy. No, he hated illegals because they were *broke*. They paid their cover charge with surly need, buying the barest level of liquor to keep them on an even level.

Get some real money. Start a bigger place. Move uptown.

Bernie scratched his belly, looking over his glass at the two company men. The whisky was old and tired, but the price was right. Bernie was on one side of *The Hole's* worn bar, the syndicate reps across from him. "It's legit."

The one from Reed snorted. The man wore his company-cool attitude, douche sunglasses on inside. "It's hardly *legit*, Eckers. If it was legit, we wouldn't be dealing with you."

The Metatech suit was just as big an asshole as the Reed douche canoe. No sunglasses, but he wore arrogance like other people wore deodorant. Metatech was too good for this part of town. They dealt in mil-spec hardware. Brokering arms deals with wicker-basket dictators. Selling WMDs to governments big enough to pay. But he was here anyway, because ol' Bernie had a deal. Not something they needed. Better — something they *wanted*. Metatech tugged his cuffs, looking at Reed. "How you feeling?"

Reed frowned, lips making a moue under the douche shades. "I feel fine."

Bernie glanced at Metatech, then at Reed. Normally these assholes shot each other in back alleys. Concern for each other's welfare was off-script. *Best be careful, Eckers.* "Great. You're feeling fine. Would you feel better than fine making money?"

"Because," said the Metatech asshole like Bernie hadn't spoken, "I saw you get shot."

"What?" said Bernie. He was pretty sure he'd have noticed something like that. "I didn't get shot."

"That's right," said Reed, glancing at Metatech for a long, cool, douche-powered second. "It's a neat trick." He tapped the side of his nose.

Metatech sighed. "Fucking Reed."

"Yes," said Reed. "At least we don't do so much shooting."

"Seriously," said Bernie. "What the fuck are you guys talking about?"

"It's not your concern," said Metatech. He leaned forward, elbows resting on the bar. "Who do I have to kill to get a drink around here?"

Bernie felt his heart increase its pace, struggling a little with the direction the conversation went. Metatech *could* kill him. Probably wouldn't. At least, not until their business concluded. *Probably.*

A drink, then. Sure. Whatever. Bernie reached under the bar, hand dropping to the rack of glasses. He touched the shotgun strapped under the bar, a solution for emergencies *The Hole* might have.

"I wouldn't," said Metatech.

Bernie froze. "Wouldn't what?"

"The shotgun," said Metatech. "I just want a beer. Don't need a glass. Don't want to shoot you either."

Reed nodded, as if they'd had an asshole convention and agreed on terms before walking in. Maybe they had. "Not until we know what this is about, anyway."

Bernie removed his hand from the shotgun, nice and slow. He turned, sliding open a door frosted over with old ice. It hid many wonders, such as cheap beer. "Whatever. It's just a glass. There's no shotgun."

Metatech laughed then, some genuine mirth crinkling his eyes. "You don't deal with us very often, do you Mr. Eckers?"

"You? Fuck no. First time I've seen you assholes."

"Not us," said Reed. "People like us."

"Company men," suggested Metatech.

"No," said Bernie. "You're all motherfuckers."

Metatech pulled his hand from under the bar, placing a sidearm on the top. It gleamed with military precision, promising an efficient death. Bernie wasn't sure what it fired, and he didn't want to find out. The metal made a dull clunk against the wooden top, just one more mark on the old brown surface. "Careful."

"Hold up," said Bernie. "I invite you to my place of business—"

"*The Hole*," said Reed.

"S'right," said Bernie. "*The Hole*. Ain't no other like it."

Reed looked around, taking in the stage hiding in its shroud of gloom. "That's the truest thing you've told us today."

"Like I said." Bernie looked at the Metatech sidearm, waiting on the bar like it needed a purpose. He hadn't seen anything quite like it before. The barrel looked too big, too *wide*, for such a small weapon. Bernie put two beers on the bar. *Be cool. It's just a business meeting.* "You guys need me to open these?"

Both company men shook their heads. Reed opened his with a twist of his wrist. Metatech popped his cap with a fucking *thumbnail*.

"Sure, okay," said Bernie. "You don't need an opener. Good. Fine.

I invite you down to my place, my *home*, wanting to do a little business. And you come in here, full of company attitude. Syndicate men, getting in my face." He grabbed his glass from the counter and took a hit of the whisky.

Reed and Metatech looked at each other. Reed sipped his beer. "Your home? You live in this shitty dive?"

Metatech frowned, ignoring Reed. "You said you wanted to do business."

"S'right," said Bernie. "Got something."

"What kind of something?" said Metatech. He hadn't touched his beer. Metatech had the air of a man who'd found cheap beer could hold unpleasant surprises, the sour taste hiding all manner of horrors. It was true, but not this time. Bernie wasn't stupid enough to poison a company man.

They'd just send another. "*Syndicate* something, if you know what I mean."

"Apsel," said Reed and Metatech together.

"What?"

Metatech laid his hand over the sidearm's grip. He spoke low, almost like he was talking to himself. Working a problem through in his head before taking action. "You're trying to sell us Apsel 'something.'"

"What?" Bernie squinted. "Why would you say that?"

Reed put his beer on the bar top, shifting the bottle between his hands. It made a low grinding noise, like a back-alley clinic's bone drill on *extra slow, extra painful*. "Because Apsel aren't here."

"Maybe I don't like Apsel as much as I like you guys," said Bernie.

"We're motherfuckers," said Reed.

"All of us," agreed Metatech. "One motherfucker's much like another. It's the money on the table that matters. You're a fixer, Eckers. You care about the percentage."

"Right, which brings me to the next point. The money," said Bernie.

"No," said Reed.

"No?"

"No," said Metatech. "We don't talk about the money. We talk about the product first."

"Can't tell you about the product," said Bernie. He leaned forward, trying for conspiratorial. Just three guys, all on the same team. He looked between the company men. *Same team, my ass. These assholes are absolute, total motherfuckers.* "But you can trust me. It's good shit."

"I don't think I would trust you, Mr. Eckers," said Reed. "Not in business. Not to serve me beer that's not watered down—"

"Hey!" said Bernie. "It's straight from the bottle!"

"And definitely not with my life. If you can't tell us what the product is, you should tell us where it's from. What it's worth."

"Millions," said Bernie.

"Millions," repeated Metatech. "That's a broad spectrum."

"It's the truth," said Bernie. He held up his hands. "Okay, okay. You got me. It's Apsel tech. Straight from one of their R&D heads."

"Ah," said Metatech. "Is a defection part of the deal?"

"Last time we got one of your cast-offs, the product was defective," growled Reed.

Bernie looked down at his belly, thinking of a tight young body held against his in a back room. "It wasn't defective. You just didn't use it right."

"And you say *we're* the motherfuckers," said Reed.

"A defection. Sure. It's a part of the deal. I don't care about that," said Bernie. *Fucking Haraway.* "You get the brain with the box."

"Box?" said Reed.

"Yeah." Bernie nodded. "It'll come in a big metal box. You can take it out on the same forklift you bring my piles of money in with."

"You seem pretty sure we'll want to buy it," said Metatech.

"Yeah." Bernie grinned.

"We're not getting anywhere with this," said Metatech. He snatched his weapon up faster than Bernie could blink, pointing the barrel at Bernie's forehead. "What's it going to be, Eckers? We leave you dead on the floor, or you tell us why you're trying to set us up."

Red glowed at the bottom of the sidearm's barrel, like a dragon's eye. Bernie watched it like it was a snake. "I, uh."

"Come now," said Reed. "You know the *rules* of this game. We're not going to give you money unless we know what's in the box. We're certainly not going to bid against each other without some foresight. It just doesn't work that way." He straightened his sunglasses, ignoring the weapon trained at Bernie's head.

"Uh," offered Bernie.

"See, the problem is that we've already met with Apsel. Just a little earlier today," said Metatech.

"You ... what?"

"We," Metatech nodded to Reed, "met with Apsel."

"You met with Apsel?" Bernie swallowed, his throat drier than the Vancouver desert. *Motherfucking Haraway.* "What did they say?"

"They said not to buy the box," said Reed. "They said it'd mean war."

"War?" Bernie thought this whole thing was getting out of proportion. It was just *money.* A *good deal* for everyone. "There hasn't been a syndicate war in—"

"We know," said Metatech. "Only an idiot would try to broker a deal at this level."

Bernie's mouth opened and closed a couple of times. He could feel sweat trickling down his back, his too-tight shirt sticking to him. "I'm not trying to—"

Reed kicked through the bar's wooden front. Splinters and glass sprayed Bernie's legs as glasses died in droves. The company man leaned in, grabbing the shotgun. "No shotgun, you said." Reed hefted the weapon, glancing at Metatech. "Think we should believe him on the money?"

Metatech hadn't moved a millimeter, which meant his sidearm still pointed at Bernie's head. "No."

Reed checked the shotgun's breech. "Loaded." He cranked the lever, a shell spinning out the side. "Seems to be well-maintained."

"Yeah." Sweat trickled down Bernie's face. *Be cool. You're dead if you panic.* "Shit happens here sometimes."

"Shit is about to happen. Right here, right now," said Metatech.

"I swear!" The situation was unraveling. Bernie tamped down on panic, wondering if his life was measured in minutes rather than years. "I'm not trying to rip you guys off!"

Reed glanced at Metatech, then back to Bernie. "No, I guess you're not." He brought the shotgun down against his knee, the weapon snapping in half at the breech. Metal and shells rained to the floor.

Bernie could feel a warm wetness in his pants. He was going to die here, and it was all that bitch Haraway's fault. "Goddamn Haraway."

Metatech leaned forward. "What did you say?"

"I—"

"*Jennifer* Haraway? Atomic Energy? Apsel Federate?" The Metatech man paused, looking at the beer in front of him. His sidearm still pointed at Bernie's head, like a promise. "I might even forgive you for trying to lace my drink. If Haraway came with the box..."

Bernie swallowed, struggling for words that might save him. *Any* words. He opened his mouth, but no sound came out.

"What's in the box?" asked Reed.

"The rain," said Bernie. "The rain's in the box."

CHAPTER THIRTEEN_

"I love it when you bring me presents," said Sasha. A slab stood between her and Mason. The metal was cold, but the body on it didn't care.

It was the Reed operative.

Mason dragged the carcass to one of the Federate's labs. He'd invoked privacy controls, the windows now coal-black. Sound inversion fields stopped their conversation from being overheard. Even in the heart of the Apsel tower, you could never be too careful.

"You're welcome," said Mason. He lifted the body's arm, letting it fall back on the table. The knuckles were scraped and bloody. *It's not like it's easy to carry a dead guy on a bike. Sue me.* "But it's not really for you."

"Oh, don't be like that," she said. "I've taken off my wedding ring and everything." Her tone was playful, but the lab was professional and clean. *Pristine. That's the word.* Not a tool out of place. Mason didn't expect anything else. It's why he always went to Sasha first.

Carter's voice came over the room's sound system. "Have you two finished?"

Sasha looked up. "Why don't you come down, Carter? This will be fun."

"I don't do field work."

"This isn't field work," said Sasha. "This is my lab. It's *inside.*"

"You're about to cut open a dead guy, which is *waaaay* out in the field. Me? Computers. I do computers."

Sasha winked at Mason. "She's going to miss out on the orgy later."

Carter gagged. Mason threw Sasha a quick smile. "I'm not sure if 'miss' is the right word. She's been cranky since she lost a fight with a hacker earlier today."

"I didn't lose a fight. The guy *died.*"

"Sure." Mason nodded. "He died. I also went blind. Way to have my back."

"You've got no sense of the dramatic," said Carter. "Coburn?"

"Yes, Carter?" Sasha put on a medical visor, the clear perspex covering her face. "Changed your mind?"

"No. I just want you to cut Mason first."

Sasha grinned. She selected a small rotary saw, clicking its switch a couple of times, the machine whining. "So. Anything you want to tell me about this guy before I do the autopsy?"

Mason walked around the medical slab, pushing a console out of the way. He checked the Reed body one more time, taking in the expensive suit. It was a robot but dressed for success. Mason offered Sasha Reed's sunglasses. "He was wearing these."

"I'm not sure if that's quite ... wait a second." Sasha held the saw out to one side, cocking her hip. She tapped her jaw, making no move to take the sunglasses. "Wearing them inside?"

"That's right. Inside. Weird, right?" Mason tossed the glasses into a tray beside the slab. "He seemed otherwise fine. A bit of an asshole, maybe."

Sasha leaned over the body. "We'll have to take the suit off first. Fibers will clog the saw, you know how it is." She gave Mason her patented once-over. "We can see if he's in as good condition as you."

"Oh, please," said Carter. "I'm going to be sick."

Mason laughed, then helped Sasha take off the Reed body's

clothes. The suit was tailored. It fit the body like the Reed guy spared no expense dressing his robots.

"Here," said Sasha. "Help me roll him over. He's heavy."

"Yeah," said Mason. "I had to carry him. I know he's heavy. It's why it's called dead weight."

She frowned, tapping a display set into the slab. "Says he's one thirty-seven kilos. He doesn't look fat."

"No. He works for a syndicate. He can afford a clinic." Mason shrugged.

"I don't think you're telling me everything I need to know," suggested Sasha.

"Maybe not, but there's not much more to tell." Mason thought back to the meeting with Metatech and the Reed asshole. "We had beer. Got in a fight. Turned out, he was a robot that bleeds." He went through Reed's jacket. Spare weapon. Energy cartridges for it. A pack of cigarettes.

"A robot?"

"Did I forget to mention that? Been a busy night." Mason turned the cigarettes over. *What does a robot need cigarettes for?*

"You were going to let me take a saw. To a robot. With a probably-still-live power core." Sasha reached for the cigarettes. "You mind?"

"You always say there's no smoking in here." Mason handed her the pack, keeping one for himself.

"I'm not going to smoke," she said, tapping a cigarette from the pack. "They look normal."

"They're cigarettes," said Mason, raising the cigarette to his mouth.

"There's no smoking in here," said Sasha.

Mason looked over the top of his lighter, then lit the cigarette. He took a deep pull. "Well, that's a piece of pure grade shit."

"Why? Is it a cigarette?"

Mason took another pull. "Oh, sure. It's a cigarette. The man has no taste though. They're Camels." He stubbed it out on a tray beside the slab, pulling Treasurers from his pocket.

"There's no—" Sasha stopped at the click and snap of Mason's lighter. "I don't know why I bother."

"Me neither," said Mason, blowing smoke toward an air vent. "It's like you've just met me or something."

"My lab is going to smell like a bar for a week."

"You'll need someone to throw up in here for that," said Mason. "Get some whisky, too."

The Reed body waited, naked. To Mason's eye, it looked like any syndicate enforcer. Guy worked out. Watched what he ate. Spent time at a clinic to smooth out nature's bullshit. The gaping through and through bullet hole didn't take anything from it.

"He looks ... complete," offered Carter.

"Very," agreed Sasha. "Can you flip him for me?"

Mason turned the body, his bionics making the task effortless. Complain as he might about dragging a hundred thirty-seven kilos of robot carcass up here, but his augments trivialized it. Sasha didn't have the same mods.

She wasn't built for the street.

"What's that?" Carter dropped a red box on Mason's overlay, highlighted the base of the robot's spine.

Mason leaned forward, touching the robot's skin, tracing tiny numbers and letters. "Good eyes, Carter."

"It's a serial number." Sasha squinted. "Definitely a robot."

Mason pointed at the bullet hole in the robot's back. "He might be a robot, but a lot of blood came out of there."

"Yes." Sasha's voice dropped all hint of play. "He's surprisingly detailed. If we didn't have the evidence, I don't think you'd be able to tell." She walked around the slab. "Where did you say you found him?"

"Bar," said Mason. "We had a beer."

"*He* drank beer?"

"Yeah," said Mason.

"Robots don't drink."

"That's why we're here." Mason sighed. "If it was an easy problem, Carter could have—"

"Fuck off," said Carter.

"I only meant—"

"You should stop talking," suggested Sasha. "You don't understand women at all."

"He rents women. Mason doesn't have to understand them." Carter sounded *off*, like her engine wanted to do more than idle.

"Did it just get colder in here?" said Mason. "It feels colder." He stubbed out the Treasurer against the slab, flakes of silver and ash falling to the ground. "So, doc, you going to figure out how it works?"

Sasha considered the body. "Yeah, I really think we need to. Carter?"

"Yes, Sasha?"

"Can you," Sasha wiggled her fingers in the air, "do your thing?"

"Hack the robot?"

"Sure."

"If you turn it on, I can hack it," said Carter.

"It's not on?"

"Does it look on?"

"I'll leave you to it," said Mason. "I need to speak to Harry." He pulled another Treasurer from the pack, lighting it as he left the lab.

Mason found Harry in Apsel's main hangar. The place was noisy, the thick miasma of oil, metal, and ozone in the air. Techs scurried. Total conversions tried not to stand on them. Mason laid his proposition on Harry, waiting.

"No." Harry swiveled. He regarded Mason over a workbench that sat between them, spare parts and tools strewn over it. Cables stretched from the back of his chassis into a panel set in the wall.

Something exploded a few bays down, sparks and burning fluid spraying into the air.

Mason and Harry watched as repair crews rushed forward, extinguishers blasting white foam over the blaze. Might have been a total conversion's chassis overloading. Too many mods with too little control, and accidents happened.

"It'll be fun." Mason turned away from the dying conversion. He looked up at Harry's massive bulk. Harry was two to three times the height of a normal human, a titan of gleaming black metal. No hint of his humanity remained.

Except for his voice. That was the Harry Mason remembered. "That doesn't sound likely, does it? The last time—"

Mason held up a hand. When he spoke, his voice was softer, almost lost in the noise of the service bay. Harry's audio would pick up his words just fine. The audio was top-shelf, just like the rest of Harry's modifications. Modifications Harry needed after their ... encounter. "I remember."

Harry leaned forward, servos whining. His hand, a mass of metal bigger than Mason's chest, pressed against the workbench with a creak. "Do you?"

"Yeah." Mason flexed his hand, remembering. He looked at it, then back to Harry. "I'd rather it was you out there."

"Why do you think you need me there?" Harry straightened, the cables from his back slapping and clacking together. "You Specialist Services assholes—"

"You used to be Specialist Services."

"Yeah," said Harry. "Before this." His huge hand gestured down at his metal chassis. A new body, after the old one was too broken for syndicate work.

"It's a good look," said Mason. "Black goes with anything. Tactical."

Harry paused, then laughed. "All right, Floyd. Tell me what you think is going down. Why you need me."

"Sure." Mason leaned against a bench. A harried tech walked by, head down, muttering to himself. Mason looked after him. "Problem?"

"No problem. He always talks to himself," said Harry. "Psych doesn't come down here. We need these guys too much."

Mason pulled out a cigarette, looking at the silver filter before lighting it. "The problem," he blew smoke toward the ceiling high above them, "is I'm going to be grossly outnumbered."

"I kinda figured," said Harry.

The same harried tech walked by again, looking at Mason. "There's no smoking in here."

Mason nodded, pulling the Treasurers from his pocket. He offered the pack. The tech looked around, nervous as a bird, before his hand stabbed out to grab one. He took the offered light, walking away while drawing on the cigarette.

"I don't know how you get away with shit like that." Harry looked after the tech, shaking his head.

"Don't listen to what he said. Listen to what he wants," said Mason.

"Did you read a book on Zen? One without pictures?"

"I sometimes watch cartoons when I can't sleep. Here's the thing, Harry. Carter's tracked down a set of ... *coincidences*."

"Like?"

"We found some evidence. A notebook with the name *Eckers* written in it. Didn't know it was a name at the time, though."

"But you know for sure now, right?"

"More like an educated guess." Mason craned to look at the ceiling. The hangar was high, and he wondered what kind of machinery needed this kind of space. Space was ... *expensive*. "Our suspect had a meeting with someone. Her calendar was wiped."

"How do you know she was having a meeting?"

"Carter's very clever. She tells me so all the time."

Harry barked a laugh. "Yeah, my handler's the same."

"I'm right here," said Carter, her link voice loud, like she was leaning into the mic. *Making sure she's heard.*

"Aren't you supposed to be helping Doc Coburn?" Mason said over the uplink.

"I can do two things at once."

Harry watched Mason. "She's talking to you right now, isn't she?"

"Yeah," said Mason in the real. "She's right here."

"Same, same," said Harry. He cocked his head as if listening. "I don't know why they hire the angry ones. When's the meeting?"

"It's already happened." Mason dropped his cigarette, lighting another. "Her calendar said she was meeting with, ah, Bernard Eckers."

"Fixer?"

"Amongst other things."

"Why is he still breathing?"

"I said I wanted you on the team, didn't I?" Mason leaned forward, trying for a little Christmas cheer. "I don't want this to come out the wrong way, but it's not because of your good looks."

"We're going to meet Eckers?"

"Already tried that. He wasn't home. Doesn't matter. Old Man Gairovald's after a different outcome."

"You spoke to Nancy?"

"I spoke to Gairovald." Mason waited for that to sink in.

Harry's feet flexed, scraping the concrete floor. He clanked around. "Look ... *shit*. Can you uncable me?"

Mason walked behind him. "Hell, is there supposed to be crap leaking out of here?"

"No," said Harry, sounding edgy.

"Good. It's not."

"You're an asshole, Floyd."

Mason grinned, pulling the cables free. Lights flickered in the cavity they'd come from before an armored casing hummed into place.

"Better," said Harry, flexing. "I hate that thing."

"You hate eating?" Mason ducked out of the way, getting the

visual safety of the workbench between them. Harry said he didn't hold a grudge.

But accidents happen.

"It's not really eating," said Harry. "I mean ... it's eating but not. It's a simulation. Feels like I'm having a royal feast. Just before you came down? You interrupted truffled eggs."

"Truffled eggs?"

"They were pretty good, too." Harry waved his massive arms with a hiss of hydraulics. "But it's not the same."

"Maybe you should work for Reed Interactive. Their eggs are probably better."

"That's not funny."

"It's kind of funny."

Harry stared at Mason for a couple heartbeats. "Anyway, it's not the taste that's the problem. It's because I know there ain't no eggs."

Mason sat on the bench. "Maybe it's you that's been reading Zen."

Harry faced Mason, torso swiveling independently from his legs. "So. Eckers."

"We're going to go plug a leak."

"Figures. Why today?"

Mason flicked ash from his cigarette. "Because Carter's been sniffing the net. There's been an increase in syndicate activity around the bar Eckers owns."

"Syndicates? Which ones?"

"As near as she can tell, all of them. Now, anyway. Initially?" Mason shrugged. "Metatech. Reed."

"You're thinking you're going to get shot again." Harry's voice was light, but it triggered Mason's memory.

Harry Fuentes pointed a gun at Mason. The dark held them closer than the rain. Mason shifted closer, the barrel of Harry's weapon digging into his shoulder. "Here. Take the shot."

"Okay, Floyd. You know what your problem is?"

"Why don't you tell me."

"You're too much of a damn arrogant son of a bitch." Harry's shot rang out, spinning Mason. *Pain bloomed in his shoulder.*

"I get shot a lot." Mason pushed the memory away. "That's not the problem. The problem is not being able to shoot back hard enough."

Harry flexed big metal shoulders. "I'm your man."

"You didn't need much convincing," said Mason.

"No. I'm pretty much always up for a fight."

Mason smiled, sliding off the bench. "It'll be tonight. I'll swing by later. We can work through a plan."

"Why not now?"

"Sasha's working on something for me. I need to go check on it."

"Coburn? Say hi to her from me."

"No problem. Harry?"

"Yeah?"

"Thanks." Mason turned to go.

"Mason."

"Yeah, Harry?"

"Why me?" Harry swiveled, gesturing down the bay. "There's a lot of enforcers at Apsel. Why this particular model?"

The fire burned so hot, the lattice trying to pull his hand away. He heard Harry screaming from inside the car, flames blasting out the windows. Fire so intense the air burned.

Mason forced the lattice aside, grabbing the edge of the door. He yanked it open, reaching for what was left of the man inside. His overlay lit bright with warning icons, flashing and alive against a haze of static. Mason felt his hand spark and flare, the skin on his face starting to smear from the heat.

Mason flexed his hand again, looking back at Harry. "No reason, Harry. No reason at all."

○

"The problem with you is that you don't listen." Sasha wasn't her usual measured self, link voice brittle. *Working with Carter might make a person feel that way.*

"She's right. You don't listen," said Carter.

Mason considered the armor suits in their glass lockers. The Federate's gold falcon flew on the breastplate of each. Empty visors looked down on the room like ancient guardians. "I listen fine. It's a robot." He was in one of the Federate's armories. Steam from showers misted in, a team having returned from a mission. Macho camaraderie wafted in with the steam.

That's what a team's like. You need to split your trust too many ways.

"No, it's *not* a robot," said Carter.

"*You* said it was a robot," said Mason. He considered a light armor suit. *No. That shit'd get torn in half tonight.* "Looks like a duck, right?"

"It's not a robot. It's not a duck either. It's what we're trying to tell you." Sasha sounded exasperated, like someone might after spending a day at a care facility for the mentally disabled.

"Got it, not a duck." Mason took a pull from his cigarette, the silver filter bright from the armory's ceiling lamps. "Which means it's a robot."

"You try, Carter." Sasha sighed.

"Okay. Mason?" Carter turned out those four syllables in slow motion like she was trying not to lose her shit.

"Carter." Mason walked the line of suits, coming to stand before a heavy armored model. The bulk of the plating made it look plus-sized. *Not that either. Couldn't even scratch myself. No mobility.*

"It's a ... I guess we don't have a word for it. It's *like* a robot."

"Right." Mason stared at the ceiling as if he could make eye contact with Carter in the heavens. "I got that part."

"But it's *actually* a remote."

"Like a drone?"

"It's probably better if I show you."

"Show me what?"

"This," said a voice behind him.

Mason spun, the lattice dragging his limbs hard, the Tenko-Senshin already out. The Reed body stood, head tilted to one side, neck broken. The eyes looked past him, dead and glassy. Its shoulders were slumped.

"Gotcha," said the Reed body.

"Gotcha," said Carter's voice over the link at the same time. She laughed.

Mason struggled against the lattice for a second, the Tenko-Senshin shaking in his hand, whining in the quiet of the room.

"Don't shoot, all right?" Carter spoke over the link, the Reed body holding up its hands in surrender. "It's me."

"It's me," echoed the Reed body. The left side of its mouth dragged like a stroke victim's.

"I'm never taking you out. Not bowling, not dancing." Mason's breath steadied, but his hand still shook, the lattice hungering. *Easy. Calm your shit.*

"It's not a robot," said Sasha.

Mason lowered the Tenko-Senshin, slipping the little weapon back into its holster. He walked around the Reed body, then poked its shoulder. It swayed gently.

"Hey. Don't do that. This isn't easy." Carter sounded annoyed.

"Definitely not a duck," said Mason.

Sasha spoke, her voice rushed. "Like we were trying to tell you, this is new tech. Brand new. So new, it's not on the market. It's a ... *construct.*"

"It's got that new car smell," agreed Mason. He poked the construct again. "Not on the market?"

"We'd know if there was anything like this."

Mason did a circuit of Reed's construct. "It's like some sort of remotely piloted robot?"

"It's not a..." Sasha wound down in defeat. "Yes. Okay. It's a remotely piloted robot."

"I didn't take much science at school," said Mason. "It looks like a really cool robot, though." He pushed its shoulder, harder this time. It swayed, stepping sideways. One of its feet gave way and it stumbled to one knee.

"Ow. I told you not to do that," said Carter.

"Stop pushing me," said the Reed body. The words were slurred, the head panning to him.

"Can you turn it off?" said Mason. "It's reminding me of a clown."

"A clown?" said the construct. Mason could hear *Carter* in the voice. It had the same emphasis, the same pauses she did. But the construct spoke with a male voice.

"You know. Clowns at kid's parties. Ronald. Whatever." Mason looked down at the Treasurer he'd dropped. It had gone out. He pulled out another one, lighting it, then offered the pack to the Reed robot. "Smoke?"

"I don't ... hell, this isn't *me*. Sure." The construct's hand was clumsy and jerky, knocking a cigarette from the pack. The silver foil spun end over end before it hit the ground.

"Did you get into computers because you're some kind of cripple?" said Mason.

The construct got to its feet, jerking like a marionette. "I..." It slurred to silence.

"This is easier," said Carter over the link. "I've sort of ... *compromised* the interface. This isn't how it's natively controlled."

"What do you mean?" asked Mason.

"We're *pretty* sure you're supposed to direct connect with one of these." Sasha sounded doubtful.

"Neural tap?"

"I thought you didn't go to school," said Carter.

"Not for science, no. Girls." Mason eyed the construct. "This is crazy."

The construct managed to grab an armor rack. It hauled itself upright. "Can. You. Get. Me. The. Cigarette." The words were slow and clear, like a drunk person pretending sobriety.

"I think I'm getting the hang of it," said Carter. The link crackled for a moment, the body sagging to one knee. "Wait. Don't help. Don't help."

Mason picked up the fallen cigarette, lighting it. "Let me know when you're ready."

The construct reached for the cigarette, the hand shaking. Its eyes locked on the glowing tip. It grabbed at the air once, twice, before snaring it. It stuffed the crumpled filter between its teeth.

"How'd I do?" said Carter.

"Great. Really great," said Sasha.

Mason dragged on his own cigarette. He leaned against an armored suit. "They'll come looking for it."

"Sure they will," said Carter. The construct took a pull on the cigarette at the same time as she was speaking. It coughed, then blew a stream of smoke out. "They'll never be able to bust in here though."

"There's one thing I don't get, doc," said Mason.

"Yes?" said Sasha.

"This thing took some fire, right? I'm pretty sure it ... *died*."

"It's still dead. We had to, uh, patch it up first. It won't be good for field work. We can strip it down. See how it works."

"'Patch it up?'"

"It had a hole in it. It's remarkable, really." A little excitement leaked back into Sasha. "It's a lot like a real body. It's got blood, or something like it. It's got a lattice."

"A lattice?" Mason flexed his hand. "Why's it got a lattice?"

"You want me to guess?"

"If that's the best I can get, sure. Why's a robot got a lattice?"

"I'm pretty sure it's got a pilot." Sasha sighed. "Or, it had a pilot, before Carter jacked it."

The construct shuffled down the room. "I was able to practice walking on the way here."

"How'd she jack it?" Mason waved the cigarette at the construct. "To be honest, I'm not sure she did such a good job."

"I'm right here," said Carter, the link buzzing. "If I had to guess—"

"Christ, it's like working with amateurs," said Mason. "We're on the corporate dime, people. What do you mean, *guess?*"

"If I *had* to guess," Carter leaned on the word as the construct turned, "I'd say someone like a company enforcer."

"Specialist Services."

"Sure. Anyway, they'd throw you into a tank, wire you up to some kind of neural net, and map you right into the body."

"So, the pilot—"

"It doesn't feel like piloting." Mason could feel Carter's uncertainty. "Not if what I'm seeing at this end is anything to go by. I can't know for sure from the interface I've hacked together."

Sasha cleared her throat, but on low volume, like she had something to say but didn't want to get in the way of a good thing. "It'd be like being there. Full sensory mapping."

"Jesus. Reed's made its agents into risk-free remotes." Mason considered his armor choices again. Maybe heavier armor *might* be a good idea.

"I don't know about risk-free." Carter's tone was *don't be a dick, Mason.* "There's all kinds of risk."

"Like what?" Mason wondered about the safety of tonight's mission, and how much armor he'd have to wear to still be sucking oxygen tomorrow. "The Reed asshole got shot, and he... *it's* still walking around like a registered voter."

The link went silent. Sasha took the bait. "It's fucked. It looks braindead."

The construct took a step closer, head twitching. Carter said, "Mason, I can taste this cigarette. When you pushed me over—"

"I touched your shoulder. It's not my fault you're inept." Mason tossed his stub to the floor, grinding it under his heel. He took another from the pack.

"It felt uncomfortable. Falling down? That hurt."

"You sound surprised."

"I'm guessing the first design application of this wasn't military," offered Sasha. "All the senses are ... *real*. Full fidelity."

"Ah." Mason snapped his fingers. "Reed Interactive. It's a sex toy."

The construct jerked. "What?" Carter sounded alarmed, like she'd patted a cat but found it slimy. The construct looked toward its pants.

"Don't let him worry you, honey." Sasha was all business. "It could be used a hundred different ways."

"I feel sick. I don't know where this thing's been." Carter sounded like she'd stepped back from the mic for some air.

"Carter."

"Yes, Mason?"

"How ... deep are you jacked in?"

The construct flailed, teetering. It righted itself. "And she saves! I think I'm getting the hang of this." Carter sounded impressed, a little bit on the smug side. "I'm not very deep. Have you ever seen a puppet show?"

"A what?"

"Never mind. Surface contact only. I'm not ... invested." The construct winked, the eyes staring past Mason. Its eyelid had a tic. "I'm just pushing buttons at this end."

"Could you fight?"

"Against who?"

"I don't know. Me, say." Mason offered another cigarette to the construct. *To Carter.* The whole she-it thing was messing with his head.

"Thanks," said Carter, the construct fumbling a filter from the pack. It took Mason's offered light, blowing smoke. "I probably couldn't fight fish in a barrel in this thing."

"Shoot," said Sasha.

"What?" The construct blinked owlishly.

"It's 'shoot.' You shoot fish in a barrel."

"I really like these." The construct drew on the cigarette. "Maybe I should take up smoking."

"You've never tried?" said Mason. A red stain spread on the construct's shirt. "Uh."

"No," said Carter, the construct taking a deeper drag.

Silence. The construct froze, smoke curling from its nose. "Carter?"

The construct fell. Mason nudged it with his toe. *Definitely a registered voter.*

"Well, shit," said Carter.

"What happened?" said Sasha.

"I'm pretty sure it just died again."

"That would make sense. If it was a person, we'd be telling it ... him? It. We'd be telling it to rest up. Plenty of fluids. That kind of thing."

"There's one thing I don't get." Mason turned the body over. "Hold the phone. Can you start this thing back up again?"

"Sure, if you bring it back up here," said Sasha. "It's pretty much dead there, though."

"What don't you get, Mason?" said Carter.

"Why the sunglasses?"

"It's the eyes," said Carter. "Caught a glimpse of myself ... Itself? I saw its eyes in the elevator mirrors."

"I figured the eyes were all kinds of screwy because it was a dead guy." Mason turned its head. It *felt* like a human. Skin still warm. Soft flesh. A little stubble.

"No. I think there's a point of view problem," said Carter.

"A what?"

"Or focal point issue." Sasha sounded more certain, now they were entering her field of expertise. "Carter and I are still talking about that."

"Yes. There are divergent theories." Carter didn't sound like both theories held equal weight for her.

"Fine. You two can start a group. All I really need to know? How to tell one of these apart." Mason let the head go, the soft thud as it hit the armory floor just like a human's would sound.

It wasn't good to dwell on how he knew the sound of a human head hitting the floor so well.

"I'd check the eyes. Anyone with sunglasses? Shoot them in the head. First." Carter paused. "I'm *pretty* sure the head is the kill spot."

"That seems overly enthusiastic. What if there's some guy just wearing sunglasses?" asked Sasha.

Mason stood, finding himself in front of a suit of armor. It stood in a glass case like the rest, but the front was stenciled *APSEL FEDERATE — MILITARY APPLICATIONS.* The suit was the only white one Mason could see, the Federate's falcon emblazoned in black on the chest. "Carter, what's this one for?"

"You want me to call Frank?"

"Who the fuck's Frank?"

"Francesco. Head of Military Applications."

"No." Mason remembered his meeting with the division head. "He'll lie."

"Ah." Carter made the noise sound like agreement. "Here it is. A demo model. Urban pacification. It's had a test run. We've even got a signed sales contract subject to the usual."

"The usual?"

"Test run, blah blah, pursuant to subclass ass, paragraph boredom."

Mason laughed. "Got it."

"Whatever. Fairly standard loadout. We've even put an Everlife fusion power system inside."

"Okay." Mason peered inside the case. "Why's it still boxed up?"

"Maybe they don't want it scratched before the test run."

"It's perfect." Mason touched the case's access panel, unsealing the glass. It whispered open, soft puffs of cold fog curling out to nestle around his feet. Mason pulled off his jacket, putting the Tenko-Senshin on a bench. "I think I'll take it for that test run."

CHAPTER FOURTEEN_

"I don't know why you didn't requisition a bigger team." Carter's voice sounded clear despite the rain against Mason's helmet. The new *urban pacification* armor had good audio, and better audio insulation.

Just the kind of thing you need when rioters scream at you. Mason looked through *The Hole's* skylight. A man and woman waited inside looking nervous, along with some illegal merch to sell. About what he'd expected. "You're clever. Why do you think I didn't want a bigger team?" The bar looked as he remembered.

"Because you want to fail?"

"Change the question." Mason shifted his feet, careful not to scrape his boots on the roof's tiles. They were old and chipped. Lichen clung with determination despite the acid rain. *Life wants to live, and sometimes, make a little bank.* It came down harder than it had in days. Active camouflage in his armor's skin held light close, making Mason hard to see. "What do you get with a bigger team?"

"More dudes. You get a lot more dudes. They draw enemy fire, so you don't get shot. Again."

"Right. Can you give me a scan of the area?" Mason waited,

almost invisible in the rain. The benefit of top-shelf armor wasn't *just* being invisible. It was being invisible *and dry*. Not a leak anywhere.

"Sure." Carter paused. "Wait. A what?"

"A scan. I'd like to see how many dudes are out there."

"You're an asshole."

"Maybe. But if we had more dudes, as you put it, there'd be a bigger fingerprint. A signature, saying loud and proud that the Federate was here. With me and my active camouflage, we keep this on the down low. Uncle Gairovald won't be on the news."

"He doesn't care about the news."

"He cares about his stock price." Mason gave a quick visual scan of the area. No one had joined him. "And the news affects the stock price."

"I might have misjudged your intelligence. This whole forward-planning thing you're doing? It caught me by surprise. You're still an asshole, though. When do you want Harry to drop in?" Carter's voice held the barest hint of admiration. *I'll take it.*

"When I'm ready," said Mason. He checked the skylight again, the room still empty except for two important people, one of them Apsel's own. And the box.

It sat in the middle of the room, Apsel's falcon big and black on the lid. He couldn't see from this angle, but he reckoned it'd be stamped with *ATOMIC ENERGY DIVISION*.

Mason remembered black lipstick against the silver foil of a cigarette. He pushed the memory aside. If she was here, that was just bad luck. It was just he didn't want her going down as collateral damage. *Hell. You don't even know her name. You've done worse. Focus, Mason.*

"You could take the shot from here," suggested Carter. "That's the mission. Kill the thief, destroy the tech."

"Try to keep up." It wasn't often Mason was a step ahead of Carter, and he didn't mind admitting he enjoyed it. *That's why you're in the field. This is why Gairovald trusts you. You don't take the easy path. And you never make mistakes.* "How do we know she's the thief?"

"Well... Because she deleted all records and ran from the syndicate."

"Eh." Mason nodded, pretty sure Carter watched from one of the many cams around the area. "It says she's shady as an old porch on a hot day."

"So, take the shot."

"Hmm."

"Hell, Mason. I don't have time for this."

"We've got all the time in the world. Until the buyers get here, anyway. What if she's shady for a different reason? Or there's another thief? We need to cover all the angles. Make sure she's alone."

"Then you take the shot?"

"Something like that. I'm still working out the finer details." He glanced at the case next to him. Rain ran dark rivulets down it. The Apsel falcon glinted. *Good enough for all manner of problem-solving.*

Mason looked back into the room. Carter dropped targeting reticules on his overlay. She marked the first one *AF HARAWAY* in big letters. The second she marked as *JD UNKNOWN.*

"He's not John Doe Unknown. He's Bernie Eckers," said Mason.

"How do you know?" asked Carter.

"It's his bar."

"Right. What if it's some other asshole here for a drink after work?"

"Touché." Mason sat on the roof, the light from the skylight struggling to find purchase on his armor. Water flowed off him, causing the active camouflage a little trouble. *Damn this rain.* "I hate the waiting."

"You could have brought a chair. Or, wait. Hey. You could have just gone in the front door."

"You've got no sense of style."

"I work in computers. What did you expect?"

"It's why you never go dancing, am I right or am I right?"

Carter sighed. "You're not going to let that go, are you?"

"I'm just saying there's something wrong with you. You work too much." Mason didn't want to admit it, but a chair wouldn't have been a crazy idea. Finding a chair with active camouflage? *Tricky.*

"You don't complain when I get you intel."

"I'm not complaining. I'm concerned."

She barked out a laugh, the link crackling like it chuckled along.

"Hey. What was that?" Mason stiffened. He felt tension between his shoulder blades, like he was being watched.

"What was what?"

"The link."

"On it." Carter's voice dropped all trace of humor. "They're here."

"Who?" Mason reached for the case.

"Uh." Carter paused. "All of them, I think." A map appeared in the lower right of his overlay. Mason zoomed it, the map filling his vision. Green road lines sparred with red buildings. The 3D model was complete down to the old wires strung between buildings. Hell, Carter had marked the sewers, complete with rats.

Those might be for artistic effect.

Mason saw two convoys of vehicles approaching. Carter marked them, *RI* from the north and *MT* from the south, text sliding over each vehicle's icon.

"Just Reed Interactive and Metatech?" Mason frowned. *The show should be bigger.*

"There's like twenty cars coming. From each syndicate. You wanted more?"

"I expected more for this level of tech."

"You're welcome." Carter sounded smug.

"For what?"

"I ... fiddled a few things."

"You 'fiddled?'" Mason looked into the room before checking on the map again. *Nope. No one magically appeared. No extras entering from stage left either.* "Where did you send them?"

"Different bar."

"Same city?"

"Maybe," said Carter the way people meant *not even a little bit.* "You do your job, I'll do mine."

Mason opened the clasps on the case, letting a breath out he hadn't known he was holding. "Thanks."

"You still get Reed and Metatech," said Carter. "They've got good deckers. Couldn't cut 'em out. Not all of them, anyway."

Mason opened the case, the rain eager to fill the corners. The weapons he'd selected waited inside, uncaring of the water. They were designed for far, far worse conditions than this.

He zoomed the map out, dropping it to the corner of his overlay. A lone icon caught his attention. It hadn't been there before and wasn't mixed in with Reed and Metatech forces. "Carter?"

"Mason."

"Is that icon *me?*" The icon sat on *The Hole's* roof where Mason stood. He zoomed the picture. "It doesn't look like me."

"You don't look like much at the moment," said Carter. "You're wearing light-refractive armor, so I needed to be creative."

Mason pulled two submachine guns out of the case, setting them on the roof. *SMGs are good for close work. High enough rate of fire to make people cautious. Big enough caliber to make an impression.* "Who is it? I don't recognize him as one of ours."

Carter laughed. "That's not surprising. It's Gene Kelly."

"Gene who? Who's Gene Kelly?" Mason searched the Federate's corporate directory. "I get a Gene Kelly in Policy. It's a woman, though. This picture is a ... what was the word you used?"

"Dude."

"This Gene Kelly is a dude. Not the woman in Policy."

"Look it up," suggested Carter.

Mason hefted a rifle from the case, checking the action. It gave a soft whine as if it were eager for the night to begin. He sighted along the barrel, then put it on the roof next to the SMGs. He then switched an SMG on. It gave a brief hum, the status lights along the top of the barrel cycling from red to green. His overlay gave up data on Gene Kelly while he worked.

It didn't find anything in the Federate archives. The information came from the public networks. "Ah."

"Ah?" said Carter.

"He was a dancer."

"I thought you'd appreciate it. Hey. Game's on. I get groups fanning down the side of the building toward the rear. It's going to get messy in there."

"I certainly hope so." Mason stood, the rain hissing down his armor. "I didn't want to get dressed up for nothing."

"You want Harry?"

"Not yet. Let's get the link up though." He put the request through. Harry came online, his face showing in the top left corner of Mason's overlay. *That's not his face. There's nothing left of his* real *face.* "Harry. What's up?"

"It's cold up here, Mason. It's really fucking cold." Harry looked pissed off, like *he* was the one standing for an hour in the rain.

"Do you need a hug?"

"I don't need a hug. I'm just making conversation."

"It's raining down here. How's the weather inside, Carter?"

"It's good. I've got the air conditioning at twenty-one." She had smug dialed a little higher.

"Fuck you both. This better be worth it."

"I promise, before the night's done, you'll get to shoot someone." Mason looked up, rain falling over his visor. He could see nothing but clouds, but somewhere up there...

"That's all I care about." Harry sounded satisfied. "Am I cleared to drop?"

"No. That's what I'm calling about. You get Carter's map update?"

"Yeah. There's a lot of assholes where you are." Harry paused. "Who's Gene Kelly? You got someone from Policy on an op?"

"Look it up. Public networks. Can you handle a force of that size?" asked Mason.

"Is the Pope still a God-fearing Catholic? Assuming I don't ice up, I'll be fine." Harry paused. "*Is* the Pope still a God-fearing Catholic? I haven't kept up with the news feeds."

"Metatech's out there. They won't be using pop guns." Carter made the *MT* icons flare briefly. "Those dudes."

"Dudes?"

"Dudes," she agreed.

"I see 'em. Do I sound worried?"

"You sound cold. Do you need a blanket?"

Harry laughed. "I get this shit from my own handler, Carter. I don't need it from you too."

"Carter, be nice to Harry."

"Why?"

Mason locked the SMGs against his belt, then racked the rifle on his back. "Because I'm pretty sure he's going to save my life tonight."

CHAPTER FIFTEEN_

Bernie paced, letting his gaze linger on Haraway one more time. She was worth looking over, and he had the time and opportunity. Haraway seemed too agitated to notice.

Rain hissed, soft and muted on the roof tiles. *Thank Christ it's not steel sheeting.* That'd be loud, and with all the rain in Seattle, shit'd get old, fast.

What *wouldn't* get old was that clinic-perfect body Haraway wore. Bernie figured it wasn't the meat she'd been born in. None of the syndicate people were *original*. Didn't stop a man from enjoying the view, though. "Want a drink?"

She jerked, like he'd yanked her from deep and important syndicate thoughts. "What?"

"A drink. Do you want one?" Bernie walked behind the bar. "A little southern hospitality, maybe." He waved a bottle.

"Sure. Fine."

Bernie found clean glasses, pouring while glancing over her again. Those syndicate bitches were *fine*. A splash of liquor escaped the glass. *Plenty more where that came from.* "Here."

She joined him at the bar. "Thanks."

He nodded, trying for eye contact. *Eyes aren't in the chest, Eckers.* "No problem."

"Mr. Eckers." Haraway didn't touch her drink, instead examining the hole those company assholes punched through his bar. "Is this going to be clean?"

Bernie leaned back. His eyes were drawn to the box. *APSEL FEDERATE — ATOMIC ENERGY DIVISION*, whatever the hell that meant. Atomic Energy and rain? *Who gives a shit. It's the percentage.* The metal was flat and gray, heavy locks above a panel. Flat and gray didn't matter. The money mattered. "Clean?"

"Clean." She had the look of someone struggling for more appropriate words. *Haraway's new at espionage.* Not that Bernie was experienced, per se. He just had a better idea of what the world owed him. She drank, coughing. "Jesus. What is this?"

"A little somethin' somethin'. We make it out back. House special."

"Special's one word for it." Haraway took another sip. Only one of her eyes screwed up this time. "Is this a negotiation?"

"The drink isn't a negotiation." It was, given sufficient quantity and enough time, an all-access pass. Bernie held his leer in check.

"No. This." She used her glass for emphasis, taking in the bar, the box, the stage, and for all Bernie knew the universe with a wave. "The syndicates deal in good faith, right?"

"Kinda sorta." Bernie thought back to the two company men in his bar. One of them snapped a gun across his leg like it was matchwood. "They *really* want what you've got. That makes it a little easier." He glanced at her breasts again.

Haraway didn't seem to notice, looking at the box. "Do you have the generator ready?"

"Yeah. See the cables on the stage?"

She twisted, giving Bernie a good look at her tight body in profile. *Damn. Maybe you should look for that bonus, Eckers.* "Yeah, I see them."

"Just plug 'em in. They're normally for music shit. Lights, amps. I dunno, whatever the hell those musos use."

Haraway looked doubtful. "Music?"

"It's loud. It'll be fine. Trust me."

She looked over her glass. "What a curious phrase. Why would I do that?"

"You company types, you're all the same." Bernie tried for a little honest indignation. "Regular guy like me, just trying to get by? You think we're trying to steal from you."

"Yes, I know. That's why I said it."

"It's not like that." Bernie put his empty glass on the bar, reaching for the bottle. "Another?"

"No." Haraway shook her head. "I'm still working on this one."

"Your loss." Amber liquid splashed into his glass. Bernie's hands shook a whisker, so he gripped the glass hard and took a slug. *Just something to settle the nerves.* "I got you the place. I cleared it out. Friday night, busiest night. I'm losing money here. And I got you my contacts."

She looked at the door. "They're late."

"They're always late. It's how they work."

A soft rumble grew outside. The sound of vehicles, drawing closer. Bernie slapped on a smile, hoping the liquor left it level. "There. Nothing to worry about."

His hands still shook. *Nothing at all, Eckers. You keep telling yourself that.*

CHAPTER SIXTEEN_

Mason kept an eye on the overlay as syndicate reps walked toward *The Hole*. He crouched beside the skylight, watching as the bar's big wide door swung open.

Metatech. Reed. He knew both men. Metatech strode in front, the man's suit immaculate. He shook water from an umbrella. Reed closed the door behind them both, water falling from his long coat. Mason's optics picked out water spots on the agent's sunglasses.

Gotcha, asshole.

"Mason, odds are good that's one of the remotes."

"No shit."

"That's not the cool thing. Check this out." Carter sent street CCTV feeds to his overlay. The images came fast, cascading into the corner of his vision. Reed and Metatech operatives were stationed outside, next to their vehicles.

The Reed men all wore the same face. "Fuck the what?"

"I told you it was cool." Carter gave a happy sigh. "This deal will teach us so much."

"I thought you said there'd be a pilot." Mason had trouble processing so many people wearing the same shell. It was unwholesome.

"We're still pulling it apart back at the ranch. I mean, sure, there's definitely *a* pilot, but—"

"The lecture can wait." Mason peered through the skylight. He placed a hand on the acrylic glass. The armor's glove acted as an inductive microphone. The overlay tossed the images of Reed's multiman aside, replacing them with an audio graph. The levels jumped as the people in the room below spoke.

"Eckers, we're here," said Reed.

"What, no hello?" The short fat man *was* Bernie Eckers.

"Hello," offered Metatech, moving toward Haraway. He held out a hand. "You must be Doctor Haraway."

She shook. "I'm not a ... never mind. You are?"

"I represent Metatech."

"I'm with Reed Interactive." The Reed man turned to take in the empty bar. "I expected more interest here."

"It's cozier this way." Eckers pushed his belly out like a stage prop. "Who'd have thought. C'mon, Doc. Let's do this."

"You're going to see something special." Haraway looked at the three men. "Don't you want to record this?"

Reed tapped his head. "It's all online. Don't worry about us."

Metatech nodded, hand to the box, palm up. "If the box really does contain the rain..." He trailed off, inviting Haraway to fill the gap.

Mason could see her frown from all the way up here. "Wait. The rain?"

Metatech and Reed looked at each other, then at Eckers. Reed spread his hands. "The interest is conditional on a number of factors. Mr. Eckers suggested that the recent atmospheric effects are controlled by Apsel technology."

Metatech nodded. "Yeah. And the technology would be up for sale. But what we were really interested in—"

"We've of course heard about Jennifer Haraway, head of Apsel's Atomic Energy Division." Reed rode over the top of Metatech as he unbuttoned his jacket. "The acquisition of scientific minds is a top priority for us."

Metatech looked at Reed, then at Haraway. Mason couldn't tell if he wanted to murder the Reed asshole or not. *I would.* "It would be a package deal."

Haraway glared at Eckers. "That's not a part of the deal. Tech for cash. Simple. Clean."

"Fellas." Eckers pushed his way between them. Mason shifted around the skylight, trying for a better view. A sweat stain sat like an oil slick on the man's back. *Nervous.* "Before we get too carried away, we should see the demonstration."

"Of the atmospheric effect?" Metatech examined his fingers. Mason's optics showed immaculately manicured nails, clinic-perfect. "I'd be uncomfortable if we were wasting our time here."

"Yes," agreed Reed. "This endeavor has a significant dollars-per-hour investment in syndicate resources."

Eckers moved to Haraway, lowering his voice. "C'mon, doc. Turn the thing on."

"The rain's not in the box." Haraway held up a hand before the other men could interrupt. "What's in the box is much, much better than the rain."

The two syndicate men waited. Metatech crossed his hands in front of him, the cuffs of his tailored shirt poking out from under suit sleeves. The Reed man nodded. "As you say, doctor."

"I'm not a doctor." Haraway moved to the box. She tapped on the panel. The clamps snapped open, the top retracting. Soft smoke drifted on cold feet over the sides and onto the floor. "You're probably wondering why I'm not concerned about you guys stealing this from me."

Reed offered a delicate cough. "We're bargaining in good faith, Doctor Haraway. It would be bad for future business if word got out Reed Interactive couldn't be trusted in... *financial* matters."

She looked over her shoulder. "Right, financial. One of you bozos tried to use it already, and you know what happened."

"Wasn't us," said Metatech.

"No," said Haraway. "It was him." Reed shrugged, as if saying, *sometimes these things happen.* "Anyway, now you know what happens now if you don't use it right." She dragged power cables to the box, thick black things that clattered against each other. They snaked across the bare concrete. "It needs a lot of power."

"Got it." Metatech offered a smile, his white teeth worth a month's salary. "That's what you guys are good at, after all."

Haraway plugged cables into machinery Mason could only partially see. "Yeah. If you think that's Apsel's only gig, this is going to blow your mind." She flicked a switch, a bass hum coming from the box.

The syndicate men didn't move, but Eckers stepped back like a super-sized nervous rodent. "Doc, what's going on?"

Haraway ignored Eckers, typing on a console in the box. The console was set against a metal structure. Tubes. A solid core. Struts.

"Carter, what the hell is that?" Mason had seen a lot of Apsel tech in his time. This looked like exactly none of it.

"No clue. I can tell you what it *isn't*."

"Yeah?"

"It's not a reactor." Carter paused, Haraway continuing to work beneath Mason. "Okay, I got nothing."

"Nothing?"

"*Nada.* We don't know what that is."

"Apsel made it. We've got to know what it is." Mason felt unease grow like a poisoned flower in his gut.

"Yeah, you'd think that, wouldn't you?" Carter sounded pissed off. He understood. Her whole job was information. "This mission is starting to feel—"

"Stretched," interrupted Mason. He took the rifle from his back, keeping his glove on the skylight. "Scope creep. I'd say the parameters of the mission have become elastic."

"Sure, elastic. That's a good word for it. When are you going to break up the party?"

Mason thought that through for a couple heartbeats. "In a minute. You know what?"

"No, I can't read minds."

"I can't *wait* to see what's in the box." Mason smiled despite the rain spitting and hissing around him.

Haraway still worked the keyboard. Metatech shifted, the movement small. "Is this going to take much longer?"

She looked up. "No. Here we go." Haraway tapped a final key.

The lights in *The Hole* dimmed. That wasn't the extent of the power draw, the street lamps around Mason flickering, then dying. A bolt of electricity, bright as the sun, arced from the box. Eckers ran behind the bar, crouching low.

Metatech looked at Reed. "This is ... unexpected."

Reed gave the tiniest of nods. "Yes. Although I still don't—"

A storm erupted from the box, arcs of lightning converging in the air. Mason's overlay stuttered, static falling like snow, and the suit lost audio from the room.

The electricity hit the same spot repeatedly. Mason could only see empty air at the impact point. There was a massive snap of discharge. Mason's suit died, his link to Carter gone. "Fuck me," he breathed. Mason looked into the room, unblinking. He didn't care his active camouflage was out. Everyone was looking at the same thing.

A perfect sphere of energy stood in the room. The floor looked cracked underneath it, as if pressed down by a massive weight. Lightning continued to arc from the box, feeding the sphere. The walls of the sphere softened until they were gone.

Mason could see a circle of desert sand in the middle of the room. Sunlight fell on it. *Sunlight ... but it's night here.* On the other side of the sphere, three people stood.

They hadn't been there before.

His link came back with a snap. "Mason!" Carter's voice was frantic. "Thank God, you're—"

"*Now*, Carter. Get Harry here now!"

The link hissed like a snake. Harry's icon appeared on Mason's overlay. Harry looked like he was about to get a happy on. "About goddam time."

Harry's dropship computer spoke over the link. "HALO insertion beginning on my mark. Distance to fall, eleven thousand meters. Time to impact, forty-seven seconds. Beginning burn, mark."

Mason stood. This wasn't a sniper kill and clean mission anymore. There were live assets at play. He slapped the rifle onto his back, then drew the SMGs. He clicked the suit into combat mode, the reactor grumbling in satisfaction.

Cherenkov blue flared through the rain from the winged falcon on Mason's back. He fired the SMGs at the skylight, falling like a burning star as he held the triggers down.

CHAPTER SEVENTEEN_

The dawn smiled, fingers of their tired red sun greeting them over desert sand. Laia shivered, huddling with Zacharies in the cold.

The Master held up a hand. "Come." He pointed to the sand. "Make a fire."

Zacharies looked around, the sand stretching desolate as far as they could see. "A fire? Master, there is no—"

A glare from the Master silenced him, Zacharies pulling knees close for warmth. He spared a glance for his sister.

"I can do it." Laia stood.

The Master glared, the folds of his hood dark against the dawn. "I didn't *ask* if you could do it."

"Yes, Master." She looked down, fingering the collar at her neck. The metal made it so hard to think, to focus. Laia held her hands up, then let them fall, her shoulders slumped.

The whip tumbled free in the Master's hand, tails touching the ground. They left small trails in the sand, like the passing of snakes. He looked to Zacharies. "And you will cook."

"Yes, Master." Her brother walked to the divan, unwrapping a small bundle. Zacharies freed a pot, dried fruit, and oatmeal. He didn't look at the whip.

Laia knew looking at the whip drew attention to it. It felt like a live thing, wanting to be used. Laia shuddered, tugging the collar again. "Master?"

He walked to her, bowing his head for a second. She felt the release, like a hand unclenched from her mind.

It would be hard, yes. But for just a moment, she was free. Free to use her gift, to see the world around her with other eyes, to call the light. Laia stretched her arm to the sand at her feet. She reached deep inside it with her gift. There was life in these tiny rocks. They remembered what it was to be the mighty castles of ancient empires, spires tall before her father's father's father had bowed beneath the master's whips.

"Come," she said. *Burn bright, show me your kingdom's power. One last time.* The sands shifted, a slight vibration.

The memory in the sands trembled in anticipation.

Fire sparked and spat, the stones remembering. Forgotten keeps roared a new memory to the dawn. The ghost of the mighty and tall rose, sand burning a bright recollection. They yawned, stretching one final time, glowing white with heat, before melting into glass.

She felt the collar's clutch once more, the lock back on her mind, the hand at her throat. Laia stumbled, exhausted in the dawn of a new day, and would have fallen into the molten sands at her feet if her brother hadn't caught her.

The Master looked at the sands at her feet, considering her exhaustion. "A pity." The whip dangled from his hand as he turned away. "Breakfast and be quick about it."

Zacharies helped her sit, then turned over the heat from the sands. Porridge steamed. He took care to prepare breakfast just so, but his eyes never left the Master, Laia seeing them smolder with a heat of their own.

○

Zacharies' back was torn and bleeding, the whip rearing again.

Laia sobbed. "Master, please!" She reached forward, then covered her head as the whip licked at her. The strands of old leather and metal slashed, the pain burning bright across her arm and her jaw. She cried out.

Her brother struggled, trying to get to his feet.

The Master spun to Zacharies, hand raised, fist clenched. Zacharies screamed, falling to one knee. "I do not like the way you look at me, boy. I will teach you respect. I will break it upon your body and work it on your mind."

The whip lashed Zacharies. His body spun, a piece of skin hanging loose at his shoulder. It glistened red. Sand clotted the wound.

Laia tried to stand, but the grip on her mind wouldn't allow it. Her legs felt like stone. Her master came to stand over her, one gloved finger tracing the cut at her jaw, then down her neck toward her small breasts.

"I do not wish to mark your face again, little one. Your ugliness would not please me in the evenings. But your mind?" He raised his hand, and the pain blazed bright behind her eyes, a red poker stabbing into her skull. She shrieked with the pain, falling. "I can leave you a vacant-eyed doe. I can burn the thoughts from your head, given enough time. And we have plenty of time."

The light of the old red sun walked its slow steps into the sky, unconcerned. *If only the angel would come! If he would drop once more, stepping onto the blasted circle in the desert... All this would stop.*

As if it had never been, the pain in her head vanished. Laia fell with the relief, retching.

The Master's head turned to the circle of blasted and crushed sand they'd pitched their small camp beside. "What...?" His voice trailed off, slaves forgotten.

Laia could feel it too, the sense of ... *something.* A pressure built. She saw Zacharies' hand reaching to the depression. Laia forced herself to go to him. He was bigger than her, and she was so tired, but she hauled him back from the perimeter. Her small footprints marked the sand as she staggered back.

The Master continued to ignore them, looking at the air above the cracked ground. He walked around the circle, steps careful and slow, his shadow leaning away as if afraid of the dim morning light.

"Something is coming." It wasn't clear who the Master spoke to. "It wants to come back. It was *here*."

Fear held Laia's heart. *No, please.* If the demon came back, not the angel...

A tiny grain of hope, smaller than the sands beneath her, kindled into life. The demon might have been here. It might have fought the angel. The demon could be running, in fear or pain.

Such hopes were dangerous.

A tiny star gleamed above the crushed sand and glass. Pressure continued to build, her ears popping. A bolt of lightning arced from the light, falling short of the circle's edge. It left a trace of red and yellow across her vision.

"Please, brother." Laia got her shoulder under Zacharies. "You must get up. You must be *ready*."

Zacharies looked at her, one eye swollen. She could feel his breath rattle as she held him. But he tried to get up. They rose together, unsteady, leaning against each other.

The lightning coiled and struck again.

It's trying to escape. It's a lion in a cage.

"The fury." Her voice was lost against the rage of noise. Laia squinted, pointing at the circle of light. "Brother! The angel!"

Zacharies looked at the sphere, one hand — *broken nails, broken bones* — held in front of his eyes. "It is the devil, Laia."

The Master walked to them. "The devil? No, slave. Something worse. Something much worse." He laughed, a deep sound from his belly.

The air snapped and popped, a blast of wind spitting sand away from the sphere. The lightning stopped, the three of them blinking in the silence. The air rippled. Through it they could see a room, the floor hard and real, solid stone. The desert's sand was gone. Laia saw four people through the newly-formed rent.

A star, blazing blue and white, fell to the ground on the other side. Wings of blue spread on its back. She could see the ground on the other side crack and fragment as it landed.

Wings of blue. The angel.

Laia grabbed her brother's arm, running toward the sphere. Her hand touched it, cool and quiet against her skin. She blinked, pushing through.

Fire burned around her, and she fell to the floor. Laia huddled over her brother.

Silence fell, and she looked up. She saw the angel's perfect boots, craftsmanship of the heavens. He stood in front of her. Laia looked up, seeing the blaze of its face against the black of the room. Force poured from it, terrible as the dawn, and she cowered in fear.

The Master stepped through behind her. He faced the angel. "You will kneel. You will kneel, or you will know pain beyond imagining." He raised a gloved hand, closing his fingers into a fist.

CHAPTER EIGHTEEN_

"I feel like I got my balls hanging way out here. You know what I mean?" Harry flexed his feet, Earth huddling below. City lights hid behind Seattle's ever-present clouds, whites and yellows only visible from the tallest corporate towers.

It was a nice view. And, blessed mercies, this side of the clouds he avoided acid rain. It played havoc with his chassis.

"You want me to be honest?" Lace coughed, the link crystal clear. Harry could hear a little smoker's hassle in her throatiness. *She might need to spend some time in the clinic.* "It might sting a little."

"I love your honesty, Lace. It's why we make such a good team."

"You don't have any balls," she said.

Harry winced. "I don't think you should be quite that honest. You might hurt my feelings."

"I'm not sure you've got feelings either. It's all in your head. Positive thinking, positive results, Fuentes." She tacked targets onto his overlay, pinpricks of red light waiting in the city far below.

"Jesus, that's a lot of dudes."

"Yeah, but they're all normals." Lace sounded bored, like she'd rather be watching paint dry. "Well, normal-*ish*. Not enforcer class."

"Tell me and again, be honest. Do you know what you're talking about? I don't think you've ever been in the field."

"I live vicariously through you." Lace didn't have to say, *it's all I've got left.* "They're easy targets for a big man like you."

The link hissed. Harry saw icons leave the overlay. "Hey. Did you just lose Carter and Mason?" He looked with the best optics money could buy at the city. The area Lace marked with targets darkened beneath the blanket of clouds. "What the hell is going on down there?"

"Wait one," she said, her voice flat. "Crap. They're gone. They're just—"

The link flared back, hard and sharp in Harry's mind. It lashed with static, Harry's overlay a confusion of crossed messages and errors.

"Now, Carter. Get Harry here now!" Mason sounded panicked, his icon on Harry's overlay flickering.

"They're back," said Lace.

"About goddamn time." Harry looked at the drop ship above him, holding steady in the cold, thin air. He shrugged his big metal shoulders, the drop harness creaking.

Harry initiated the burn.

The ship above him confirmed his orders, the AI speaking over the link. Her voice was quiet. It felt right with so little atmosphere. "HALO insertion beginning on my mark. Distance to fall, eleven thousand meters. Time to impact, forty-seven seconds. Beginning burn, mark."

He felt the sudden hard push of the fusion drive, fingers of fire blasting into space. The Gs felt like a fist slamming him toward the ground.

Harry let out a whoop. Whatever had happened before the accident—

The pain went beyond words. He was trying to scream, but his throat had burnt out, lungs pumping flames instead of air. The lattice thrashed, flailing, useless. He was stuck in his seat, the wheel pressing him into the burning plastic. His hand clawed the dash, fingers sloughing off like soft butter.

—it let him do this kind of shit, and it was nothing a norm could do.

"You still ... me?" Lace cut out, the link crackling against the burn of the drive. Harry felt the subtle shifting of the gyros holding him steady, his vision vibrating with the rockets. The red dots blurred, scan lines vibrating in his overlay.

"Sort of. You're breaking up. Can you scrub the signal?" Harry didn't need Lace for this part, but he'd need her later.

"On it." Lace tightened the link, target markers for the enemy clearing. His overlay gave Harry their likely loadouts.

"Are those assholes wearing sunglasses?" asked Harry.

"Looks like it. The Reed Interactive guys, anyway."

"What's with that?"

"Carter says they're robots."

"They're remotes," said Carter, cutting into the link. "Constructs. They're not *robots*. Look, it doesn't matter. How far out are you?"

Harry checked his overlay. "Thirty seconds. How bad is it?"

"I don't know." Carter sounded more cranky than usual. *Maybe she's stressed.* "Mason's in the middle of something. He doesn't usually talk to me when he's working."

Harry punched through the cloud deck, lightning crackling around him as he burned for the Earth. Underneath the clouds he fell through rain, lashing him as he dropped. Streaks of water ran across his chassis, blasting to mist as they passed through the rocket's trail of fire.

Time to get busy. Harry marked a van on the street within Reed's convoy. "Okay, Lace. I'm going in hot on that one." Rockets roared above him, his armored feet shuddering in the thickening atmosphere.

"Not Metatech first?" Lace sounded doubtful.

"You want to do this?"

"Yeah. Actually, yeah. I'd love to." She sounded wistful.

Christ, Harry, way to go. Why don't you just call her Hot Wheels while you're at it? "Sorry, Lace. You see—"

"It's okay. At least I've got nice rims. You're in a metal coffin."

"Metatech armor their vehicles. I don't want to hit one of those things." Harry's chassis was strong, but Metatech was mil-spec. Best not to test immovable objects and irresistible forces, especially when you were one of them.

The dropship's AI updated the link. "Initiating breaking burn in three, two, one, mark." The rocket above stuttered out, then the drive below lit. A line of fire lashed out, a torch cutting off the view below him.

The overlay continued to mark targets. *That's a lot of dudes. Mason, what have you got us into?*

He felt the force of the braking burn. If Harry still had teeth they'd have snapped shut. He tried to swallow, the old reflex still there, metal arms reaching out to steady him he plummeted.

"Overtime." Harry kicked the system on. He got her answering click over the link.

The overlay stuttered to white but still showed his descent speed. He slowed, but when he hit the van, going through to the tarmac below, he was doing just under thirty meters per second. His metal legs braced for the impact, but one hand still reached forward with monkey instinct to help with the impact.

The fall's shockwave blasted outward, the van exploding into a fireball, shrapnel tossing burning shards. Men standing near him were knocked from their feet as the ground bucked.

The sound was deafening, windows in the buildings around blasting inward. Harry stood, chassis causing the air to shimmer with heat. The harness on his back clanked and rattled as the weapon rails rotated over his shoulders.

"Game time." Harry switched his external PA system to *high* and *loud*. The lenses in his faceplate burned red. Harry leaned forward, flames from the van rising around him. "Under the Syndicate

Compact of 2087, Apsel Federate invokes its right to recover intellectual property and—"

A round impacted the front of his chassis, knocking him back a step. His overlay complained about *high-velocity ordnance*, highlighting a man who'd recovered his feet. Harry's overlay tagged him with Metatech's crossed saber logo. Harry's optics zoomed. *That asshole has a Metatech coilgun. A goddamn mil-spec coilgun.*

No point crying about it.

Before the man could finish cycling the weapon for a second shot, Harry fired his own coilgun. The force of the weapon shoved him back, chassis be damned, Harry stepping through the van's burning debris.

The man's torso exploded into red mist, his legs staggering before falling. Rain wicked the mist away.

Silence fell for a heartbeat of time. Reed men looked at each other, then at Harry. Metatech men looked at their fallen comrade, then at Harry.

Every fucker is looking at me. Awesome.

Everyone moved at once.

Harry stepped from the wreckage of the van, metal feet clawing up chunks of tarmac as he stepped onto the street. The cleats on his feet fired, driving pitons into the street, and he swiveled his torso to face the Reed contingent.

The plasma cannon mounted on his other shoulder hummed online. The reactor on his back lit, the Apsel falcon bright against the night. Falcon wings stretched blurred fingers of light against the shadowy buildings at his back.

Harry keyed a targeting solution, firing the cannon. Bolts of plasma roared across the street. Night turned to day as cars shattered and melted, Reed operatives turning into human torches, stumbling before falling forward.

There's some weird shit right there. None of them screamed. *Still. Not my circus. Not my monkeys.*

His coilgun spun over his shoulder, firing rounds down the street.

The noise was like God's jackhammer, white lines tracing through the air. The coilgun tore through machines and bodies alike, super-heating metal and destroying flesh.

Another coilgun round hit the side of his plasma cannon, shearing it from the harness. Harry stumbled as one of his cleated feet tore loose. He let his torso swivel with the impact, his own coilgun coming over his shoulder toward the Metatech line. The asshole who'd shot him was behind an armored van. Harry fired, the stream of coilgun rounds shearing the vehicle in half, turning the man's body into mist and memory.

Harry laughed, releasing his remaining pitons. He walked down the street, the coilgun hammering the dark as small arms fire rattled against his chassis. Harry stepped through a burning vehicle, snatching a Reed man from the ground. The man shouted, but Harry slapped his hands together, pulping the body in an instant.

The coilgun ran dry. Harry blew the harness bolts, metal frame spinning into the night. He held one of his arms out, the fingers articulating back, exposing the fusion cannon inside. The reactor on his back flared like the sun, and a stream of white fire carved a molten track through tarmac, vehicles, and enemy syndicate assets.

He wondered how Mason was doing and glanced at *The Hole*.

No news was good news, right?

CHAPTER NINETEEN_

The back of *The Hole* was quiet. Dark. Almost, if Sadie didn't think about it too much, *safe*. After she played, she came back here. To relax. To celebrate.

To fight with Aldo Vast.

Sadie tried to muster anger but came up with contempt. "That's your problem. You're an asshole."

"Hey, screw you." Aldo paced. "I haven't done anything—"

"Yeah, you have."

"Like what? Name one thing." Aldo's voice rose, and he pointed a finger at Sadie. *God, I hate it when he points.* "Come on, tell me. What have I done that's so bad?"

She looked at his finger stabbing the air. Sadie noted how his movements had too much jank to them. Wrong drugs, or wrong dose, it didn't matter. Aldo was just *wrong*. She turned to the mirror. Her fingers found lipstick on autopilot. Sadie pursed her lips at her reflection. "How about Janice? That'll do for a start."

"Jan ... what?" She could see his mouth hanging open in the mirror.

"Janice. You know her." Sadie turned to face him, lipstick in one hand. The other hand chopped out to just over her own shoulder height. "She's about this tall. Blond hair. Pretty, if you like that kind of thing. Oh, shit. That's right. She plays bass in our band, too. That's where you may have seen her."

"What?" said Aldo.

Sadie threw the lipstick onto the dressing table. "You've been fucking her."

"I—"

"I don't even care." She picked a different color, a darker shade, red so twisted it was almost black. "Because I know I don't love you anymore."

"Who told you I was ... Janice and I were...?" Aldo's voice quietened to a stillness, anger leeching it dry and bare. "I'll kill them."

Sadie shrugged. "Janice."

"Janice told you?"

"She didn't mean to, of course." Sadie picked up a brush, teasing her hair. "Or, she did."

"She did, or she didn't, Sadie." Aldo's Adams apple bobbed like a drunk goldfish. "Look, stop screwing around, and just play a straight song. We can talk this out—"

"She asked how our breakup was. How I felt." Sadie leaned toward the mirror. The damn lights were useless. "Trying to make sure there were no hard feelings."

"Janice wouldn't—"

"That's what I thought." Sadie turned to face him. "You're a user and a taker, Aldo Vast. I loved you once, but you stopped the music."

Aldo's hands clenched. "This is bullshit. You've got it all wrong. Janice, she's trying to get between us—"

"Why would she do that? You're already fucking her!" Sadie's voice rose at the end toward a scream, then she got a hold on it. "Just get the fuck out."

"We're playing tonight."

"I can play without a drummer." Sadie waved her hand at the door, turning away from Aldo. "I don't need a drummer. Go screw Janice some more."

She saw him come up behind her, the mirror showing the war of anger and sadness in him. Aldo touched her arm. Sadie shook it off. His lips twisted into something ugly as anger won. Aldo grabbed Sadie, spinning her around.

"Now you listen, Freeman." Drug wizened he might be, but he was still stronger than her. Aldo pulled her close. Sadie could see the light glint in his eyes. "You and me, we're not done."

She shoved him. He grabbed her with his other hand. They stumbled, rocking back against the dresser, and one of her wrists slipped free, her elbow clipping him in the jaw. It wasn't much of a hit. She hadn't even *meant* to strike him. But there was no mistaking how the music changed, his eyes going flat and dead centimeters from her face.

Aldo brought his hand against her face with a crack. Sadie's head snapped back, smashing into the mirror. She tasted salt and copper and spat red in his face.

"You bitch!" he yelled, anger wild and free. Aldo's hand clenched into a fist, and he punched her in the face. Pain bloomed in one of her eyes. The force knocked her free from his grip as she fell.

Sadie couldn't see right, the eye he'd hit refusing to focus. She groped for her bag, managing to slip a hand through the strap just as Aldo's hand closed on her hair.

She screamed as he pulled her upright. Aldo twisted her head around, driving a fist into her stomach. He raved. Sadie couldn't make sense of his words. Her head rang as Aldo hit her again, a sound without end.

Had she been hit? How many times? Sadie couldn't remember. Her good eye found the bag she held. Sadie's fingers closed around the grip of her small, black taser. When Aldo twisted her to face him, she fired.

His eyes bulged, and he bit his own tongue as his throat locked tight. Aldo didn't make a sound, falling with a thump she felt rather than heard.

Sadie spat blood, spatters hitting the floor. She turned her head, neck stiff. Sadie's jaw clicked. She looked at the bag, then to the taser in her other hand. The crossed sabers of the Metatech logo were above the charging lights of the weapon, red marching to green again. Sadie backed into the mirror, turning to see her face.

She looked away. Maybe she wouldn't play tonight. Her vision wandered the room until she saw Aldo. He groaned, his movements stiff. Her hearing came back, and the first thing she heard was Aldo mewling like a dying cow.

The second thing she heard was the fury of the gods.

From the front of *The Hole*, it sounded like the bar had been struck by lightning. The boom was followed by shattering glass, the ground shaking.

Sadie stumbled into the dresser. She threw a hand out, cutting herself on the broken mirror. Sadie looked at the bright red line on her hand, then at Aldo, and finally at the door.

Fuckit. She wasn't playing tonight anyway. No sense staying in the dressing room. She'd just want to kick Aldo. Her hand found the doorknob as if by magic, and she started a slow shuffle toward the front of the bar.

The wall was cool against her face. Sadie leaned on it, eyes closed. One of them was swollen shut, and she needed to rest the other one.

She tried to push herself up, but her body felt heavy. Sadie couldn't think straight. *Where am I? Why am I out here?*

Open your eyes.

It seemed so hard. Sadie breathed, feeling something loose in her jaw. She swallowed blood, then grunted her one good eye open. The wall in front of her was ordinary, a mix of graffiti and blood.

Blood? Whose blood is that? Her hand explored her face. Sadie winced. Her hand came away, sticky and red. *Why can't I open my other eye?*

A door slammed open to her right, and she turned to look. A man crashed into the corridor. He had a fragment of something shiny, something sharp—

A broken mirror. My mirror. Aldo broke my mirror.

—held in his hand. He spun, seeing her. Something nasty worked its way from his eyes to his lips, a smile twisting them.

"You *bitch*. You fucking bitch." He moved toward her, listing to his left, knocking into the wall.

Sadie drew a breath. She couldn't remember where she was going. Sadie used to have a weapon, but she didn't know where it was.

Run. You've got to run.

She turned away from Aldo and ran down the corridor.

CHAPTER TWENTY

O vertime.

Movement slowed to treacle's lethargic pace, the light bleached out. Mason dropped toward the floor, the SMGs firing as he fell. Glass shimmered and spun around him, the moment held in overtime's close embrace.

One syndicate agent stood near where he would land, hand already reaching into his jacket. *Metatech*. Mason's overlay tracked the motion, marking *MT* above the man's head. It stenciled *UNKNOWN* next to the weapon he drew.

A second man stood by the bar, sunglasses turning up as Mason fell. *Reed*. The agent's head turned before Mason finished punching through the skylight. The overlay marked him as *RI* and noted the sidearm leaving his jacket as *LOW THREAT*.

Mason turned his attention to Apsel's interests. *Haraway*.

She stood, a fly in amber, motions slow in the real. He could see the shock start to move across her face. Mason could ignore her for the moment. She had no weapon, and no one was shooting at her.

He felt the tremble of the reactor at his back as he dropped. Status icons painted his overlay with green as the armor's systems came online. He landed in a crouch as glass shattered in a ring around him. The concrete floor of *The Hole* cracked as one of his knees hit. Mason lost grip on one of his SMGs. He stood as Metatech's weapon cleared his holster.

"I'm real sorry about this," he sent to Metatech as the link popped and cracked between them. The man's sidearm had almost swung to bear as Mason's fist connected with his jaw. The inductive taser loop in the gauntlet fired, and the man tumbled to the floor, sidearm falling away.

Mason spun toward the Reed man, the taser system's icon on his overlay showing *ready to rock* already. Reed fired on Mason. The impact rocked him as the round hit his helmet. Mason stumbled back.

His overlay updated, replacing LOW THREAT with IMME-DIATE THREAT. Mason smiled, and he extended his free hand toward Reed. He lit the magnetic coils in the glove, and the agent's gun spun from his hand, sticking to Mason's palm. The bar's taps groaned, and Mason felt pulled toward them. He clicked the coils off, Reed's weapon dropping to the ground.

Overtime sloughed away. Mason clicked his armor's PA system on. He swallowed the taste of oranges and almonds, then turned to Haraway. "Jenni Haraway, you are under investigation for theft of Apsel Federate technologies. Under the termination clause in your contract, you are—"

Mason saw real fear in her eyes. "Please. You don't understand. They have—"

"—subject to assessment and revocation of that selfsame contract." Mason glanced at Reed, then back to Haraway. "Under the subclass B of that same paragraph, if you're found to have received monetary or other gain by brokering that technology to another agency, organization, or department, the termination clause can be deemed ... final." Mason picked up his fallen SMG, sighing. "Gairovald is very angry, Jenni."

She swallowed, glancing at the sphere that hung in the air. "Do you ... do you know what this is?"

Mason pointed the SMG at her. "I'd have to be honest and say I don't care." The Reed agent worked his way along the bar but made no move to interfere. Mason let his armor track the man, keeping his attention on Haraway. "Do you have any items to issue in your defense?"

"Yes," she said, looking at her feet. Mason saw *guilt* and *pain*, gone as quickly as sun in winter. "This whole situation is sublime."

"Mason," said Carter, the link edged with static.

Haraway continued. "It's a full clusterfuck."

"Mason," urged Carter. "Shoot her. Shoot her now. The mission, Mason."

"What you need to know is that I'm under a code of parlay. The Federate knows." Haraway peered at Mason, as if able to see inside his visor. "Do you know what I'm saying?"

Carter sighed. "Mason, I've got a problem. Don't shoot Haraway."

"Wait, what?" Mason's SMG had Haraway dead to rights. "I've got a bit of a situation here."

"Gairovald is very explicit. He's said to extend Haraway every assistance."

"Gairovald?" Mason looked at the Reed man, then at Haraway. "He said that?"

"New mission," said Carter. "New rules. I just work here, okay? No one tells me shit. It just came through. Extend all assistance to Haraway."

"That's it? Extend all assistance? What the blue fuck does that mean?"

"It means you gargle balls if you have to. Get her out of there."

Mason spoke over the PA system. "There has been a development."

"There has?" Haraway smoothed her hands on her pants.

"Doctor, I've been asked to extend you every assistance." Mason swung the SMG toward the Reed man. "And you, asshole, need to stop moving around."

Reed smiled but stopped walking. "Of course."

Haraway looked at the sphere, then back to Mason. "Okay. What we need—"

Two figures stumbled from the sphere, a young man and a younger woman. The girl was holding the boy up, and they collapsed to the ground. Mason's optics mapped over them, highlighting *superficial wounds* before updating with *malnutrition bordering on starvation. What the hell are they wearing?* Their clothes bordered on rags.

Haraway looked to be having a moment. "Jesus *Christ.*"

Mason turned to the two on the floor. "Orders, Haraway? I need a mission statement."

"Help them. God, look at them."

Mason stepped toward them, boots crunching on broken glass. The girl looked at him before cowering away in fear. A third person, a man with no obvious injuries or starvation, stepped through the sphere.

The man looked into Mason's visor, saying something, the language hard. Mason's overlay cycled, *NO LINGUISTIC MATCH* flashing in the corner of his vision. The man's hand raised into a fist.

Mason raised an SMG. "Okay, sparky, chill out. You need to—"

The pain that flared in his skull was like nothing he'd felt before. It was an amalgam of being cut, burned, and crushed. He cried out, falling to one knee, SMGs clattering to the ground. Mason grabbed the sides of his helmet, screaming as something red and angry pounded inside his skull.

The impact as Harry hit the street outside rocked the bar, windows exploding a deadly rain of glass inside. The man in front of Mason stumbled, pain gone. Mason looked at the girl, his face right in front of hers. *That is raw terror.*

She said something, *NO LINGUISTIC MATCH* flashing on the overlay again. The man started to regain his balance. Mason's lattice took over, shoving him to his feet, overtime falling into place. The man's eyes widened in what would probably become surprise if Mason left it long enough. The rest of the asshole's face was hidden, a wrap — *a keffiyeh? shemagh?* — covering everything below the eyes.

The pain hit again, but the lattice twisted and bunched. Mason's hand smashed out, connecting with the man's jaw, the induction taser firing. The pain dropped as the man crumpled. Mason stood, looking at the girl. He felt pretty good about how things turned out as Reed smashed a chair against his back.

The armor took most of the blow, but he had to take a step to catch his balance. Mason turned his visor toward Reed, the blue of its eyepieces flaring. Mason swung a fist at the man's face, but Reed ducked away.

Mason twisted his neck, spine popping. "That wasn't very professional." He heard Harry saying something outside, then the heavy sound of a coilgun firing, the bass rough edges of a plasma cannon mixed in for good measure. *At least someone's having a good time.*

Reed cocked his head. It was hard to get a read on the man through the sunglasses. "You've got no idea what you've got here." The words came over the link, the other man in overtime as well. An explosion came from the street, firelight flickering through broken windows.

Mason looked at the crate, Apsel falcon clear on the side. "Looks like it's some of our shit, doesn't it?"

"Mason, you need to destroy the crate and get Haraway out." Carter's voice was flat with tension.

"What about this asshole?"

"It's a remote." There wasn't room in the stretched moment of overtime for much, but he was sure she was pissed about something. "Do whatever you like."

Mason took a knee, reaching for his rifle. Reed was already moving, running toward the bar, his steps looking slow against the overtime.

The rifle's stock against his shoulder, Mason fired three shots. Reed stumbled at the first, jerked and twisted at the second, and then fell at the third. The body skidded across the concrete, a wet stain of red following.

His lattice nudged at him, tired and sluggish. He shrugged it off, but dropped the overtime, his mouth flooding with the taste of chocolate. Mason racked the rifle, then collected his SMGs. He checked the weapons, locking them in place on his belt.

Mason looked at the girl and boy at his feet. The girl's eyes were wide, her mouth open. The boy — maybe more than a boy, a late teen — was out, unconscious or dead. *Not much you can do about either. The mission.*

His feet crunched against glass on the floor as he walked to Haraway. "We need to clear the area."

"Mason Floyd." Haraway nodded, like she remembered him from somewhere. Maybe she did. He'd cleaned enough of her division's dirty laundry. "Help me pack this up."

Mason laughed, the PA system roughing the edges of it. "I'm not a porter."

"But you've got to—"

"I've got to keep you breathing. I've got to make sure Federate tech doesn't fall into rival syndicate hands. Pack your own bags."

Her eyes widened a moment before he heard a sharp intake of breath. Mason spun to see Reed wrestling with the girl. The syndicate agent had managed to pull the boy from her and was hustling him toward the door. The girl was trying to stop Reed, but she was a kid and he was a super-enhanced killing machine. Hardly seemed fair.

"You don't fucking die, do you?" Mason pulled an SMG from his belt. "You're like a zombie robot."

The girl turned at Mason's voice. Reed pushed her away. Her heel snagged, and she tumbled. *Way to go, asshat.*

Reed held the boy in front of him as a human shield, smiling. Too-bright blood seeped from his lips. "Low-risk acquisitions, Apsel. It's the way of the future." His sunglasses were gone.

"What's wrong with your eyes?" Mason squatted next to the girl. He helped her up, then steered her behind him toward Haraway. "Tech still a bit janky?"

Reed spat on the ground, red and wet. "It's not productionized yet."

"You look cross-eyed." Mason shrugged. "Whatever. You're not making it out that door."

Reed shook the boy, the kid's head lolling. *Out like a light.* "You going to stop me? I've got quality bargaining capability here."

"There's a total conversion outside. He'll stop you."

"No, he won't." Reed shook his head. "If I see an enforcer when I walk outside, this kid'll be turned into a set of parts."

"Why do I care?" Mason scanned the room. *Limited options.*

"I heard the doctor. New mission, right Apsel? This way, you still get to *try* to collect on your orders. You won't succeed, but you can give it your best shot." Reed backed through the bar with the boy, making for the door.

"Carter." Mason's link was cluttered with static. "Get Harry out."

"On it." The link snapped like a flag in wind at her words. "How you going to play this?"

"No clue. Getting two kids and a wizard out wasn't part of the original mission brief."

"Wizard?"

"Later." To the Reed man, Mason said, "Harry's leaving."

"Harry's the enforcer?"

"No, he's a circus clown. Yes, he's the enforcer."

"You talk big, Apsel, for a man with limited options."

Mason looked at the sphere still glowing in the air. He glanced behind, where Haraway held the girl. "Maybe. But I've recovered all the assets from the original brief. This? Maybe it'll affect the percentage of my bonus, but that's probably negotiable."

Metatech's gun pressed against the side of Reed's head, firing. The remote's head sprayed into fragments, and Metatech grabbed the boy before he could fall.

"Thanks." Mason lowered his SMG. "Sorry about the taser."

"Don't thank me," said Metatech, holding the boy in front of him like a shield. "Same deal. I'm out with the kid."

"That's just super," said Mason. *I love how this day is turning out.* He turned to Haraway. "Out the back."

The girl in her arms struggled, trying to break free. Mason crouched in front of her, holding up a hand. He lowered the PA system to a whisper. "Not like this. There will be another time."

Mason had no idea if she understood him, but she stopped struggling with Haraway. Mason nodded, his armor's blue eyepieces reflected sparks in her eyes. He stood, facing Metatech. Mason keyed the link to Carter. "Is Harry gone?"

"Harry is pissed."

"But is he gone?"

"Maybe." Carter's voice held the certainty of sand. "He hasn't stopped swearing at me."

Mason turned the PA up. "Okay, Metatech. You're clear out the front."

"It's just business," said Metatech. His face crinkled, and it took Mason a moment to place the expression.

He looks sad. How about them apples?

"It's always business," growled Mason. "I'll be seeing you real soon."

They looked at each other before Metatech gave a single nod. He shouldered the kid, jogging for the door. Mason stepped to the Apsel crate, unclipping a small explosive device from his belt.

"What are you doing?" said Haraway.

"Clearing the scene." Mason dropped the explosive into the crate. "Back door. Go."

Haraway gaped at Mason. "You don't know what that's going to do to—"

"No," agreed Mason. "We've got about fifteen seconds before we find out. I'd recommend running, doc."

"There are still enemy syndicate representatives holding at the rear of the building, Mason," said Carter. "What's your play?"

Mason tossed a glance at the unconscious man sprawled on the ground, shemagh over half his face. He looked over at where Eckers had gone to ground behind the bar. Mason replayed Haraway's instructions on his overlay, the woman etched against the top right of his vision.

I need a mission statement.

Help them. God, look at them.

Mason didn't answer Carter, running for the door behind Haraway and the girl. He didn't look back at the sphere, shifting in the air, lightning sliding across its surface in uneven bolts. He saw Bernie Eckers make his way to the asshole who'd come through the gate with the kids, dragging him behind the bar.

Neither of them was the mission. The mission was Haraway, the girl, and the boy. One thing at a time.

Mason ran past Haraway. Doors marked the walls to the left and right of the corridor. "Stay close, doc. But stay behind me." The sprinklers in the ceiling sprayed water, slicking his armor, the white coming clean as the dust washed free. Haraway's hair plastered to her head. She held the girl close to her.

The explosion from the bar rocked them sideways. Mason steadied himself against the wall. The timed charge had gone off, Apsel's stolen tech gone. *That's part one of the mission brief put to bed.*

"Keep a hold on her." Mason risked a look at the girl. Her eyes were trying to look at everything at once. The kid had something Latin in her under all the dirt and grime. "I'm going to get us out, but you need to help me. Know how to use one of these?"

He offered her an SMG, grip first. Haraway shook her head. Mason sighed. "Like I said, stay on my six."

"Six?"

"Do you not watch movies?" Mason started walking, SMG pointed in front. His overlay chattered to itself, painting doors, the

suit including a thermal map of the rooms. *Where is everyone?*
"There's no one here. They've all gone."

"Eckers said he was going to clear the place out. For the..."
Haraway trailed off, sounding like she needed a drink more than any
other human alive.

"For the what?"

"It doesn't matter," she said.

Mason frowned. *The mission. That's what you get paid for.* He
moved down the corridor, thermal playing out cold and empty rooms
in blue. A haze of red worked its way behind a door at the end of the
corridor, and Mason switched his optics to visible light.

A woman stumbled through the door. Her hair slicked against her
head, eyeliner running dirty tears down her face. *Her. From the bar,
before.* She looked like she'd been in the shit, one eye swollen shut.
She stared at the three of them, dazed. Mason's optics tracked her,
overlay updating. *Facial bruising. Dilated pupils, most likely a
concussion.*

"Hey," he said, the PA system raised loud enough to be clear, but
not so loud as to terrify. "You know where the back door is?"

The woman's eyes swept past them, then back to the door she'd
entered through. A shaky hand pulled it shut, and she backed toward
Mason, Haraway, and the girl.

"Mason." Carter still sounded stressed. "Mason, you need to get
out. Reed are staging a deployment at the front."

"Metatech?"

"Pretty sure he got clear."

Mason walked to the woman. He took one of her arms. She
looked at him, as if seeing him for the first time. Her lips were shiny
and wet from the sprinklers. "Who the fuck are you?"

The door she'd closed yanked open, a man coming through. Long
greasy hair matted his head. He held a fragment of something sharp
and silver, the edges of his hands cut and bleeding around it. "Bitch,
I've got you now."

Mason smiled. *This asshole.* "Excuse me," he said to the woman, stepping around her.

The man looked at Mason, taking a step back. His eyes flicked to the Apsel falcon on Mason's armor. "This doesn't involve you, company man."

"Fair enough. Do you know a back way out of here?"

"Yeah," said the asshole.

"Where is it?"

"Oh," the asshole turned toward the door he'd come in through, "through there, take the second door on your left. You'll find a room where you can go fuck yourself."

"Okay." Mason pointed an SMGs at the asshole's left leg. He pulled the trigger, the weapon roaring. Cords stood out on the man's neck as he screamed, a high-pitched sound. Both his hands went to grab his leg, the fragment of mirror falling forgotten. He slid to the ground, the wall behind him stained black and red.

The woman looked at the man on the ground. "I know a way out."

"You do?" said Mason. "Look, I don't want to rush you, but—"

"I can't quite..." She stepped up, put her hands against the wall, and kicked the man on the ground in the stomach once, twice, three times. She breathed heavy after that, unsteady on her feet, but her eye was clear as she looked at Mason. "I remember, now. It's through here."

CHAPTER TWENTY-ONE

J ulian stood in *The Hole*, taking it in.

The floor was scorched where the ball of lightning dropped three strangers into their midst. The bar looked like a pile of matchsticks, shattered glass resting amongst the wreckage. Whatever Apsel had dropped in the case did a number on this place. They'd find nothing here worth salvaging. *The technical term is 'proper fucked.'*

He took a pull from his cigarette. The tip of the Camel flared, as if sharing his anger. Julian glanced at the hole in the floor where the Federate's box had stood. The concrete rim still glowed where the charge exploded. Whatever device their agent used was burning a channel into the Earth. It smoldered three stories deep.

Julian wouldn't climb in to check on whether there was anything worth saving. *Someone on a lower pay grade can do that.* Heat roiled from the pit, the air dancing above it.

Men and women swarmed around him. Heavy light stands stood, illuminating the bar. Drones flitted through the air, stabs of red and blue lasing out to map the scene. Rain lashed and howled outside the building, gusts blowing water in through the hole in the roof. Julian flicked ash from the end of his cigarette, raising a hand to adjust his sunglasses. He walked to the body of his last remote. *Those fuckers blew its head clean off.*

He wasn't sure how the Apsel agent managed that. One minute, Julian had been about to get away free and clear, a new acquisition for Reed Interactive held close. The value of that acquisition was questionable, bought at a significant cost in vehicles and remotes. At least Metatech were paying the same bill.

It wasn't clean for any of them, even Apsel. They'd be scrutinizing their local operation, trying to plug a leak. That meant a little breathing room out on the streets. Metatech would want their percentage too, but Julian couldn't even find their operative's body.

Of course. Julian had been shot by Metatech, not Apsel. He noted that on his internal ledger, adjusted his tie, and nudged his downed remote. "We need to make these stronger."

"Sir?" A tech paused beside him.

"The remotes." Julian pointed with his cigarette. "They don't hold up in the field."

The tech looked at him, then down at the headless remote. "I ... see. I'll put it in the report."

"Be sure you do." Julian dismissed the man, moving to the small huddle of people around Eckers. He pushed through to stand before the fat man. Eckers shied away from Julian, voice drying up from whatever lies he'd been dropping like coins into a wishing well.

Near Eckers lay another man, silver recovery blanket wrapped around him like a shroud. His shemagh had been removed, revealing a face that could only be described as classically handsome. He was free of any clinic enhancements. A scan had shown him to be an illegal without augments of any kind.

Time enough for him when he wakes up.

"Mr. Eckers." Julian smoothed his tie. "It's so good to see you again."

"Uh," offered Eckers. It was a pretty good start, considering his circumstances. Surrounded by syndicate people, an agent in front of him, Julian felt a tiny shred of respect the other man hadn't tried running away.

"I'm curious about something." Julian swept his arm, encompassing the ruins of the bar. "We came here to negotiate in good faith. To purchase something from you, and I quote, worth 'millions.'"

"That's right." Eckers made to stand.

Julian pushed him back down. "There's one small problem."

"A problem?"

"The problem is simple." Julian smiled, showing perfect white teeth. "We've *paid* millions. Vehicles. Remotes. Let's not talk about the billable rate of all these people. We've paid, Mr. Eckers. We've paid a lot."

"But—"

"The problem is we've paid a lot and have nothing to show for it. Reed Interactive is not the most militaristic of the syndicates. You know this. We deal in ... softer services."

"It wasn't—"

"But rest assured, Bernie — may I call you Bernie? Rest assured, Bernie, that we will either have what we've paid for, or you will never be seen again." Julian flicked a speck of dust from the sleeve of his suit, then leaned close to Eckers. "Do you understand what I'm saying to you?"

Eckers sneezed, and Julian drew back. Old flesh habits died hard; it's not like the remote could catch anything from Eckers, or anyone else.

"I been trying to tell these assholes," Eckers nodded to the small group around him, "we were set up."

"Apsel knew," said Julian. "They knew, and they sent a recovery team."

"Hey, that's not on me." Eckers stood. "Look what they did to my place. That shit's on you." He pointed at Julian's chest.

Julian looked down at the finger, then back to Eckers. "It's on us? I'm interested to see where you're going with this."

"I know who I told about this meet," said the fat man. "I told exactly two assholes. You and that other clown—"

"Metatech. You told us and Metatech."

"Yeah," said Eckers. "So, the leak's with you."

"That's an interesting theory," said Julian. "I have another. Would you like to hear it?"

"Whatever." Eckers shrugged. "You got a smoke?"

Julian offered the Camels to Eckers, lighting one. "Okay, Bernie. Here's my theory. You told Reed and Metatech you had Apsel tech to sell."

"Yeah," said Eckers. "Because I did."

"Sure." Julian spread his hands. "But what if — and this is hypothetical, of course — you only *pretended* to have Apsel tech to sell?"

Eckers looked over his cigarette. "I'm not sure I follow, company man."

"What if this was all a pretty interesting ruse from Apsel? Take out rival syndicate resources and create a diversion?"

"A diversion? Have you seen my fucking bar?"

"Yes." Julian nodded. "I've also seen destroyed assets outside of a *significantly* higher value. Do you understand my position?"

Eckers took a long drag on the Camel. "I'll play along. What do you think this was a diversion for, company man?"

Julian grabbed the front of Eckers' jacket, jerking the fat man closer. "We'll find out." He put his foot behind Eckers' ankle, sweeping the man to the floor. The breath shot out of the fat man as he fell. Julian grabbed a chair, slamming the legs around Eckers's shoulders, a cross strut pressed against the man's throat. Julian straddled the chair, looking at Eckers while the man thrashed. He took a pull from his cigarette. "Bernie, there are two ways this can go."

Eckers continued to flail, veins on his neck standing out. He gagged.

"See, Bernie, the two ways are like this. First way, I find out what's going on here, and you and I part as friends. Comrades in action, with a common story to tell our kids." Julian drew on his cigarette again. "The second is only good for one of us. I leave here with an unpleasant story to tell my kids. You leave here in a box, and no one cries at your funeral because they don't even know you've died. You just disappear." Julian leaned forward. Ecker's lips turned blue. "Am I being fairly clear?"

Someone to Julian's right spoke, but he couldn't understand the words. *NO LINGUISTIC MATCH* appeared on his overlay. The asshole with the shemagh had woken up. He looked at Julian as if he expected the syndicate agent to say something.

"You're in luck," said Julian. "I've got someone else to talk to as well. I'll need to split my attention between you two." He stood, pulling the chair from the fat man's throat. Eckers gasped a lungful of air as Julian turned to the other man. "Hi. I'm a representative from Reed Interactive, and we're quite curious about the events of this evening."

The other man stood, tightening his shemagh as he glared at Julian. He spoke again, his tone angry and commanding. Julian flicked his cigarette butt away. "I understand you're confused. You don't know why the evening turned out this way. In that regard, we're in the same boat. Ships on the same sea, if you like."

The man took a step toward Julian, his eyes narrowed. He said something short and sharp in his no-linguistic-match language, breath puffing the front of the shemagh as he raised a hand.

Curious. Julian offered the man a cigarette, noting how the asshole's eyes widened in surprise or shock. "You don't smoke?" Julian shrugged, lighting a Camel for himself. He blew smoke into the other man's face. "You should give it a try."

The other man blinked, coughed, then took a step back. The storm howled outside, rain finding its way in through the hole in the roof and the blasted windows. A couple of techs swore. Julian ignored them, watching as the man raised his hand again.

Eckers howled. Men and women around the room clawed at their heads, screaming. Julian looked around, then back at the asshole. His eyes were savage but widened when they saw Julian still standing.

"Ah, you didn't expect that, did you?" Julian listened for a moment longer to the screaming before slamming a fist into the man's stomach. He dropped like a sack of meal as the air went out of him. Julian drew on the cigarette before stamping down on the man's hand. There was the crunch of bone, and the man cried out.

Julian leaned forward. "I'm not really here. Whatever meat-based shit you're trying to pull? We'll work it out. It's the kind of tech Reed is interested in. But first? It's time for some education."

A tech staggered close, hand to his head. "Sir," he wheezed.

Julian turned. "Can't you see I'm working?"

"Yes, sir. But they're not." The tech jerked a thumb at a group who were supposed to be working by the windows. Cracked and broken glass above them let the rain inside. Three men, two women. All were standing dumb as stones. *More curious.* Julian pulled out his sidearm. "Clear the room."

"Sir?"

"The room. Clear it."

The tech nodded. People were moving as orders passed over the link. They hurried outside, huddling against the rain. Julian walked to the five people near the window. "Hey, assholes. You're not getting paid by the hour. Get back to work."

None of them moved. Their eyes were blank, staring into space. Julian waved his hand in front of a woman's face. Her eyes didn't track.

A man to his left twitched, looking at Julian. He tried to grab the agent, but the lattice pulled Julian aside. He shot the man in the head, pulpy red spraying the wall. The body dropped. The other four turned as one to Julian. They shambled forward. "Eckers," called Julian.

Eckers stood behind the asshole with the shemagh. "You know how I said the rain was in the box?"

"Yeah." Julian pushed a woman back. He hated killing company assets. It had a small but statistically relevant negative effect on his bonus. *Still, you don't have to kill them.* He raised the sidearm again, shooting her in each leg. She dropped without the usual scream he'd expected, trying to claw toward him. It bore further examination.

Best keep another alive too. He shot a man in the legs, eying up the remaining two. Julian shrugged then shot them each once in the head. The two left alive continued to drag themselves across the floor. Julian walked back to the man from the sphere, looming over him. "What did you do to my people, asshole?" The man on the ground grinned through the pain of his broken hand as he spoke. *NO LINGUISTIC MATCH* flashed on Julian's overlay again. "For crying out loud."

From outside, someone yelled in alarm. A woman screamed. There was a shot, then another, followed by the bass roar of a plasma weapon.

Julian looked at Eckers. "Don't move. I'm going to check this out."

"Sure." Eckers looked at the man on the ground, massaging his throat.

Julian walked to the door, opening it. Rain lashed the street. The men and women of his team clawed at each other as the wind howled. A woman near a vehicle fired her plasma rifle into the press of chaos.

It was a lot to take in.

Julian stepped into the rain, raising his sidearm. He shot the woman with the plasma cannon, her head exploding into ruin. The lattice pulled him hard to the left, a shotgun blast hitting the wall where he'd been standing. Julian kept firing until his weapon ran dry, then ejected the magazine, slapping in another one. He grabbed a screaming, gibbering man who ran at him, fingers clawing Julian's face. The skin of his remote unmarked, Julian threw the man into the press of bodies.

He keyed his uplink. "I'm going to need another team. And a Psych unit." Julian turned away from the madness of the street, returning to the bar. He locked the door behind him.

The asshole with the shemagh grinned at Julian. The grin fell away as Julian walked to him, reaching for the chair he'd used on Eckers. "We've got about ten minutes until the second team arrives." Julian hauled the asshole into the chair. "Let's see whether we can find common ground in that time, shall we?"

CHAPTER TWENTY-TWO_

The light stabbing at Sadie's eyes felt like a physical thing. A knife, right into her brain. She wanted to throw up as constant motion jarred her. Sadie was in what looked like a van. The feeling of nausea grew, raging like a dragon, and she almost retched.

Instead, Sadie said, "Get that thing the fuck out of my face." The light drew away. It was replaced by a woman, blond hair around a too-pretty face. Sadie turned away, coughing. *Company woman.* "You got a cigarette?"

The company woman frowned. "You've got a concussion. I hardly think—"

"You a doctor?" The vehicle bounced.

Surprise crossed the woman's face, like she was used to people knowing who or what she was. "No."

"Okay then. You got a cigarette?" Sadie rubbed her face, pulling her hand back with a hiss of pain. What the hell?

Aldo grabbed her face, smashing her into the mirror. Glass fell away behind her, and she tumbled to the floor.

"Fuck." Sadie spat as she remembered, but the taste of Aldo Vast wouldn't leave.

"What is it?" asked the woman.

"I left my guitar back there." Sadie's palms itched to hold it. She rubbed them against her leather pants. "How you getting on with that cigarette?"

The woman turned away, a hint of a smile about her. Voices came from the front of the vehicle. Someone familiar.

Do you know a back way out of here?

I can remember now.

Someone *company*. She could remember what he looked like, but not his name. Sadie touched her face again, careful as she let her fingers walk across her lips. Her lower jaw hurt, and her teeth felt loose. One of her eyes wasn't working right, but her head didn't hurt so bad anymore.

The company woman offered her a pack of cigarettes, silver foils winking in the gloom. Sadie pulled one out, accepting the offered light. The woman had to strike the lighter twice before it caught.

"Not a smoker then?" Sadie drew the delicious taste of the Treasurers in deep. *Damn*, they were good. The air cycler in the van wicked away the smoke as if it had never been, the interior cool and clean.

The woman pocketed the pack. "No."

"He's got good taste." Sadie glanced at a small huddle near the van's side door, then turned to the front. She could see the back of the driver's head, the helmet a subtle white in the dim interior. The huddle moved, an arm extending to pull the blanket higher. "We got another passenger?"

"Yes," The company woman offered her hand. "I'm Jenni. Jenni Haraway."

Sadie returned the shake. "Apsel?"

"What?" said Haraway.

"I said, 'Apsel.' Like, are you with him?" She pointed with her chin to the driver.

The driver glanced back, face hidden behind the helmet. "Don't waste your time, Haraway. Bonus Round doesn't trust people like us."

Bonus Round. Sadie smiled, then swallowed it. *These are*

company people. You can't trust them. She raised her voice. "That's right, company man." Sadie laughed. "What are the odds?"

Haraway turned to look at the driver. "You know each other?"

The driver focused on the road outside. Sadie couldn't see the dash from where she sat, but the soft amber of the display reflected against the side of his helmet. The rain outside made visibility zero, the van's windshield overlaid with wireframes of vehicles and buildings. He shrugged. "Sort of. I don't mean to be rude, but—"

White speared across the windshield as the night lit bright white, the amber wireframes invisible for a second. The driver swung the van hard right, Sadie falling to her side. Haraway grabbed onto a wall strap. The person in the bundle of blankets rocked against the wall.

The van clunked as the driver worked the controls. Its drive kicked hard, and the machine pushed forward.

Haraway glanced at Sadie, fingers gripped tight on her strap. "It's been an interesting evening."

"Where's Aldo?"

Haraway looked puzzled. "Who's Aldo?"

"My drummer," said Sadie. "Something else, once."

"Long black hair? Thin guy?"

"Yeah. That's him."

Haraway sighed. "I wouldn't ... let's just get out of this first, okay?"

Sadie glanced front. "He's an asshole."

"Who?" Haraway followed her gaze. "Mason?"

Mason Floyd. The name clicked back into place. Sadie took another pull on the cigarette. "Either one, I guess."

"Mason's ... efficient," said Haraway. "I'm lucky he and Carter were there."

Sadie looked at the bundle of blankets. "That Carter?"

"Her? No. Carter's—"

"Company. I get it." Sadie ground the cigarette out against a van wall, ignoring Haraway's frown. "Who's that, then?"

"A girl. I guess mid-teens."

"Not with Apsel?" Sadie took a better look at the van's interior, picking out the colors. *Ah. This isn't an Apsel van. No asshat gold falcon.* "Your evening's not going well, is it?"

"Why do you ask?" Haraway steadied herself against the wall as the van rocked again. Mason swore, then started tapping buttons. The drive spoke back, the whine increasing until it was ultrasonic. The wall of the van vibrated.

"Aside from you fuckers abducting me?" Sadie laughed. "It's not your van."

"Not our van?"

"These aren't Apsel colors." Sadie waved an arm, a gesture that said *look at all this shit.* "Not very German, is it?"

Haraway frowned again. "It's a Reed van, I think. I'd have to admit to not being really on form at the time."

"You got another?"

"What?" Haraway looked confused. "Another van? Why?"

"Cigarette," said Sadie. "That last one was good."

Haraway looked at her for a second, then laughed, handing her the pack and lighter. "Help yourself."

"Thanks," said Sadie around the edge of a filter. She flicked the lighter on. "I could get used to being abducted by the company."

"It's not like that," said Haraway. "How much do you remember?"

"Not a lot," said Sadie. "I remember him, though."

"Mason?"

"Yeah."

You'll find a room where you can go fuck yourself.

Okay.

A single hammer drop of sound, and Aldo's leg was in tatters. He fell, screaming.

She shuddered, hugging herself. "Not from tonight. I remember that, but..." Sadie hid behind another drag on the cigarette. Her hands shook, so she clenched them into fists.

"Haraway," said Mason. "Look, I don't mean to break up your Kodak moment, but—"

"Coming," said Haraway, but she looked at Sadie. "I'll be right back."

"Take your time," said Sadie. *Bonus Round.* The man was company from his expensive-yet-bad haircut to his very expensive-and-good shoes. Thought he owned the world. Sadie looked over at the girl huddling inside the rags, scooting over. "Hi."

Wide eyes. Dirty face. The girl said something Sadie couldn't understand. *Not the first time you haven't understood something.* Sadie smiled. "I don't know what you're saying, but sure." She held out the pack of Treasurers.

The girl looked at them then back to Sadie. She didn't move.

"It's not poison," said Sadie. "Not the worst kind, anyway." She pulled a cigarette out, lit it from her own, and handed it to the girl. "It'll help." Sadie took a pull from her own cigarette.

The girl watched her, putting the silver filter between her lips. *Thin. Hungry. Been on the streets a while.* She drew in a big breath, coughing. It was a hard sound in the back of a van used to syndicate luxury.

Sadie laughed. "Yeah, first time's always rough." She drew on her own cigarette again.

The girl watched her, before examining the filter of the Treasurer, silver in the van's dimness. The girl took another puff, smaller this time, coughing anyway.

Sadie smiled at her. "You have no idea what the hell is going on, do you?"

The girl said something back, the babble of sound almost familiar.

"Me neither," said Sadie. "Look, sit tight. I'll see what these company fucks have got us into, okay?" She stood, legs shaky, steadying herself against the van's wall. Her head still pounded, and she took a moment before moving to the front. Haraway huddled behind Mason.

"There's got to be a way," said Mason.

"I'm not that kind of scientist," said Haraway.

"You know fusion reactors — Jesus!" Something bright scarred the street, Mason yanked the controls as they swerved. Sadie could see vehicles streaming past them as Mason pushed the van faster and harder. She saw a number on the HUD, 257 big, bright, and orange, watching as it ticked up to 258, then 259. It ducked down to 242 as Mason yawed around a truck, the bigger machine roaring as they blew past it.

"Is that the speed?" said Sadie. "Tell me that's not the speed."

Mason looked at her. The helmet made him look like a machine, no skin visible at all. "Can you do anything to help?"

"I don't know," said Sadie, putting a little *fuck no, but no way I'll give you the satisfaction* in her tone.

"Then get in the back." He turned to the front. "I need to lose these assholes, and I need to do it before we run out of traffic."

"What about Carter?" asked Haraway.

The night flashed again, and something high in the sky flared into an orange cloud. The amber of the windshield faded back in.

Mason laughed. "Don't worry about Carter. Worry about the tracker in this van."

Sadie nodded, moving to the middle of the van. She looked around, feeling like the world was *finally* coming back into focus. Her head still hurt but her thoughts moved at the pace she expected. *Jesus.* Blood coated the wall opposite the girl. Sadie looked at the racks of weapons on the walls. No seats. She swung back to the girl. "These vans are used for two things." Sadie pulled a rifle from the wall. "They either send a bunch of dudes to kill people, or they send a bunch of dudes to capture people."

The girl gabbled back.

"That's right," said Sadie. "Not a comfortable bus." She checked her weapon, then pointed it at the van's floor. Sadie squeezed the trigger, the weapon barking loud, muzzle flash strobing bright. The floor shredded, the tarmac racing by, an ugly blur in the dark. Air howled, blasting rain into the van. Sadie's hair billowed around her face.

"Christ!" yelled Mason. "What the hell are you doing?" To the company man's credit, the van didn't crash, holding position in the traffic. Red warning lights flashed from his HUD, an alarm sounding.

"Solving your problem." Sadie had to raise her voice over the road noise. "They won't be tracking us anymore."

"They what?"

"The tracker. On the van," she said. "They mount them on the underside, in the middle."

"How—"

"Look, company man," said Sadie. "Just drive the van. When someone you love more than air is taken by a company for re-education, you can think about how you'd disable their trackers and get them back."

Haraway looked between the two of them. "Is it gone?"

"Carter thinks so," said Mason. The air flashed again, the rumble of an explosion much closer this time. "She's cleaning up."

Sadie tossed the gun to the floor, watching as it rattled and shook. "What next?"

Mason glanced at her, white eyes of his helmet giving nothing away. "I need to get us lost. I know a place."

The girl spoke again, more gibber-jabber. *She's tough.* Most people would have freaked in this situation. Freak or not, shock would come soon enough. "Mason, how about some food?"

"You're hungry?"

"No, I want to puke." Sadie jerked a thumb at the girl. "Your cargo looks like she could use a burger, though. Like, *actually* starving."

Mason left a hand on the wheel, turning to glance at the girl. "Yeah, okay." The van slowed. "Haraway?"

"What?"

"You're in charge. Where to?"

"Well..." Haraway looked lost.

"Okay," said Mason. "Get comfortable. Take Bonus Round back with you."

"There aren't any seats," said Haraway.

Mason shrugged. "See that girl on the floor?"

"Yeah," said Haraway.

"See her complaining about no seats?"

Haraway closed her mouth, pushing past Sadie as she went to the van's rear. *Bonus Round.* Sadie smiled again but was sure she shouldn't be.

CHAPTER TWENTY-THREE

"How fucked is he?" Harry swiveled, taking in the hangar. Twenty operatives, give or take. A lot of dollars-per-hour to have standing around, dicks in hand. Or, figurative dicks, because most of them were total conversions like him. Big chassis, armored agents, ready for war.

War. A goddamn syndicate war.

Not a lot of meat left in their shells, though. The hiss of hydraulics overlaid the whine of machinery as operatives jockeyed for position. Techs were absent, this well above their pay grade. Seeing the boss? Rare, and it needed clearance. That clearance only came with being company from your armored shell to your interior power core.

"Hard to tell," said Lace. Her link voice he'd know anywhere. Better than his own skin, if he still had some. "Carter says she lost him."

"*Carter* lost someone?"

"That's what she said," said Lace, voice testy. "It's hard to know for sure."

"Why?" Harry shook his arm. A fragment of metal fell from a joint. "Carter and you not seeing eye-to-eye?"

"It's not like that, Harry." Carter's voice was crystal clear on the link as her icon appeared on Harry's overlay. "Wait a sec. I'll be right back." Her icon vanished.

Lace sighed, sounding tired like the stims weren't keeping her up like they should. "She can cut in on us."

Harry clanked across the hangar, moving to take position. He wanted a good spot. "I don't get it."

"The link is just for you and me."

"With you so far."

"So, Harry Fuentes, how does she talk on *our* link?" Lace had a little fire in her voice, like if stims wouldn't do it, she'd keep herself awake through bile and fury, but tamped down to a corporate-acceptable level.

Harry tapped an armored toe, *clank clank.* "Hell if I know. You asked her?"

"Yeah. She laughed." Lace sighed. "She's pretty good. It's like she thinks it's a game."

"Isn't it?"

"Well, Harry, I don't know," said Lace. "It's probably a game right up until the link gets jacked, someone hacks your core, and you blow your reactor."

Harry looked at the platform at the front of the hanger. A podium stood on it, an Apsel falcon gold against a black background. Gairovald liked his corporate colors. Harry looked at the others in the room, a soft hum emanating from his chassis. "He's late."

"Don't change the subject," she said. "You want your core to blow?"

"I don't know." Harry's big metal hand rubbed the back of his head, old meat memory taking over. He stopped, looking as big metal fingers clicked open and closed, then dropped his arm to his side. "Would it stop your bitching?"

"Your problem is you don't appreciate artistry."

"Artistry? This mean you've worked out how Carter hacked the link?"

She sighed again. "No."

"Keep working on it," he said. "You'll get it."

"Yes," said Lace.

"You'll keep working on it?"

"Maybe, but not that. Yes, in answer to your earlier question."

"You know I hate this game, Lace. You change the subject six goddamn times and get hurt when I don't know what the hell you're talking about."

"You asked," she said.

Harry replayed their conversation on the overlay, looping back the last thirty seconds. "Technically, I didn't ask."

"It was implied."

"So, he's running late?"

"Is that a question?"

Harry clenched a metal fist. Lace's laugh came down the link. "How late is he?"

"About five minutes. His air car landed a couple minutes ago. He should be with you about ... now."

A door next to the podium opened, Gairovald Apsel walking through. Two men in black suits kept stride with him. Harry's optics zoomed in on Gairovald, noting the small flower on his lapel. "Is that an orchid? It looks like an orchid, but tiny."

"Shhh," said Lace. "You'll miss the briefing. He has people to engineer his flowers."

Harry stopped shifting, chassis settling, a soft whine escaping as it parked.

"Good morning," said Gairovald, his voice coming in the real and over the link at the same time. "I'm sorry about the hour."

"He's handsome," said Lace. "Better than his photo. He can wake me up at four AM anytime."

Harry ignored her. Gairovald continued, "Earlier this evening, one of our operatives attempted to recover lost Federate intellectual property. This IP was stolen from us by a senior within the R&D team." He raised a hand, to forestall questions. No one would be stupid enough to interrupt the boss, though. "A file will be supplied with all the details." He cleared his throat, taking a sip of water someone had left on the podium. "It appears our operative was a part of the heist."

"What?" said Lace. "What did he just say?"

"On your overlays are the details of the two people in question." Gairovald showed perfect teeth. "Jennifer Haraway, recently head of Atomic Energy, and Mason Floyd, one of our senior Specialist Services agents. They are to be considered your top priority for recovery." Gairovald straightened a cuff. Harry didn't think it needed straightening, but he hadn't worn a suit in a while. "Recovery, or termination."

"Fuck *me*," said Harry. "*Fuck* me."

"He didn't just say that, did he?" said Lace. "What does that even mean?"

"Quiet," said Carter. No icon accompanied her link chat this time. "The worst is still to come."

"The worst?" said Lace. Carter didn't reply.

Gairovald walked from behind the podium, standing before the operatives. Some shifted nervously, but most just idled. It was a total conversion stance that said *I'm bored, what's the bonus on this one?* "Harry Fuentes."

Harry jerked, kindling his chassis to life. He stepped back a half meter, an agent next to him scrambling out of the way. "Watch it, asshole," said the agent.

"Sorry," said Harry, then turned the PA down as it boomed across the hanger. He faced Gairovald. "Sir."

"You were on this evening's mission?" Gairovald looked at one of his shoes, the shiny black leather a dark mirror, before glancing at Harry. "Mason requested your involvement?"

"I ... sir. Yes, sir." Harry shuffled, metal feet scraping the concrete floor. "Sir, what is this about?"

"Don't worry, Fuentes," said Gairovald. "You're not under investigation."

"I'm not?"

"No," said Gairovald. "We've reviewed the footage, and it looks like you engaged as instructed."

"Sir?"

"Floyd went into the structure?"

"*The Hole?* Yes, sir." Gairovald waited. Harry felt like he should fill the silence. "He went in through the roof."

Gairovald waved the comment away. "We lost contact with his link. Interference."

"Yeah," said Harry. "About that. I lost him for a while too."

"It looks like he deployed tech to hide his movements," said Gairovald. "Carter's still piecing it together—"

"Carter?" If Harry still had eyes, he would have blinked in confusion. *Carter is Mason's handler. You don't set a handler on their own agent.*

"As I said, Carter's still piecing it together. She has a recording of Floyd requesting you pull back. The link record is audio only, and even then it's full of static."

"Yeah," said Harry. "I got that instruction."

A small smile from Gairovald let Harry know he'd said the right thing. "We also have your reaction on file." He took another sip of water. "We were wondering if we could use your ... relationship in a strategic manner."

Harry looked at the agents around him. All optics were on him. "I'm not sure I follow, sir."

Gairovald nodded, taking in his unease. He raised his voice. "The rest of you can go. You have your mission. Find Haraway. Find Floyd. Remove them from the field, by any means necessary. Fuentes, please stay."

Operatives filed from the hangar, one or two looking at Harry as they passed. Harry waited for them to go as he spoke over the link. "Lace?"

"Yeah." She sounded worried. *Lace is never worried. Cranky, sure. Angry for no reason? You bet. But she never gets worried.* It wasn't how she'd been forged.

"Can you talk to Carter?"

"Yeah," she said. The link clicked off, leaving Harry alone with Gairovald and his guards.

"Fuentes?"

"Sir."

"Fuentes, how well do you know Mason Floyd?" Gairovald stepped down from the platform. His guards followed, a few steps behind.

"I don't know," said Harry. "I don't play poker with him."

"Are you friends?"

Harry screamed and screamed, but no sound came out. His lungs were full of fire, the lattice thrashing and flailing against the wheel. The door ripped open, a man's hand reaching to grab what was left of Harry—

"Not really," said Harry. "I shot him, once."

"I know," said Gairovald. "For all that, he saved your life."

Harry was rolled across the road, each tiny bump in the asphalt an eon of pain. The cold wet of rain washed what was left of his body. Burnt skin on his leg cracked, flaking away. Harry kept trying to scream, but there wasn't enough of him left to make a sound.

"I guess." Harry looked down at his chassis. "Yeah."

"I think he chose you for this mission because you wouldn't ask questions," said Gairovald. "I think he played you."

"Sir?" Something cold and heavy settled where Harry's stomach would be if he still had one.

"He picked the one man as backup who wouldn't second-guess him. The one man who *owed him.*" Gairovald walked around Harry, Harry swiveling his chassis to follow. "Do you think that's fair?"

"It might be," said Harry. "Mason's a bit of an asshole."

Gairovald smiled again. "Yes. Yes, I think he might be." He continued around Harry, looking him up and down. "How is the chassis?"

Harry paused, surprised at the question. "It's..." He didn't know what to say.

"Tell him it's amazing." Lace's voice was hard on the link. "Don't think, just say it."

"It's amazing," said Harry.

Gairovald nodded. "We did the best we could with you, Fuentes. There wasn't much left to work with. Not after Floyd recovered you."

Harry stopped swiveling, leaving Gairovald to walk his quiet circuit. "Recovered. There's a word."

"That's what he did, though. After his handler sold us out. We reviewed the evidence, of course. It wasn't clear whether Mason should have guessed his handler was a thief, so we let it slide." Gairovald walked into Harry's field of vision again. "We don't let things slide twice. Do you understand?"

"Say you understand," said Lace.

"I understand," said Harry. "I appreciate the opportunity, sir."

"To help with Floyd?"

"No, sir." Harry's hands clicked as they opened, and he gestured at himself. "For the second chance. For the conversion. I..." He trailed off, struggling for the right words. Mason was better at this corporate bullshit.

"Yes?" Gairovald looked up at him, face blank, eyes empty. Harry was reminded of a snake watching a mouse, for all that Harry was massive to Gairovald's human-normal height.

"Mason saved my life, but the Federate put me back together. Made me who I am today."

"Nice," said Lace.

Gairovald nodded. "Of course, Fuentes. You were — and still are — an excellent asset. We look after our own."

"Thank you, sir."

Gairovald waved the thanks away. "Think nothing of it. You've more than repaid the investment."

Time to get the details. "Sir?"

"Yes, Fuentes?"

"What is it you want me to do?"

"Floyd will contact you." Gairovald strode away, leather shoes whisper quiet on the concrete floor. He spoke over his shoulder. "When he does, agree to meet him. Find him for me."

"I understand, sir. I'll find him," Harry raised his metal hands, clenching and unclenching them, "and remove him from the field."

Gairovald nodded as he reached the door. "Exactly. Good morning, Fuentes." Gairovald left, his guards a double shadow behind.

"That was intense," said Lace.

Harry looked around at the now empty hangar. He'd been standing for a couple of minutes, not moving. His chassis hummed, patient. Ready.

"I said," said Lace, "that was intense."

"I heard you," said Harry. "What's with the audio prompts?"

"Did Gairovald say you were a great operative?"

"Yeah, I think so," said Harry. "Whole thing was off the chain."

"What I mean is, you're a moron," she said.

"What?"

"He was *testing* you." Lace talked fast. "He was testing you to find out how deep it went."

"I—"

"Don't talk. I..." Lace trailed into silence, the moment stretching between them.

"I know," said Harry. "It's okay."

"No, it's not." The link was quiet, then her voice came back, small and still. "He can't take you too. I won't have anything left."

Harry didn't say anything for a few moments. He clanked across the hanger. *Still no techs. Nobody else at all.* Maybe they were giving him a few precious moments to come up with a plan. *More likely, they're waiting for you to hang yourself.* Harry looked at his metal hand, the Apsel falcon a black outline. "Lace?"

"Yes, Harry." Her voice was clearer. "We're a good team. Forget I said anything. I'm sorry—"

"No one will touch you again. Do you hear me?" He left the hanger, not looking back. "Not ever."

He thought she was gone until she said, voice soft as a moth's wings, "I hear you."

CHAPTER TWENTY-FOUR_

The forecourt was empty of other vehicles, the pumps standing alone, tin soldiers in a row. A couple of charging stations stood off to the side. One looked broken, interior components exposed, wiring trailing through puddles. Demand for standard fuel types dropped now Apsel shipped reactors for cars.

Mason left the van, pulling off his helmet. Rain howled around the forecourt, but he welcomed the freshness after the hours locked in the armor. Mason spat out the taste of roasted chestnut, the shaky fingers of overtime still stuck inside his head.

"She remembers you," said Carter. The link felt strained between them, static sanding the consonants down.

"Who?" Mason walked toward the front of the station. A light flickered above the doorway, spasmodically trying to keep the darkness away. A canopy above kept the rain's sting at bay.

"The illegal," she said. "You know her. Black lipstick."

"Oh," said Mason. "Bonus Round. Yeah, I got that."

"She's not your type," said Carter. "Right? Because if she is, you'll fuck up the mission. Say it."

Mason nodded, running a hand through sweat-slick hair. His

white boots spread ripples through the puddles. Mason's reflection stretched out in the water, taller than he felt. "Sure. Carter?"

"Yeah?"

"What's my type?" Mason paused with his hand on the station's door, looking through the glass. *One man behind the counter. Two more in the aisles.* He sighed, then pushed inside to stale air. The place was more tired than Mason was, linoleum peeling from the floor, but the shelves were well-stocked.

"We're not having this conversation. Where are you taking the payload?"

Mason stopped between the checkout and the aisles. The two men in the aisles looked at him before turning away. "What do you mean, where am I taking them? Back to HQ. Where else?"

"That's not a good idea," said Carter. "You're compromised."

"Hold that thought." Mason walked to the counter, dropping the man behind it a quick smile. The guy was a little older, gray showing through his uneven shave. Working here, it was unlikely he could afford a clinic, and it showed. "Hey."

"Hey." The attendant took in Mason's armor and SMGs at his belt. He sniffed. "Help you?"

"Maybe," said Mason. "I need ... lemme see. You got any language packs?"

"Sure." The attendant glanced at the Apsel falcon on Mason's armor. "English? Or German, maybe?" He coughed, a wet sound, then pointed with his chin. "Back there. Next to the sodas and road beers."

Mason nodded his thanks, then moved back through the store. He snagged a basket, carrying it in his left hand, tossing the helmet inside. His rubber soles squeaked across the tired linoleum floor. "What do you mean, 'compromised?'"

"So, about that," said Carter. "It's a bit crazy up here."

"Right," said Mason. "The mission—"

"It's not the mission." Carter paused. "Okay, you're right. It's the mission. Sort of. This evening there may have been violations of the Syndicate Compact."

Mason frowned. He paused in the aisle. "Where the hell ... oh, here they are." He found the language packs hanging on an old wire frame, a Reed logo in the top corner. "You reckon the kid is more into strawberry or chocolate?"

"Does it even taste like strawberry?"

"You're right. Chocolate it is." Mason grabbed one of the packs from the shelf, flipping it over to check the back. "Okay, it's English."

"Don't forget the mix," said Carter.

"You saw back there? At *The Hole*? Guys with guns, right?" Mason tossed the language pack into the basket.

"Yeah," said Carter. "I saw."

"You saw me shut the room down. That was me, right?"

"That was you."

"I'm okay managing to shut down a room full of assholes, but you don't trust me to go shopping by myself?"

"Of course not," said Carter. "Don't forget the mix."

Mason sighed, walking past the two men still in the aisle. He nodded to them as he made his way to the refrigerator at the rear. "Explain why Old Man Gairovald trusts me with the big jobs but you don't trust me to shop solo."

"It's not worth the trouble," said Carter. "So, the compromise I was talking about."

"Yeah. *We* didn't violate the Compact." Mason grabbed a couple of liter bottles of water from the refrigerator. After a brief pause, he grabbed cans of energy drinks too. "It was our IP."

"Maybe," said Carter. "That's not the important part. It's pretty clear that Reed and Metatech violated the Compact. There'll be consequences."

"Sure," said Mason. "What's the problem?"

"You are," said Carter.

Mason stopped in the aisle, looking at the attendant behind the counter, then to the two men. "I'm the problem?"

"You have a history."

"I was cleared."

"It's still a history," she said. "Gairovald's reviewed the ops footage."

"So?"

"Try to look at it from his perspective," she said. "He sent you out to kill a thief."

"With you so far." Mason looked into the basket, then cast an eye around the store. "You think we need food?"

"Almost certainly," said Carter. "The thing is, he sent you to kill a thief, and no thief was killed. He changed the mission parameters to support Haraway. He thinks you're going to bring back new assets—"

"The girl." Mason frowned. "And a boy and a man."

"—but that came after, and you've only got *one*. What he's got is a lot of footage of an op gone bad. Damage to company assets, all of that. Here's the important part, though."

"I'm listening."

"You didn't kill a thief." Carter paused. "Are you hearing me?"

"There wasn't a thief to kill," said Mason. "There was just Haraway. There, under Gairovald's orders."

"Right," said Carter. "Where'd the device come from?"

"Uh."

"Haraway's playing the middle, Mason. She's not the seller." Carter coughed. "How many Federate operatives were at the scene?"

"Shit."

"How many, Mason?"

"Two." He looked into the basket he carried, then started another go-around the aisles. *What the hell do kids like to eat, anyway?* She looked a little anemic. Protein bars? He found some with a Reed logo that looked safe enough. It felt like a betrayal buying other company products, but it wasn't like there were options here. He wished it wasn't *Reed's* product. "Me, and Haraway."

"And you're both still breathing," said Carter. "You need to stay with Haraway. Find the real thief. Don't blow her cover."

"Isn't her cover pretty blown?"

"Not necessarily. Anyone gets that footage, it looks like a grab mission gone wrong. Lawyers will be crawling all over it for years trying to work out who screwed up the worst. The thing is, right now, that's *you*. They're going to pin the tail on the scapedonkey."

"Is that even a real thing?"

"I'm getting it squared away. It won't be a problem once Gairovald's cooled down. And once you kill the thief. They've got the chair set up for you. If you come in, you're not going to leave as anything except a brain in a box. Unless you kill the thief."

"What about you?"

"Don't worry about me," said Carter. "I got this end. I'll square it away. You find somewhere to hide."

Mason put the basket on the counter. The attendant started to ring it up, putting items into a brown paper bag. Mason reached into a pouch at his belt, pulling out a wad of cash. The attendant's eyes widened a little, but he didn't say anything. "I think I know a place," said Mason, still on the link.

"Where?" Carter sounded concerned. "You can't stay in the city."

"No," said Mason. "Look, the problem's going to be my link."

The attendant cleared his throat. "That'll be thirty-four fifty."

Mason peeled off a fifty, putting the rubber band back around the roll of notes. "Keep the change." He grabbed the bag, then shouldered his way out onto the forecourt. A squall of rain lashed above him like a whip. Mason made it to the van, yanking the side door open.

Haraway looked stressed. Bonus Round looked bored. And the kid looked scared. Mason shrugged, hefting his helmet. "Look," he said, "I've got one more thing to take care of. Can you prep the language pack?"

Bonus Round snorted. "You're going to put that shit in a kid? She's not even linked."

"Right," said Mason. "That's why she gets a pack. Give her this one first." He tapped one of the boxes.

"I know how they work," said Haraway. "It's not rocket science."

"Says the woman who couldn't find a tracker in the van." Mason slid the door closed.

"She's right," said Carter.

"Who?"

"Bonus Round," said Carter. "The illegal."

Mason walked back to the station's entrance. "I thought you said they're not illegals."

"I'm trying to use small, familiar terms so you don't get confused," said Carter. "The reports on the virus in the packs on the developing mind are inconclusive."

"I don't have a way to get a link into her." Mason put his helmet on just outside the station's door. "Not out here."

"Mason," said Carter.

"Yes, Carter?"

"What are you doing?"

Mason shouldered his way into the station, one of the SMGs snapping out and up. The two men from the aisles looked up in surprise. One held a small pistol to the attendant's head. The other was stuffing cash from the register into a bag.

"Hi," said Mason over the armor's PA. "I forgot to buy cigarettes."

The targeting solution fell into place on the overlay, red frames boxing the men. The SMG barked twice. Both thieves fell back, one spinning into a stand of jerky, the other dropping behind the counter. Mason walked to the bodies, checking them with a boot, then pulled off his helmet. "Got any Treasurers?"

The attendant's skin was pasty underneath the poor shave job. "What?"

"Treasurers," said Mason. "Cigarettes."

"No," said the attendant. He looked like he was having trouble processing the situation, eyes wide and blinking. "Say. Why'd you come back in?"

"Like I said, I forgot to get cigarettes. What else you got?"

The attendant swallowed. "How about some Camels?"

"I hate Camels," said Mason. "They remind me of an asshole I know."

"Sure, okay," said the attendant. "I'm ... sorry. I'm having trouble here."

"Right," said Mason. "What about throwing me a couple packs of Marlboros?"

"Okay," said the attendant, handing them over. "No charge."

"No, it's fine," said Mason, pulling out the roll of cash. "How about a hundred?"

"For what?" said the attendant. "You saved my life."

"No," said Mason. "No, I didn't. I wasn't here."

"You ... what?"

"No cars in the parking lot. I got to thinking, how'd these guys get here?" Mason peeled the plastic off one pack of cigarettes. "Got a light?" The attendant held out a box of plastic lighters. "Thanks." Mason took a couple. "Need a spare. So anyway, I figure these two guys here, they've come from somewhere local, looking to score a hit."

"Why?" The attendant looked at the bodies, then back to Mason. "I need to call someone."

Mason held up a hand. "In a minute. Thing is, no one shops out here."

"You do," said the attendant.

"Yeah, but maybe I needed a fuel cell." Mason looked at the back of the store. "There's better places to shop if you want milk. No offense."

"None taken," said the attendant. "You don't need a fuel cell."

"Stay with me," said Mason. "So, the thing is, I wanted to go somewhere there weren't other people."

The attendant's eyes widened. "Like witnesses?"

"Exactly like," agreed Mason, taking a pull on the cigarette. He made a face, blowing smoke out toward the ceiling.

"I won't tell anyone." The attendant licked his lips, eyes bright with fear as they looked at Mason's SMG.

"I know," said Mason. "Because if you do, I'll come back." He

smiled at the man, dropping two fifties on the counter. He headed for
the door.

"Wait," said the attendant. "Just ... hang on."

Mason turned. "What is it?"

The man swallowed. "Thanks."

Mason nodded. "Can you take care of the CCTV?"

"Yes," said the attendant. "I'll tell them it was a gang shooting.
The other guy got away."

Mason shrugged. "Up to you. Just remember what we talked
about." He pushed the door open and headed back outside.

○

The van door swung closed. Mason tossed his helmet to the seat
beside him.

"Get what you needed?" asked Haraway from the back.

"Let me the fuck out," said Bonus Round. "I'm not up for your
syndicate bullsh—"

Mason slammed his fist into the dash. He hit it again and again.
He yelled and screamed at the dash. Plastic cracked and splintered,
the metal underneath deforming. The windscreen's overlay flickered.

He stopped, breathing hard, looking at the ruined dash.
"Haraway."

His audio picked up the rustle of her coat as she moved
closer. "Yes?"

"Is there anything you'd like to tell me about the nature of this
mission?" Mason didn't turn to look at her, staring instead at the
cracked dash. *Compromised.*

"What do you mean?" Her breathing quickened, his overlay
picking out stress markers in her voice.

"Particulars," Mason said. "Details. The little things that might
get you killed."

"No, I don't think so." She hadn't moved, her voice still the same
distance behind him.

Mason looked at her. He tried to keep his voice steady. It came out flat. "You're sure?"

Haraway shook her head. "No, I'm not sure."

Mason watched her for a second. "Good enough."

"Good enough?"

"Yeah." Mason keyed the van's drive, the system low and quiet. "You didn't lie to me then."

"No," she said. "I didn't."

"Good," said Mason. "You lied to me before."

"I—"

"Or maybe you weren't a hundred percent straight." He shrugged. "Because everything is fucked."

"I don't know—"

Mason held up a hand, not looking at her. "Carter's doing what she can. But I need you to think. Think *hard* about what you're doing." He faced her. "Do you know what 'compromised' means?"

She looked at her hands, her voice small. "Yes. More than you know."

"Right," said Mason. "We're compromised. Think about a plan. I'll get us off the grid."

"Where?"

"You'll see." Mason slipped the van into gear. The machine complained, a grinding noise coming from its belly. He frowned. "Last time I was compromised, a man died, and two people were crippled." He didn't know whether he could face more of Haraway's half-lies, half-uncertainty, so he keyed the privacy screen between the cabin and the driver's compartment.

Mason glimpsed Bonus Round's face, her eyes wide as she stared between the two of them.

Yeah, you got it right. Syndicate bullshit.

CHAPTER TWENTY-FIVE

"Comfortable?" Julian lit a cigarette as he observed his prisoner. The man was held to a chair by gleaming bands. He stared at Julian, eyes wide, but not with fear. No, this freak wasn't scared. He was *pissed off*. Julian smiled, blowing smoke into the asshole's face. *Time to teach a little fear.* They were at Reed's Seattle HQ, in one of the processing rooms. The perfect place for terror.

"I appreciate you can't understand a word I'm saying," he said. "We're going to fix that right up. Square the problem away. Before, at *The Hole?* We can both forget it ever happened."

The man spoke, *NO LINGUISTIC MATCH* flashing on Julian's overlay. Julian could see gaps in his teeth, the gums still bloody and raw. Julian yanked out quite a few before believing the man couldn't understand him. Sometimes you had to break a few eggs.

The tech beside him took a half-step forward, adjusting his collar. "Sir?"

"Yes?" Julian glanced at the tech. *Obviously hasn't got used to piloting the remote yet.* "You good to go or not?"

"It'd be easier if I was here," said the tech.

"Trust me," said Julian. "You *really* don't want to be here. Remotes are the only way until we understand how it works." He slapped the tech on the shoulder. "Besides, you'll get used to it. It's better than your real body."

The tech nodded. "Good to go. On your word."

"Consider the word given." Julian gave a magnanimous wave of his cigarette. The tech moved to a console, pressing buttons. The chair the man was strapped to rotated and elongated, stretching him out to face the ground.

A clamp over his forehead locked the asshole's head in place. The inverted chair left a space at the back of the man's skull and neck exposed. Julian took a last pull on the cigarette, then stubbed it out on his palm, flicking the butt away. Best not to have airborne contaminants during surgery.

A surgical machine extended from the roof, the metal arm articulating out to hover over the man's neck. The man spoke again, *NO LINGUISTIC MATCH* flashing on Julian's overlay. He stiffened as a hypo touched the back of his neck.

It was a simple contact anesthetic. Seemed reasonable.

The man shouted, but the machine didn't stop. A circular saw extended, the whir high. There was a deep buzz, then the slight smell of burning meat as the saw cut the back of the man's skull open.

He's really *yelling now.* Julian glanced at the tech. "Is he in any pain?"

The tech shrugged as the machine continued to cut. "Shouldn't be. Anesthetic's strong, and there's very few pain nerves in the brain itself."

"That's a shame," said Julian.

"I'm sorry?" said the tech.

"Nothing," said Julian, watching as the saw retracted. The back of the man's skull was open, bone glistening wet and red under the lights. The surgical arm extended another mechanism, a chip held out. Laser light stabbed down, medical green mapping of the man's exposed brainstem. The machine reached forward, holding the chip in place. The chip would self-guide the rest of its install into the brain itself. The arm spun again, inserting titanium screws to fix the chip against bone.

Lasers stabbed out here and there, cauterizing. The man had stopped yelling, instead jerking against the restraints as nerves were burned away.

"We don't normally do these on adults, do we?" said Julian.

"No," said the tech. "Complications."

"Fixable?"

"Usually," said the tech. "It's almost done. What do you want laid in first?"

Julian smiled. "How about some English? This asshole and I still need to have a good, long, honest talk."

"Okay," said the tech. "Anything else?"

"See if you can put his teeth back in," said Julian. "I might need to pull them back out. Ping my link when you're done."

○

The man was still clamped to the table but had been turned upright. The back of his skull was painted with synthetic skin. Good as new.

"How are you feeling?" Julian peered at him.

"You will release me, or I will kill everyone you love." The asshole sounded like the words came easy to him. Used to being in charge.

Julian smiled, offering him a cigarette. The man didn't budge. Julian shrugged, lighting his own. "Sounds serious."

"Release me now." If looks could kill, this asshole would have put all of Seattle in the ground with his glare.

"I don't think so," said Julian. "I'd like to talk to you about something." The man stared at him, naked hate in his eyes. "I take it by your silence you're happy for me to talk. Back there, at the sphere. You remember?"

"Sphere?" The word was out of the man's mouth before he could stop himself.

Julian nodded. "Ball of light. About the size of a hotel lobby, give or take. Lightning and shit coming off it." He pulled on his cigarette. "Know what I'm talking about?"

"The gate," said the man. He swallowed, like he'd remembered what fear felt like.

That's right, asshole. You're saying things without wanting to. Welcome to your new link. "The gate?"

"I..." The man struggled, swallowing what he was going to say.

"It's okay to fight it," said Julian. "It helps us map your brain. It'll work better in the future. So, this thing? It's a gate, okay, I get that. What's on the other side?"

"Your destruction," said the man. "An end to everything you know. We will come here and enslave you—"

Julian cut him off with a wave of his cigarette. "Right, okay. How's that going for you so far?" The man stayed silent. "That's what I thought. I'm going to step out on a limb here and say this shit was about as surprising for you as it was for me."

The man pulled against his restraints, then relaxed. "We came through. After it."

"Yeah. With a girl and a boy. No guns."

"Guns." The man turned the word around in his mouth. "I know the word, but I don't know what it means."

"This is a gun." Julian pulled out his sidearm. He held it up, releasing the safety. "It works like this." He pointed the weapon at the man's leg, still clamped to the chair, and pulled the trigger. The weapon barked, red spraying against the chair and the floor behind it. The man screamed, thrashing against his restraints. Julian holstered the sidearm. *"That's* a gun. Now you know."

The man panted, his face gray and sweaty as blood leaked from his leg. "You will pay for that. I will burn the memory of it on your children's minds. They will never be free of it."

"Right," said Julian. "But you can't do anything, can you?" He tapped the side of his head. "You need a meat body to work with."

The man spat at him. "What kind of man are you?"

Julian smiled. "That's the spirit. Mutual understanding. We can talk this through, find some common ground. Me? I'm … special."

"You're not a man. But you look like a man."

"Yep," said Julian. "Anatomically correct."

"No," said the man. "In your … inside. There are…" He struggled with the words. "There are meat parts."

"A few," said Julian. "Not enough to fill a coffee cup with. Not enough for you to make me bat-shit crazy like you did to my team."

"No," agreed the man. "But enough for me to begin to see what you want."

Julian felt a small chill go up his spine. His sidearm came out of his holster as the lattice drew it smooth and fast, centered on the man's forehead. "You can read my mind?"

"Not really." The man's face lost more color, the pool of blood under the chair growing. "But I know what you are, now."

"Okay, asshole," said Julian. "What am I?"

"A slave," said the man, his teeth pulling back in a bloody grin. "Like all the rest."

Julian looked down the sidearm at the man's face, then holstered it. "You had me worried there for a second."

"What?" said the man.

"We're all slaves," said Julian. "I'm happy with that as long as I'm on a steady percentage."

"Percentage," said the man. "So much of this is unfamiliar. This world, this manner of speaking, of telling lies and truth at the same time. You surround yourselves with toys and ornamentation, but none of you know about true power."

"True power?" Julian frowned. "I'm not the one stapled to a chair."

"No, you're a puppet. But I can give you what you want, Julian Oldham. I can give you everything."

Julian stared him. "How did you know my name?" He checked the link, trying to find a feedback loop, something he'd missed.

The man smiled. "There's enough space in a cup of coffee for many things. Your name. Your heart's desire. It's the same thing."

Julian looked at the man's clamped hands and wrists. "Do you even know what a cup of coffee looks like?"

"No," said the man. "It's as unfamiliar as a ... percentage."

Julian smiled. "This thing you can do." He pulled a fresh cigarette from the pack. His words were softened by the cigarette as he lit it. "Read minds. Shit like that."

The man looked at Julian. "Yes?"

"What sort of technology is it?"

"It's not a technology." The man chewed on the word. "*Technology*. Like the thing that lets me speak your words."

"Yeah, the link," said Julian. "That's tech."

"Real power isn't a technology," said the man.

"Okay," said Julian. "What is it?"

"It's the right to rule," said the man. "It's a gift from the spirits."

"Spirits." Julian took another pull on his cigarette. "Fuck off."

"It's what I came here for."

"Like some kind of spirit animal?" Julian wiggled his fingers in the air, the cigarette trailing smoke. "A wolf, or a coyote? You didn't seem to need it back at *The Hole*."

"The what?"

"The bar," said Julian, his cigarette leaving a lazy trail in the air. "The gate. It was at a place called *The Hole*."

"Ah," said the man. "It's not an animal. The spirit and I are ... joined. Each separate has power, but together..." He trailed off.

"Together?" said Julian. "What happens when we get both of you together?"

The man looked down at his bloody leg. "I don't think you'll get to find out. I think you intend to kill me here."

Julian laughed. "You aren't from around here, are you? Why do you think we put the teeth back in your head?"

"I'm not sure. The reason I would do it is so I could pull them back out again."

Julian nodded. "Do you know where you are?"

"I am in a room, in a strange place, on another world," said the man.

"No," said Julian. "I mean, where *here* is."

"No."

"Reed Interactive. Our business is dreams. Do you think we might work together?"

"Trade is spineless work for the lower castes. Commerce is a game for the weak minded, the slaves, the bearers of burdens."

"Where you come from? Sure. But here? Business is the way your ass is getting out of that chair. The *only* way."

The man's eyes narrowed. "You are proposing an alliance."

"If you like." Julian looked to the ceiling. *Best not to give anything away.*

"You know what I think?"

"No."

"I think that when you learn how I do what I do, when you capture my spirit and tether it to this Earth, you will kill me."

"Not at all," said Julian, meaning *yes, of course.*

The man thought for a minute. "We may be able to do business. Will you do something for me?"

"You're not in much position to ask for favors."

"It's a small thing." He glanced at his bleeding leg. "Can your technology fix this?"

"Well, shit," said Julian. "Of course. It'll do other things too."

"Like what?"

"Let's see if we can get you a cup of coffee, for a start." Julian felt excited. They might get somewhere. "A point of reference is always good."

"Tell me, Julian Oldham," said the man. "Does the rain usually make people see things in your world? That might be a good point of reference."

CHAPTER TWENTY-SIX_

"I know a place," said Carter.

"I was thinking downtown somewhere." Mason slipped the van out of the station's lot, easing into the traffic. "Get into a love hotel or something." Rain lashed the windscreen, the amber wire-frames standing out against the darkness.

"A love hotel?"

"Yeah, like the ones that do circus sex," said Mason. "Room for four? No problem."

"There's a *small* problem," said Carter. "I don't think you've thought it through. Like I said, I know a place."

"What problem?" said Mason. "Love hotels are off the grid."

"Not really," she said. "I could find you there. Also, it's not credible."

"What's not credible?"

"You, servicing three women in one night. Night after night." Carter sighed. "You're ... well."

"I'm what?"

"One night? Maybe," she said. "Three nights? A week? A month? And one of them's a teenage girl."

"You can buy anything," said Mason. "What if I'm not a very nice guy? What if I like underage sex? It's a good cover."

"Do you want to hear about the place I know about?" she said. "Anytime at all?"

Mason drove through the rain, steering the van around traffic. "What do you mean, you could find me?"

"I could find you," said Carter. "I know where you are right now."

"Yeah, but the link," said Mason. "Of course you know."

"Okay," said Carter. "I know other things. I know where Harry is. He's at the Federate, being asked to kill you."

Mason drove in silence for a few moments, easing to a stop at an intersection. Neon signs flickered, a red one promising HOT FOOD as it blinked on and off. This part of town still used the real rather than overlay ads. *At least it's in English.* "That's not great."

"No," she said. "He'll wipe the floor with you. Get into the corners with your face. Real thorough."

"Thanks," said Mason. "I mean, it's not great they got to him that fast."

"You're not asking the right questions," said Carter.

"I'm not? What questions should I be asking?"

"For a start, you should ask me which place I know of. A place you'll be safe, and no one will find you."

"Other than that?" The intersection lamps cycled, their pure green LEDs turning the rain a different color.

She sighed, the link bringing it through clear. "They've asked me to find you, Mason. They've asked me to find you and kill you."

"I know," said Mason. "It's why I didn't ask."

"You ... knew?"

"Yes," said Mason. "It's what I'd do. First, they'll investigate you. Run a few routines. Check your house. Maybe your friends." He smiled, even though there wasn't much to smile about. "Your dance class."

"I don't dance."

"Then, once they're sure you're not a total loss like me, they'll get you to prove it."

"I haven't done this before," she said. "I don't know what to do."

"Yeah," said Mason. "You do. You know exactly what to do."

"I'm not going to do that," said Carter. Her words were brittle, like they might break apart at a touch. "They can't make me."

"Oh, Carter." He laughed in the real. "Carter, Carter, Carter. They won't make you. Not at all."

"But you said—"

"They don't *make* you do anything," he said. "If you don't do it, you'll just disappear. Maybe your family. Your friends too. It'll be like you didn't even exist. They'll find your dance class and erase it like a bad mistake."

"Mistakes, by definition, are bad," she said. "That was redundant."

Mason shrugged, tapping the steering wheel as he drove. "Not always. Not for everyone."

The link hissed for a few moments, the silence stretching between them. "Okay," she said.

"Okay," said Mason. "You've got to turn me in. I understand. It's just business."

More silence. "Mason?"

"Yes, Carter."

"They watch me all the time."

"I know, Carter. I know."

"How?" she said. "How can you know?"

"You ever wonder who makes people disappear? Who's the fucker who knocks on your mother's door? You ever wonder what kind of person can burn down a dance studio with everyone inside?" Mason took the next left, driving at random, the downtown traffic slow as treacle. Neon signs continued their assault on the rain's veil, the van's overlay fighting to clean up the picture against the visual noise.

"No," she said. "I don't wonder. I don't want to know."

"No," said Mason. "Probably not. Goodbye, Carter."

"Mason, wait."

He held onto the link. Carter could be tracking him now, sending them to him, but he didn't think so. "I'm still here."

"Do you trust me, Mason Floyd?"

Mason sighed, the cabin small and empty around him. "Maybe," he admitted. "What with?"

"With your life," she said. "Would you trust me with your life?"

He tapped the steering wheel again, then pushed the van into a gap in the traffic. There was a snarl ahead, an accident causing people to drive like imbeciles. *Would you trust me with your life?* Mason sighed. "Yeah."

"Okay," she said. "Here's what you've got to do."

"I'm listening."

"You need to go where I can't find you."

"I'm doing that," he said. "Sex motel, remember?"

"No," she said. "I'm better than that. *I'll* find you."

"You got a better idea?" he said.

"Yes," she said. "That's what I've been trying to tell you. I know a place."

"What kind of place?"

"It's the best kind," she said. "It's a place that doesn't exist."

Mason drove through the night, surprised when the fingers of dawn tried to push through the rain. The van hummed along the old road, his overlay showing the route. He'd been running without headlights for a hundred klicks or so.

A few hours back someone had hammered on the van's internal privacy screen, maybe Haraway, but he'd ignored it and they'd stopped. Mason wanted to be alone for a while longer.

The trees alongside the road were old, dead and blasted, twisted fingers eager to hold the clouds above. The ancient tarmac underneath the van was rutted and pitted. It was as if no one had been out here in a long time.

It's the best kind. It's a place that doesn't exist.

The lattice pulled his hand, steering around a pothole, the van moving smoothly despite the speed. He checked the HUD, seeing the big numbers tick between 200, 201, and back again.

"Mason," said Carter.

"Hey," he said. "You can't find me, remember?"

"Yeah, that's what I'm calling about," she said. "Soon, I won't be able to."

"I don't understand."

"Do you know how to wire a place up?"

"What?"

"This place is off the grid, but ... it's got a sort of grid of its own."

"Okay," he said. "That's good?"

"It might be. I'm trying to work out how to get in, but it's ... it's *old*. Father Time's never heard of it. It's old, and it's shitty, and I'm just—"

"Carter."

Silence followed for a heartbeat, then, "I'm sorry."

"It's going to be okay."

"How can you know?" There was something hard and frightened in her voice. "They're right here!"

The van bounced and jerked as he hit rubble on the road, the lattice kicking a little under his skin as he got the van back under control. "Carter?"

"Yeah?"

"Fuck 'em, okay?" Mason looked at the coming dawn. "They're an international cunt circus. Fuck those fucking motherfuckers."

She laughed, ragged at first, then long and clear. "I haven't heard that one before."

"Yeah," said Mason. "It's about right, though."

Carter sobered. "I might not be at my best. I haven't had a break in a while."

"Me neither. Still, my seat's nice. Those Reed assholes have comfortable cars."

"The grid, Mason," she said. "Remember the grid."

"What about it?" He thought he could see a structure in the distance, a smudge of black against the coming dawn. "I think I'm almost there."

"You've got a way to go yet," she said. "The illegal?"

"Bonus Round?"

"Or Haraway," said Carter. "Either of them."

"Either?"

"See if they can help you. You don't have to do this alone," said Carter. "Find a store. Anything with tools. For working with cables, or wires."

"A store?"

"There's not much time left." The link crackled and popped through Carter's voice, cutting out for a second. "Mason?"

"Yes?"

"I'm sorry."

"What for?" But the link was gone, lost and dead like the trees lining the road.

Mason stood in the rain, hair plastered on his head. He hauled the van's door open.

"You motherfucker." Bonus Round crouched in the doorway, her eyes wide as she looked around. "Sweet Jesus."

Haraway joined her, looking into the rain in the smudged light of dawn. "Mason, where are we?"

"We got here off the two-forty. What was left of it." He shrugged, looking at the rotted buildings that lined the road. No skyscrapers. Nothing but old, disused junk. "I passed a sign. Richland High School. So, I guess this is Richland."

"Where the fuck is Richland? I've never heard of it," said Bonus Round. "Where is this place?"

"Wait here," said Mason. "I'll get you something for the rain."

"You're not covered," said Haraway. "What about you? Where's your helmet?"

"Carter said they could track me through it," said Mason, "so I left it about a hundred klicks back."

"You—"

"Don't sweat it, doc. It's why they pay me the big bucks." He walked through the rain, white boots crunching through fragments of gravel littering the road surface.

It probably didn't much matter. Dead from the rain, cancer, or from an Apsel bounty, dead was dead. He strode across the big wide street to a building that had the look of a general store, door hanging free of its hinges. Mason picked it up, grit sloughing free. He tossed the door inside, stepping after it.

Water dripped at the back of the store. The floor was rotted, and mold crawled up the walls. *Paradise.* Mason stepped through the aisles. Most shelves had fallen, but a few still held goods ready for sale. *No looting. Plenty here worth taking. What happened to the people?*

He found a rack of cheap umbrellas, plastic sleeves wrapped around the metal frames. He smiled at the color options, picking three out, all the same. Mason gave a last look around. He thought a figure shambled at the back, but it was gone when he blinked.

That's not ideal.

He walked back to the van, handing the umbrellas out. The girl turned hers over like it was a snake, unsure what to make of it.

"What shit is this?" said Bonus Round. "This the only color they had?"

Haraway looked like she wanted to take charge. "I hardly think—"

"No, probably not," said Bonus Round. She pulled the sleeve off her umbrella, opening it. Its pink canopy arched above her.

"It's very you," said Mason. "It goes nicely with—"

"Go fuck yourself, company man," she said. "Pink? Really?"

The girl looked at Bonus Round's umbrella then back to her own. Haraway reached down, pulling the cover free. "Like this, Laia."

"Laia?" said Mason.

"It's her name," said Haraway. "The language pack."

"Right." Mason crouched in front of the girl. "You're Laia?"

"Yes," she said, then looked at Bonus Round's back. "Sadie says you're an asshole." Her accent was thick, like she came from a Latin country. *Spanish, maybe Italian.*

Mason looked over his shoulder at Bonus Round. *Sadie, huh?* "She did, did she?"

"Yes." Laia looked into his eyes. "It's inside you."

Mason stood, taking a step away from the girl. "What is?"

Laia looked at the clouds, holding her hand out to the rain. "The demon. It's inside you."

"I—"

"She doesn't make a lot of sense," said Haraway. "It's like she's speaking English fine, but doesn't know the right words."

Laia touched the collar at her throat. "Can you get this off?"

Mason looked closer at the collar. It looked like a couple hicks hammered it out of spare steel. "Maybe. I'll need some tools."

"Hurry," said Laia. "Hurry, or the demon will eat your soul."

CHAPTER TWENTY-SEVEN

This was the most comfortable cage Laia had ever been in. The walls were smooth, beautifully made, and the floor was lush, like the finest garments. That was if you ignored the hole in the middle where one of the women used a weapon of impossible power.

While they couldn't get out, cages didn't have weapons inside. Which meant this wasn't a cage, but a carriage. *The angel secured us inside to keep us safe.* She'd never been in a carriage.

Laia watched the two women with her. They were well fed and healthy. The one in black had been beaten, but her injuries looked recent. And *beaten* didn't feel like the right word.

She had been *fighting*. Neither of them walked with a limp or carried a cane. They hadn't undressed, but if they had Laia was sure their backs would be free of lash scars. Laia wanted to be able to speak with them, to hear how one who was not a Master could carry her head high.

How they could fight.

They weren't the only ones. The angel could fight. Before he'd put them in here, she'd seen the angel face down her master. His eyes had burned blue-white. Maybe the heavens were filled with warriors and asked mortals to join them when fighting injustice. Whatever was going on, Laia knew one thing.

Her master wasn't her master anymore.

She wondered where Zacharies was. The angel had sent him away with another man, dressed impossibly fine, and they'd spoken words as if they'd known each other. Laia wondered what it would be like to know an angel and to speak with one. She'd been worried about Zacharies, but after thinking about it, she knew the angel wouldn't have sent her brother off if there was danger.

Would it? Laia had felt the thrill of fear when the carriage moved. It leaped forward, the speed of it pushing her to the floor. She'd felt pinned, the majesty of the heavens holding her still.

You weren't afraid of the carriage. Laia remembered the angel's star-brilliant eyes. Who was she to think she could talk to angels? The prophecy only said the angel would save them, not how. Laia had sat on the floor, eyes wide, and watched the women speak with the angel. They were able to talk in its language. Laia couldn't and felt fear because she wasn't sure she'd be able to convince the angel to help.

The woman with the black hair and blacker lips showed no respect. That was surprising. Were angels so common here? Was this Heaven or Hell?

Perhaps angels *were* common here. *A world free from injustice.* Laia had seen so many strange things since arriving. Lights without fire. Men and women walking tall and free. Weapons of impossible power. And an angel.

It's all true.

She remembered crystals falling with the rain as the angel fell, blazing a trail from above. He'd knocked her old master down before his will could be stolen. The angel was so fast, he could only be divine. He'd looked at Laia with eyes made of hard light, and she'd felt like he looked at her soul. Turned it this way and that and found her wanting.

But he took me with him.

Laia had forgotten her fear, remembering being led out through beautiful passages walled with the finest materials. Their surfaces had been smooth. Laia had trailed her hand across them, unable to find a seam or defect. But the passages hadn't smelled right. They smelled old, dead, and rotten.

Like the rain.

At least that was familiar. So many strange things, like the wool floor of the carriage, and yet the stinking, vile rain poured from the sky as it did in her world.

Whenever she tried speaking with the two women who shared the carriage with her, they hadn't understood. The one with no respect had given her a smoking stick that tasted good but made her lungs burn, like the *lamesh* weed from the marshes.

When the carriage stopped, the angel brought water, which the blond-haired woman had mixed with a powder. Laia had drunk it all, the taste something marvelous. And so sweet! When she'd been offered more a little while later, the carriage moving swift and sure around them again, Laia drank it all. It made her head feel heavy, her brain *itchy*, but not in an unpleasant way.

She'd slept, exhaustion dragging her away. Laia didn't know for how long, but when she woke light seeped in from the front of the carriage. Laia felt them slow, the change in speed what woke her.

"I'm going to punch his lights out," said the woman with the black clothes and blacker lips.

I understand the language of the angels!

The blond one frowned. "I wouldn't recommend that. He's not known for his tolerance."

"How many times have you been dragged from your home in the night?" Laia watched the woman's black lips curl with anger.

Tolerance. The word snagged at her mind, the itching behind her eyes coming back. She knew the word, but not the meaning.

"What does tolerance mean?" Laia sat up, steadying herself as the carriage listed.

"Now there's a thing," said the one with black lips. "She's Spanish."

"She's not Spanish," said the blond, tossing perfect hair. "Her mouth isn't used to making our sounds."

"I know how it works," said the other one. "Christ, Haraway. I'm a musician, not brainless."

Haraway. A name, not a word. The blond woman was Haraway.

Laia leaned forward. "Where is the angel? Is he all right?"

The other two looked at each other, and Black Lips cocked her head. "Come again?"

Laia gestured to the front of the carriage. "He was with us before, but there's a barrier there now. I can't see if he's okay."

Black Lips looked at her for a few moments, then laughed, deep and loud. "Oh, honey. He's *no* angel. He's a fucking asshole."

"He's just following orders, Sadie." Haraway frowned. *The other one is called Sadie.* "My orders."

"Yeah? So, who's the asshole then?"

Haraway kept her frown on, staying silent for a few more moments before turning to Laia with a smile. "Hello. I'm Jenni Haraway. This is Sadie Freeman. What's your name?"

"Laia."

"Pleased to meet you, Laia. How are you feeling?"

"I'm..." Laia thought about it, wanting to give the truth to these people in the land of angels. "I miss my brother. Will he be all right?"

"Which one was your brother?" asked Haraway.

Not the slaver. Not the devil. Not the one who cages your gift. Laia touched the metal at her neck. "The other one with a collar."

"Right," said Haraway. "He's probably okay."

Sadie snorted but didn't say anything. Haraway glanced at Sadie before continuing. "He's with another syndicate."

Syndicate. Another word she knew but could give no substance to. Laia scratched her head. "I'm speaking but not ... using *my* words, am I?"

One of Haraway's eyebrows lifted. "You don't know what a language pack is?"

"Maybe she's never wanted to have that shit in her brain," said

Sadie. "Some people would prefer to get next to the metal. More predictable than a virus in their heads." She shuddered as if either path led to horrors. Laia was going to ask what she meant, but the carriage stopped. "You company people? You're all the same."

The side of the carriage opened. Through the door, Laia saw a dead city huddling in the rain. Sadie said, "You motherfucker." Then, as she saw the ruin outside, "Sweet Jesus."

She couldn't see what Laia saw, though. The rain was *alive* with the demon. The angel stood in the downpour. Laia could see his face for the first time. He had a hard jaw and blue eyes. Perfect. Beautiful. Terrible.

She could see the demon was already inside him.

Laia looked at the fire, thinking. *Mason Floyd.* The angel had a name.

She took another bite of the food stick she'd been handed. It was delicious, full of substance and strength. It smelled of nuts and something called *chocolate. Chocolate* had been in the drink she'd had earlier. This place *must* be Heaven to have chocolate.

Yet, around her was a dead town. She could see it would have been fine before it fell. Built to a quality her own world couldn't touch. They'd left it, and all the people, to die.

Which meant it wasn't a Heaven Laia could understand. The angel *Mason* had served them. Laia was prepared to forage for food before he'd handed out food sticks before walking out into the burning rain.

He didn't flinch, tall and strong as he'd walked into the demon's caress.

Haraway chewed her own food stick. "What did you mean when you said that he had a demon in him, Laia?"

Sadie spoke while chewing. "I figured it for some kind of *hentai* reference."

Hentai. Another word of meaning and no substance. "What is *hentai?*"

Sadie swallowed. "Nothing for you, that's for sure." She stood, walking to the edge of the room, looking out through the gap of crumbled wall. The set of her shoulders said: *I'm angry.* Sadie looked into the rain after Mason, and she was angry. *How can you be angry at an angel?*

Haraway scooted forward. "Does the demon have something to do with the rain?"

Laia stared at Haraway for a few moments. *Has she been touched by the sun? Her thoughts have no strength.* "The demon is the rain. Every child knows that."

Haraway smiled. "Pretend I haven't been born yet."

Laia sighed. "The Masters bring storms. When crops are needed, the rain comes, and the guilty are punished."

"How?" asked Haraway. "How are the guilty punished?"

"The rain." Laia swallowed, thinking. She pointed past Sadie. "The demon is in the rain."

Haraway ran a hand through perfect hair, sighing. "Okay. That's what I'd call circular logic."

"Where is Mason?" said Laia. "Even an angel can't stand in the rain."

Sadie snorted. "I told you, kid. He's no angel."

"I saw him fall from the sky. The air burned."

"Maybe it did." Sadie shrugged, glaring back at the rain. "I wasn't there."

"He saved me," insisted Laia. "From my master. He saved you, too."

Sadie turned, her eyes hard. "What?"

"The angel saved you from the man who hates you for how well you play." Laia wondered how they could not see things so obvious. "With hair black like yours but made dead and flat from the poisons he takes."

Sadie and Haraway both looked at her before Sadie said, "I don't remember anything about that."

"About what?" Mason stood at the rain's edge. Laia could see that his face was gray, his eyes too wide. He held a bag.

Sadie spun, taking a step back. "Jesus, Floyd, don't sneak up like that."

Mason whispered, "It's the only way I can stay hidden from the dead."

Haraway stood, walking to Mason. She took the bag from him and set it aside before looking into his eyes. "Oh. *Oh.*"

"What?" Sadie looked torn between wanting to hit Mason and being concerned. Laia understood. The demon was their common enemy.

"He needs treatment," said Haraway. "For the rain."

"I can do that," offered Laia. "If you can get my collar off."

"Shit." Sadie ignored Laia. "He's the only one who knows anything about this place. We're fucked without him."

"I know," said Haraway. "He's taken us off the grid."

"I can do it," said Laia. "Help me take the collar off."

Mason looked between Sadie and Haraway, his teeth chattering. Laia moved toward the bag Mason brought, trying to understand the fastening. It was a row of tiny teeth, the metal ends interlinked like miniature fingers.

"There's nowhere off the grid," said Sadie. "If there was, I'd have bought real estate there."

"Well, it's here," snapped Haraway. "*I* can't get a signal. Can you?"

Sadie tapped the back of her neck. "No link. I don't put that shit in my head." She pulled out a small rectangle, thinner than the parchment they used to record tithes. "Phone's got nothing."

Laia managed to get the bag open. She saw a big metal pair of scissors, the handles long, the cutting ends short and thick. She took it from the bag, setting the blades to her collar. Laia tried to work the handles, but they were too long, and she almost couldn't hold them. *I must. I must do this!*

"Well, you'll just have to trust me," said Haraway.

"Not likely." Sadie tossed a glance at Mason. "He doesn't look good, though."

Laia wedged one handle against the ground, heaving on the other. The big scissors cut the collar with a solid *snick*, teeth snapping shut next to her skin. The broken collar fell with a clatter, giving her a farewell kiss as it nicked her jaw. Blood welled but Laia ignored it as she felt the hand at her throat relax, the world's colors coming back. She stood, walking toward Mason.

Haraway spared her a glance, then turned back to Sadie. "We need him."

"We?" said Sadie. "Or you? I'm used to getting along just fine without—"

"What, like how well you were doing with your boyfriend back there?" Haraway snorted. "Please."

Sadie shrugged, reaching into a pocket in her black jacket. She pulled out a crumpled pack, silver edges peeking through her fingers and lit a ... *cigarette.*

Laia ignored them, taking Mason's hands in hers. The angel flinched, trying to pull away before squinting at her. "You're ... *her.* I ... *remember* you."

"Come inside," said Laia. "Come out of the rain. It's burning you."

"I'm scared," he said. "They keep coming."

"Who keeps coming?" Laia drew him inside, the water trickling down the white armor he wore, the fingers she held hard and cold. *Gloves.* The word held itself in her head.

"All of them," said Mason. "All the people I've killed. I drowned them in my head, and they won't stay dead."

The other two women fell silent. Laia pulled Mason close to the fire. He followed, docile like a small child, kneeling before her. She leaned next to him, whispering into his ear. "Close your eyes. There's no one here."

Mason looked to the gap in the wall before shutting his eyes, hands still in hers. Laia knew the terrors the demon could bring. *The angel has courage.* She reached out with her gift, going below the white suit, the flesh beneath, and seeing the blood beating in his veins. Her mind touched the flow of a million tiny living things and saw the demon riding along with them. Laia saw the metal within him, how his arms and legs were no longer *his.* She ignored the beating heart of fire in his chest, powerful enough to blind her if she stared at it.

She closed her own eyes, breathing out as she *pushed.* The demon was surprised, struggling, and Mason gave a small cry.

"Shhh. I've almost got it." Laia held a million pieces of the demon in her mind, then slammed down on it. She laughed with the joy of her gift as she pushed the demon out through his skin into the air.

Mason coughed, shuddering, his eyes snapping open. He leaped to his feet, hand coming up in a fist above Laia.

Sadie's hand was on his wrist. "No. *Look.*"

Mason followed her gaze. A silhouette of mist faded away, the shape of his crouching form, as a small breeze from outside picked it apart and drove it away.

"What..." He pulled his wrist free, coughing, then hurried to the break in the wall. Mason threw up into the street.

Sadie took another pull on her cigarette, blowing the smoke out. "There's something you don't see every day."

CHAPTER TWENTY-EIGHT_

"How's that?" said the man with perfect clothes. Zacharies' collar lay on the table between them, cuts made by a small device more precise than the finest saw. Zacharies felt those cuts added form and structure to the rude work of the collar, like even destruction in this world was beautifully done.

The collar sat beside a plate of bagels. Zacharies did his level best to work his way through them. He rubbed the marks on his throat. He would carry scars. "It is..."

"Better?"

"Amazing," said Zacharies. He could hear the world again. "Thank you, my friend."

The man smiled. Zacharies had never seen someone with such perfectly-straight, brilliant-white teeth. "It's nothing. You must be worried about your sister."

"Yes," said Zacharies. "How do we get her back?"

"It's tricky." The man looked around at other people bustling from table to table. How he ignored the heavenly scent of the food, Zacharies didn't know. "My ... colleague? The guy from Apsel Federate."

"The angel?" Zacharies spoke around a mouthful of food. "I should have believed Laia. I was such a fool."

"Angel?" A hint of the man's perfect teeth glinted, then he relaxed into a laugh. "I get it."

"Something is funny?" The words felt clumsy in Zacharies' mouth. The man explained the metal seed they'd planted in his skull was letting him speak with their words. They still felt alien, like he wasn't meant to know the tongue of the angels.

"A little. There's nothing heavenly about him."

"But I saw—"

"Armor. You saw urban assault armor. Or riot gear, maybe. I don't know, it's Federate tech, and there's a fine line there anyway. A bit out of spec, but it got the job done."

Armor. Where Zacharies came from armor didn't grant people the power of gods. "I know what I saw."

"Yeah, okay. An angel, then."

Zacharies spread his hands. "My sister's younger than me. Idealistic." He tried the word on for size, finding it a good fit. "Laia's a ... *believer.* And what she believes always comes true."

"Really?" The man straightened his shirt. The movement looked so casual, but if Zacharies had a shirt that fine he'd be very careful about touching it. The stitching was too fine to be seen. "Always?"

"Yes." Zacharies watched the people moving around in chaotic symphony. "Not always clearly, but she sees."

"What do you mean?" asked the man.

Zacharies considered him, wondering if the word *friend* would fit. It also felt right. "Look here." Zacharies lifted a bagel from the plate. He'd eaten six of them, his mouth bursting with the wonderful saltiness. Zacharies bit into his seventh. "This food is exquisite."

"It's just a bagel. Not a very good one. The cafe on this level's barely average. Apparently, engineers don't care."

A man in a white coat approached their table, reaching for their spare chair. "This seat taken?"

"Fuck off." Zacharies' friend adjusted his tie. The man in the white coat paled, walking away.

"It's things like that. They make me confused." *This place is full of such contradictions. Could we not have spared the chair and shared these wondrous bagels?*

"He was an asshole," offered the man. "Works in Weapons Applications."

Weapons. Applications. "How do you not know how to apply a weapon?"

"Exactly." The man made a fist, pointing with his index finger, bringing his thumb down. "You just point and shoot."

"That's his job?" Zacharies wiped his fingers on his new shirt. The cloth was so fine it felt like a sin. He stared at the empty plate. His belly was more than full. Zacharies was in the city of angels. *I didn't believe. I should have believed.*

The angels surrounded themselves with ordinary people and made them perfect.

"You want some more?"

"We should ask around." Zacharies looked around. Surely one of these others needed food. "Others may be hungry."

The man laughed again. "They might be, at that. But they can get their own damn bagels."

"They don't need to eat?"

"They need to eat all right. If you decide to stay with us ... no one ever goes hungry at Metatech."

Zacharies looked down at the collar, fingering the sheared metal. "My sister?"

"She'll be welcome. We're a family-first company."

"What will it cost?" Here, the word carried a same-but-different feel. *Cost* meant the whip, the iron, the fist. Zacharies felt it true here too, in less obvious ways. But if he could get Laia here, he would pay. For her.

"Ah. That's the thing." The man picked up a piece of Zacharies' collar. "You said this was holding you back."

"Yes. Removing it was like taking a hand from around my throat."

"Gotcha." The man leaned forward. "What does that mean, exactly?"

"It's like..." Zacharies turned toward a window. It took up an entire wall, a portal out to the demon-filled rain lashing the glass. The pane was crystal clear, showing him all of the demon's fury. "It's like always being under a cloud. Then walking out into a clear day."

"Sure." A slouch, a sigh. "Still don't know what you're talking about."

"Okay." Zacharies drummed his fingers on the table. "Who is the Master here?"

"Master?"

"Yes." Zacharies nodded. "Who holds your leash?"

"That's a funny question," said the man. "Or a funny way of asking it."

"You have a master, surely."

"I've got a *boss*, Zacharies. I'm no one's servant."

"You keep servants? Not slaves?" Zacharies looked at the plate again. "I think I would like another bagel."

"Not something else? You've eaten a lot of bagels, man."

"I can have other things?" Zacharies hadn't dared ask.

"Sure." The man glanced away, eyes growing distant for a second. "There. I've got something on the way."

"How?" Zacharies hadn't seen him make a gesture and had seen no servant.

The man tapped the side of his head. "The link, kid. You'll work it out."

Zacharies frowned, lifting his broken collar. The crude metal was dirty and black. "Who tells you when you may use your gift?"

"Gift? I'm not sure I'd call shooting fools in the head a gift, but whatever."

"No." Zacharies shook his head. "Your inner gift."

The man frowned before glancing at the empty plate. "You're not allergic to wheat? Not having a chemical imbalance?"

"I don't think so," said Zacharies. "I don't think I've eaten this much before."

"Me neither," said the man. "Seven bagels is some impressive shit. Zach?"

"Yes?"

"We don't have magic inner powers and weird monkey friends in the sky. I get *missions*. I fix problems." He sighed. "You said you could show me your gift."

"Yes. Once you removed the collar."

"Right." The man stared at the collar. "It's removed."

"I need permission. From a Master." Using the gift without permission brought agony. Zacharies glanced down, shying away from the remembered whip.

"Was this Master the asshole who came through with you?"

"Yes."

A grin. "He's not going to be anyone's master for long. Reed have a reputation."

The night closed about him, the pain in his mind extreme, as Laia whimpered in the darkness near the Master. If he could just get free...

Zacharies shook off the memory. "A reputation? Will they hurt him?"

"Absolutely. Probably a great deal."

"Good." Zacharies spat the word out.

A woman wearing green arrived at their table carrying two plates. "Who wants the steak?"

The man nodded at Zacharies. "He does."

"Okay." She put a plate in front of the man. "Yours must be the omelet."

"No. They're both for him."

"I see." She winked at Zacharies. "Growing boy." A twirl of green, and she was off.

Zacharies' eyes were drawn to his plate. The smell of the meat made his mouth water and his stomach yearn, despite being over-full. *This is Heaven, without question.*

He made to grab the food, but the man's hand on his wrist stopped him. "Not like that. Fuck's sake, Zach. Were you raised in a barn?"

"I ... Yes."

A blank stare, then a nod. "Okay, fair enough. The knife and fork."

Fork. "I don't know that word."

"Knife?"

"Fork."

"It's that thing beside you that's not the knife." The man picked up the knife and fork, showing Zacharies how to hold them. Zacharies took the implements from him, his grip clumsy. He managed to more mash than cut a piece of steak before getting it into his mouth.

"This is very good." Zacharies wanted to talk, but he wanted to eat as well, so he spoke with his mouth full.

"It's *okay*. Like I said, this place is just a bit shit."

Zacharies chewed. *How do I decide what to do without a master?* "If there is no Master..." He trailed off.

"Kid? Here, we do what we want."

Zacharies frowned. "Anything?"

"Not *anything*. The police need paying if we go too far."

"Police?"

"Assholes," said the man.

Zacharies considered that. "There are a lot of assholes here."

"More than you know. Let's see it."

"See it?"

The man reached into his jacket pocket, pulling out a small rectangular box. He pulled a stick from it, putting one end in his mouth, then lit it with another box that made flame. The man inhaled, then blew smoke toward the ceiling.

Zacharies watched, forgetting to chew. The man noticed him staring. He offered the rectangular box to Zacharies. "Smoke?"

Zacharies ignored him, pointing at the smaller box. "That makes fire?"

"Yeah. You've not seen a lighter before?"

"Laia usually does that," said Zacharies.

"Your sister has a lighter?"

"No, she is..." It was hard to find the right words. This language of angels was so strange. Zacharies moved some steak around his plate. "Her gift is smaller and bigger than mine."

"What?"

Zacharies sighed, putting down the knife. It really was very good *steak*. He reached out a little way. His gift walked the air between them, standing invisible on the table. He felt the plates, the vile evil of the collar, and the table.

His mind touched the small rectangle held in the man's hand, and he tugged. The man's eyes widened as the lighter slipped from his fingers, spinning silver in the air as it slipped across the table to Zacharies' hand.

The man goggled. "What the *fuck*."

Zacharies voice was small. "I'm sorry. My gift is tiny."

"Tiny." The man drew on his cigarette, hands shaky. "You call this a gift?"

"Yes."

"How many people on your world can do this?"

"A few. The Masters watch babies, selecting some."

"Some?"

"Yes." Zacharies looked down. He didn't feel like eating steak anymore.

The man watched him in silence for a moment. "Fair enough, kid. Assholes."

"Yes," agreed Zacharies. "I think my world is full of assholes too."

The man laughed. "No shit? Assholes on two worlds. Who'd have thought."

Zacharies smiled again, timid as the dawn. "Who'd have thought." He held the lighter out.

"Keep it." Zacharies' friend pushed his chair back, crossing his legs. "Your sister has a bigger gift?"

"Bigger and smaller." Zacharies waggled his hand in the air, *so-so*. "She is stronger but works on smaller things."

"Smaller?"

"It's hard to describe." Zacharies held up the lighter. "She can make fire."

"Hmm. We'll look into that when we find out where she is. How much can you do?"

"Do?"

"You took my lighter."

"I'm sorry." Zacharies held the lighter out again.

"Don't apologize. Not here. Zach, can I give you some advice?"

"I'd like that. This is all very strange."

"There's a bunch of assholes in R&D who are going to want to get in your head. Peel it like a grape." Zacharies swallowed but said nothing. "So, here's the thing. I like you. And I don't like R&D."

"I don't understand," said Zacharies.

"Don't apologize," said the man. "That's it. Do what you do. Do it large. And if someone wants to peel your head like a grape?"

"An asshole?"

The man smiled over his cigarette. "Sure, an asshole. Don't just take their lighter away."

"I think I understand," said Zacharies. "You want me to use my gift."

"I don't think you *do* understand, but it's a start. Before we see those guys in R&D, what can you do?"

"Lift things. Move things."

"How many? How heavy?"

"Not many. Not heavy." Zacharies thought back. "I can lift a chair holding a man and supplies for a week. I can carry that across the desert."

"Right." The man blew smoke at the ceiling. "Quite a lot, then."

"My powers are small," said Zacharies. "Not like the angel."

The man laughed again, eyes crinkling with mirth, before scrubbing out his cigarette on the table. "He's not an angel. Let's go watch you mess with someone's day." He stood, holding a hand out to Zacharies. "Since we've decided not to lose you to the butchers in R&D, you can call me Mike."

Zacharies took Mike's hand. His grip was firm. Zacharies wondered why Heaven was full of assholes, but he also wondered how he'd found a man who was kind and decent.

○

"I don't know how to explain it better." Zacharies frowned. "I ... *touch* it and *ask* it to move."

They were in a room with bright lights and things called machines, plastic and shiny metal. Screens glowed. A tech Mike called Yelden was with them, and the three of them stared at a chair, center stage. The chair didn't look welcoming, despite being made in the same perfect way as Mike's clothes and teeth. It had straps. Zacharies hadn't liked it as soon as he'd seen it, so he lifted it from the ground.

Yelden watched the chair, doubt in his eyes as he crouched low to check the air under it. He turned to Mike. "Seriously, if this is some kind of joke—"

Mike spread his hands. "It's no joke. Mind if I smoke?"

"There's no smoking in here," said Yelden. Zacharies watched as Mike nodded, pulled a pack of cigarettes out, lighting one. He offered the pack to the tech, who looked at it before taking one. "Thanks."

"No problem," said Mike around the edges of his cigarette. He looked to Zacharies. "It's not a trick, right?"

Zacharies frowned. "I don't know if I understand the question. Your language is strange."

"He means you're lying." Mike blew smoke. "Are you lying, kid?"

"I don't think so." Zacharies held a hand out, palm up, to the chair. "I asked it to—"

"Spin in the air?" Yelden watched the chair rotate. "Hang on. I'm going to call Kerney down here."

Zacharies glanced at Mike. "Should I put the chair down?"

"Not yet." Mike straightened his sleeves, leaning closer to Zacharies. "Remember what I said about assholes?"

"Yes." Zacharies considered the chair he held with his gift. It was very light, lighter than anything that size had a right to be. "What is the chair for?"

"Exactly." Mike nodded. "Grapes. Keep your head together."

The door behind Zacharies opened with a soft hiss of air, and he turned to see another tech enter the room. The man's hair was a mess, and he had a stain at the edge of his lips. "Fuck is it? I'm in the middle..." He stopped, taking in the chair, mouth open.

"Kerney," said Yelden. "I need a consult."

Kerney stared at the chair, then did a slow walk around it. "You've—"

"I haven't done shit." Yelden took a pull on his cigarette. "I just wanted to see if the look on your face was the same as mine."

Kerney stopped walking, glaring at Zacharies. "Who the hell are you?" He turned to Mike. "There's no smoking in here."

Mike nodded, grinning around his cigarette. "That's right." He blew a cloud of smoke, soft and gray, at the ceiling.

"Fucking Specialist Services," said Kerney.

"What was that?" Mike leaned forward, hand cupped to his ear. "I didn't catch what you said."

"Nothing." Kerney blurted the word.

Zacharies looked between them. *Someone is in charge in this room. It isn't Kerney.* Kerney gestured at the chair. "May I?"

"Be my guest." Yelden shrugged, hands in his pockets.

Kerney reached out, stopping the chair from spinning. Zacharies could feel Kerney's touch like a light in his mind, the pressure on the chair's arm full of life. Kerney drew his hand back, turning to a table. He grabbed a steel tray, tools and instruments clattering to the ground.

"Hey," said Yelden.

Kerney ignored the other tech, passing the tray through the air around the chair. "There's nothing holding it up."

"That's not quite true, is it?" Mike ground out his cigarette against the side of a machine. He pulled another from his pack, lighting it. Zacharies saw the brief flare of fire reflected in his eyes. "Because it's not holding itself up."

"It is." Kerney waved his tray at the chair. "There's nothing—"

"It's an inanimate object," said Mike. "*It* doesn't do anything."

"Semantics," said Kerney.

"I thought you guys were scientists," said Mike.

Yelden was about to say something before Zacharies spoke. "I asked it to do that."

All three men turned to look at him. Yelden spoke first. "You said something like that before. Like you talked to it."

"It's not ... *talking*," said Zacharies. "You do not have gifted people in your world?"

"Our world?" Yelden looked sideways at Mike.

Mike shrugged, the gesture small. "Roll with it."

"Okay," said Yelden. "There's lots of gifted people. People who can do math faster than a computer, or someone who can hit a curveball out of the park."

Math. Computer. Curveball. Zacharies frowned. "I don't know these words. Not yet."

"Don't sweat it, kid," said Mike. "The link will work it out for you over the next couple days."

"He's got a new link?" said Kerney. "He's what, eighteen? Nineteen?"

"Maybe." Mike blew more smoke at the ceiling. "Hard to tell."

"Hell with this." Kerney walked to Zacharies, glaring at him. "How are you doing it?" He reached toward Zacharies. Zacharies stepped back, the chair jerking in the air, following his direction of movement.

"Yeah, that's where you guys come in." Mike sighed. "If I knew how he was doing it, it'd be in my report already."

Yelden's eyes were wide. "Are you saying—"

"He's a telekinetic." Kerney moved closer to Zacharies. Zacharies stepped further back, the chair drifting again. "The military applications..."

"Please," said Zacharies. "I just want to find my sister."

"You have a sister?" said Yelden. "Can she do this?"

"Apparently not," said Mike. "She does another thing entirely."

"Her gift is different." Zacharies shrugged. "Bigger and smaller."

"Right." Kerney rubbed at the stain on his lip. "Protocol is clear. We need to get him in a chair."

"Go ahead." Mike edged toward the side of the room.

"Are you giving authorization?" asked Yelden.

"No," said Mike. "I'm just an observer."

Yelden turned to Kerney. "Security is on the way."

"Security?" said Zacharies. "What needs to be secured?"

The door whispered open, three men stepping through. They wore clothing of a strange cut, the material hard, strong, rigid against his mind. They held weapons. Zacharies' eyes narrowed, recognizing the shape of the devices from what the angel had carried. "Are these men angels?"

"No." Mike was behind him. "You don't need to go easy on 'em."

Yelden pointed at Zacharies. "Detain him."

One of the three newcomers took a step forward, then stopped, looking at the chair. "Is that chair floating in the air?"

"Kinda," said Mike. "You need to think carefully, sergeant. How do you want this day to end?"

The sergeant looked over at Mike, then back at Zacharies. "Don't take this personal, kid." He pulled a small device from his belt, pointed it at Zacharies. The device hissed and spat a dart.

Zacharies stopped the dart in the air. He touched his fingertip to it, causing it to bob and turn a lazy spiral. "Please. I want to find my sister."

"Kid, the fastest way to find your sister is to get taken seriously."
Mike gave an embarrassed cough. "I take you seriously. These guys?
Orangutans."

The sergeant's face twisted in a snarl. He waved his men
forward. Zacharies felt their intent, their *need*. The man to his left
took two steps. Zacharies made the chair move, black leather and
metal surging across the room. The man to the sergeant's left raised
his weapon in surprise, firing. The rounds tore through the chair as it
raced for him. Bullets tore an arm from it before it slammed into the
guard, knocking him through the air and into the wall.

The second man raised his rifle, pointing it at Zacharies. His face
spoke of animal fear.

*Reach deep. Into the stone and rock. It's dead, long turned, warped
by the hands of men, but it will suffice.*

The floor ripped, cement and tiles showering up. A slab of
concrete the size of a man rose from the ground to stand between the
guard and Zacharies. The guard's weapon fired, bullets hitting the
concrete. Chips and splinters sprayed.

"I said, cease fire!" The sergeant knocked the other man's weapon
down. "Christ. What the hell—"

"That'll do, kid." Mike stepped away from the wall. "Well
played."

Yelden and Kerney got up from where they huddled behind lab
equipment. Zacharies hadn't notice them move. Yelden started
with, "What?"

"He, umm," said Kerney.

"I think the best thing we can do right now is help Zach here find
his sister." Mike did a slow turn. "What do you fellas think?"

The sergeant walked to the cement block standing in the air like
the chair had. He glared at the floor underneath as if the whole world
lied to him. "He's ripped a hole in the floor. He ripped a fucking *hole*
in the *floor*."

"Yeah. Make sure you put it in your report. C'mon, kid." Mike
led Zacharies from the room.

Zacharies stopped in the corridor outside, glancing back. Kerney and Yelden looked at the hole left by the cement slab. The sergeant bawled at his man. The third man was still out cold. "Mike?"

"Yeah, kid?"

"There are a *lot* of assholes in Heaven."

Mike laughed, turning. "Yeah, kid."

"What ... what happened there?"

Mike shrugged, walking down the corridor. "You made some enemies."

Zacharies frowned. "Why did I do that?"

"So you can find your sister."

Mike continued walking, Zacharies hurrying to catch up. "I don't understand."

"No, I expect you don't."

"Will the link tell me?"

"Shit like that isn't on the link."

"Then why?"

Mike stopped, turning to look at him. "Kid?"

"Yes, Mike."

"This isn't Heaven. It's just a world, and not a very good one."

"But—"

"Wait." Mike held up his hand, face serious. "There aren't angels, and there aren't demons. There are just people."

"I *saw* him, Mike. He fell from the sky."

Mike frowned. "He wasn't an angel."

"My sister said he was," insisted Zacharies. "Laia is always right."

"Fair enough," said Mike. "Look, it's..."

"Yes?"

"There were two ways this could go. Either they'd strap you to a chair and pull your head open, or..." He trailed off, looking at his shoes. "*You* make people fear you. I can't do that. I can't always be there."

Zacharies thought of Laia, crying in the night. "No, you can't. You can't always be there."

"This way, I don't have to be." Mike walked on.

After a moment Zacharies followed. He still thought about his sister. Zacharies hoped she was right about the angel. If he was an angel, he would be able to protect her in the night.

The way you never could.

Zacharies shook his head, but the thought stayed. It rang true, and he hated it.

CHAPTER TWENTY-NINE_

"Your problem is you've got no sense of gratitude." Mason looked through the gap in the wall, staring out at the rain lashing and coiling in the street outside. He touched the old brick, some of it crumbling away. The lattice shuddered inside him, a flash of remembered nausea clenching in his gut.

"Right." Sadie turned, her glare set to kill level. Mason could see the anger bunching under her skin, like it was a part of her flesh and bones. The way she moved her head, the way she stood, and the way she looked at him said *I despise you, company man.* It might have been fair. "I should be *happy* you dragged me out to the middle of Fucksville?"

"This was not my first choice of place." Mason kicked a stone, watching it skip over broken asphalt, the rain welcoming it. This building, like the street outside, hadn't seen maintenance in years. How many was difficult to tell. Fifty? A hundred? How long did it take for concrete corners to weather smooth? Or for red signs to bleach white?

"Oh yeah? What was your first choice? A graveyard?"

"A sex hotel."

"A..." Sadie gaped, raw anger stopping her words. "A *what?*"

"Sex hotel," repeated Mason. "Look, much as I'm enjoying your rant, I'm going to get more cigarettes."

"Don't you dare walk away," said Sadie. "Don't you *dare*."

"I'm not walking away. I'm walking out there. You can come with."

Mason watched her watch the rain, the corners of Sadie's eyes softening for just a moment before the hard steel returned. "Whatever, company man. Go get yourself killed."

He shrugged, pulling out the rumpled pack of Marlboros. *One left.* Mason tucked the pack back into his armor's pouch, turning to Haraway. "Look after the kid, okay?"

Haraway looked pale, drawn and thin. She hadn't wanted to get into the conversation between him and Sadie. Fair enough. Mason hadn't really wanted to either. The rain was as much of an escape as a grocery run.

Sound. Shapes in the rain.

The lattice pulled his gaze to the street, but there wasn't anything there. Mason watched through the break in the wall for a few moments. "Laia."

The girl was at his side almost straight away. Mason didn't like the look in her eyes that screamed *adoration*. She followed his every moment. "Yes, lord?"

He winced at the same time Sadie snorted. "It's just Mason, kid." He pointed into the rain. "Is it still there?"

She nodded, eyes solemn. "It's everywhere. Always. It's not leashed here."

"Here?" Haraway leaned forward, some of the weariness leaving her face for a moment.

"This world has no Master. Like me." The girl shrugged, a small smile dimpling her face. "Water flows when it has no container."

"But you pushed it out," said Mason. "You made it leave. Leave me."

"Yes." Laia frowned, looking at his face, his body, then his legs. "It's gone, lord ... Mason."

Good enough for me. There really is something in the rain. Mason sniffed. "Okay."

"You're really going back out there?" There was something Mason could mistake for concern in Sadie's voice, if it hadn't been hammered paper-thin by fury.

"Yeah." Mason stretched his shoulders, his armor's plates moving over each other. He unslung his rifle, offering it to Sadie. "You know your way around one of these. I saw your work in the van."

Her eyes widened. "You're giving me a gun?"

Mason frowned. "Sure. Why not?"

"Because..." Sadie stopped, looking at the gun. "I—"

"You figured we pulled you out, abducted you like some asset, and we're going to run down your brain in a company lab, the doctor here frying your insides like a good steak." Mason looked to Haraway. "Honestly? Between you and me, I don't think she's up for it."

Sadie's gaze followed his. "It's just—"

"Forget it." Mason offered the rifle again. "Know how to use it?"

"I guess." Sadie's fingertips touched the rifle. "Aren't you afraid I'm going to...?" She lifted her chin in a *you-know* gesture.

Haraway's voice was wry. "I'll admit, I'm a little worried about that too."

Mason held Sadie's eyes. "No. I'm not worried about that."

"But I might—"

"I'm not worried about that either." Mason shrugged. "Take it or don't."

Sadie took the rifle, Mason watching as she struggled with the weight of it. The rifle was heavy, designed for someone with bionics. Sadie wasn't weak, dropping it like an idiot, but it didn't look like she'd be able to sling it like a pro.

"What about a SMG?" Mason unclipped the SMG from his belt. "Smaller. Faster."

"A norm's weapon?" Sadie's lips narrowed to a hard line. You could cut sheet steel on them.

"Do I look like a normal?" Mason put the SMGs on a rotted counter. "I'm going hunting."

"Hunting?" Haraway frowned. She looked between Mason, the rifle, and the SMGs. "It's a dead city. What for?"

"Cigarettes." Mason stepped out into the howling rain.

He found cigarettes three blocks away, an old convenience store set within crumbling brick walls. The water hissed and spat, driving into his eyes, and he almost missed the doorway, the sign above it a blank rectangle, the words faded and lost. The door tore from the frame as he opened it.

Mason took shelter inside. The blue from the fusion reactor on the back of his suit pushed a soft light through the store, a soft cape spreading around him. Old magazines sat on shelves, rotten pages loose, glossy stars lost to history on the ancient covers.

Magazines. Now there's a thing the world hadn't seen for years. Not where Mason walked, anyway. Sadie might still know a place or two to buy them, but the market for unlinked entertainment couldn't be large enough to justify the work.

Bonus Round. Sadie. It'd been a mistake to bring her along. Another bad call in a really bad day. She was a damn illegal, or close to. When the Syndicate Registration Act passed, she'd be getting a link or a free trip to jail. He shouldn't care, except...

It's not fair. You picked her up from her home, a place you blew to pieces, and dragged her to a ruin dead people named Richland. You can tell yourself you were doing the right thing, but the right thing would have been to walk away.

Mason strode the aisles. He ignored products scattered across the ground. The cigarettes were huddled on a rack, packs covered with writing. He picked one up.

What the hell is a Surgeon General? And where the good goddamn is Richland?

The town wasn't on any map he had stored in the overlay. He came up empty every time he tried to search for it. He'd found a Rich*mond*, but Richland? Ghosts and echoes.

Mason looked around the store, taking in the aisles and their products. Brands stacked in shelves from companies he didn't recognize.

"Carter," he said out loud, "how old is this place?"

The link was empty, gone, no reply coming. What had she said?

It's got a sort of grid of its own.

Water dripped from his hair. Mason stared into the rain, pulling the plastic wrapping from one of the packs of cigarettes. *Marlboros, the soy bacon of cigarettes.* He lit one, taking a long pull before blowing smoke. The sweet smell of burning tobacco shouldered its way through stale air, like the cigarettes were trying to get Richland to remember what people were like.

How did a place stop existing? The stores were old, but there weren't signs of looting. The shelves were stocked, products standing or falling where they'd been left. A whole town had stood here one day, and then the next day, nothing.

Where did all the people go?

The fusion reactor at his back hummed soft and low, the suit idle. Mason watched the rain, the lattice tugging as he remembered. Mason grabbed a dirty plastic bag from one of the checkouts, tossing cigarette boxes into it. No one had stood at the checkout for years beyond counting.

It's a place that doesn't exist.

Mason walked into the rain, switching his optics to infrared. His overlay pulled structures shrouded by rain's cloak into focus. In the distance, curved stacks caught his eye.

My God.

It was an old nuclear facility. Looking back the way he'd come, he made out the break in the wall where he'd left the others. Mason remembered Laia's eyes, and the way she'd looked at him.

Do you trust me, Mason Floyd?

What with?

With your life.

"Carter, where have you sent us?" The rain didn't answer.

Mason set off at a jog, the armor hissing under the rain as he made his way toward the stacks shouldering the load of the sky. What had Carter said just before the link dropped?

I'm sorry.

The twin cooling towers were old, a crack running up the left one. Trees at the edge of the facility were blasted, ancient, dead. Nothing grew here and hadn't for a long time. Mason breathed hard, the run longer than he'd expected. The lattice shuddered under his skin, tasting the rads peeling off from the building in front of him.

It was only a few stories tall, windows empty, most broken. Like the rest of Richland, no signage remained to tell him what people called it. But Mason knew *what* it was. A fission power plant. The best answer people had before Apsel's clean reactor tech arrived.

He walked through the main door of the facility, the rain lashing at his back, a squall following him inside. Mason stood in the gloom of the first room. An old sign, covered with verdigris and dirt, claimed this was a *RECEPTION*. A desk slouched, a chair in rotted ruins behind it.

Mason felt the lattice pull under his skin, pushing him toward the door. He almost listened. Mason shouldn't *be* here. It wasn't his problem.

He reached into the fire. It burned white hot. The man inside the inferno thrashed, blind eye sockets gaping. Mason tore the door away, the squeal of hinges lost in the roar of the flames. His hand charred, catching on fire. The lattice thrashed, wanting to run.

It'd do as it was told. Mason moved past the dead reception and deeper into the building. Ancient electronics struggled in a semblance of life, and a single ceiling lamp flickered to life, old, red, and tired. The light was flattened by the blue from the reactor at his back.

Mason saw an old skeleton stretched out on the ground. There wasn't any tissue or clothes left. Just the skeleton, wearing an old wrist watch, the crumbling plastic falling away. He picked up the watch, looking at the face. He rubbed grime away with the rubber tip of a gloved finger.

Casio. A company he hadn't heard of, one that didn't exist anymore. Mason wondered which syndicate owned their IP and knew which model of watch replaced this one from decades ago.

Mason tried to picture this as a place with people, doing their jobs. Trying to make a living. He imagined he knew what had happened. There were a lot of rads. None of that explained why no one knew of Richland, the memory of the city excised like cancer.

He wondered how the person at his feet had died. He looked over the skeleton again, poking through the bones. Dust drifted, and he coughed. *There.* The bones of the rib cage were chipped and shattered. It was a small clue, hardly conclusive.

Could be vermin. Could be gunfire. Mason looked around the dark room, red light seeping in from the ancient emergency light.

Probably gunfire.

Mason went further into the gloom, the blue of the reactor at his back casting shadows that caressed the walls. He keyed the suit's lights, the chest plate throwing clean luminance from under the hard shell. The strong white light shoved back the dark. Mason froze as something scurried away at the edge of his sight.

Rats that survived the cascade of radiation from a reactor breach didn't exist outside of horror movies, did they?

He followed the corridor to the end, walking past doors long gone. He paused at a gaping entrance, the edges ragged. Mason fingered the old metal, feeling the bend in it. So much time had passed, but the fingerprint of explosives was hard to miss. Someone had come here with a real hard-on for busting their way through.

Who the hell breaks into a nuclear reactor?

At the end of the corridor, old elevator doors stood open and broken. The shaft was dark, the car gone. As he walked closer, the light from the suit edged its way into the shaft, hard shadows thrown back from the cables hanging down.

Mason stood at the edge, looking up. The machinery at the top of the shaft was mostly gone, an old gear wheel large and pitted hanging onto a warped clamp. He let his gaze fall down the shaft, the light from the suit stopping before the bottom.

He reached for the ladder set into the wall of the shaft and started to climb down.

○

The control room was old like everything else, but the bodies were different.

They were dried husks, not skeletons. The rads here were higher. A normal would be dead by now. Mason's lattice bunched and twitched under his skin. Nothing could live down here, not people, or the bacteria that fed on the dead.

The glass wall at the front of the room was shattered, a few pieces stuck in the frames. The suit's light pushed into a vast chamber beyond, old girders spanning a pit sunk into the ground. Somewhere above, light from the sky broke through, the dimness of it lost against the suit's brilliant light. Rain poured in, pattering against a massive concrete and steel structure standing vigil in the gloom.

Meltdown. They'd put a lid where the reactor used to be.

Mason's overlay hissed with static, his optics hazing in a struggle with the radiation. He stepped over to a body. It wore armor. Nuclear plant workers didn't wear armor. Not anywhere Mason had heard of. They wore safety coveralls and radiation warning badges.

He stepped away from the body, looking at now-white fabric worn by another man face down on the ground. Shot in the back, body stretched out, hand reaching toward a control panel. Mason stepped to the panel, wiping away years of grime. There was only one thing of importance. A shutdown button.

Mason looked back at the hero who'd died while trying to initiate safe shutdown. "You didn't make it, did you?" His voice sounded thin to his own ears, the massive space of the reactor chamber beyond gobbling up the sound. Words didn't have the strength to touch the concrete mass standing vigil in the dark. "You didn't manage shutdown before these assholes shot you in the back."

Probably wouldn't have mattered. Shutting down a live reactor wasn't like turning off a switch. Still, the man had tried. He hadn't run from danger, he'd run *toward* it, trying to stop...

What? What had he known was coming?

Mason paced to one of the armored men. The bodies were slumped, fallen in a loose huddle, no obvious marks on them. He grabbed one, wiping grime from the chest plate.

"Jesus Christ." Mason stood, stumbling back. The lattice shivered in sympathy.

A gold falcon's wing stared at him from the armor.

It was when he reached the bottom of the elevator shaft for the climb back up the horde came for him. Bounding out of the dark, misshapen, hideous.

He looped back the live feed from his optics to his overlay. The creatures were still there, not imagined bodies of the dead, but *real* monsters. They were humanoid, skulls lumpy and bulbous, wispy strands of hair clinging in places. Their arms were thin, teeth crooked and extending outside their lips. They were dressed in tattered rags and scraps of scavenged clothing.

They howled and chittered at each other in the darkness.

"Fellas," said Mason. *Were these ... Jesus, were these people?* "I'm pretty sure you don't want to do this."

Eyes wide and black stared at him. One turned to another, clawed parody of a hand slashing at the air, then they rushed Mason.

Overtime fell in place, natural as breathing, and he cranked the suit's lights up high. The white was blinding, a cascade of brilliance burning pure against the warped bodies of the lost men and women before him.

Mason charged, spinning and turning within their rush. He moved between them, striking hard and fast. The inductive tasers in the gauntlets fired, cycled, fired, again and again. One of the hunched people was thrown clear, Mason's fist hitting it hard enough to knock it across the corridor. Another tangled with him, then convulsed and jerked as the reactive armor discharged into it.

The blue of the reactor on his back burned bright.

Two rushed him, and he slammed the blade of his hand into the neck of one. It dropped, the taser discharging. The other grabbed for his face. Mason pushed it away, stepping back. The edge of his boot was against the black of the elevator shaft. He stood, panting, overtime pulling the color from the faces around him. He felt rather than heard more of them coming from above, and up from the shaft below.

How many? How many dead come for you, Mason?

They surged at him, pushing him back.

Mason fell, white and blue spinning against the shaft as he fell into the dark below. He fought as he fell, the tasers firing as he lashed out. He snagged an arm through the ladder at the side of the shaft, felt the jerk as the ancient metal sagged away from the wall. His boot slipped on a rung, and one of the creatures leaped from the wall to latch onto him. The reactive armor fired, the thing twitching, the smell of burnt flesh in the air.

The ladder gave way, and Mason tumbled, lost, into the forgotten dark below.

CHAPTER THIRTY_

"How the fuck long does it take to get cigarettes?" Sadie crumpled the empty pack of Treasurers, lighting the last one between black lips. She blew smoke into the rain. Laia said a demon lived in the rain, so *that* fucker could get her second-hand smoke. "This company man of yours. Know what he's doing?"

She heard Haraway step closer. "Yes."

"That's it? Just 'yes?'" Sadie turned.

Haraway shrugged casting her eyes to the floor. "He's the best at what he does."

"What's that?" Sadie took another pull, eyes darting to where Laia huddled in the corner. "Abducting people?"

"No," said Haraway. "He's not very good at that at all."

Sadie coughed out a laugh. "No, I guess not. Still," she turned back to the rain, "he knows how to show a lady a good time."

Haraway stood beside her. "This isn't really what his mission is supposed to be."

Sadie gave her a little side-eye before looking back at Laia. She kept turning, taking in the black rifle leaning against the wall, the Apsel falcon on the stock. *These company types even have a design crew for pleasing color palettes on their weapons.* "Haraway?"

"Yes?"

"What does a company man need with a BFG like that?" Sadie blew more smoke into the rain.

"Don't do that," said Laia. "It doesn't like it."

"What doesn't?" asked Sadie.

"The demon," said Laia. "It knows you're here when you do that. It's trying to get in."

"The rain?" Sadie took a big draw on the cigarette and blew more smoke into the torrent. *Don't like that, do you?* "It's been trying all day."

"No," said Laia. "Not like this."

Sadie frowned. The rain howled, and just for a moment, a squall walked sideways, just like a man. "Fucking fuck." She grabbed the rifle, pulling it to her shoulder, yanking the charging handle.

"What?" Haraway's eyes were wide. "What is it?"

Sadie ignored her, swinging the rifle through the gap in the wall. She sighted through the scope, pulling the trigger. The weapon clicked, a blue light highlighting the safety. Sadie flicked it off.

"I thought you said you knew how to use that," said Haraway.

Sadie looked through the scope, into the rain. The company weapon felt heavy, and she imagined it was a sniper's weapon. Her guitar was as heavy, but that felt alive. The rifle? It felt dead.

It's for killing. That's all it's ever done.

The shapes in the rain were gone, the rangefinder in the scope finding no targets. "I could have sworn…"

"What? Freeman, what did you see?" Haraway grabbed Sadie's shoulder.

"It's probably nothing," said Sadie. "Damn rain."

A creature swung inside, crashing into her and knocking the rifle away. It landed on her chest, clawed hands reaching for her throat. Saliva stretched between its teeth as it gnashed in her face. Sadie held it back, bringing her knee into its groin. It croaked, curling around its pain.

Sadie scrambled out from underneath it, then kicked it in the head. "Motherfucker!" She brought her boot down on its face. It wasn't human, or at least, not anymore. Disfigured and twisted, mottled skin stretched over bones.

"Sadie!" Haraway fiddled with an SMG, trying to get the weapon to respond. "How does this work?" More creatures boiled out of the rain, pouring through the gap in the wall. The gun in Haraway's hand roared its defiance, the rounds tearing and chewing bodies.

The weapon stuttered dry, clicking over and over. Sadie placed a hand on top of the weapon, pushing it to the floor. Haraway's eyes were blank, uncomprehending as she stared at the pile of corpses.

Sadie walked to Laia. "You okay?"

"Yes." The girl huddled in a blanket. "I told you, it knows you're here when you do things like that."

Sadie picked up the rifle. "It knows, huh?"

"Yes."

"Okay." Sadie moved to the gap in the wall. "What's it going to do next?"

Before Laia could reply, something howled out in the rain.

CHAPTER THIRTY-ONE_

Julian thought Reed Interactive was the best of all worlds. They had a good marketing division. Agents like himself had the freedom to work as the company *needed*. The benefits were excellent, and the company HQ was a marvel of design, all clean lines and open space. A haven from the world outside. No one here was messy or dirty, and they all worked together to raise the value of their stock options.

And they made good products.

The clean, off-white corridor stretched in front of him, empty and blank. *Perfect.* A team had probably spent hours working out what color it *shouldn't* be before they'd landed on this one. It was like the whole building readied itself for an imprint, a slice of synthetic reality for whatever you needed it to be.

Julian adjusted his sunglasses. He took out a pack of Camels, pulling one free with his lips and lighting it. He leaned against the corridor wall. *What's the game plan today?*

He'd gone pretty hard on the asset in their last session, using the pliers until there was nothing left of his mouth but blood and mucus. The tech would have put him back together by now. Julian took another pull on his cigarette, frowning. The asshole was resistant.

Almost like he had nothing to tell. That was impossible, of course, because he could do things to people's minds. Reed would do anything to get its hands on that technology. Create reality for people? Sure, there was a business model in that, but to *change* people, make them do what you wanted...

Julian allowed himself a smile. The percentage in that would be unbelievable.

The corridor remained deserted. Until they figured out how the tech worked, they needed to keep the asset separate from normals. Julian had ordered remotes only. Better safe than sorry.

This corridor wasn't just *clean* and *empty*. All the doors were blank, not a label in sight. If you didn't know what was behind 'em, you didn't have clearance. Julian stood before one, using his link to authorize entry. The door lights blinked red, red, then green as it hissed open. The room looked dark, a single bright lamp casting light on a chair.

"I've been thinking," Julian walked inside, "that we might not have..." He stopped talking, mouth open.

The chair was empty.

He walked to it, leather soles whispering across the tiled floor. The clamps were open, *unlocked* rather than cut or forced. The metal was smudged red where the asset had abraded skin as he thrashed under Julian's questioning, but nothing else. The chair was unmarked, the black surface smooth and bare.

"Shit!" He kicked over a small cart beside the table, scattering plates. The sound of breaking ceramic made him pause.

A cart. With plates.

They weren't supposed to be here. Someone had brought the prisoner food against Julian's instruction. It was important he build a bond with the man, be the source of pain and relief in equal measure.

Think. Focus.

That there was a cart here at all wasn't the problem, was it? If a colossal fuck-up like this could happen, then it was likely other instructions wouldn't have been followed.

Only remotes.

Julian brought the lights up, rendering the scene in stark contrast. Traces of blood and vomit on the floor. His examiner's table holding bloodied tools, a set of pliers next to surgical shears on a tray. An ashtray, the filter of a Camel ground out on it.

He moved to the cart, righting it. Standard Reed catering, hot and cold compartments, with a handle for a human operator. A human operator on a pay grade so low they'd never see a remote in a year of Christmases. A human operator so incompetent they'd spend the rest of their life in a cell, mind-wiped and empty-eyed.

Not yet. Where was the prisoner?

Julian brought up the room's cam feed on his overlay as he walked to the door. It hissed open. He switched his optics to thermal. The floor's blue showed faint yellow bare footprints, the spacing suggesting a person hurrying away. The imprints were faint, the heat easing away, but still only minutes old.

He might still be able to catch the bastard.

The footsteps led toward an old service elevator at the back of the building, used to bring supplies between floors. At this time of day, the elevator would be unused. Julian had to give it to the asset: the asshole chose the right path for down and out.

That shaft led deeper than the ground floor. It was sunk into the old rock under the city's floor, below parking levels. Down there was a sheltered facility. Rainproof. Bombproof.

Not idiot proof though. "Oh, holy Christ."

He ran to the elevator, sending out a region-wide call. "This is Julian Oldham, Specialist Services. I'm en-route to sub-basement level eight in pursuit of a critical asset. The asset is to be considered extremely hostile. Lethal force is not authorized, repeat, shoot to incapacitate only. Asset is believed to be in control of Reed staff already. He's on his way to the crypt."

No more than two seconds passed before his link was flooded with comms requests. He ignored them as he sprinted for the elevator, issuing a priority override to it. It was waiting, open and empty by the time he got there.

The elevator dropped into the depths of the Reed building, vibrating at the speed of descent. "Oh, holy Christ," Julian said again. He reached into his jacket for his sidearm. *What a fuck-up.*

○

The floor's lights were out, unresponsive to Julian's link commands. The first man he'd passed stood slack-jawed, drool coming from his mouth. Julian's optics kicked the light amp up, picking out a dark trickle from the man's ear. His white lab coat shoulder was spotted with it, the blood almost black. *A hemorrhage in the guy's skull?* Julian moved on, sidearm pointed into the darkness.

The woman he'd found next wasn't still. She slammed her forehead against a pillar, the white concrete holding up the darkness above. The front of her face was gone, a ruin of blood and bone, but she'd kept pounding her head against the concrete, leaving a sticky red residue on the cold stone.

Julian's optics showed more Reed staff in the dark, links still live even though their minds were gone. The whole floor hid in shadows, lights from server racks blinking in the dark.

It was cold, tendrils of fog snaking across the floor. The crypt's temperature was always low. Some science nerd had tried to explain it to him before they'd interred Julian, something about *circuits* and *superconducting in the brain.* He hadn't listened. It didn't matter, because it wasn't the ambient temperature of the crypt that made Julian shiver. On the short elevator trip down, his link had thrummed with the screaming of people in pain.

Agony. The word you're after is 'agony.'

Their minds burned a final incandescent flare over the network before they went silent. There weren't any *words.* Julian had moved from foot to foot in the elevator, wanting it to go faster, at the same time wanting it to slow down.

But he had to go. If Julian were a gambler, he'd have bet he knew where the asset went.

He stepped over the form of a man sobbing in the darkness, eyes clawed out by his own hand. The man grabbed Julian's leg. "What will you trade me?"

Julian shook free, tugging at his suit's crease. "What?"

The man held something. "For these pretty marbles. What will you trade me? White marbles are always worth the most." The overlay highlighted what the man held, and the lattice bunched, pulling Julian away.

My God. Julian tugged his collar, pulling the lattice under control. You couldn't make progress without investment. Sure, most of the people here couldn't be made right, but once Reed had the kind of technology that could make a man claw his own eyes out, they could take over the world.

He lifted his weapon. Julian had slid a set of tranqs into it, more than enough to take out a man. Julian wasn't going to take chances. He watched the overlay, the live feed at the right of his vision showing the corridor to the main crypt area. The asset hadn't gone that way yet, so there was still time.

Someone screamed in the dark. His overlay mapped the audio, showing the source was in front of him. Julian broke into a jog. He caught a flash of movement, the overlay dropping a targeting wireframe over a person. He fired, the body spinning. Julian didn't slow as he moved closer.

Shit. Just a tech. *Not the asset.*

A familiar voice spoke from the darkness. "Julian Oldham."

Julian looked around. His optics had nothing. "Yeah?" *Keep him talking.*

"Julian Oldham, I'm so glad we have this time to talk before the end." The asset sounded calm. In control.

"Before the end?" Julian walked toward the crypt, the overlay showing the audio's likely source. *Just down here.* "The end of what?"

The man's laugh echoed in the dark. "The end of you, of course.

The end of all you hold dear. The end of what you love and strive for. Because, Julian Oldham, I made you a promise."

You will release me, or I will kill everyone you love. Julian frowned. "Yeah, about that."

"Oh, it's too late to bargain." The asshole was using the PA system. *Had* to be. His voice filled the room.

"There's just one problem," said Julian.

"What's that?"

"You've still got to get into the crypt. I'm pretty sure I'll find you before that happens."

"Really?" The asset sounded surprised. "Why do you think that?"

"I know this place." Julian stepped through the dark. It felt solid, smothering, his lattice shaking under his skin. "You don't."

"No." God*damn*, but the guy sounded so agreeable. "But I've lifted what I need from the minds of your servants. So many petty concerns in their heads. So much freedom of thought. You should run a tighter ship. This has been too easy."

"So, you know this place. Big deal. You've still got to get into the crypt." Julian arrived at the crypt's door, the white vaulted metal looming in front of him. The status light on the front blinked red.

"No, I don't."

The crypt's door slid open as Julian realized: *red light*. Red wasn't the right color. The crypt yawned before him, stasis coffins laid side by side in the dark. Julian could already tell most of the status lights were also red, a sea of dots blinking their silent scream.

The asset stood beside one coffin, the lid open. Julian raised his sidearm. The link snapped, fluttering in his mind, and he stumbled.

"You see, I'm already here." Julian heard the asset's voice from two places. One, at the door, where he — *a remote, solid, secure, stable* — stood, and the other, in the coffin, where he — *a body, weak, fragile, insecure* — lay, squinting in the brightness of the coffin's wakeup lamps.

The remote's link broke. It fell to the ground. Julian looked up with his own eyes into a face cruel and hard. "Julian Oldham." The asset rubbed a stain of dried blood on his lips. "I think it is time for you and I to become ... better acquainted."

Sleep sickness made Julian's face numb, his body sluggish. The lattice under his skin tried to fire, but his arms only twitched. Overtime wouldn't kick in.

The pain started, beyond anything he'd felt before. Through the pain, he could hear the man's voice in his mind. "Don't cry. This is the start of something beautiful. This is the start of the rest of your life."

CHAPTER THIRTY-TWO_

"How's the fit?" Mike looked at Zacharies, something in his eyes measuring, calculating. They were in a room, two machines vaguely in the shape of men standing in a vaulted space that reached high and wide. Black and crystalline, the walls didn't reflect light. They seemed to hold it close, like a promise. Or revenge.

Zacharies touched the front of the suit they'd given him. It was form-fitting, emblazoned with a sigil of crossed sabers. "It feels tight, Master."

Mike laughed. "I'm not your master, kid." He stopped laughing, but a smile stayed in his eyes. "Hell. I'm not sure anyone's big enough for that job."

Zacharies touched the front of the suit again. "It feels very fine. I'm sorry if I caused—"

"Zach?" Mike held up a hand. "I get it. Shit's gone weird, yeah?"

"A little." Zacharies nodded. "I don't understand how this Heaven of yours works."

"No one does, kid. That's the thing." Mike gestured at the room around them. "Take this place, for example."

"What of it?" Zacharies scanned the room. He knew the words

for *machine* and *computer,* but they still lacked meaning. "I don't know what any of this is."

Mike frowned. "No, I guess you don't. Okay, let's break it down. You remember the R&D freaks?"

"The men who wanted to, you said, 'peel me like a grape.'"

"Yeah, those guys." Mike pulled out a pack of cigarettes, offering them to Zacharies. When Zacharies didn't take one, Mike shrugged. "Suit yourself. Anyway, those assholes put a call in."

"A call?"

"Right. So, these guys around you, they're going to try to peel you like a grape instead. Different way, though. Outcome's the same." Mike pointed to one machine. "That guy? I was on a mission with him three, maybe four years ago. Real psycho. No offense."

"Go fuck yourself." The machine rose with a hiss and a whine. Huge metal legs stamped forward, the clank of metal against the floor a hard scrape of noise.

Zacharies stepped back, stumbling into another machine behind him. It hummed into motion as well, standing above Zacharies. Their voices were hard, like metal would sound if given life. "Watch where you're going."

Zacharies felt fear, cold fingers in his gut. He looked at Mike. "What are these things?" Zacharies didn't understand how they spoke. They were metal, weren't they?

Mike looked at the first machine. "Total conversions. Lots of steel, a little plastic, and a handful of ceramic. Whatever else is pure asshole."

"Hey," said the first. "Watch what you're saying. You want to get pulled apart today?"

"Yeah," said the second. "Place like this? Accidents happen. No cameras. Specialist Services guy like you could just go missing."

Zacharies turned between the two machines. The second one spoke differently, a softer way of rolling its words. "They ... they are people?"

The first leaned back, shaking as it laughed. "The kid catches on fast."

"Yeah," said its partner. "A little too fast. What if we fixed that?" It moved forward, large legs clanking. Two quick strides brought it to Zacharies, a metal fist raised in the air.

Somehow, Mike was there. Zacharies hadn't seen him move, but the man stepped in front of him, hands up. "Guys, don't. This isn't part of the test."

The first machine lumbered around Mike, its body groaning low, a bass rumble rising slowly in pitch. "Or what? You look a little out of your depth."

"Or I will pull you the fuck apart." Mike smiled. "Maybe not today. You've got to go in for a service sometime. When your chassis opens? I'll be there with a pair of bolt cutters."

No one spoke, the only noise in the room the mechanisms inside the two — *Men? Machines? What are they?* — machines. Zacharies panted, his pulse pounding. He threw a quick glance at Mike, but the man wasn't watching him. Zacharies could see the trickle of sweat at Mike's brow.

He realized that this was the first time he could remember another, other than his sister, standing in front of him, taking the whips of the slave master. The thought caught him off guard.

"Naw," said the second machine. "Not if I pull you apart here." A heavy fist swung through the air with a whine. Mike danced back, leather-soled shoes whispering against the floor.

The first machine snatched him up. Mike thrashed, an arm trapped next to his body. The machine brought its other arm up.

"No!" Zacharies' gift lashed out. He felt inside the machines.

Metal, new forged, the strength of a thousand people. There, at the core, the shell of a man, hidden deep in a cage of Heaven's forging.

The first machine's raised arm whined, stuck. It turned to look. "What the hell?" The arm broke off, spinning across the room in a spray of sparks and metal fragments. The machine stumbled, dropping Mike.

Zacharies turned to the second machine, movement in the corner of his vision warning him. A weapon of some kind ratcheted from behind it, coming over its shoulder and locking in place. Zacharies *pushed* with his gift, feeling how it was made.

Tiny fragments, each strong and deadly. Too many for a person to hold, tubes of steel held in a belt of interwoven links. Impossible heat. A weapon of the gods.

Zacharies raised a hand. "No. This weapon is for the angels. It is not for you." He chopped down, the weapon shearing away, rivets popping to bounce against the hard floor. The machine hissed, swiveling around it's middle, then took a step forward. Zacharies swung his hand sideways, palm open, and the machine flew through the air to crash against the wall, the sound mighty and terrible.

Zacharies walked to Mike, offering his hand. "Master?"

Mike took his hand, wincing as he stood. "I'm not your master, kid."

"A Master cares for his slaves." Zacharies frowned, looking at the fallen machines.

"I didn't do much of that," said Mike. "I'm pretty sure you cared for me."

"I'm no Master." Zacharies looked at his hands. "It's never felt this strong before."

"No shit." Mike pulled out his pack of cigarettes. The box was crushed, but he pulled a crumpled cigarette from it anyway, lighting it with a hand that still shook. "What do you call people back home who look out for you?"

Laia. "We call them family." The first machine struggled to its feet. Zacharies stepped around Mike, raising his fist. The machine rose into the air, legs and remaining arm flailing.

Mike put a hand on his shoulder. "Zach? Put him down."

"But he—"

"He's an asshole," said Mike. "You got to think, though. You want to be an asshole too?"

"Yeah." A nervous laugh broke from the machine. "Listen to the man, kid. You don't want to end up all messed up like me. Put me down. All a big misunderstanding."

"A misunderstanding? You were going to hurt my..." Zacharies trailed off as he looked to Mike. He wasn't sure what word to use in this language of the angels.

"Friend," said Mike. "You can call me a friend, kid. Here? We've got families too, but friends are better. They're the family you choose."

Friend. The link shifted the word in his head. Zacharies let his hand fall, the machine crashing to the floor. "Friend?" He watched the machine clamber upright, sparks cascading from its shoulder.

"Yeah, kid. Friend." Mike held out his hand in an *after-you* gesture. "C'mon. Let me buy you lunch."

"You can eat after this?" Zacharies felt the sweet sickness in his belly, his blood still rushing, body ready to fight or run.

"Yeah. Gotta eat. Keep up your strength." Mike walked toward the door, taking a wide path around the first machine.

"Mike?"

Mike paused, turning back. "Yeah, kid?"

They're the family you choose. "I don't think I've ever had a friend before." He looked down at the suit he wore, the crossed sabers on his chest. "I think I'd like one. I'd like that very much right now."

"Sure." Mike shrugged. "You can buy me lunch tomorrow."

"Heaven is very complicated." Zacharies sat, another empty plate in front of him. He'd eaten two lunches of something Mike called *scrambled eggs and bacon.* The bacon was crunchy and salty. Zacharies had never tasted anything quite so good. Mike had said *everything was better with bacon.* They were in the same cafeteria Zacharies ate the bagels in. He'd wanted to come back here, the memory of the food making his mouth water.

"A little complicated, sure." Mike tapped ash from his cigarette.

They'd paused on the way to get a pack of cigarettes from a machine of metal and lights.

"You have no slaves, and no masters." Zacharies frowned at his plate. *So perfectly made.* "Yet you have masters, and slaves."

Mike tipped his hand back and forth in the air, *maybe*, the cigarette trailing smoke. "Sort of. Maybe the best way to describe it is to say you choose your master."

"What if you don't want a master?" Zacharies' flash of anger was hot and quick, his voice overloud. "I'm sorry. I didn't mean—"

"It's okay, kid." Mike pulled on his cigarette. "Not many people run solo these days. A few on the edges. Illegals, mostly."

"Illegals?"

"No link," said Mike, tapping the back of his neck. "No trace. Off the grid. Illegal."

"What makes them *illegal?*" Zacharies turned the word over in his mind.

Mike frowned. "You want another coffee?"

"Yes please. May I ... may I have cream again?"

Mike laughed. "Sure. It'll be here in a sec. You can order coffee too, if you like."

"How?"

"The link lets you do things. Order coffee. Order a hooker. Whatever." Mike looked away.

"And ... illegals can't order coffee?"

"Sure they can, but not from anywhere that doesn't suck. You need cash, something close to the grid but not on it. Borderline living. Not my thing. Not my thing at all."

Illegal. The link chattered away, the meaning of the world falling into place in Zacharies' mind. "What crime did they commit?"

"Who?"

"The illegals. What crime did they commit to be illegal?"

"They're not linked, kid." Mike sighed. "Maybe it's not *technically* illegal. Will be soon. There's a new law coming."

Zacharies touched the back of his neck where a machine had kissed his skin. He couldn't feel a mark there, but knew something was inside him, talking to him, helping him understand words in a language he didn't speak. "What do you mean, it will be soon?"

"It's like this. It's kind of ... *useful* for syndicates to know where people are, what they buy, who they're buying it from, and what relationships they have. Who they argue with, or the porn they download."

"Porn?"

"Later," said Mike. "So, we applied a little pressure on the civilian government."

"You are the masters of the Masters?"

"No, we're—"

"You are making people do something they don't want to do, are you not?"

The coffee arrived, the waitress putting cups on the table. They both ignored her, silence a heavy thing between them. Mike spoke first. "It's better this way. The possibilities—"

"I don't know, Mike. I think..." Zacharies trailed off.

"What, kid?"

"I don't think Heaven is the place where people are made to do the things they don't want to do. Heaven's a place of possibility and freedom." He stopped, the words having come out in a rush like they wanted to be free of him. It was something Laia would have said.

"Freedom, huh?"

"Yes," said Zacharies. "It shouldn't be illegal to make your own choices."

"Even if it's better this way? Look at us. We're talking because of the link."

"Even," Zacharies leaned forward, "if it meant bacon every day."

Mike laughed, a clean and happy sound. His eyes sparkled as he looked at Zacharies as if seeing him anew. "Zach? I'm pretty sure we need you around here. Will you stay?"

"Stay?" Zacharies looked at his *coffee with cream*. "I need to find Laia."

"Yes," said Mike. "I promise we'll find your sister."

"Because you want me to stay?"

"No," said Mike. "Well, yes, that too. But because that's what friends are for."

CHAPTER THIRTY-THREE

S adie's breath came hard as she steadied the rifle against her shoulder. The weapon cracked, bucking against her shoulder, and one of the misshapen, hungry things in the rain spun, falling. The weapon cycled, a soft whine rising above the level of her hearing. She spat, grit and bile hitting the ground.

Haraway was to her left, holding an SMG with a hand that shook with fatigue. Laia huddled behind them, eyes wide with fear.

Fucking company man. Left us here to die.

Haraway threw her a glance as if she heard Sadie's thought, hefting her SMG. "This one's almost empty." They both looked at the second SMG where it lay on the ground, the weapon having run dry what seemed an age ago. "How's the rifle?"

"Hell if I know." Sadie looked through the scope. "It's not like we've been dating long. I guess he's fine. First time out. Exciting evening. Didn't go how either of us expected."

Haraway gave a tight little laugh. "Freeman—"

Sadie pulled the rifle's trigger, the shot tumbling a body in a whirl of too damn many arms and legs, the rain following the creature to earth. The whine cycled for the tenth time. Or was it the twentieth?

Her head pounded. She wanted a drink, something warm and

amber, a rock of ice the size of an asteroid dropped in the bottom of the glass. *But no, it couldn't be a simple night with a decent drink and good music — it had to be monsters.* Sadie fired, missing, something cackling and screeching outside.

"You're a good shot," said Haraway.

"I missed," said Sadie.

"That time," agreed Haraway. "I thought you said you were a singer."

"I sing." Sadie pulled the trigger again. A crack, a whine. "I do other shit too." She thought of her father, her lips settling into a flat line, and she shot something else in the rain.

A crash against the brick beside Haraway. The woman spun, SMG hammering the wall. Ancient plaster shattered. An answering scream, half rage, half pain came from the other side. Laia whimpered.

"Be the end soon," said Haraway. "I didn't figure it'd be like this."

"What, torn limb from limb in a town that's not on a map, tossed under the bus by the company you work for?" Sadie snorted.

"Yeah." Haraway smiled. "I also figured it'd all work out."

"What would work out?" Sadie frowned.

"Marlene." Haraway looked like she wanted to say something else.

"Who's Marlene?"

"Doesn't matter now," said Haraway. "Think they'll rush us again?"

"I would," said Sadie. "They gotta be running out of dudes, though. One thing's bothering me."

"Just the one?"

"For now." Sadie glanced around, making sure there weren't more surprise assholes coming for them. "This place was deserted when we walked in. Where'd they all come from?"

"The rain," said Laia.

"Sure," said Sadie. "They fell from the sky."

"No," said Laia. "The demon brought them."

"Sure," said Sadie again. "But no. Someone's pissed 'em off."

"Who?" Laia's voice was small, almost lost in the hiss of rain. "There are so many of them."

Sadie glanced at the girl. *Chin up, kid.* "There's someone that springs to mind."

CHAPTER THIRTY-FOUR_

Mason looked up the shaft, darkness looming above suit light's reach. He steadied himself against the wall. His leg wasn't working right. The lattice shifted under his skin as the overlay chatted in his vision, diagnostic routines indicating FRACTURE: FEMUR.

It could wait.

The bodies around him were ... *lumpy*. There was no other word for it. Mason could see that under the suit's lights. Their stark brightness made the shaft a haunted house scene, the shadows tall and sharp on the walls. He looked to the side, a tunnel running into the dark.

The overlay said the reactor room lay that way. Down in the dark, things had made their home next to a cracked casing leaking rads. His vision frosted with static for a second, and he debated about whether he *should* go down the tunnel. After all, he'd find what was waiting.

Fuck that noise. It was time to get the hell out of here. Mason set his hand on the ladder lining the shaft's wall and climbed. Mason's link turned off the pain in his leg, but it still wouldn't hold his weight properly. His whole side was going to bruise. He remembered the fall.

Tumbling in the dark, something screaming and clawing at his face. He hit the shaft wall, the impact tossing him in another direction, wind rushing past as he spun. The sound of the taser firing was almost constant until he slammed into the ground, something in his leg giving with a crack.

The fall *had* been a long way, hadn't it? Augmented bone and bionic augmentations had their breaking points.

The ladder groaned, the old metal complaining under his glove. He saw it bend, the metal pulling away like taffy, before it gave way, dropping Mason to the bottom of the shaft again. He covered his head with his hands as pieces of metal rained down.

Silence. Mason looked back up the shaft, the metal ladder gone from just above his head to a good three or four stories above him. He sighed, glancing at the tunnel running away from the shaft into the dark. To the reactor casing, and a family of monsters who'd made it their home.

"This day just keeps getting better." No one answered him. Mason squared his shoulders. *The mission, Floyd.* He still had a job to do.

The tunnel was newer than the facility above. Things had clawed it from raw rock. It didn't go very far before opening into an empty chamber. No reactor housing, no construction, just an empty room. The overlay hissed, his vision scattering as the lattice bunched and moved, looking for a way out.

There's a lot of rads in here, but where are they coming from? Mason looked up at the roof. The room stood out as he switched his optics to low light. It was clear there was no containment breach. Why? Because there wasn't a reactor here anymore.

Also, he was still alive. The protection in his skin was enough to keep the rads out, and no *way* he'd be able to stand next to a breached reactor. No tech Apsel had could do that. The overlay hissed again, his vision flickering and rolling.

Mason walked to the middle of the chamber, turning. Now he was here, he could see the floor was curved. He looked at the walls carrying the same indentation. A sphere, pushed in here from somewhere, punching the raw rock aside. Wherever the portal opened to, well, they'd got a reactor in the face. The thing was just *gone*.

Mason looked at the roof. There was something up there, a block of black metal wedged into the concrete. "I'd bet that's giving off a lot of rads." The darkness ate his words. Someone had left a radiation weapon here, to hide the fact they'd taken the real reactor away.

That someone wore Federate armor. And they'd wiped all memory of the act away. They'd made a whole town vanish.

Something hissed in the darkness. Mason brought the suit's beams up brighter. A man, freakish and twisted, shielded his eyes against the light, hissing again. Ragged clothing whirled as he turned and ran, ducking into a tunnel.

A tunnel that might lead out.

Yeah. Good idea. It was time to leave, touch daylight again, and get away from the atomic weapon wedged in the roof.

Away from the Apsel accident and its missing reactor. Away from the evidence of a sphere that shoved the walls of the containment chamber aside. Mason had seen a device that made spheres in the air. People had come through it. Made sense you could send things the other way, like a reactor. The sphere device was old. As old as Gairovald and his Apsel syndicate. Maybe even as old as Richland, a town torn from memory.

Mason jogged into the tunnel, his gait lopsided with his broken leg. The lattice worked hard to keep him steady, the pain locked off in a corner of his mind.

He didn't have time for mysteries. That was someone else's mission.

○

Moving through the tunnel felt oppressive. Moisture seeped through the walls, like cold sweat. The suit's lights pushed the shadows away, but his audio picked up movement ahead.

And movement behind.

Mason drew the Tenko-Senshin. The little weapon hard-linked through his glove, it's tiny AI babbling. It sounded almost happy. He raised it as he jogged through the tunnel, the lattice making his footing sure even on the tunnel's uneven surface. This one was hand-carved, just like the last.

He saw a side branch ahead, his overlay adding it to the map in the corner of his vision. Mason slowed, looking down the tunnel. A monster leaped at him, clawed hands reaching. The Tenko-Senshin screamed, flechettes ripping through its body, the air sparking with the heat. Mason held the trigger down, a part of the thing's body tearing away, flames peeling from flesh before it hit the ground.

He stopped firing, silence held at bay by the hum of the reactor at his back. Mason coughed as the smoldering body smoked. He heard no other movement, the sounds behind him gone. *Keep moving.*

Mason turned back to the main tunnel. He paused after a few meters. Mason could taste the change in the air. Mason switched off the suit's lights. His optics picked out light from ahead, delicate, faint like morning mist. He broke into a jog, favoring his leg, and emerged into the rain.

Mason closed his eyes, breathing deep. *Free. Safe. Outside.* Water washed over him, not burning, pure and clean.

He heard the crack of a weapon. Mason's eyes snapped open. The town lay blurred by the rain, but there was no mistaking the Federate's rifle he'd left with Sadie. His gut twisted with fear as he noticed the ground outside the tunnel was trampled, the mud churned by the passing of feet.

A lot of feet.

He ran back to the place he'd left them, the lattice shrieking and shuddering against the pain from his leg. Misshapen forms loped alongside him, visible through the rain. A huge creature roared, and he raised the Tenko-Senshin, but it vanished in a squall, lost as the rain howled.

The mission.

Mason pushed himself faster.

CHAPTER THIRTY-FIVE

Rain cascaded against the monster, matting remnants of hair along the shiny, slick surface of its skull. It was huge, over two meters tall, and covered in rippling muscles. Sadie considered the signpost it carried, the monster holding it like it weighed no more than a flyswatter. *Maybe it eats the other ones?* It wasn't spindly, roaring its rage into the storm.

Sadie shouldered her rifle, pulling the trigger. The weapon clicked, then beeped three times, short and insistent. *Empty.*

The creature bared teeth, rushing their small shelter. Haraway raised her SMG, firing wild, precious rounds lost in the uncaring rain.

The thing slammed into the wall of their shelter. Old brick cracked, dust falling from the ceiling. Laia screamed. Sadie spun, trying to grab the girl in her panicked flight, but her fingers closed on empty air. "Laia!" The girl was gone, dashing past the monster as rain hammered earth.

The monster ignored Laia, leering at Sadie. Rotted teeth lay like crooked tombstones in a mouth like wet clay. It reached for her, jagged nails at the end of a massive hand.

Fuck this thing. Fuck this place and fuck these company assholes.

Sadie tossed her rifle, catching the barrel. She swung it like a bat, the heavy stock hitting the monster's hand. It roared, stepping back. Glaring, it crunched away, steps churning dirt into mud. *Laia.* It was following smaller, easier prey.

Sadie glanced at Haraway, then to the rain. "We have to help her."

"Probably," said Haraway. "How?"

"I play guitar. How the fuck should I know?" But Sadie's feet seemed to know. She ran outside, the water drenching her in an instant. Sadie squinted, spotting something huge and shambling. She ran toward it. *Only an imbecile runs toward monsters.*

Other, smaller creatures called to each other at the edge of her vision, pacing alongside, marking her progress. Sadie's breath came ragged, chest heaving as panic rose, but she pushed it down. *There.* Through the rain she could see light bobbing toward her. It cast Laia's small frame into contrast.

It also cast the monster's frame into stark relief. Its shoulders bunched as it roared defiance.

The light slowed, steadying. Sadie realized she still held the empty rifle, dropping it to the muddy street to clatter at her feet. For just a moment, the rain stopped, the sky taking a great breath in. Sadie saw Mason push Laia behind him. His face looked pale in the light, his armor brilliant, challenging the rain to do more.

The creature ahead of her hefted its pole like a club. It charged at Mason, lumbering strides closing the distance. Sadie watched, heart pounding. Mason was a company man, deserved everything that was coming for him, but he'd done something no company man she'd ever seen do.

He put himself in harm's way for someone else. It was an act with no percentage in it. Sadie was sure Mason could dodge the monster, but if he did, the creature would kill a child.

Laia, run! But the girl didn't move, frozen in fear, her eyes wide and staring.

The club swung. Mason got under it, arm raised. Wood cracked, splintering shards flying to be lost in the rain. Mason fell to one knee, but he'd raised a small, black sidearm. Sound hit Sadie, a metallic roar like a thousand chainsaws. Light danced in the air as the rain hissed and coiled, steam billowing. The creature in front of Mason twitched and shuddered, and — *impossible!* — caught *fire* in the rain.

It screamed as Mason's weapon flensed flesh from bone. It fell.

Sadie watched Mason turn to Laia. The girl answered his question with a nod, their words torn away by the wind. Sadie walked toward them, then froze as a creature howled to her right. A smaller monster, this one the size of a man, scampered through the mud on all fours like a dog. It leaped at the company man.

Mason tried to twist aside, but his foot slipped in the mud. *He must be hurt. No syndicate agent slips.* Sadie watched, hand over her mouth, as he went down. His weapon spun into the rain. The creature chittered, jaws wide. Mason slammed his fist into its face. His glove flashed, rain hissing as he struck, and the creature dropped, twitching.

"Are you okay?" Sadie reached Mason. His lips were blue, face strained like he'd sprinted a marathon. He stared past her. Sadie turned, following his gaze. Another creature had picked up his little gun. It fumbled with the weapon, then pointed it at Mason.

"That's not going to end well for you." Mason's words slurred, like he was drunk. *Drunk on exhaustion maybe.*

The thing pulled the trigger. Lightning arced from the creature, crackling through the air. The monster exploded into mist, red mixing with the rain, slurry splatting to the broken street.

Mason limped toward Laia. Sadie jogged to where the creature died, the air smelling of ozone. She picked up the company man's weapon. It was a snub-nosed black sidearm. A red light slowly blinked on the side. Sadie looked at the circle of charred dirt and flaked asphalt where the creature had stood. She examined the weapon again. Tiny letters were etched onto the grip. *Tenko-Senshin Intelligence Systems 12.*

She'd never heard of Tenko-Senshin and wondered which fascist syndicate erased them from existence. Sadie turned toward Mason, then froze. Two monsters hunched in the rain between them. Sadie called, "Mason?"

He turned, took the situation in with a glance, then stepped forward. The company man stumbled after a single step, the movement looking like it cost him more than pain. His leg sagged like the bone inside was made of cardboard.

One of the things leaped at her. *Don't shoot it. God, don't shoot it. You saw. You saw what happened to the other one.* Sadie whipped the Tenko-Senshin up anyway. The other monster closed on Mason, the man swatting it aside.

She hit the ground as the creature landed on her. The rain was in her eyes as the monster screeched. Sadie swung the sidearm, but her angle was wrong, the blow doing nothing. Jaws gnashed, snapping before her face. She tried to get an arm up. Sadie could see the hunger in its eyes.

The thing's weight left her, bright blue-white light washing over her. Mason staggered back, the monster thrashing in his grip. He held it in with one arm, punching it with the other. The company man moved like a broken machine, movements mechanical yet jerky.

The other creature jumped him from behind, latching onto his back. Sadie scrambled back as Mason dropped to one knee in the muck, struggling with the creatures. He tossed the one he held away, then tore the one from his back, flipping it over his shoulder.

The thrown one scuttled in the mud. It came up with the remains of the signpost the larger creature used. Sadie saw nails jutting from the end, watching in horror it ran at Mason, swinging.

"Mason!" she screamed. He turned, but not fast enough, the nails slamming into his neck. Mason coughed blood, then ripped the weapon from the monster, his neck spurting red as nails tore free. He hefted the post, then smashed it into the creature. Wood splintered into kindling as the creature tumbled away.

Mason looked at her, smiling with bloody teeth. "I'm sorry, Sadie." He took a step toward her.

The creature jumped from the rain's murk, knocking Mason to the ground. Sadie lifted the little gun up, holding the trigger down before she could think about what she was doing. The air before her filled with fire, searing heat on her arms. The creature on Mason ignited, parts flying off to hiss and sputter in the rain.

I'm alive. There wasn't any lightning.

She looked at the weapon and its blinking red light, then back at Mason. He tried to get up, coughing bloody fluid. Mason fell forward, one hand out. He crouched, shivering in the torrent. The last creature lunged at him with a scream. Claws scrabbled at his armor before it sank its teeth into his neck. He cried out, trying to push it off.

Laia screamed, a raw, animal noise, anger and fear twisting her face. She ran at the creature. It bared teeth at the girl, maws red with Mason's blood. Sadie could see what would happen, the snap of its jaws, and Laia would be gone, another lost to forgotten Richland.

Red mist exploded out the back of the monster. It fell to the ground like a dropped toy, arms and legs bouncing as it hit. All its blood floated free, the storm carrying it away in a bloody squall.

Sadie stared at the fallen creatures, Mason's body, then at Laia. *Holy shit.* She shuffled forward, putting an arm around Laia. The girl sobbed. Sadie hugged her close. "It's okay. It's—"

"No," wailed Laia. "They've killed him. They've killed the angel."

Holy fucking shit.

Sadie walked to Mason's body. She nudged him with a foot. No response. The armor he wore pulsed with light, red and white, a cross beaming from the chest plate. A woman's voice spoke from the suit. "A medical emergency has been noted. Please stand clear."

"Who's that?" asked Laia.

"Someone we should listen to." Sadie pulled Laia back, hands on the girl's shoulders.

"Please stand clear," repeated the woman's voice. "Subject is coding. Conductive environment noted. Please stand clear or risk immediate death by electrocution."

Laia twisted from Sadie's grasp, face her. "We can't leave him."

"We're not." Sadie wiped rain from her face, for all the good it did. *Plenty more where that came from.* "You think this is Heaven?"

"Not anymore," said Laia.

"Have a little faith, kid, and step the fuck back. Syndicates don't let their very expensive angels fall."

Laia frowned but backed away from Mason. The armor's red-white cross flashed twice. The voice, soft, calm, and probably recorded in a nice dry studio, said, "Thank you. Administering epinephrine. Encouraging implant systems to produce plasma. Defibrillation in three, two, one..."

There was a hum, and Mason's body stiffened.

"Cycling," said the suit. The hum sounded once more. Sadie thought the air tasted of metal, like the tension before a concert. Mason's body convulsed.

"What's it doing?" Laia's voice was harsh with a terrible amalgam of fear and hope.

"Cycling," repeated the suit. Again, the hum. This time, smoke curled out from armor's joints, to be beaten down by the rain.

CHAPTER THIRTY-SIX

Mason woke to warm, flickering light and the smell of woodsmoke. He hurt everywhere, the lattice shaking and grumbling under his skin. His overlay was awash with errors. Mason groaned. They were in the broken shelter he'd left them in. The walls looked worse for wear, but he felt surrounded by hope as three pairs of eyes watched over him. Sadie looked like she'd parked her anger three blocks back. Haraway was spent, a dollar used to cover a five-dollar bet. Laia's eyes were round, the girl smiling like the dawn.

"You look pretty good for a dead guy," offered Sadie.

He opened his mouth, but the words wouldn't come. Mason didn't have any anger or witty retorts left. Sadie handed him a tin cup. He gulped water. It tasted of metal, dirt, and *being alive*.

Laia came closer, raising a tentative hand to touch his face. Mason pulled his head away. He didn't like the way she looked at him. He didn't deserve *adoration*. Not for what he'd done, and for who.

"You were dead," she said.

"No," said Mason. His voice sounded like some asshole had packed his throat with gravel. "Not quite."

"Yes." Haraway spoke from where she stoked the fire, hair falling around her face. "All the way dead."

"You really are an angel." Laia beamed. "To rise from the dead? It's a miracle."

Mason looked at Haraway. "Really?"

Haraway shrugged. "You seem to have come back online okay."

"I feel like shit."

"Ever been dead before?"

"No."

"Exactly." Haraway didn't sound satisfied. She sounded tired, resigned, and worn thin. Like this wasn't the mission she wanted. Not for any of them.

Mason stood, flexed his shoulder. His overlay started its assault of messages again. Mason cleared them. Maybe he'd find time to be dead later. Right now? *Status.* His neck felt sore. He probed the injury. His skin had already healed over, because it wasn't really skin. He looked at Laia. "I'm okay. Really. And I'm not an angel, kid. Just another company asset."

Sadie snorted. "He finally speaks the truth."

"There are gaps. What happened?" Mason wasn't sure if he wanted to know what he'd let happen to them while he'd been chasing after Apsel mysteries and mistakes.

Sadie shifted from foot to foot. *Nervous — about what?* She pulled out the Tenko-Senshin, holding the weapon with exquisite care. As she handed it to him, Mason glimpsed angry red on her arms, hidden by her sleeves. "I ... borrowed this."

"Okay." Mason didn't take the weapon, instead pushing her sleeve back. The burns were livid and angry. "You fired it."

Her eyes darted to the hole in the wall. To the rain and dark outside. "Yes."

Mason smoothed her sleeve in place. "You've got questions."

"Yes." Sadie nodded, her words tumbling free. "Before you ... Before I picked it up, one of the ... things, those monsters—"

"People." Mason's voice was quiet. "They used to be people."

He watched as she tried the thought on for size. "One of those people tried to use it."

"Yes. I remember that."

"It died."

"Yes." He watched her eyes, not moving.

She bit her lip. "Why?"

"Because it was an enemy." Mason shrugged. "Tenko-Senshin made things that aren't really weapons. They're ... works of art."

"Art?"

"Sort of." Mason sighed. "Tenko only made twelve that I know of. And that's a guess, because of the number on this one. There are records of another nine. He was a crazy old man."

"I couldn't *not* do something." Sadie swallowed. "I could have died."

"Yes," agreed Mason. "That's probably why you didn't."

"Probably?"

"I don't know how it works. It didn't come with a book. I think it found me, if we're trading truth." Mason took the little weapon from Sadie. It beeped, the hard link coming through his glove, its little AI chattering happily. He looked at Laia. "You okay?"

"They were people?" The girl looked confused, like she'd been told purple was a flavor.

He crouched. "Yeah. They were."

"They didn't ... I didn't mean to..." Tears were in her eyes.

"Laia," said Mason.

"I reached out." A sob caught in her throat. "I felt inside it and *pushed*. I pushed all the way. I didn't know my gift could do that. I've never—"

"Laia, stop."

Her eyes were wide as she stared at him. "I felt it die. *I* did that."

Mason sighed. "Yeah, I guess so."

"What?" said Sadie. "That's all you've got?"

"No. Wait here a second." He looked at the three of them, huddled in a dirty room around a fire that tried to push the night away. Favoring his leg, the bone growth still playing catch-up, he stepped out into the night.

The rain slowed to a trickle, then stopped, leaving the air quiet and still. Mason walked up the road a block or so until he found a store he remembered from earlier. He shouldered the door, the lock popping open. Mason walked inside, grabbing what he needed.

As he walked back, his feet slowed. He breathed the night in. Calm sat in the air, and he drank it up.

You're alive. A young girl saved your life today.

Voices came from their camp, firelight dancing through the cracks and gaps in the walls. He let the sound walk around him, not really listening to the words, leaning back against an ancient post.

A girl saved you. Isn't it your mission to look after her?

He looked at what he held. It'd worked in the past. When he had doubts, questions he couldn't answer, or when the voices of the dead wouldn't be still.

She saved your life.

The mission was to recover the asset and protect it at all costs. Mason thought back to the room in the nuclear facility, bodies dried and preserved by the radiation threading through them. He thought about the Apsel logo, and the cavern full of radiation where a sphere to another world had punched the rock walls aside like soft clay.

He wondered where the reactor had gone, and why Apsel Federate had sent a team in at all. Why there was a dirty bomb in a nuclear facility, and why a whole town had been left to die. How the people of Richland had twisted, bodies turned into monsters.

Radiation didn't do that. That was a deliberate act from a different arm of science. Something viral, shifting people into animals. For what? To stand guard over a dead city?

A girl saved your life today, and you owe her, Mason Floyd.

He stood, leaving the post and his contemplation behind. Mason entered to the firelight's embrace through a gap in the wall. Three pairs of eyes looked at him. He smiled. "I've got just the thing. It answers all questions." He held up a bottle, the whisky warm and dark against the light from the fire.

"You've got to be kidding me," said Sadie.

"You got a better idea?" he asked.

"No, I meant, you didn't get any glasses."

"I'm not proud." Mason twisted the bottle open. He took a pull, the liquid burning down his throat, then handed it to Laia. "Here."

"Will it make me forget?" She looked at the bottle. "Will it take it back?"

"Yes," said Mason. "For a little while."

You've finished *Chromed: Upgrade!* I hope you loved it.

If you want to know what happens next, check out the sequel, *Chromed: Rogue.* It's more kick-ass cyberpunk sci-fi where heroes save the world through action scenes and clever dialogue. An excerpt is available at the end of this book. Buy it here:

[https://www.books2read.com/ChromedRogue]

WAIT. Don't go!

Thanks for reading my book. If you liked it, would you share your experience with your fellow organics? Reviews are helpful to readers by ducting like-minded people to books they'll enjoy.

Review *Chromed: Upgrade* at **your retailer** and **Goodreads** [http://hit.mondegreen.co/ReviewUpgrade]

FYI, an angel gets its wings for every five-star review.

ABOUT THE AUTHOR_

Richard Parry worked as an international consultant in one of the world's top tech companies, which sounds cool, but it wasn't all cocaine parties. He lives in Wellington with the love of his life, Rae. They have a dog, Rory, who chases birds. The birds, who have the power of flight, don't seem to mind. Richard's online hood is:

www.mondegreen.co

GET UPDATES

Want to be the first to know next time I have some Inner Sanctum™ data (like releases, cover reveals, specials, and free reads)? Get on my mailing list. Signing up nets you *Escape* and *Sleepless* as a welcome bundle.

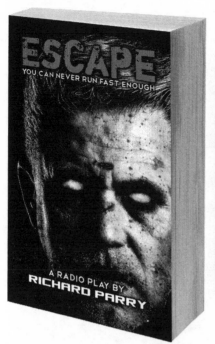

HTTPS://WWW.MONDEGREEN.CO/GET-ON-THE-LIST/

ALSO BY RICHARD PARRY_

THE EZEROC WARS

The Ezeroc Wars universe is big (and growing!). Get the reading guide here:
https://www.mondegreen.co/ezeroc-wars-reading-guide/

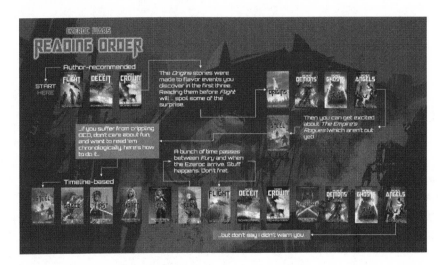

A colony world goes dark.

When Grace Gushiken and Nathan Chevell of the *Tyche* are hired to deliver a new transmitter for a downed Guild Bridge, they find the Absalom Delta colony deserted, its people enslaved by the insect-like Ezeroc. The aliens have descended like locusts on humanity, consuming all in their path. No one is safe. Even the Republic Navy is powerless against them. The ship and her crew need to test their skill and their luck to survive. Will Grace and Nate be able to work together to get away? Or will fears and rivalries from the past destroy humanity's hopes, ceding victory to the Ezeroc?

Tyche's Journey

Book 1: https://www.books2read.com/TychesFlight

Book 2: https://www.books2read.com/TychesDeceit

Book 3: https://www.books2read.com/TychesCrown

Tyche's Progeny

Book 4: https://www.books2read.com/TychesDemons

Book 5: https://www.books2read.com/TychesGhosts

Book 6: https://www.books2read.com/TychesAngels

TYCHE ORIGINS

An empire falls.

Before there was a *Tyche*, the crew were scattered. Nate wore the Emperor's Black. El helmed mighty destroyers. Hope joined the new Republic's reclamation projects. Kohl fell in with the Yakuza. And Grace was a prisoner. Grab their origin stories as they become the heroes the universe needed them to be.

Collection (origins 1-6): https://www.books2read.com/TycheOrigins

Or get them à la carte...

Origin 1: https://www.books2read.com/TychesFirst

Origin 2: https://www.books2read.com/TychesChosen

Origin 3: https://www.books2read.com/TychesHope

Origin 4: https://www.books2read.com/TychesFury

Origin 5: https://www.books2read.com/TychesGrace

Origin 6: https://www.books2read.com/Gravedigger

FUTURE FORFEIT

Not sure where to start? Get the reading guide here:
https://www.mondegreen.co/future-forfeit-reading-guide/

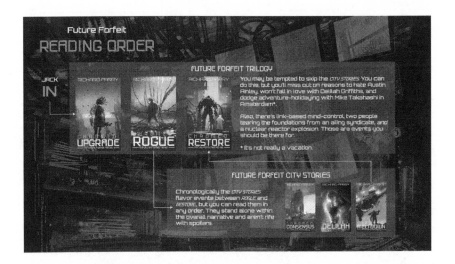

It's 2150AD. There hasn't been a corporate war... until now.

Mason Floyd is an augmented syndicate enforcer at the top of his game. His job is asset protection and acquisition, no questions asked.

Company tech is stolen on Mason's watch. Rival megacorps want it, and they don't mind killing him to get it. Framed for the theft, Mason runs. He tangles with off-grid rockstar Sadie Freeman on the grimy seam between the powerful and poor. Together they uncover a secret an entire city died to keep.

Hunted and desperate, they must team up to survive. Together Mason and Sadie can save the world. Apart, both are lost. They must trust each other or die.

Megacorps. Cyborgs. AI. Gene-spliced monsters. Syndicate enforcers. Off-grid illegals. Supersoldiers. Rock music. Violence. Einstein-Rosen bridges. Liquor. Enhanced reflexes. Power armor and energy weapons. Full body replacements. Swearing. Mind control. Telekenetics. G-Men. Drugs. Neural links. Orbital cannons. **THIS IS CYBERPUNK.**

Book 1: https://www.books2read.com/Upgrade

Book 2: https://www.books2read.com/ChromedRogue

City Stories 1: https://www.books2read.com/Consensus

City Stories 2: https://www.books2read.com/Delilah

City Stories 3: https://www.books2read.com/Meltdown

Book 3: https://www.books2read.com/ChromedRestore

NIGHT'S CHAMPION

Could just one night change your life forever?

Valentine Everard and Danielle Kendrick have the Night's Favor: they are werewolves. There are many who would steal the Night's dark gift from them. The Night's Champions must face down the corporate interests of Big Pharma, battle with masters of dark Vodou, and make their last stand against both vampires and the Riders of the Apocalypse. Armies fall. Zombies roam the street, and no one is safe. The world is close to its final Judgment. What can a handful of souls do against the powers of the heavens?

Book 1: https://www.books2read.com/NightsFavor

Book 2: https://www.books2read.com/NightsFall

Book 3: https://www.books2read.com/NightsEnd

GLOSSARY_

A**binal** A planet ruled by telepaths. Masters use "demons" to control weather and people.

Active camouflage Light-refractive tech where crypsis is achieved through cameras to sense the visible background. Peltier panels and other coatings dynamically change camouflage appearance, rendering the wearer nearly invisible to visible and thermal detection.

Agent A syndicate field agent. Synonymous with enforcer.

AI Artificial Intelligence. So-called expert systems and machine learning are a long way from true sentient AI. Some success in military applications, particularly friend-or-foe recognition, has given researchers hope for true machine intelligence. So far, success remains elusive.

APC Armored Personnel Carrier. Designed to minimize risk to agents while transporting equipment and people into combat zones.

Apsel Federate One of the three major syndicates. Apsel control the energy market through their high-quality, safe fusion reactors. A connected, always-on world needs clean, renewable energy.

Bionics Life-like augments for the human form. Bionics can be arms, legs, hearts, lungs, eyes, and more. Human modification can be purely cosmetic (see: clinic) through to extreme (mil-spec augments to make humans faster, stronger, and much harder to kill).

Chassis Slang: the part of the bionic frame total conversions associate with their missing body. While dependent on the agent and Psych profile, this is most often the torso component of the biomechanical structure.

Chromed Slang: those equipped with obvious offensive bionics.

Clinic Facilities for enhancing human attractiveness. Clinics can reduce or reverse obvious signs of aging, alter bone structure, and change hair and eye color. Clinic services are expensive, their clientele usually higher-paid syndicate workers. Many health-care plans include clinic services to ensure salaried employees can work longer hours.

Coilgun Also known as a Gauss rifle, these weapons use electromagnets as a linear motor to accelerate projectiles. The resulting high velocity payloads deliver tremendous kinetic energy on their target. They are different from railguns; railguns require sliding contacts ("rails") to pass current through their projectiles. These rails suffer wear.

Company [wo]man An employee whose allegiance to their employer comes before personal beliefs, loyalty to fellow workers, or even family.

Console A computer. See: deck.

Construct A non-organic humanoid.

Cybernetics see: bionics.

Cyborg A human augmented with bionics.

Deck Slang: a (usually portable) console.

Decker Slang: a skilled hacker or handler.

Dispenser Automated calorie dispenser, most commonly used for beverages and instant foods.

Dropship In-atmosphere or sub-orbital mission deployment aircraft.

Fixer Slang: a dealer and contact-broker.

Handler Support operative for field agents, usually operating from safe company headquarters. Handlers are typically gender-preference compatible, leading to better bonding with their assigned agents.

Hard link (see: link) Link connectivity established through direct rather than wireless connection. Hard links are more robust, higher bandwidth, and difficult to hack.

HUD Heads Up Display.

Illegal Slang: someone without a link.

Keffiyeh (also: **shemagh**) Headdress fashioned from a square scarf.

Klicks Slang: kilometers.

Lamesh weed A narcotic plant found on Abinal. It grows in marshy areas.

Language pack Tech to deploy languages to the brain. Memories as someone learns a language (or other skill) are tagged by a virus, then deployed to other brains by water-soluble code packs.

Lattice Tech hardwired to an agent's nervous system. Outfitted with prediction and response routines, lattices allow faster-than-though threat responses. Interfaced via link to optics and overlays, they can yield precision combat maneuvers for ranged or close encounters.

Link Slang: uplink. A tech interface allowing communications and data download to the brain. Links are used to order food, communicate on networks, install new skills, and have a range of military applications as well. Links serve as the information substrate for other modifications. Syndicates seek to make non-linked humans illegal (ref: *Syndicate Registration Act*) as links have certain direct-marketing advantages.

Master A powerful telepath who can subvert human will with their mind.

Medivac An emergency healthcare service, often military.

Medivacs are usually armed and armored aircraft designed to take a near-death human to an optimal care facility.

Megacorp Slang: syndicate.

Memory sliver A portable data storage device, often very small. Slivers may be implanted into humans acting as data couriers. Data crystal, memplant, and data sliver are synonymous terms.

Metatech One of the three major syndicates. Metatech specialize in mil-spec weapons and bionics. They often deploy agents as mercenaries, operating as a PMC (private military contractor). Their specialty is warfare.

Mil-spec Slang: defense standard equipment, often called military standard. Mil-std, mil-spec, and MilSpecs are synonymous terms.

Monoblade A bladed weapon with at least the edge forged from monomolecular structures (see: nano filament).

Nano filament Slang: monomolecular wire (often a weapon) made from nanotubes of cylindrical nanostructure. These have properties useful to electronics, optics, and other materials science technologies.

Nanotech Slang: nanotechnology. Describes tech manipulating matter on an atomic, molecular, and supramolecular scale. Often used for fabrication of macroscale products, especially (often weaponized) robotics.

Off-grid Slang: referring to an area or person not in the linked world, not surveilled, lost, or missing.

Optics Slang: ocular implant to replace visual organs (eyes).

Overlay HUD displayed on optics.

Overtime A mil-spec upgrade increasing reaction time. Overtime modules manipulate the body's endocrine system while decreasing nervous system response time. They effectively "overclock" humans. Short-term side effects include light perception and other sensory stimulus issues; many agents complain of phantom flavors or sounds. Long-term side effects include endocrine overload, burnout, and brain death.

Psych Slang: psychology assessment team, used to check field readiness of agents. Psych often use re-education to reduce the effects of PTSD or non-loyalist behaviors.

Railgun A device that uses electromagnetic force to launch high-velocity projectiles. The payload is accelerated along conductive rails.

Re-education (Often forced) Programming of humans to change allegiances, thought patterns, and behaviors. Re-education was perfected by the criminal justice system and has been adopted wholesale by syndicates as another tool in their arsenal.

Real Slang: the real world, also called "the real."

Reed Interactive One of the three major syndicates. Reed control the entertainment market. Their products include digital holidays, virtual relationships, and an array of family-friendly network programming.

Remote See: construct.

Rogue An AI (non-sentient expert system, as true AI doesn't exist) no longer under human control.

Seeker A zombie-like slave to a Master. Typified by all-white eyes and an altered body temperature.

Sexbot or sex robot. Human-like, anatomically correct (or exaggerated) constructs for sexual pleasure.

SMG Submachine Gun.

Syndicate Compact Signed in 2087 between over a hundred syndicates, the Compact was designed to forestall war on a planetary scale. It allows for recovery of stolen assets in clear breach of intellectual property law, reparations between corporations, and a no-compete clause for senior company [wo]men. Signed into law in most geopolitical regions, it's cited as protection against all-out syndicate conflict.

Syndicate Large (typically global) corporation.

Syndicate Registration Act A proposed legislative change allowing forced introduction of links into all humans from birth, plus retrospective introduction into non-linked adults. It is widely supported by all major syndicates and geopolitical entities. The proposal includes recommendations for non-compliance, which include a range of responses from incarceration to termination.

Syndicate Riot Act Active legislation in most geopolitical regions allowing syndicate assets to disperse citizens if suspected of intent to riot.

Tenko-Senshin Slang: Tenko-Senshin Intelligence Systems. Imaburi Tenko started a specialist weapons company before falling off-grid. His weapons are known as works of art, available only at astonishing sums. They run AI (expert systems) with a variety of features, notably to protect their owners. At least twelve were made before Tenko disappeared. Mason Floyd is in the possession of the twelfth Tenko-Senshin weapon, a small pistol that fires flechettes carved from a metal block by a laser. It then accelerates these using an internal railgun assembly, firing projectiles so fast they superheat air. Its internal AI has advanced friend-or-foe capabilities. Tenko was nothing if not creative.

Total conversion Slang: a human mostly converted to bionics, leaving no visible trace of the original meat body.

Tranqs Slang: tranquilizers.

Uplink See: link.

Vibroblade Slang: weapon with a thin blade that vibrates at a high frequency.

Wireframe Overlays and HUDs commonly use wireframe models over the real.

ACKNOWLEDGMENTS_

Thanks go especially to Arran and Erin for their merciless demands for more in the Future Forfeit universe. I released the original *Upgrade* in October 2014, and it was only with the support of friends and fans like them it's become the remaster you hold in your hands today.

I'd like to thank Hugh Herr for helping me understand that humans can never be broken. And Steve Ramirez and Xu Liu for ideas on how to alter memories with lasers (and eventually, a drink that tastes like chocolate that can teach a teenage girl from another world how to speak English). Raffaello D'Andrea gets a nod for showing what machines can do if only we have the right math.

And here at the finish: my Rae. You believe, even when I don't. Will you stay with me until the end of time?

— R. P.

October 2018, Wellington

EXCERPT: CHROMED: ROGUE_

COMPANY PEOPLE_

There was a time when coming to this part of Seattle wouldn't get you shot. Lace hadn't had a promotion in years. Her home stagnated along with her salary. Harry wasn't sure how she made it home each day, but maybe there were still enough people who wouldn't gun down a woman in a wheelchair.

What used to be tree-lined boulevards slumped into scraggly wooden skeletons. Harry thought the dead trees looked like they could use some company but had been planted too far apart to huddle together for warmth. He didn't want to stick around for long.

He clanked across the street, the sound of horns coming loud and fast to his right. Harry swiveled his torso, raising a metal middle finger to the driver of a low-slung combi van. The van was coated in graffiti. Hard to tell whether it was intentional, or the owner made the mistake of leaving it outside one night. The driver looked on, wide-eyed, at Harry and the cart he hauled behind him.

It might have been surprising seeing a company total conversion dragging shovels.

Harry made the dubious safety of the sidewalk. Despite the shitsville state of the neighborhood, the link worked fine. Fine enough that Lace's sighs and general tone of derision made it loud and clear.

He cleared his throat. "What I don't get is why the big man was so convinced Mason would be in contact."

"With you." Lace spoke slowly and clearly, like she was trying to teach a chicken algebra. He knew she'd be eye-rolling. "That he'd be in contact with *you*."

"Yeah." Harry held back a sigh of his own. *Won't help.* "That."

"Gairovald's right."

"You would take the boss's side. Carter been in touch?" Harry's overlay showed he was nearly at his destination. He remembered a small townhouse, fence bright and green back when he still had a real body that could feel the sun. Harry hadn't been invited here in five years. *Time to change that.*

"She said she'd lost Mason." Lace sounded surprised, like someone managed to turn lead into gold. "Can you believe that?"

"No, not for a minute."

"You don't think she said that?"

"I don't think Carter's lost Mason." Harry's chassis wound down, the massive four-meter high bulk of it slowing with engineered precision as he arrived. The townhouse was where it should be, but the fence sagged. Only flakes of faded green paint remained, clinging on like an old man's memory. The front gate had gone, lost in the intervening time he hadn't been welcome. A fine drizzle of rain overlaid the scene.

"I..." Lace's voice cracked like an eggshell.

"It's okay, Lace. I know they're watching you."

The link hissed for a moment. "Yeah. They watch all the time. They're assholes."

"We used to do that job."

"Be an asshole?"

"If that's what it takes. When someone goes off the rails, you need people who can pull the pieces back together." Harry reached out a big mechanical hand, the hiss of hydraulics vying against the street noise. A piece of the rotted fence fell, flaking into the dead flower bed behind it. "That was us. We were that team."

They used to be such beautiful flowers. Harry remembered seeing a bee, a real live bee *here* at the edge of the city. He'd been sipping a mojito, the sun making him sweat almost as much as the frosted glass. He looked at his metal hand, remembering his flesh and blood limb. The overlay dropped a wireframe on his new limb, telling him it was in perfect working order.

Perfect working order. He hadn't had a mojito or broken a sweat in five years. Harry felt he'd *worked*, but maybe not *lived*.

"Pieces?" Lace's voice was almost a whisper. "That's what we did? Picked up the pieces?"

"Yeah. One second." Harry cut the link audio, tearing the fence down. He caught the action of a guy up the block. Harry waited as the man jogged closer.

He was average height. Above average concern, his brows furrowing into a thin line. He looked the type to start some shit, if Harry was a normal like him. He stared into Harry's optics, struggling for the right thing to say. He settled on, "Uh."

"Hi." Harry's PA amplified his voice too much in the real. He turned it down. "Sorry."

"It's fine. Uh."

"Help you?" Harry relaxed as much as the chassis would let him, crouching low, trying to look smaller. This guy had *cojones* the size of melons to come up to him, and Harry liked that in a neighbor. Especially Lace's neighbor.

"We don't..." The guy's off-the-rack shirt stuck to him, the rain's drizzle adding mugginess to the day's sins. The shirt looked hand-me-down, maybe used by someone else before it got to its current owner. "We don't get a lot of your kind here."

"Sure." Harry paused, swiveling his torso to take in a forming crowd. "What's your point?"

"Uh. See, she's not home, and I kind of try to keep an eye out." His eyes darted to the Apsel falcon on Harry's chassis. "I'm sorry about this, but I have to ask. Why are you here?"

"It's okay." Harry wondered what Mason would say. "I'm just here to ... make it right."

"Make it right?" The man laughed, but there wasn't any trace of humor in the sound. "How can you do that? There's not much left."

"I know." Harry held up his metal arm. "These are strong. Stronger than anything I used to have. I can put them to work." He extended his hand. "I'm Harry Fuentes. We used to ... I work for the Federate."

The man reached out, tentative, trying to work out how to shake Harry's massive hand. He settled for wrapping his palm around a couple of Harry's fingers. "Julio. Man, I'm pleased to meet you. *She'll* be pleased to see you. No one from the Federate comes down here anymore."

"Julio, you're one brave motherfucker. Brave, or dumb as a box of rocks."

"Yeah." A smile worked its way onto Julio's face. It looked like it belonged there, like he'd been wanting an excuse to smile all week. "That's what my old lady says too."

"Great. I understand. Look, I'm going to..." Harry trailed off, looking at the cart beside him. How did you explain fixing a fence as a way to mend the hollowness in your gut?

"Sure." Julio smiled again. "You need anything, you ask."

Harry watched as Julio walked away, the crowd drifting with him. The overlay did quick ID scans of people's faces, dragging information from the link. When it finished, he knew who they were, and where they lived. The link told him everything except why they were here.

He turned it off. Harry didn't need the uplink here. As soon as he cut it off, it snapped back on. He would have sighed, but it wasn't worth the static.

"What are you doing, and why have you shut me out of your link?" Lace sounded brittle, anger vying with concern. "I'm only getting audio from you. It's like you've fallen off the edge of the world."

Edge of the world. "Something like that," said Harry. "Just a little personal business."

"You don't have personal business." The link snarled, hissing and popping. "I'm getting interference."

"I'm not shopping, if that's what you're asking." Harry stamped into the yard, scanning the dead grass and blasted plants. A small lemon tree clung to life near the front door beside where the steps used to be. A ramp leaned there now, because Lace couldn't use stairs. Not after what Harry had done.

"You still do that job, don't you?" asked Lace.

"Which job?"

"Being an asshole."

"What is it about my personal business that interests you so much?"

"I don't mean to pry. But what could you possibly need?"

"Something I'm not going to tell you about."

"People here are getting nervous." The overlay said Lace's voice carried stress markers.

"No, they're not," said Harry. "And if they are, you can tell them to fuck off."

"How do you know they're not getting nervous?"

"Because I'm online and haven't left the city. Geofencing would have triggered. I'm not anywhere near Mason. If there was a risk I'd bump into him, city CCTV would have got him first. We'd know what underwear he had on today. The Federate has bigger things to worry about than my personal business."

"If it's not shopping, what is it?"

Harry shut down the link, *then* sighed. It'd taken him a little while to find the right tools, ones that he could hold and use like the man he used to be. It'd taken him longer to do that without Lace working out what he was up to.

She wasn't stupid.

He pulled the cart into the yard, hooking a piece of digging equipment up to his chassis. Finding farming equipment with the same mounts as Apsel combat hardware hadn't been as hard as he'd thought. Some bean counter in Finance had embarked on a standardization program years back, making "industrial" the same thing as "military." It was a mistake that had cost millions, but there were still a few pieces of industrial equipment in warehouses. It'd just been a matter of getting them delivered without anyone knowing.

Carter probably knew where he was. She knew a lot more than she let on. She hadn't said anything to Lace, though.

The reactor on his back hummed as he turned the cracked earth over. The fans in the chassis kicked in, venting heat out the back as he shifted dirt. He built a pile of dead foliage, flowers that used to be red or blue now a uniform brown, dry, brittle.

There weren't any bees. Not anymore.

Harry returned to the trailer. The plants in the back were the best he could find. And hell, at least they were alive. He looked at his metal hands, then at the plants.

Shit. It's not like he was built for delicacy.

Julio stood at the fence line, holding beer in a generic brown bottle. No syndicate branding. Home brewed, maybe. If so, it was flat-out illegal. There weren't any yeasts left that weren't under patent. "How's it going?"

Harry swiveled. "So-so. What do you think?"

"Very ... flat," offered Julio. "You want a hand?"

"I couldn't ask that of you." Harry's chassis hummed. "It's my problem."

Julio set his bottle down at the crumbling fence line. "Hey, company man. I'm not a charity. I'm hoping I help you here, you help me out too." He pulled a plant from the cart, glancing at Harry's hands. "Didn't think it through, did you?"

"Not this part," said Harry. "The rain stopped, so I figured it might be safe to try planting something again."

"It's okay. You get started on the fence."

"Thanks." Harry clanked around the fence line, tearing posts from the ground, crumbling concrete yielding from the earth. Once the old supports were gone, he hefted a posthole digger from the cart, working his way around the property. Each point where the overlay suggested the optimal place to dig, he hunched, the chassis bracing. Pneumatic rams in his arms fired. Each hole was perfectly carved, cut instantly into the dirt.

Sometimes being less than a man made things easier. But only sometimes.

Julio and Harry worked throughout the day. Harry did the hard, heavy things. Julio helped with the delicate jobs, occasionally heading off to get more beer. By the time they were finished, the day had turned to dusk, light failing under hard gray clouds.

Harry put equipment into the trailer before turning to Julio. "Thanks."

Julio shrugged. "Think nothing of it. She deserves it."

"Yeah, she does. Thanks anyway."

"Doesn't look done yet." Julio spoke with the expert air of a man who'd dug more than one garden.

"No. She's on the clock. Double shifts. Won't be home for a while."

Julio nodded. "You've still got time, then."

"Yes," said Harry. "What about you?"

"I got everything I need." Julio sighed. "I'm pretty sure—"

"You said I could help you out," interrupted Harry. "You probably weren't thinking about me keeping quiet."

"Quiet?"

"The illegal beer."

"There'll be another time, Harry." Julio laughed. "But you did help me."

"I did?"

"Yeah." Julio retrieved his bottle as he walked out of the yard. "Because you helped *her*. That's how it works."

"Around here?"

"No, it's how it works everywhere. You company people? You've just forgotten."

Harry watched him go. He checked what they'd achieved in Lace's garden. Dusk made shadows of everything, but he could imagine what it would look like when the sun returned. It wasn't much. It sure as hell was what she had had before.

He fired up the chassis' lamps. Plenty more needed doing, but what he and Julio had done today was a start.

CHAPTER ONE_

F ixing Richland? Impossible. But Sadie hoped fixing Richland
enough so they could get a tiny sip of power was possible. With
a reactor meltdown in the heart of a nest of monsters, it was unlikely
to be prime real estate anytime soon. They needed enough power for
the little things.

"I don't get why we're out here." Haraway kicked a stone, sending
it skipping away. "It's late. There are zombies."

"They're not zombies." Brushing black hair over her undercut,
Sadie grabbed two harnesses from the van. They had lights, which in
her view was essential for grubbing around in a city full of monsters.
"I'm going with mutants."

"Zombies, mutants, whatever. I don't read fiction."

"Didn't look like fiction to me." Sadie handed Haraway a harness.
The company woman's clinic-perfect blond good looks were
unmarred by roughing it. Sadie pulled her own harness on. The black
nylon straps felt unforgiving through her shirt, like even syndicate
designers hated illegals.

I'm not illegal. I don't want their shit in my head.

Haraway held her harness at arm's length, like it was a snake.
"What am I doing with this?"

"Putting it on."

"I—"

"Don't tell me you don't do fieldwork. This was your idea, remember?"

Haraway tossed Sadie a crooked smile. "All this?" She raised her hand, as if saying *behold this dead city*. "It's new to me."

"That's no problem. Put the harness on."

Haraway ran a hand through hair that looked like it needed to spend more time in the company clinic. "Why aren't we inside with them?"

"You wanted power."

"Power can wait until tomorrow. We don't need to turn power on at midnight."

Sadie tightened her harness. "You kill anyone today?"

A couple of seconds passed. Haraway sighed. "I shot ... *things*. I don't know if I killed them."

Sadie offered a sigh of her own. "In there," she jerked a thumb at the gap in the wall, "there's a girl who'll be afraid of the dark forever if we don't get the lights on. Because we couldn't hold a fucking line. Because we couldn't *see*." Sadie wanted to say, *see your company bullshit* or *see what you've done, what you've always done*, but she stopped at Haraway's expression. The woman looked like a tree felled in a storm. Still had leaves, sure, but might be dead soon.

Haraway's voice was soft. "I get it. More than you know." She straightened, dragged her head through the harness straps, then turned on the lamps. Beams of light pushed against the dark. Rubble raised fingers of shadow against the buildings. "It's quiet, isn't it?"

"Long may it last." Sadie hauled a toolbox out of the van, offering it to Haraway.

Haraway took the box from Sadie. "Everything here is ruined. It's broken down, used up. You can't kickstart a reactor."

"You're the scientist. I'm here for moral support."

"Moral support?"

"It's what I call sticking an axe in anything that tries to eat your face when you're coming up with the real answer."

Haraway laughed. "Fair play, Sadie Freeman."

Sadie leaned against the van, a smile she hadn't realized was there falling from her face. "I play guitar. I don't know what I'm doing here."

"You're not a prisoner, Sadie."

"I know." Sadie scuffed her boot against rubble. "You don't give prisoners weapons."

"Right, you're a part of the team."

Sadie straightened, anger's fire going right to the heart of her. "Don't you dare. Don't you fucking *dare*."

Haraway took a couple of steps back. "I don't—"

Sadie stalked toward her. "You people shoved me in a van. Brought me here. I didn't choose to be here. I'm not a part of your *team*." She spat the last word out, bringing her face close to Haraway's. "I'm not *company*."

Haraway held a palm out, the movement slow. "Freeman, I didn't plan it like this. You weren't supposed to be here."

Sadie glared. "What do you mean?"

Haraway turned, shoulders slumping. "It doesn't matter. Just ... I'm sorry. You weren't supposed to be here."

Sadie grabbed Haraway's shoulder. "Hey. Don't turn away!"

Haraway slapped her hand away, eyes bright. The bright white lights of Haraway's harness glared, and Sadie couldn't make the other woman's face out. "Don't touch me. You have no idea what this has *cost* me. You're worried about being on an unplanned camping trip? Shit happens. Deal with it."

Sadie felt her anger growing, fingers curling into a fist. *Steady. Listen. Not to what she said, but what she meant.* She made her hand relax. Haraway was rigid, caught between staying and running. "Can you do me a favor?"

"Oh, you want a favor? From the *company*?"

"Not really," said Sadie. "From you. Could you turn your lights off? They're in my eyes."

The moment stretched, then Haraway laughed, a broken, fragile sound. She turned the harness lights off.

"Thanks." Sadie blinked, trying to clear her eyes. Night vision? Gone. "Do you think you can do it?"

"I don't know. It's been hard to get here."

"What?"

Haraway shook her head. "What were you asking?"

"I wanted to know if you can get the power back on." Sadie kept her voice low.

"Oh." Haraway looked into the street, quiet for a moment. "I thought you meant something else. It doesn't matter. I can get the power back on, sure."

"How?"

"We're going to find the distribution center. Be a building. Lots of cables. Can't miss it."

"Okay."

"We're going to hook the reactor in the van up to it."

Sadie looked at the van, trying the idea on for size. It didn't fit. "It's a van. It can't possibly power a town."

"Why not? It's got a reactor in it. One of *our* reactors. This is what we do, Freeman. The Federate makes clean, limitless energy."

"Reed put an Apsel reactor in their van?" Sadie frowned. "I thought you syndicates tried to shop local."

"When we can," said Haraway. "Reed bought this van from someone who used our reactors. Sort of a supply-chain thing."

"You know a lot about this," said Sadie.

"I make reactors. I know where we sell them."

"Okay." Sadie thought about it. Reactor in a van? Sure. But powering a city? "How are you going to make a reactor in a van power a city? They seem different levels of hard."

"Now *that* is a trade secret. You leave the science to me. If we can get to the distribution center, I can make this van give us as much power as we need."

CHAPTER TWO

P rophet stood with his back to Julian. The Master looked out the
window of Reed Interactive's Tower Prime. They were in the
highest executive suite. The previous owner ... fell.

Clouds reached, gray and ugly, over the city below. Julian blew
across the surface of his coffee before putting the plastic lid on. "I'm
sorry, Master. I still have some ... trouble understanding how this
works." He stood back — *quiet, respectful, or the pain starts again* —
but he could see the flash of lightning. The boom came less than a
second later. *Motherfucker calls himself Prophet.* Julian clamped
down on the thought. Things like that led to more pain.

"You do not need to understand. That's not your function."

"Of course, Master. It's just that—"

"Does pain excite you? I've known some like that." Prophet didn't
move. "They need to be discarded. Too hard to shape, like clay that's
been already fired."

"Master, please." *Incentives. Go with incentives.* "I feel if I don't
do my best for you, you may hurt me more in the future."

Prophet turned slowly, his face pulled tight with anger. "If it's my
wish you feel pain, then you'll be *hurt*." Julian held himself still. "But

you have been a useful tool, Julian Oldham. It is a poor craftsman indeed who doesn't listen to the hum of the tools under his fingers."

"Master?"

"Speak, Julian Oldham. Speak, and I will listen." Prophet turned to the window. "If your words do not please me, then there will be pain. Do you understand?"

"I understand, Master." Prophet could lift the thoughts from Julian's head, so this was some kind of sick test. *Was there a right answer?* Julian looked down at his hands, the shake in them something that hadn't gone away since the night he'd awoken in the crypt.

Julian's mind shied away from the memory. *He knows what you're thinking. Lead with it.* "Have you heard the word incentive, Master?"

"The taste of this word is familiar, but I do not know its meaning."

"It is a mechanism of sorts. It influences the way people make decisions." Julian's breath came short and shallow, fear stirring his thoughts in a way no boardroom presentation ever had.

"Ah," said Prophet. "Is this from those imbeciles in Marketing? They have not pleased me. Vacuous, intangible morons."

"No, Master. I mean, yes, Marketing are morons. This is not their term. This is..." Julian struggled with the *right* words. The words that would prevent pain. "It is economics."

"Is this to do with this thing you call money?"

"Yes, Master."

"I do not need money." Prophet stared down at the cloudscape. "Do you see how they scurry and run? Of course not. You have only your eyes. But I can see their *minds*. All those people live their lives wrong. They make mistakes, cause harm, and disrupt the natural order. I have been sent to return them to their place. Order will be restored."

"Yes, Master." For a moment, Julian forgot who he was speaking to. "It is just that—"

"You contradict me?" Prophet's shoulders bunched before relaxing. "No. I said I would let you say your piece. Say it and be done."

"The right incentive makes people do a thing, and at the same time believe they wanted to do it." Julian felt his nerve trickling away, water down a drain. *Harden up. Make the play.* "They do what you want, but think it is their choice."

"They will do that anyway."

"Of course. But they will do it faster with the right incentive." Julian took a half step forward. "Out there, your ... agent—"

"The demon. What of it?"

"As you say. Your demon—"

"It is not mine, any more than my arm is mine. We are the same thing, Julian Oldham. Why is this so hard for you to understand?" Julian could feel the touch, light and delicate as a feather, as Prophet reached for his mind. The pain would start soon. "You still want to speak your mind, while you have one. Know that my patience grows short."

"They hide, Master," said Julian. "Before you came, people learned to hide from the rain."

"You can't hide forever."

"No, but if people didn't want to hide, how fast would you get what you wanted?"

Prophet stood quiet for a moment. "You think that the right incentive would make them stand in the rain as it poured down, burning at their minds?"

"Not quite, Master. How flexible is the demon?"

"Flexible?"

"Yes, Master. Let me explain." As Julian laid out his ideas, Prophet relaxed, then smiled.

This time, it wouldn't hurt.

Julian met Bernie Eckers at *The Hole*. The bar was dark. It and

Eckers smelled of stale beer. The pudgy, sallow man's shirt was stained with sweat and grime. He faced Julian from behind the bar, using the wood like a shield. Julian chose the fixer's place of business figuring it might set the human cockroach at ease. He'd laid out his proposal like fresh chum, but the shark in Eckers hadn't bit. Not *yet*.

"I don't get it, Oldham." Eckers rubbed his belly where his shirt didn't meet his buckle.

How he'd managed to escape the grip of the Prophet was a curiosity, but in this instance it worked for Julian's plan. He might get out of this *and* make decent cash. Prophet didn't want money. He wanted control. Prophet was the biggest asshole Julian had seen in Reed's C-suite, but he didn't seem averse to Julian making a little on the side so long as he remembered who was in charge. Julian's angle was to give Prophet the control while keeping the proceeds. Nice and simple.

"You don't have to get it. It's a simple proposal, Eckers. You sell it, you keep a percentage." It was hard to not murder the fat man. Julian's last couple days had been harder than normal. *You need him. At least for a little while.*

"I get that part. Why are you coming to me? You Reed assholes have all kinds of channels for this. You already distribute stuff at a scale I can't touch."

"Sure, we distribute a lot of entertainments that have been proven to be profitable. Those have a history of clinical trials."

Eckers shuffled behind the bar, favoring a leg. "Trials." He held up a tumbler, and Julian nodded. Eckers splashed amber liquid into the glass and pushed it over. "Last time you were here, you broke my shotgun and blew a hole in my roof." He looked up at the ragged hole that let light and rain in. Both fell in roughly equal measure against the old concrete floor. It cast the inside of *The Hole* into relief where the tired bar wanted to stay covered in quiet gloom.

"No, those Apsel motherfuckers blew a hole in your roof." Julian shook his head.

"Whatever. You're all company to me."

"The difference is twofold." Julian forced a smile. "First, we're